GUNRUNNER'S DAUGHTER

E.M. CUMMINGS

BLACK ALCHEMY BOOKS, LLC

CONTENTS

To Mr. E.M. Cummings,

Thank you for finding the diamond in the rough within me and my first draft of this novel. Your unwavering support has been instrumental in our mutual growth. Neither of us would shine as brightly today without your continued loving encouragement and unending patience.

AUTHOR NOTE

Dear Readers,

As a reader myself, I have a confession to make: I hate author notes and almost always skip them to get right into the story. As an author now, I've also rewritten this note at least as many times as I rewrote this novel (hint: five different times). So, to save us both a lot of time and encourage you to read this, here is a bulleted list of the main thoughts from all five of those other author notes:

- This is a dark romantic thriller novel. There are dark and intense themes and moments.

- General content warnings include foul language, violence, trauma, manipulative relationships, dysfunctional relationships, substance use, dubious consensual acts, death, dark themes, disturbing imagery, and dark humor. All the fun stuff, right? Yeah, I know why you all are here.

- The main character of this novel is no Jane Eyre; she does not cling to her principles and her God. She is morally gray and makes decisions that align with that. I mean, come on, the title of this book is literally *Gunrunner's Daughter.*

- IF YOU EVER ENGAGE IN ANY KIND OF SEXUAL SIT-UATION IN REAL LIFE, MAKE SURE YOU GET FULL, SOBER, "HELL YES" CONSENT BEFORE ENGAGING IN ANY SEX OR KINK.

- Please be cautious if you explore any of these kink scenarios. However, under no circumstances should you attempt to recreate the scene from Chapter Twenty-Five!

- Dimiter's name is pronounced dih-MEE-ter. I don't know why he insisted on spelling it the way he did.

- I have made a full album that accompanies this novel. You can stream it on SoundCloud (Sinful Spins) or purchase it from Bandcamp (Sinful Spins).

Well, with all that said: Please fasten your seatbelt, keep all hands and feet inside the ride, and prepare for a wild adventure!

Thank you,

E.M. Cummings

A Note on the Music

♫ A Note on the Music ♫

If you are reading the ePub version of this book, you will find song references marked with musical notes (♫). The underlined text between the notes is clickable and will take you directly to the corresponding song on Spotify.

For print readers, the same musical notes (♫) indicate songs, and QR codes will be provided at the end of each chapter. Scanning the QR code with your phone will take you to the song that corresponds with that section of the book.

If you'd like to listen to the full album, you can access the complete playlist here:

♫ *Gunrunner's Daughter: The Album* ♫

Enjoy the experience of reading and listening together, immersing yourself in the world of *Gunrunner's Daughter* like never before.

Happy reading—and happy listening!

PROLOGUE

I t was exclusive knowledge that my mother hated me. It was about to be common knowledge, though, that she was a cheating whore.

I opened the home-office door, expecting to see my father's warm smile beaming at me, to be met with my mother's infidelity.

A stranger had her sitting on top of my father's desk. They were kissing feverishly and undressing each other. I couldn't help but stare at them with morbid curiosity as they acted out their passions.

The man pulled away from my mom, his hand embraced her face with a gentleness not belonging to my father. He gazed at her with a lust and passion I had never seen before. Then his green eyes drifted over to me. A small gasp escaped his lips, which were smeared red from kissing.

My mother's head snapped around, following her lover's view. Her eyes brimmed with disgust and hatred when they found me.

"SOFIA YOU LITTLE BRAT!" she screamed.

I dashed down the hallway as my mother gave chase. Pushing myself to run faster, faster, faster.

Mother stumbled as she tried to grab me. She kept clumsily bumping into the walls of the mansion in pursuit.

Is Mom drunk?

I navigated the maze of our mansion, trying to lose my chaser, when I ran right into someone's side. As I recovered, I looked up to see my father smiling down at me.

"Here's my little Angel," he said, picking me up into a hug.

Tears of relief fell down my face. My saving grace was here to rescue me.

"Woah, woah, woah, we don't cry in this family," Father brushed my tears away.

"Mother," I said as my tears continued falling.

"Yes, what about your mother?"

I told him everything I had seen. The touching, the kissing, the chasing after me. Just as I finished, my mother charged into the hallway. She stopped running when she saw who was with me. The color drained from her face as she approached us, walking now. I've never seen my father's face so red as he watched her.

Bane, my twin, walked in on the scene with an inquisitive look. He scrutinized our parents and felt the growing tension between them. Without saying a word, he grabbed my hand and dragged me away into his room. I allowed him to pull me up onto his bed and into his arms. He held my face on his chest, and we waited for the storm outside to begin.

All at once, shouting echoed through the hall, loud and violent.

"Hey, how do you feel about reading a book?" Bane asked me, his fingers running through my hair in a comforting gesture. I nodded at him meekly. He got up and went to his bookshelf, scanning for something promising.

"Have you read any Rotten Ryan books?" Bane called back to me, still scanning his bookcase.

"Who is that?" I asked.

Bane grabbed a book and got back into his bed. He curled his arm around me as I laid on his chest.

Outside, a vase shattered against the wall.

Bane read his Rotten Ryan adventure book to me. We could hear the fight drifting around the mansion. Still, my brother tried to speak up over the screaming.

BANG

The sound of a gun stopped my twin. We laid still and quiet, holding out breaths. The house seemed still and silent.

BANG

Another gun shot rang out. I squeezed Bane, and he held me tighter. Neither one of us said anything else for the rest of the night. We feel asleep in each other's arms.

The next day, an agonizing stillness had fallen over the house. I woke up my brother, and we tiptoed around the mansion to investigate. No one was in sight, but the house was absolutely wrecked.

A small clattering drew my attention. I grabbed Bane's arm and pulled him toward the sound. We ended up in the main dining room. The cook was putting the finishing touches on a large breakfast when we arrived. He gazed at us woefully.

"Your father commanded me to make an extravagant breakfast for you," he said before leaving.

Bane and I took our normal seats on either side of the table. We exchanged a knowing look after surveying the spread of food.

Bad news.

It was only a few minutes later Father entered the room reading his morning newspaper. He sat at the head of the table and hummed casually to himself.

"Dad-" Bane started.

"Eat," father said from behind the paper.

"What happened to-" I tried.

"Nothing," he directed. His unspoken command was final: no more questions.

Bane and I exchanged a long look before serving ourselves. We never mentioned our mother again.

BANE'S GUNRUNNING BUSINESS RULE NUMBER FOUR:

Be bold, just not with Father.

I repeat, NOT WITH FATHER.

CHAPTER ONE

Emilio Zoric, ♫ my father, was the most notorious arms dealer in all of Europe. He obscured his booming empire, which we all just referred to as the family business, with a diverse range of companies under the Zoric, LLC name.

Bane went on his first 'special trip' with Father right after we graduated from secondary school. I, however, was just banned from the business.

"This is unfair!" I shouted from the front door. Dimiter, my tall, blond, and recently appointed guard, held me back from running after my family.

"Go find a husband!" Father yelled as he got into the family limousine. Bane looked at me with pity as he followed.

I threw my elbow into Dimiter's core, hoping he would drop me. Instead, he held me tighter into his arms, reminding me who was stronger.

I growled, infuriated, as my father and brother drove away from the mansion.

"Maybe it's time to find a hobby," Alexei, my also new, brutish guard, suggested.

"Yeah, one where you can find a fine young man to date," Dimiter added, dragging me safely back into the house and letting go of me.

I sneered at them and skulked back to my room to plot my revenge.

The next trip, I snuck onto the family plane an hour before the scheduled departure.

I waited gleefully in one of our leather chairs with a newspaper, ready for my family's arrival. It took three hours before I heard my father's voice as he bounded up the stairs.

"If you don't find her by the time I return, I'll make you disappear!" he was shouting.

The plane door opened, and I looked over my newspaper at him.

"Where are we going, Papa?" I asked.

My father's face turned bright red, the telltale sign of his anger.

"Alexei! Dimiter!" He shouted.

Bane poked his head in the door, then smiled devilishly at me.

"That's smart. They can come to keep me safe. Where are we going?" I asked as the men boarded.

My father ignored me.

"Come on, Angel," Dimiter sighed, extending his hand to me. I glanced at it before settling more comfortably into the plane's leather chair.

My guards looked at my father.

He stared back at them, annoyed.

"I'm already late. Are you going to deal with this or not?"

Alexei nodded once, then moved toward me. He grabbed my core and threw me over his shoulder.

"WHAT DO YOU THINK YOU ARE DOING?" I shouted.

"My job," Alexei responded coolly as we moved up the plane.

"LET ME DOWN," I slapped at his back, feeling a tinge of excitement at being manhandled.

Alexei didn't let me go until we were back inside the mansion.

"We're going to have to keep a better eye on you," he muttered, crossing his arms.

Dimiter mimed the gesture with a bemused smile on his face.

I scowled at the men, then left for my room. As I marched around the corner, though, I crashed right into one of my father's house guards.

"Oh, I'm so sorry, miss," he said, rushing a protective arm around me.

I stared up at the man and found myself not minding being wrapped up in his powerful hold. He was my age, with a buzzed head and captivating hazel eyes. His uniform was tight in all the delicious places.

"Are you ok?" he asked sincerely.

"She's fine," Alexei grumbled, ruining our moment.

I glared over at my personal guard.

Alexei was shaking his head curtly and mouthed the word NO.

I smiled sardonically at him, then leaned in and kissed the guard on the cheek.

"I am now," I reassured him, then reluctantly untangled myself from Hazel Eyes.

The young man looked down at me, surprised. He held a hand to his cheek where I had kissed him.

I managed one more glance at my guards before continuing to my bedroom. Dimiter was bemused and Alexei was pinching the bridge of his nose, exasperated.

The hazel-eyed guard was forgotten until a week later.

I was hiding in a disregarded room at the front of the mansion, lounging on an ugly floral chaise lounge and plotting my next act of insubordination when I heard it. The echo of controlled footsteps sounded down the hall, and I mentally braced myself for Alexei to find me.

He was always the one to find me.

Instead, to my delight, Hazel Eyes peeked his head into the room. He traced down my body with his brilliant eyes, then winked. Without further ceremony, he left and returned to his duties in the hall.

I rose and leaned out the door to observe the man as he worked.

The guard marched to the next room and peered in. After confirming that it was, in fact, still empty, he turned to me. With a seductive look, he formed a V with his fingers and displayed his tongue between them.

I smirked, which motivated him to stir his tongue. With an intense flutter, I felt pure desire build inside of me at the idea of sitting on his face. Before I could take a step closer, though, he straightened, turned, and walked to the next door opening.

As quietly as I could, I crept out into the hallway and snuck into the next room. Slipping in unseen, I hid by the door.

It was only a moment later that the guard stuck his head into the room. I went in for a kiss, hoping to take the man by surprise.

Hazel Eyes, however, saw the motion and attacked.

With a smooth and swift movement, I found myself wrapped up in his powerful arms with both of my hands trapped in his.

"What a delicious treat I have found," he purred into my ear. Then I felt a trail of soft kisses down my neck and to my shoulder.

"Want to take a lick?" I breathed, grinding myself against his front.

"Unfortunately, I need this job more than I want to fuck the boss's daughter."

With a flourish, I was twirled into the room as Hazel Eyes untangled us and took a step back out into the hallway.

While my guard peered in to the next room, I tiptoed behind him into the successor.

A beat later, my prize stuck his head in to look around and pointedly ignore me.

Standing right in front of him, I lowered the front zipper of my dress until both of my considerable tits fell out. Then, I grabbed and played with my nipples until they were hard.

Hazel-eyes stopped looking around the room and stared openly at my bare chest.

"I can make you need me," I purred.

The guard took three decisive deep breaths before stepping back out into the hallway. As he marched forward to the next room, his eyes remained glued to my breasts.

I looked out into the hallway.

Hazel Eyes was not looking into the next room. While he was standing in front of it, he was looking back to where I stood. An impressive enough tent forming in his pants.

Stepping out into the hallway, I undid the rest of the zipper, removing my tight black dress.

The man stiffened.

I stepped toward him, running a hand up my naked body. Then I took another slow and deliberate step forward, playing with my breast.

Desire burned in his eyes as I approached.

Finally, as I stepped in front of him, I placed both hands on his chest and ran them down his body until I grabbed his erect package.

"I can't wait to feel this inside of me," I whispered.

His penis throbbed in my grip. Without delay, I was swept into his arms, our lips locked in a passionate kiss.

After allowing a good feel for each of my breasts, I pulled my new toy down the hall. The guard refused to take more than a few steps before stalling to kiss me somewhere new. First my cheek, then neck, shoulders, chest, breast, nipples.

We fell into a closet together.

Safe, now, inside the forgotten room, he pushed me back and up onto a shelf.

His mouth slide down my body to his prize.

I felt one large lick up my slit, and then he buried himself into me, massaging my sweet spot expertly. It seemed his earlier showcase of talent was not an over exaggeration.

It only took a few minutes, but I had to pull myself away from his lips before I exploded on them.

"Fuck me," I insisted.

He ripped his clothes off and rubbed on his long, hard member.

"Are you sure you can take all of me?" he teased before moving himself swiftly to my inviting opening.

I felt him slide into me slowly, stretching my slick hole as I took all of his engorged cock. As the last of him inched into me, a small, pleased moan escaped him. Hazel Eyes kept himself rooted into me. His lips fell onto my exposed nipple and he sucked slightly.

Clearly, he wanted to take his time, but I was impatient. I spasmed my muscles around his erection, and the guard stood up straight, moaning.

The man's brilliant eyes locked with mine. They were thirsty.

"Naughty girl," he whispered on my lips before kissing me. His hips pounded in and out of me briskly. I moaned, feeling the friction of him moving inside me.

"Fuck," I cried out loud.

"Shh!"

Hazel Eyes shoved himself into me and covered my mouth. He waited frozen for several minutes to listen for signs that anyone heard us. I tried to move myself around on his sizable member, but his grip prevented it.

Finally, my guard became convinced no one heard a thing. He grabbed my chin in a tight grip and held me up to his face.

"Sorry," I mouthed.

Hazel Eyes kissed me, then began thrusting with a lustful fever.

I stretched out on the shelf to better enjoy his rhythmic pounding and had to bite my lip to keep from screaming rapture. My guard became excited at this response and thrusted into me more rapidly. I nearly lost all of my senses to the pleasure.

Then, as I felt the last stretch of my indulgence rising, my partner's pumping slowed down to deliberate, lustful thrusts. With one more shove of his enormous cock into me, I shuddered on it.

Hazel Eyes smirked, pleased with himself.

"WHAT IS THE MEANING OF THIS?!" boomed throughout the closet.

I recognized the voice immediately.

The guard's member slipped out of me, suddenly limp, and his whole body drained of color.

"Grab him," my father commanded. Men heaved my partner away, dragged him out of the room, still completely naked.

"No!" I yelled and chased after Hazel Eyes. Father caught me and held me back.

"You told me to find a husband!" I protested, fighting his severe grip.

A gun shot sounded outside the closet door.

"Do you know what would happen if I allowed employees to sleep with my daughter? My business partners would never take me serious again," my father growled in my ear.

I stopped struggling when Alexei and Dimiter walked into the closet. When I gave up on trying to escape, Father's grasp on me loosened.

"Don't try this again."

I didn't respond. Dimiter's hand fell on my shoulder and pulled me away. I allowed my bodyguard to usher me back to my room. The idea for my new mutiny solidifying in my mind.

EMILIO ZORIC

CHAPTER TWO

For the next year, ♫ _I made it my mission to fuck every goddamn guard my father employed to punish him_. ♫ With a constant stream of ripped men to choose from, the task was easy.

My first partner, a shy red head with a Quality Penis, had been pleasing me for several months now, until we were recently caught. At the discovery of our entwined bodies, my father's anger boiled to a deep shade of red. The sign my plan was working.

Father demanded I watch as he shot Quality Penis. I studied his indignant anger instead. His need to control me burned into my psyche.

With the next partner, I pushed my luck.

Crooked Smile had a curved and very enjoyable organ. He was also a grunter. I started to respond in kind and slowly we became louder each time we copulated. We tested the limits of how loud we could be.

After Crooked Smile, word spread among the guards what the consequences were of touching me. Most of them actively limited their interactions, leaving me with no easy replacement.

I responded by walking around the mansion naked while my family was away. The move drew the attention of the men again.

My next target's stare lingered on my breasts the longest as I passed by. He found it hard to say no as I laid naked at his feet, begging to suck his veiny cock.

After six guards had to be replaced, video cameras were installed. They kept the locations of the cameras a secret to all except for the men assigned to watch them.

Unfortunately for my father, I started sleeping with the cameraman.

Due to his position, Eight Inches was convinced we would never get caught. He allowed me to ride him at his computer desk, which I insisted turned me on. I spent our time together memorizing the blind spots in the house.

The man had a fantastic package, though, and most nights; I had a hard time controlling my climax. It required several enjoyable visits.

After four months of intimacy, the cameraman had to be replaced. Alexei and Dimiter had found me finishing on Eight Inches and dragged me to my father's office.

"This stops," he commanded from across his menacing mahogany desk.

I ignored his outburst, still reeling with post-orgasmic bliss mixing with the adrenaline of being caught.

"If you don't stop this, there will be serious consequences! You are disrespecting me and the Zoric name by fornicating with the staff," he yelled, his voice moving an octave higher.

"Do you have anything to say for yourself?" he barked when I still did not respond to him. I shrugged before finally opening my mouth.

"I'm just practicing my wifely duties. I want to make sure I can please my husband," I said, smiling innocently.

My father's hot, angry blush made its way down his neck. He breathed deeply several times to maintain his temper before speaking again.

"You are grounded," he stated in a strained calmness.

"That will help me find a husband."

"Your pool, shooting range, and polo field privileges will continue to be lost to you," he continued.

"I'm not interested in pool boys, anyway."

"And part of your allowance will now go to train the new staff I have to keep replacing!" he finished, his temper slipping at the end.

I didn't respond and tried my best to stop a smile threatening to emerge. Through the endless scolding, I could see unfamiliar ticks beginning to show.

It was subtle, but I could see I was winning.

In addition to loitering around in the nude, I publicly gratified myself to entice a new partner. To ensure I attracted attention, I wailed with my climaxes. A rush of guards would dash to me in a panic, only to find me finishing on a toy.

It was a few months into this new mating tactic that Alexei let his honorable demeanor slip for the first time.

I was positioned in the middle of the library, with my favorite gold dildo between my legs.

Alexei rushed by to find me. With a glance into the room, he froze.

I moved sensually up and down on the gilded cock and noticed his breath catching. His chocolate eyes watched me lustfully. A jolt rushed through me, as I saw my guard for the man he was.

His indiscretion passed quickly, and he ran a hand through his dark, thick hair as it left. The movement caused some of his normally perfect gelled hair to come undone.

Alexei peeked into the room to see if anyone else was in there. Confirming we were alone, he entered and walked slowly around me. His eyes staying on my body as I played with myself. Finally, he settled into a chair behind me.

As I slid up the dildo, I leaned forward to show off the onyx heart shaped butt plug I had added today. A deep groan escaped Alexei before he masked it with a cough.

Dimiter walked by, also looking for me. He stalled in the doorway and glanced around the library to find Alexei and I were alone. A suspicious look crossed Dimiter's blue eyes. In a sharp tone, he barked, "What are you doing?"

I stayed on my toy and played with my clitoris as Dimiter pointedly ignored me.

"I wanted to make sure she was not corrupting the new guard," Alexei answered dourly, as if this was all just another day on the job for him.

Dimiter paused for a long moment before accepting the answer.

"The new one seems to be young and reckless," he finally agreed before walking into the room and siting next to Alexei.

"You two are making my job sound easier," I joked, sliding up the dildo again, flashing both men my butt plug. There was no answer from either of them.

I deciding to reward my guards with a show and moved faster. My moans were soft at first, then gradually grew louder. A powerful climax rose inside me. I pounded myself harder onto the dildo, moving my hands across my body and touching myself. Then the click of an unruly stride sounded, and I slowed down.

Young and Reckless was coming.

He walked casually to the doorway, then his eyes widened when he saw me. I smiled and licked my lips seductively.

He was not too bad looking, tall with chaotically spiked blond hair and gray eyes. His gorgeous face softened into a sly, crooked smile.

I backed down from peak pleasure to pace myself.

Minutes stretched by and no one moved except for me sliding on the cock.

The guard's eyes devoured me, traveling around my body and resting on the movement at my opening. He flashed a look at the other men in the room, which revived him briefly from his feverish dream. Then his eyes returned to me and I saw the senseless lust burning within. Without thinking, he moved one step into the room.

"Move along if you want to keep your life," Alexei roared behind me.

I flipped my long raven hair behind my shoulder and turned to look at him. Our eyes locked. Alexei's chocolate brown ones became darker despite his indifferent expression. I smiled at him and moved myself faster, forcing the climax. The wave of pleasure rippled inside me. I came down hard on the dildo, spasming and moaning in ecstasy. Alexei stared nonchalantly as I finished. Then he glanced back over at the doorway.

I followed his gaze back to Young and Reckless. The man was in perverted shock, his eyes ablaze as he stared at my pearl. It took him a full minute to recover. He swallowed loudly, then stepped back into the hall.

"Of course," the guard said to my men as he regained a sloppy composure. With one last look at me, he smirked before continuing his route.

"We're going to need a new man soon," Alexei sighed once the delightful Young and Reckless was out of earshot.

"I think he will come to his senses," Dimiter rebuffed.

Slowly, I slid off my toy, enjoying the friction on the way off.

Alexei sighed behind me and muttered just a little breathlessly, "Zoric has not stopped looking for new men lately. He seems to be in a constant shortage."

The following night, my father returned from another business trip. His distraction would provide me ample time to seduce the latest addition.

I put on a strappy scarlet lingerie set. Then, over it, I threw on a sheer crop top and tiny black miniskirt. A quick glance in the mirror confirmed I looked as tempting as original sin.

I grabbed a pair of tall nude pumps and slipped out of my room unseen.

The night before, I had memorized the bodyguard's schedule. I knew the man was going to be in our second, smaller dining room alone for at least forty-five minutes. As soon as I found the carpeted hallway, I put on my heels and snuck into the unused dining room.

My trophy didn't see me at first, his attention absorbed with an old china cabinet collecting dust. I cleared my throat, startling the young man, who turned toward me frantically.

"Oh, I thought you were about to yell at me to get back to work," he sighed with relief. Then his eyes raked down my body, taking in the outfit.

"They are always yelling at me here. Do this, do that, don't... touch you," he seemed to lose his train of thought as his eyes traced down my long legs.

I approached him slowly.

"I'm sorry to hear that everyone has been so unpleasant. Can I make it up to you?" I asked, grabbing his hand and pressing it to my breast.

His gray eyes held a desperate yearning, but Young and Reckless untangled his hand from mine. Then he stiffly returned his attention to the china cabinet.

"There are some beautiful pieces in here," he insisted.

"I don't care."

His restraint was a flimsy facade. I moved my hands to his belt buckle, and the man twisted his hips to make it easier for me to undo his pants. As I slid them down his legs, I lowered myself onto my knees.

"You don't care?" he breathed as I revealed his weary erection. It was clearly his last attempt to distract me.

I looked up into his piercing eyes through thick lashes as I glided my fingers up his inner thigh to my swelling reward.

"It was my mother's. And I fucking hated my mother," I said before taking him fully into my mouth. The move, thankfully, caused him to drop the conversation.

He leaned against the cabinet and sighed in sinful desire. The part of him that knew this was forbidden dissipated and his hands found their way to my long black hair. I pulled his hips toward me, shoving more of his cock into my mouth.

My work turned sloppy. We found a rhythm, and it was not long before he made The Face. The one of wanting to unload on me.

"Oh, for fuck's sake," I heard from a low voice behind me. I kept sucking despite recognizing the newcomer. Another hand seized my hair and yanked me away.

I found myself looking up into Dimiter's eyes. A touch of pride was in them, but the rest of his face was despondent. He dragged me away from the guard, who stood rigid with shock.

We made it across the room. Then Dimiter pulled out his gun and, almost as an afterthought, shot the petrified guard. The man's blood splattered all over the china cabinet.

CHAPTER THREE

"**I** can walk myself!"

I clawed at my captor's hand until he finally let go of my hair. The moment I was dropped, I tried to dash away. The blond guard expected this, though, and grabbed my arm before I could get too far. He twisted it behind my back and continued to navigate me down to Father's office.

Dimiter shoved me into my usual seat. Father was already sitting across from me in his large, dominating chair. He looked up from his papers and over toward Dimiter through his prominent, round glasses, a questioning look on his face.

"I found her sucking off the latest guard."

My dad grumbled and looked down at me, exhausted.

"I suspected he was going to be a moron. He's already been taken care of," Dimiter added before my father dismissed him with a wave of his hand.

A heavy silence settled between Father and I. An unstoppable force meeting the unmovable object.

"Angel," he started, trying to warm our conversation by using his nickname for me.

"My business is dangerous and difficult. It's not just about adventure and riches. I need you to understand I cannot put you, my precious daughter, into the middle of that chaos. Do you know how many negotiations I find myself on the wrong end of a weapon?

"Find a husband. A good, strong, and rich one. I can bring him into the business. Marry one of my partners! You will remain safe and happy while the danger resides with the men of the family."

My father leveled his eyes, hoping I would understand what he was really saying: *There is no fucking way you are going to get involved with my business.*

"Please, just give me a chance. Dimiter and Alexei can come with us," I implored.

My father shook his head.

"You are not listening to me. Your safety with Dimiter and Alexei is guaranteed here, outside of active war zones."

I said nothing, but felt exhaustion wash over me.

"I feel this has become a game to you, sleeping with my employees. It's really becoming a nuisance, though. Rumors are being spread that I cannot keep my household in order. Being undermined by your own daughter is not respectable. This needs to stop now."

He put the emphasis on NOW by slapping the top of his desk.

"Since you have put no efforts into your actual future, I've decided what you need is motivation. I am giving you six months to find someone to marry on your own. If you're unable to find anyone, I'll find someone for you."

My father glared at me, confirming his threat was sinking in. I did not indulge him with a response, and left my face carefully blank.

"And if it will keep you off of my staff, I will get you a job at one of my many legal enterprises, *but only* until you are married." He added, as I refused to respond to his terrible offer.

"Do we have a deal?" He asked.

Anger boiled beneath my surface. *With all the strength* I could muster, I restrained any reaction though, and purposefully drew out the silence between us.

"Stop acting like your mother," he finally spat at me.

The words stung like a slap. I clinched my jaw and stood to leave.

As I made my way to the door, I spotted my father's office bar next to it. On the top was a pricey vodka bottle, which I grabbed.

"Six months," my father repeated behind me. I barely acknowledged his words, just dragged the vodka off the bar and took it with me as I left.

Staggering down the hall, I started drinking freely from the bottle. My life felt like it was slipping away. A strong rage stirred inside, becoming fueled by the vodka.

If he wanted to call me a whore like my mother, a whore of a daughter he would get.

I trudged to my father's most expensive liquor cabinet and found the priciest bottle. Having freed it from its resting place, I took a drink from it to try. It was disgusting, and I spat it out immediately.

I made my way to the library and drenched the books in the nasty alcohol while liberally drinking from my vodka. When everything was sufficiently soaked, I clawed through the drawers for an ignition source. Papers and random objects flew as I emptied drawers, growing frustrated.

Thousands of candles around this stupid house and no lighter? I thought.

With half of the library drawers pulled out and dilapidated in some form, I finally found my prize.

I walked over to the curtain and tried to ignite the small pink lighter.

"Sofia?" I heard Bane call out behind me.

I turned to face my confused brother. At first he seemed concerned about me, then he saw what was in my hand.

A large whoosh of flames erupted as the lighter ignited, setting the curtain beside me aflame.

Bane rushed to my side as I poured the rest of the disgusting expensive liquor on the blaze, causing it to grow excessively. I laughed manically and watched my twin's panic. My brother tried his best to dampen the flames, but the fire had grown too large.

A rush of staff had come pouring in at Bane's shrieks. I took the vodka and left the library unnoticed. No one was around to stop me as I hightailed it to the garage.

I drove from the mansion like a bat out of hell in my bright purple

McLaren Spyder, straight to Arousal, the local upscale sex emporium.

Arousal provided quality lingerie and adventurous toys. However, it was more known for its glory holes and peep shows. The store was located in a secluded spot and its bright lights blazed up the night skyline as I approached. AROUSAL, in large purple cursive letters, had silhouettes of women on either side of it. The logo sitting on top of a large light brown building illuminated by flood lights of all colors.

I drunkenly stumbled into the emporium, still carrying my vodka with me.

Scanning the inside, I found what I was looking for, a neon red sign reading THE GLASS BOX hanging over a large, dark curtain. Soft, sensual pop music undulated from the other side.

"Can I help you?" a mature man asked me from behind the register.

"I'm here to perform," I muttered, making my way to the curtain separating the arena from the store.

"Someone is giving a show. You will have to wait," the man called after me.

I turned to look at him, gave myself another sip of the vodka in response, and stepped through the curtain.

The music was louder in the peep show arena. The area was enormous, styled in a neon crimson. It resembled a small amphitheater with rows of long benches. Colored lights adorned the outer rim to aid in finding a seat. A row of stairs led down from the doorway to the center, where a transparent Plexiglas cage was illuminated brightly. Inside, a naked woman was enthusiastically touching herself.

She had short electric blue hair tied into pigtails, and was spread out on the floor of her cage. With legs spread open, her fingers danced on her exposed jewel.

I surveyed the audience and noticed a scattering of men, and to my pleasant surprise, a few women. Most were playing with themselves, but a few were partnered.

I took a big swig of the vodka, hoping the alcohol would help me feel anything but anger. Instead, the burning sensation encouraged the wrath.

I pulled my crop top off and tossed it, attracting a few eyes from the crowd. Then I strutted my way down to the arena. At the bottom, I took my time removing my skirt provocatively, slinging it toward a man at least twice my age.

When I turned my attention toward the cage, and the woman inside eyed me cautiously. With my disruptive arrival, she slowed her act.

Stepping up to the Plexiglas, I placed my hand on the surface, reaching to the woman inside. She extended her own hand and held it up to mine. I beamed at her, and she smiled back curiously.

Our moment passed, and I walked around the cage slowly, dragging my hand and leaving a trail of smudges on the plastic. When I made it to the door, I set down my vodka and tossed my car keys. Then I opened it, provoking the woman inside.

"HEY! You have to wait!"

I looked up to see the man from the register, now pointing at me from inside the curtain. He rushed down the stairs.

I ignored the disruption and dropped to my hands and knees. Moving like a predator, I crept to the beautiful woman touching herself. When in reach, I dragged her open legs toward me, eyeing her display hungrily. A yelp of pleasure escaped as I licked her pearl. She spread her legs wider for me. In response, I moved two fingers into her slick hole. The woman arched and threw her head back as I tongued her sensitive area thoroughly.

Behind her, I spotted the register man standing frozen on the ground floor, gawking at us in perverted delight. His hands drifted to the front of his pants and he unbuckled them to pull out a growing erection. Then he stumbled backwards to the front row and began to stroke himself.

I played with the woman and moved with her as she grew closer to climax. Her moans grew desperate, and I accelerated my efforts, begging her to succumb. Finally, a powerful moan escaped her, filling the room. The woman convulsed at my lips for several moments. When she was done, she collapsed on the floor of the cage and took a long, satisfied breath.

I traced my lips up her body slowly, kissing every few inches, stopping only to suck on a nipple before continuing to my true destination. At her mouth, I kissed her hard and passionately, her lips softened into mine as she kissed me back.

"Ow!" she shouted when I had grabbed the base of her hair.

"What the fuck are you doing?" she screamed at me as dragged her up to her knees.

"I need this," I said dully, pulling her by the knot of hair and dragging her out of the cage. I threw her onto the red-carpeted floor, then grabbed my vodka again.

Standing on the stage, I surveyed the crowd. They were staring at me, most with dicks in their hands, eagerly awaiting my next move.

I entered the cage and slammed the door close. While gulping from the vodka liberally, I moved to the ground. My drunken haze liberating me.

I removed my bra and my tits plunged out. Then I traced a hand across my chest and thrust my exposed breasts into the air, showing them off to the crowd.

Many of the men resumed masturbating, with fresh additions wandering in.

At the front of the crowd, I noticed the blue-haired woman had recovered from my harsh treatment. She was sucking on two different men, both ogling at me. I knew they recognized me as Zoric's daughter, and found their stares to be unbelievably titillating.

Next, I took the vodka and poured it onto my bare chest, throwing my head back. The cold liquid hit my nipples with a rush, making them hard immediately. With one last sip finishing the bottle, I moved it to the side and out of my way.

Then I removed my underwear and, moving with intention, spread my legs wide open. I wanted to expose myself completely to the group. A fresh wave of lust drunkenly rushed over me as eyes stared at every inch of my exposed body.

Once I was satisfied everyone got a full look, I brushed my hand down to my exposed hole. Slowly, I inserted a finger, knowing I was already madly wet. When I pulled it back out, it was slick with my own juices. I sucked the finger seductively, moaning in delight at the taste of me.

One man responded by grabbing on himself tighter, his face aflame with desire.

I inserted my fingers into me again, scanning the crowd to see other favorable reactions. That's when I noticed Alexei staring vehemently at me just inside the curtain door. I smiled at him and played with my clitoris. He grabbed at the bulge in his pants, trying to hide his shameful stiffness.

I closed my eyes and moaned in pleasure several times before looking back at Alexei.

Dimiter charged through the curtain and caught my eyes. He stopped dead and gawked at my alluring figure. It took impressive strength for him to recover, but he did so skillfully. Then he moved forward and whispered in Alexei's ear, snapping him back to reality.

Both men descended on me.

I closed my eyes and concentrated on my bliss. The first gunshot sounded right as I began to climax. More rounds rang out, and screams mixed with the peppy beat. I slid down to the ground of the cage and rubbed at myself harder. The last waves of pleasure washed over me as the gunfire died down.

My eyes opened to the cage door being snapped off.

Alexei stood over me as I laid out happy, wet, and exposed.

"You're coming with me."

He approached with a blanket and draped me in it.

I purred as he picked me up in his muscular arms and carried me past the massacre. Instead of looking at the destruction, I kept my eyes on my savior. Drunk, and in a euphoric bliss.

"I hope you are happy with yourself," he mumbled as he carried me out of the store and into his car.

A strong glow started radiating behind us as we pulled away. I looked over to the review mirror and saw the emporium was ablaze.

A smile crawled across my face as I watched the flames consume the neon building.

Back at the mansion, I sat in the car, refusing to move. Alexei sighed heavily before picking me up and carrying me to the same chair I sat in only a few hours earlier.

My father glared at me from across the desk, his entire body a dark red, nostrils flaring. His normal disheveled look took on a sloppier appearance.

Around the office, it looked as if a child had thrown a tantrum. Documents he usually kept in a disarray stack on his desk were now scattered about his entire office. Books laid out as if thrown across the room.

It seemed that details of my actions had made it back to him.

I stared at my father, satisfied with myself, as Alexei explained the state they found me in Arousal. Each clarifying detail caused my father's temperament to flare higher, his self-control slipping more and more. Once Alexei finished explaining how they committed arson to cover the evidence, a fierce silence fell over the room.

A short eternity passed, with no one moving or saying anything. My father's glare was tearing into me. I could see why so many found him intimidating. Finally, he broke the silence.

"And you think you have won," he condescended.

A silent giggle made its way up to my lips. I felt it grow more into a loud deranged laugher, mostly from still being drunk.

"Angel!" my father barked.

A fresh wave of lunacy washed over me and it took several minutes for my laughter to die down. Eventually it become a small chuckle that rested into a sly smile.

"I want in the business, and I want to pick who I marry," I demanded.

My father's eyes bore flames into me. I held his gaze and remained unmoved.

"A high-level job at the bank and six months to find a husband," Fathered offered. His eyes studying me, his face tight with anger.

"THE business and two years to find a husband," I countered, moving the blanket just enough to make my father uncomfortable.

Staring very carefully into my eyes only, he spoke slowly.

"CEO of the bank and one year to find a husband, but I approve of him first."

"You are going to let me into the business and give me one year to find a husband who I can pick without your approval." I stated my demands boldly. The air became thick. My father was not one to be commanded, and especially not by his daughter.

"Angel, no," he murmured. I could hear the weariness in his tone.

"I'm never going to stop."

Father sighed deeply.

"There are more stores in this area, not to mention stripping," I added.

My father looked at me with hard, determined eyes, trying to hide how tired he was of this fight.

"Then there is the Internet, a sex tape could leak. You will have to kill so many more to stop me." I let my words hang in the air.

The silence seemed to stretch on forever as my father considered everything. We kept glaring at each other until finally; he broke off eye contact and looked down at his hands. A small sigh of resignation slipped out. He closed his eyes and pinched the bridge of his nose.

"You will have a trial period where you shadow Bane and one year to find a suitable husband. If you do not find someone after a year, you will marry the man of my choosing." He stated his agreement monotone.

A victorious smile reached my lips.

"Thank you," I whispered, then rose to take my leave.

"Angel," my father muttered as I reached his office door. I paused for a moment.

"Don't threaten me again," he said miserably. I left coolly without responding.

It had taken a little over two years, but ♫ *I was officially a gun runner*. ♫

12 Months

BANE'S GUNRUNNING BUSINESS RULE NUMBER SIX:

Think outside the box.

We encourage creative approaches to selling more firearms.

CHAPTER FOUR

"The Arousal Accident," ♫ *Bane* ♫ laughed from behind father's newspaper.

I had walked into the dining room the next morning to see my brother already seated. He was laying back in his chair, feet up on the table.

"Don't let father see you sitting like that," I scolded, grabbing some fruit that was laid out for breakfast.

"Well, if it isn't our family's best negotiator," my twin beamed at me over the paper.

I pushed his shoes off the table and he moved them down, finally sitting correctly in his chair. Normally Bane was the most conventional sibling, but he had his ways of rebelling, too.

"What are you doing here?" I asked, taking my seat across from him.

"I got a drunken, angry call last night from father. Something about his precious Angel growing up. I really could not tell if he was proud or resentful. Either way, he told me to 'drag my lazy ass' over here this morning to 'start showing your goddamn sister how to sell some guns.'" A roguish chuckle came from Bane as he slicked back an expensive haircut. He leaned back again, placing his red bottom shoes on the table, and returned to reading the newspaper.

My twin wasted no time in indulging in his own luxuries over the last two years. He moved out as soon as he could afford it and we rarely encountered each other anymore. The difference in his appearance was obvious as he seemed to reinvent himself using the money he made on the deals with father.

Today he had on a well-tailored suit that matched his gray eyes, with a colorful undershirt he only bothered to button halfway up. I studied my twin and realized this is what he thought power looked like.

Bane skimmed the newspaper and read out loud aloud, "A local adult emporium, Arousal, burned to the ground late last night. The local authorities are determining if this is an act of foul play. It is unknown if anyone was in the store during the fire."

"Put that trash away, get your feet off the table!" Father snapped as he entered the room.

Bane hastily removed his feet and sat rigidly in his chair. Father made his way around the table, snatching the newspaper out of my twin's hand and mumbling something inaudible under his breath.

The rest of breakfast went by, enveloped with a tense silence. Bane and I traded knowing smiles behind Father's paper as we picked at the food laid out. Father ignored us and read the politics section first, sipping on his black coffee. As soon as it was empty, a staffer rushed to refill his cup.

"What are you two still doing here?" He grumbled over his paper, acknowledging our presence again.

"Eating, finishing, uh, breakfast," Bane stumbled, hoping to find the words that would not cause Father's temper to snap.

"I don't remember calling you over to eat breakfast," Father responded, eyes staring sharply at Bane.

"Right, yes-"

"Go take your sister before she burns down the rest of the city," he roared, which made Bane flinch.

My brother and I stood up together in sync, almost by habit, and hurried out of the room.

"Take me where?" I asked Bane once we were a safe distance away from Father's mood.

"To New Underwood City," my brother responded tersely, clearly bothered by his recent berating.

My twin still had a long road to earning the respect he craved.

Our flight to New Underwood City was thrilling.

As we touched down on a private landing strip, a fleet of purple and gold helicopters was waiting. They were adorned with the large scripted letters of A and V on the side. I wanted to ask my twin about them, but it was too loud.

We landed on top of a large glittering skyscraper in the middle of the city. A man dressed in a bold purple and gold patterned suit moved us to an elevator on the roof. We went down two floors, and the doors opened to a wall covered in green vines. An enormous pink cursive neon sign spelling out "VOYEUR" was in the middle of the wall.

We passed the entrance to a large room adorned in shades of white with marble and gold embellishments trimming the space. Paintings, drawings, statues, and photos were dispersed around the area by a careful eye. The diligent positioning allowed each piece to be experienced separately. I spotted a photo of a woman on top of a Sybian, her head thrown back in orgasmic pleasure.

"This place is enticing," I purred.

Bane strutted past everything as quickly as possible. He turned down a hallway, and I begrudgingly followed him. My twin opened the first door on his left and entered a large, mysterious office space.

"Adonis?" He called into the room.

A delicate moan answered my brother.

In the middle of the room, a toned and naked young man was strapped onto a large black and red x-shaped cross. He was dusted with a gold that matched a cage glittering around his balls tightly.

A more mature honey blond man was kissing the neck of the younger one. His hand was squeezing around the younger man's erect shaft, which had turned red from pressure.

Bane froze, momentarily stunned. He took a full minute to recover, then mumbled something quickly before pulling me back into the art studio.

"What was that about?" I asked, watching my brother get a little flushed.

"Adonis is known for his sexual exploits. He was just simply enjoying one of them." Bane tried to laugh, clearly embarrassed.

"Want to go look at some of his collections?" He swallowed uncomfortably and moved me to the closest picture.

The first wall held black and white sketches. My favorite was showing two women kissing, one of them with their eyes open, staring out at the audience. The sketch gave the illusion of the woman following the viewer as they moved around the picture.

Further into the studio, I paused at a painting of a couple embracing. The woman was straddling the man. The painting detailing their love-making by depicting his penis penetrating inside of her.

Across from it was a painting of a woman being embraced by a man kissing her neck. On the back of the woman was the couple in various sexual positions, flowing within a cloud of colorful smoke. *It's almost as if the woman was tattooed by their lovemaking.*

I passed another painting with a woman seductively licking the side of a knife. Then I found a stretched photo of two people struggling to kiss. Hands were pulling the couple away from each other. Desire burned on the lovers' faces, a touch of pain at not being able to unite.

The last item of interest was a close-up photo of a woman's clitoris and labia taking up an entire wall itself. I had just approached the picture when a booming voice sounded across the room. Turning to the source, I found the older honey blond man gliding across the studio toward us.

His hair was well cut, parted, and gelled back stiffly. He wore white pants with a gold jacket embellished with a blue fancy pattern.

The man outstretched his hand, glittering with golden rings, to me specifically. I took it, and he opened his mouth to speak. A jumble of words fell out, and I stared confused at the man.

"Sorry, what?" I asked.

Again, he opened his mouth and began talking, but I didn't recognize any of the words.

He was speaking another language.

I pulled back my hand, stupefied and stared at Bane in horror. My twin was watching me with a half smile on his face.

"Why did you not tell me he does not speak our language?" I demanded.

"I did on the plane. You were distracted with your mirror instead of listening to me," Bane gloated.

I glared at my twin, unamused, but his delight did not diminish.

"This job is more than just traveling and a paycheck. Father will not tolerate indolence when it comes to The Business, and neither will I." My twin lost his humor when he said this.

"Ok. This business takes work, and I'll take you more seriously. Are you going to make all your teaching moments like this?" I asked, annoyed at every man in my life.

I stole a glance at the art connoisseur. He was watching Bane and me converse with a fascinated smile on his face.

"Of course not. Today, I will handle our buyer, Mr. Adonis Valencia. Tomorrow you should learn some English," Bane smiled again, pleased with himself, before turning to Adonis and launching into the foreign language.

Bane formally introduced me to Mr. Valencia, who took an interest in me right away. After shaking my hand again, Adonis smoothly turned me around and, respectfully, into his arms. While keeping one hand on my lower back, he drew me closer to the picture of the clitoris again.

"It's named *The World's Clitoris*," Bane translated Adonis's words for me.

"It is actually a mosaic using..." Bane started to translate before pausing to stare at Adonis in disbelief. Then Bane moved closer to the photo himself, not bothering to offer me further explanation.

"A mosaic using what?" I asked, inching closer to get a look at the smaller photos.

"Clitorises," Bane and I answered in unison, finally able to see the individual pictures.

Adonis, who seemed proud of himself, continued talking. He walked up to the piece and pointed to one smaller photo in particular.

"What is he saying?" I asked, eager to know more.

"He says that this is one of his own installments. He took all the photos himself after... sharing an intimate night with each woman. That clitoris was his favorite." Bane translated, his face becoming slightly flush.

"How do I say, 'I love it' in English?" I turned to Bane excitedly.

"I hardly think that is appropriate." Bane dismissed my request with a wave.

"What? If you compliment his art, maybe he will buy more?" I shot back.

Bane ignored me and turned his attention back to Adonis. The two men continued in conversation without me.

I felt someone come up next to me. A glance told me Dimiter stood towering over my shoulder. He spoke gibberish in an indistinct murmur. It took him several times to repeat it before I realized he was teaching me to say, "I love it" in English. I looked up at him, stunned, but copied the words he was whispering. Once I was comfortable with the phrase, I waited patiently for Bane and Adonis to finish.

"Ready to go back into his office?" Bane turned to me with a hand outstretched.

I ignored my brother and turned back to the mosaic on the wall.

Staring carefully at Adonis, I repeated what Dimiter told me, and a dazzling smile crossed his face.

Adonis launched into excitement, enunciating words I did not know excitedly as my brother glared between me and my guards.

Bane's trying to figure out which one it was, I mused to myself.

Adonis walked to me and took both hands in his. He kissed the top of them, then turned to my brother expectantly. Bane sighed heavily before translating.

"He wants you to know that you have a great taste in art. He also mentioned that he knew from the moment he met you, you two would become great friends." My twin rattled off the translation.

"Are you done flattering him now? Can we go do our job?" Bane sneered.

I moved my hands until I gripped Adonis' glittering, ringed fingers in mine. Then I brought them to my lips and kissed the top of them. Adonis looked at me in adornment before sweeping his arm around me again. With a great big smile, he whisked us away into his office.

The office was dark and cavernous, with navy walls and gold accents. The furniture was shades of cream that stuck out in the dark surroundings. In the center was a large fur rug and a marbled gold and black desk. The desk itself was shaped in a half circle, with beams shooting out of it as if it was a sun.

Off to one side, the gold dusted man was still hanging on the cross. His cock was fully chained in the golden cage now, a large lock sticking out of it.

Adonis took his seat in a large Gothic black chair with gold trim flaring out. Bane and I sat down across from him, and the two men started talking freely about the terms of the deal.

I looked around his office.

Directly behind Adonis's chair was a rendition of The Birth of Venus. Instead of Venus, though, a nude Adonis was painted in the center, covering his package with a seashell. I gasped when I saw it.

Adonis looked at me, a knowing smile on his face. Bane asked me what was wrong, and I waved him off, back to his conversation.

As I recovered from The Birth Of Adonis, I studied the man on the large cross. His shaggy ginger hair covered his eyes as he hung his head in a sign of submission. To my surprise, the young man whimpered.

Adonis stopped talking, holding a delicate finger in the air. He got up and sauntered over to the cross, carrying a bowl of fruit with him. Once he reached his boy toy, Adonis began feeding him grapes, one at a time. To my brother's discomfort, Adonis continued the conversation.

Bane tripped over several words as he tried to respond to our buyer with a neutral face. Whereas Adonis was nonchalant.

The boy whimpered again, and Adonis returned to his chair while my twin pulled out a few firearms to show.

I continued inspecting the tied-up man, whose head was still cast downward. He lifted it slightly and winked at me.

Bold for someone in a cock cage, I thought.

Bane nudged me to get my attention. I turned to see both men looking at me expectantly.

"He wants to know which one you like," Bane stated. I looked over the guns on the desk, then back at my brother.

"Like the best firearm out of this selection?" I asked.

"No. As in, aesthetically, which one do you like?" Bane corrected me.

"You're joking, right?"

Bane shook his head. I looked at the options laid out again.

"What outfit are we trying to match?" I asked my twin.

Bane turned to Adonis and asked my question. The art dealer chuckled, then got up. My twin and I followed. Adonis rushed in explanation as we all walked to a row of large clay statues.

The statues were of a man in uniform. All were identical, and they stood at guard with one hand out, ready for a butt of a gun.

"He is creating a modern day terracotta army and needs to know which gun looks the best." Bane explained.

I studied the statues carefully and noticed a small groove was sculpted into their shoulder to support cradling a firearm. Knowing what to do, I turned back to the desk, grabbed a few of the rifles, and brought them back with me.

As I was placing a rifle in the first statue's hand, Adonis understood what I was doing and began to help. At the end of the exercise, all four statues held a different rifle. I had one left over in my hand, though.

"Bane, can you stand at the end of the line and hold this like the rest of the status?" I asked. My twin glared at me.

"Ask the help," he insisted, nudging toward Dimiter and Alexi.

"Yeah, but Dimiter is too tall. He will throw off the visual element," I argued.

Alexei moved from his place by the doorway and next to the line of statues. I helped him adjust, so he stood just like the rest of the line and nestled the rifle to lean on his shoulder.

"Thank you," I mouthed. Alexei grumbled a "whatever," in response, but I saw a twitch of a smile.

With everything in place, I stepped back and evaluated the statues. Adonis moved next to me and assessed the different options as well. It was silent as we thought, the only movement coming from Adonis occasionally adjusting a rifle, the fixes barely perceptible.

"Is this really necessary, just-" Bane started to complain to me in our mother tongue.

Adonis and I both shushed him quickly, each holding a finger out. Alexei shook with a small, contained chuckle.

Finally, Adonis launched into a speech, pointing at several of the guns. Bane translated for me.

"He says he likes the rifles, but he is not sure if it would be better to go with a modern look or something more classical."

Adonis then pointed to my guard and spoke again. At the end of his speech, he did a sexy animal gesture at him. Alexei blushed.

"He says that he is also captivated by the Barrett because his eye keeps getting drawn to the sexy male model holding it," Bane explained. I laughed before taking the rifle from Alexei and exchanging it with one from another statue.

Adonis and I froze and pulled back. The Barrett looked great with the statue as well.

"I think this is the one," I said. Adonis murmured something in his language. I turned to my twin expectantly.

"He agrees," Bane smirked at me.

Adonis got excited and launched into another conversation with my twin. We returned to the desk, and the men concluded the sale quickly.

Bane was packing everything up when I noticed it for the first time. To my immediate left hung a very colorful painting that bewitched me.

A beautiful and busty woman was painted holding a gun indifferently up into her mouth. Enormous pink and blond hair surrounded her sharp face that held a dangerous and reckless expression. Behind her stood a man shrouded in smoke, his hands twisted around to her front, each one holding up her perfect, sizable boobs. His fingers barely covering her nipples.

I got lost in the careless violence of the painting and found myself drawn to it, trying to memorize every detail.

"He's asking if you like it," Bane said. Both men had followed me as I stared at the painting.

"Yes," I breathed, staring up, captivated. "Ask him how much is it?"

"He says it's not for sale," Bane translated for me. "It's a photo he painted, inspired by his first love. She was the only blond woman he ever wanted."

I frowned. "I mean, we have a lot of money. How much?"

Bane translated, and Adonis chuckled lightly before just looking at me and shaking his head decisively. Adonis kept my attention with his intense blue eyes. They seemed to show his frustration at not being able to converse freely with me.

I finally broke away from his gaze and looked back at the beautiful painting.

"It's too bad. I don't think I have ever found a painting I've liked so much," I said. Bane translated my words, even though I did not mean for him to.

Adonis beamed, and, through Bane, informed me, "that I have paid him some of the greatest of compliments today and that he is grateful I could join my brother in our visit."

I smiled back at Adonis and felt my heart warm a little.

Back on the plane, I fell into a booth in the cabin area. Bane grabbed champagne from our inflight bar and began pouring us two glasses. He sat down across from me and handed me mine.

"To your first sale," he held up his glass. I raised mine to his offering.

"So how did I do?" I asked. Bane shot a look over to Alexei and Dimiter lounging across from us on matching leather sofa beds. Neither man was paying any attention to us. Dimiter was playing a game on his phone, and Alexei was reading what looked to be a thick Ostrarian novel.

"Well, he bought eight thousand units," Bane disclosed.

"Wow, eight thousand for those statues?" I asked. "Is that a lot?"

"Well, since you also happened to pick out the most expensive rifle we had, the Barrett M82A1, it ended up being..." Bane paused to draw me in. It worked, and I felt myself leaning into him.

"Ended up being. How much?" I pressed when he just smiled at me.

"Sixty-four Million," He beamed.

"WHAT?" I shouted, drawing the attention of the cabin.

"Sixty-four Million," he repeated, confirming I heard correctly. I jumped up, feeling a burst of energy suddenly from the news. Dimiter stood too, and without thinking, I jumped into his arms for a hug. He laughed and twirled me around the cabin. Bane chuckled at the spectacle, taking sips from his champagne.

Being placed back firmly on the ground, I locked eyes with Alexei.

"Way to go, kid," he said, his lip curled into a half proud smile.

"Thank you," I responded, unsure if I should hug him too. Alexei decided for me by returning to his novel. For the rest of the ride home, though, I couldn't help but feel Alexei's chocolate eyes appraising me.

12 Months

CHAPTER FIVE

Father was impressed by my first sale; he gave me a ten percent cut which I used to buy a house for myself in the neighborhood. It was a sleek, modern three-story with a finished basement, which I planned to turn into a personal gun range.

I had fallen in love with the small backyard that was still big enough to squeeze in a large pool, sizeable hot tub, and Zen garden. All could be seen throughout the house, as the entire back façade was covered in windows.

After putting the money down, I found Father in his office to let him know I was moving out.

"Hello father," I sat carefully in my normal "delinquent" chair.

"What is it, daughter?" he asked, not bothering to look up while filling out a stack of forms.

"I just thought you would want to know; I'm moving out of the mansion by the end of the month," I stated. This caused my father to stop writing, and he looked up at me, hopefully.

"You found a husband?" He asked, a little too excitedly.

"No, I just bought a house and…" I trailed off at seeing a tinge of red appear on his face.

"No," he demanded, then returned to his forms.

"This is less of a question, and more just telling you," I said.

"No," he said again coolly, despite his temper noticeably rising.

"The papers are already signed," I explained. My father's head snapped up again to glare at me.

"What did I tell you? No. You are not leaving this house until you are married," Father began lecturing.

I sighed and got up to leave his office.

"Don't you roll your eyes at me, young lady," my father snapped as I stood up.

A male staffer named Savin appeared at the door. He was new, young, and eagerly trying to fill the shoes of the most recently retired house butler.

"What is it?" My father barked at Savin.

"We have a meeting to go over some of the summer house activities," Savin spoke timidly. His eyes moved between my father and I.

"I've never really noticed it before, but do you work out, Savin?" I purred to the man, moving closer to him to touch a bicep.

"Angel," my father growled.

"It's a shame I'm moving away into my own house. Otherwise, I think we could really get to know each other," I murmured seductively to

Savin, brushing my fingers up his arm to his chin. I tried to move his chin to look at me, but Savin stood still, eyes wide at my father. He trembled under my fingers.

I looked back at my father to see his face was boiling in anger. He would open his month to speak, then close it again. Finally, he barked one last "Angel!"

"Think about it," I said to Savin. With one last look at my father, I left his office.

It took Father a week to speak to me again. It was over breakfast, which I still shared with him each morning.

"You are going to need some furniture at your new place, right Angel darling?" he asked casually from behind his newspaper. I paused eating my food and just looked at my dad. He did not meet my eyes as he continued.

"I hired an interior decorator to work with you. He will send the bills my way. Consider it a moving present," he said casually. At the end of our dining, I hugged my father before rushing off to continue packing. The endearment took him by surprise. He melted into the intimate moment. Walking away, I could have sworn I heard a small sniffle, but I left my father with the dignity to not comment on it.

Decorating went on without effort. I had to travel to a few deals with Bane over the month, but my father's man had a good eye for my vision.

The windows were all outfitted with automatic shading that transitioned throughout the day. Information was fed to an automatic thermostat to update the interior temperature accordingly.

The spiral staircase in the center of the house was illuminated by hanging lights, dangled in a spiral pattern.

The bottom floor held an expansive living room, dining room, and a breakfast area.

The living room was an open concept and decorated in black and gray. A large, dark coffee table sat in the middle of it, surrounded by sleek, modern furnishings.

The second floor held the main bedroom with an attached closet. The bedroom was outfitted in dark colors, but illuminated with a maroon glow. My gigantic bed in the center of the room was placed on a platform. It faced a row of shelves that had been carved out of black cherry wood. We placed my favorite dildos and sex toys tastefully on display.

The second floor also housed the kitchen, which was outfitted in black, white, and gold. Marble counter tops with dark cabinets and matching dining sets were complimented with modern gilded chairs.

On the top floors, I had him turn the extra bedrooms into a library, media room, and sex room. The library doubled as my office, which I had moved a large desk into, to rival my father's, and then promptly ignored.

No one else seemed to be as charmed by me as Adonis.

I struggled with the language barriers, and Bane was becoming less inclined to translate for me. English, as it turned out, was the most common "business" language and very difficult to learn. I worked at it every day, putting efforts into a language book that I took with me everywhere, but kept forgetting basic words.

After embarrassing myself on several trips, I was hiding in shame at my house when my doorbell rang.

I opened the door to see Alexei standing at my porch, unsure of himself. His deep brown eyes pierced me from under his dark, carefully styled hair. He had on a black button up, pair of dark washed jeans, and boots, which made him look as serious as he took himself. In his hands, he held a book with a burgundy bow placed on top.

"Alexei," I said, a little surprised, "would you like to come in?"

"Su... sure," Alexei responded awkwardly. He cleared his throat and walked through the door stiffly as I held it open for him.

I watched my bodyguard as he shifted uncomfortably, marveling at my living room.

"You want to sit down?" I asked and sauntered to one of my couches. The move worked, and Alexei rigidly followed. He sat unusually close, his knee just brushing mine. I smiled at him innocently, waiting for my guard to do something. He stared at me for an uncomfortably long moment, clearly debating with himself if he should be here.

"What do you have there?" I asked, pointing to the book before Alexei could change his mind and bolt.

"This is for you."

He handed me the book and settled more into the couch, committing to the visit.

"Wow, English for Idiots!" I read the title out loud.

"Not that I think you are an idiot!" Alexei startled. "I just saw that you have been struggling, and the man at the store said it was the best book out there."

He blushed and buried his face in his hands.

"Thank you, I appreciate it." I pulled his shoulder toward me, trying to get his face back out of his hands.

He finally relented and turned to look at me, his face inches from mine. His eyes moved down my face and stopped at my lips. A tension between us grew, and I thought Alexei might reach out and kiss me.

"I should probably go," he said right as I suggested, "maybe we try some of these exercises in the book."

"What was that?" he asked eagerly.

"I was wondering if you wanted to try some of these exercises. Maybe practicing out loud with someone could help." I reiterated.

"Yeah, that sounds great," he responded and leaned back into the couch to make himself comfortable again.

A small giggle escaped my lips as I also leaned back onto the couch and opened the book.

An hour later, we had moved much closer together as we argued over the English language. I had propped my legs over Alexei's lap. His rough hands rubbed over them as he explained I should spend more time learning useful words and stop wasting time on trying to understand slang.

"But we run an arm dealing business. Understanding slang will be important for the black market!" I defended myself.

"Not as much as learning correct pronunciation. Here look, pronounce this," he pointed to a word in my book, which was spread open on my lap.

"Read," I said confidently.

"No, it's actually read, as in the past tense. I read my English book. Not actively, I am reading the English book. You must look at the surrounding words to determine the correct way to pronounce it," he corrected me.

"Oh, just you wait!" I playfully slapped my guard's chest, secretly pleased to confirm it was hard with muscles. "Wait until I find that one person who will be impressed that I know WAP stands for wet ass pussy." I giggled into my book, pleased with myself.

Alexei sighed with fake frustration.

"That's all well and fine, Angel, but not everyone will be so captivated by how beautiful you are as Adonis was." He leaned back, moving both arms behind his head, a cocky grin on his face.

I looked up at my guard and smiled, a warm feeling spreading through me.

"You think I am beautiful?" I whispered, not meaning to, but barely getting the words out.

Alexei's smile dropped. He removed his arms from behind his head and crossed them in front of his chest.

"I mean, uh, yeah Angel, everyone thinks you are beautiful," Alexei coughed and looked away from me, toward the general direction of the door.

I turned his head in my direction again by pulling on his chin gently.

"No. Do *you* think I am beautiful?" I asked.

Alexei stared at me for several long moments, my chest filling with warmth every time his gaze kept lingering down to my lips. Finally, he broke the silence.

"I can't do this, Angel," he said, pulling his gaze away from me and staring straight ahead. He released his arms again and caressed my legs, but more in a friendly manner than a romantic gesture.

My stomach dropped.

"I... do what?... why?" I faltered, feeling caught in a trap, unsure how to proceed.

"I mean, your father would kill me to start. I am supposed to be protecting you." Alexei ran a hand through his hair, causing it to become chaotic.

"Father would not kill you, those games are over," I dismissed his concern with a wave of my hand.

"Is it over?" Alexei asked.

I looked up to see his eyes piercing into me, anger lurking behind them.

"What do you mean?" I asked.

"I mean, how would I know I am not just another one of your guards? Sure, I am attracted to you. I also carried out my fair share of the orders to kill those I caught you fucking. I'll be honest, most of them I secretly enjoyed offing simply because they had to audacity to think they deserve to touch you," his admission caught himself off guard. He cleared his throat and took a deep breath to regain some composure.

"How would I expect any other fate if I touch you? Just because you are no longer feuding with your father, I doubt he would suddenly be ok with you sleeping with the help." He stared deep into my eyes as he said this. I felt pinned by his look.

"You would be different, and I hope you would know that Alexei. You're not the help."

I pulled myself closer to him and rested my head on his arm. A long moment stretched between us.

"Besides, you are as young as my sister," Alexei broke away from me, chuckling to himself, "I should date a woman my own age."

"You are only ten years older than me!" I exclaimed, poking him in the side to which he jumped slightly. At that, he grabbed both of my hands and held them in loose captivity in front of us.

"I didn't know you had a sister." I looked up at my captor through thick eyelashes.

He sighed.

"I... had a sister," he started.

"She was a couple of years older than you and we were close. About nine years ago when I was busy chasing a bullshit dream to become some champion fighter, she..." he choked up for a moment, "she was killed."

His words hung thick in the air.

I pulled one of my hands free and caressed his arm. This was the first time I had ever heard of Alexei having a sister, much less one that had been murdered.

"Her volatile boyfriend, who thought he was some big badass, stabbed her... all over her body. They had had some fight, and he lost control of his anger. I had hints their relationship was abusive before, but I was never sure, and did not know on how to intervene.

"My sister would have never allowed me to get involved, anyway. She was such a sweetheart, but had a temper too. That is why I think he killed her; he could never truly control her." Alexei stared off into the distance, eyes glassed over with the memories.

"I was.... I had...I didn't respond well." He admitted, a look of guilt crossed his face with another memory.

"How is anyone supposed to respond to that appropriately?" I asked, inching closer.

"I hunted him, or I tried to, but he disappeared after her murder. Probably killed by some other gang member, or that is what I tell myself, so I don't.... It doesn't matter." Alexei turned to me.

I nodded at him sympathetically.

"I realized my dream was senseless and stupid, so I moved on. Then, I found myself at the bottom of every bottle I could find for ten months straight until one day something snapped."

He sighed and unconsciously moved an arm around me, drawing me closer and into his lap.

"I don't remember how it started. I was so drunk... Some slick douche just showing up in my space and we fought. He was bigger than me, but I had this fury. I just needed to punch something. We brawled, and he knocked me down good. Then he laughed, thinking he won the fight, but I still carried this wrath.

"I lifted myself back up and started throwing punches again. He would hit me down, but I kept on getting back up again. I was just so angry. Angry at the world, angry at my sister, but most importantly, angry at myself."

I moved one of my hands to his chest. He placed a free hand over it. His eyes looked straight ahead, far away into nothing. He continued his story.

"I kept being knocked down when Ivan showed up. Ivan was the owner of the bar I had been drinking at. Apparently, one of the many nights I was drunk, I told him my... about my sister. I didn't remember it and he never brought it up again, just left me to my drinking. I was a reliable paying customer, no need to get involved.

"That night though, he stopped the fight, chased out the man and his friends, had me dragged to the back. I was barely conscious, but he took care of me. After I had slept the drunk off, I woke up to find him by my bed. First thing out of his mouth was 'do you have a fucking death wish, son?' I ignored the question but couldn't escape the next two hours of him lecturing me about my drinking, the fight, and telling me to get my life together.

"I broke down; I was so alone, like the only person who could help me with my grief was the one I was grieving, which just made the grief worse. Ivan let me cry and when I was done, he offered me a job. Told me that a job would do me good for once, get my mind out of my head and into life. I started body guarding for him at the bar. That's how I got into... what I do now."

Alexei looked at me, his eyes smoldering.

"But he told me... he told me it wasn't my fault what happened with my sister. That she was her own person and got into her own trouble. That it was the past and drinking myself to death would help nothing.

"He told me to find a new purpose in life, and I did. I promised myself to strive and protect any vulnerable person I could from those horrors of life. The abuse and pain. I've saved drunken women from being raped, others from being beaten by their deadbeat boyfriends.

"Protecting you, though, has brought me the greatest joy in life. I remember the first time I saw you, storming out of your dad's office while I was waiting to meet him for the first time. Ivan had put in the good word for me now that I think of it, but you came storming out, lipping about your father."

Alexei chuckled and smiled down at me. His hand burning on my skin.

"It's been a challenge to keep up with you, but you are so good and pure and sweet under that tough skin of yours. My world would be a much worse place without you in it." He finished his story, keeping his eyes on me.

I leaned into him, resting my head on his shoulder, processing everything.

"I had no idea... I'm sorry," I whispered into the lingering silence.

Alexei breathed heavily and whispered in my ear, "it's ok, I never told you."

I sat up to look at him. He had a tortured look on his face that pained me. Tentatively, I brushed my fingers over his cheek.

He closed his eyes and grabbed my hand. In a tender moment, he brought my fingers to his lips and slowly kissed each of my fingertips. Then, he moved our hands down onto our laps and intertwined our fingers.

The silence remained between us for several moments as Alexei played with my hand.

"So, as I was saying, you're too young for me," he cut through the intimacy of the moment.

I pulled out of his embrace, acting offended, as he chuckled.

"You mean you wouldn't want me to do this?" I asked, then softly kissed his neck down along the collar of his shirt.

He held his breath, trying to maintain his composure. I pulled the collar of his shirt down, revealing more of his chest hair, and continued my trail of sensual kisses.

Finally releasing his held breath, he gasped out, "older women have more experience. They know how to please a man."

I pulled back to look at him. He had a clever smile on his face.

"Well, if you feel that way," I untangled myself from him. His arm tightened around me, and he pulled me back into his embrace, all the way, until our lips met.

The kiss started gently. Then his hand found my neck, and he pulled me in. We melted together for what felt like forever. Once we stopped to catch our breaths, I knew what I wanted.

My movement startled him at first, as I straddled him and grabbed his shirt to remove it. A few buttons down, though, and he just pulled it off for me.

I marveled at his body.

Alexei had well sculpted abs that I couldn't help but rub my hands down. He had bulging chest muscles and biceps. I secretly wondered how he managed to not accidentally tear apart every shirt he owned by flexing.

A pleased look danced across Alexei's face as he watched me, before he became more serious again and moved closer for another kiss. He pulled me into him with those powerful arms and I became undone.

In an impressively quick move, he took off my shirt and rushed back to kissing me, his hands caressing up my naked back. As I was not wearing a bra, his thumb brushed the sides of my boobs. The sensation teased me, causing my nipples to harden.

He broke off our kiss and looked at my exposed breast lustfully.

His hands slid to the front of me, and each held up a boob. He just smiled at the sight, then he slowly leaned in and kissed my nipple. His lips brushed across my tit, and he found his way over to my other breast. He kissed it as well, then expertly sucked my tit.

I arched my back in pleasure.

Alexei continued his tender sucking on my nipple, sometimes brushing his tongue along the tip, while his other hand moved up to play with my free breast.

I was overcome with the sensation and moaned.

At the sound, Alexei moved me down onto the couch and pulled off my pants. He hovered over me, kissing my lips softly, then my he continued his kissing down my stomach, past my navel, and to my sensitive area.

I felt his tongue moving lightly between my legs, and gasped. He found my sensitive spot immediately and sucked on it playfully.

I felt myself awakening.

Alexei continued his pleasant torture on my clitoris, and I felt him move a finger into my opening, followed by another.

I clinched my muscles around his fingers and Alexei sucked at me harder.

My rapture started to overcome me. I was writhing under his lips when Alexei stopped sucking. He looked up at me mischievously as I groaned. Then he bent back down and moved his tongue around my pearl roughly. It was too much, and I gasped in ecstasy, spasming.

The orgasm left me blissful, and I smiled up at Alexei as he pulled away from me, clearly pleased with himself.

"How can I return the favor?" I asked, moving toward him to undo his pants.

Alexei stared at me, contemplating. A mix of horror and arousal in his expression. He looked down at me while sucking on his fingers, the ones that were inside of me only moments ago.

"I should go," he stated, monotone and under tight control.

"Alexei?" I asked, dumbfounded.

"I should go. I shouldn't have come here; I don't know what I was thinking. I shouldn't have touched you. I'm sorry Angel. I shouldn't have... I am so sorry. Please don't tell anybody." Alexei started rambling as he grabbed his shirt and started toward the door.

"I won't tell anyone, but-" I started and could not finish as he was out the door.

The next morning, seeing Alexei's English book open on the coffee table left me bitter. I threw it away when I saw it and hired an English tutor on the spot.

10 Months

CHAPTER SIX

"I remember my first bribe as if it was yesterday," Father smiled into the drink before sipping.

"It was with an Ostraria official. I needed a very specific shipment of firearms and had run out of options. I don't know how he had acquired them, but whispers told me he was the only source."

My father sat smiling, looking at nothing, just lost in his memory.

"I staged a happenstance meeting, offered to keep buying the man vodka shots. We kept downing them, and I was beyond trashed by the time he started to loosen the fuck up. Finally, he turns to me and says, 'If I didn't know any better, I would assume you want to make me an offer for something?' I guess he knew flattery for what it was."

Father paused again and took a slow, meaningful puff from his cigar.

A cloud of nicotine rushed out of his mouth, temporarily shrouding my father.

"I offered him money, gold, jewels, your mother, he wanted none of it," father continued, leaning into his desk.

"Finally, I just asked him what he wanted, and I'll never forget what he said to me."

"I want nothing more than for one day for you to bore your children with this story to discourage from bribing anyone?" I asked.

"No," Father ignored my comment, "I want to go to the mouse's house."

"What?"

"What exactly!" Father chuckled. "He wanted to go visit that amusement park in Havenia!"

At this point, my father genuinely laughed, his face turning a joyful scarlet color now. At the end of his glee, his crackle turning into a smoker cough. He cleared his throat with a sip of his drink, then went back to take another puff from his cigar.

"A round trip for the two of us, and one night of crocodile wrestling, ended up being cheaper than what I was originally trying to bribe him with!"

My father laughed again, but he seemed to be the only one in on his own joke as Bane and I shifted bored in our seats.

"Anyway," my father pulled out a large document and laid it out on top of the crest. "This is the current list of all the embezzlement companies currently under Zoric, LLC."

I ran a hand over all the different logos on the piece of paper. One of them had a large X crossed out over it.

"Wait, why is this one crossed out?" I leaned forward to get a look at it. Then I recognized the familiar cursive. "We owned Arousal?" I asked.

My father glared at Bane. My brother smirked back.

"I told you she didn't know, and it was just coincidental," Bane gloated, his eyes gleamed. My father grumbled, then pulled out his wallet. He threw over a couple of hundreds across the desk. Bane picked up the cash smugly.

"We *used* to own Arousal, until someone decided to test my patience and it had to be burned down. That reminds me, I got the insurance check from that and was going to put half in your account. I don't strictly want to reward your insubordination, but as it turns out, we were losing money operating that place," my father brushed at his desk casually, refusing to admit to my actions. I watched him and marveled at our strange relationship.

"However, yes. It turns out sex stores and strip clubs are great for embezzling cash." He added.

"And somehow a non-profit for war relief," I said, looking down at another logo.

Bane chuckled, "Yeah, I thought that was ironic myself."

"Are you two done wasting my time?" my father barked hotly.

"Yes, father," Bane and I said in unison.

Father opened his mouth to start another lecture, when the doorbell rang out, loudly. We all sat waiting for the chiming to pass before my father opened his mouth again.

"Excuses me," a timid voice interrupted before Father could say anything. A housekeeper was standing in the doorway with a terrified expression on her face.

"What is it?" my father snapped.

"It's for you, well for the family," the young woman gestured to Bane and I.

"Is it important?" Father asked.

The woman started to nod yes. Then slowly, dazed, the nod turned into an uncommitted no.

"Well, what is it? Yes or no, answer me woman!" my father's temper slipping into his voice.

"I don't know. It's just so... unusual," she finally sputtered out.

The three of us made our way to the front door, following the housekeeper. She opened the door for us and I couldn't help but gasp at the sight.

In our broad front doorway, two rows of women stood in rigid, straight lines to form a runway. Each one was topless, but long flowing hair covered all exposed nipples. They had on Grecian loincloths and each head was adorned with a golden leaf crown. Impressively, every woman held up a long gleaming horn in perfect alignment with each other. A purple and gold banner hung from each instrument with cursive A's displayed on the left banners and V's on the right.

The team of women began playing their instruments, playing a musical version of a popular pop song. At the very end of the runway, a man unfurled himself and turned. I recognized him immediately as the young man Adonis had chained up in his office when we visited. He was dressed in a tight black thong with large black wings strapped onto his back.

To the beats of the music, he danced gracefully toward us, careful to keep a sizable violet box balanced and upright in his hands. He spun and leaped divinely, taking up our front area as his own heavenly stage, all while holding the package safely to his chest. Finally, he leapt to just in front of us, allowing for one more dramatic twirl. Then, with his free hand, he pulled on a ribbon, which caused the walls of the box to fall open. Butterflies sprang from the gift immediately and flew away, leaving just a small Navy envelope addressed to "The Zorics" in gold calligraphy.

The show ended with the young man beaming suggestively at me. He outstretched his hand, inviting us to take the card, as the music faded behind him.

I clapped excitedly, which made the dark angel in front of me smile brighter. My father groaned behind me.

"This is exactly why I don't deal with that..." I looked at Father to see his face had turned raging red. He struggled to find an appropriate word. "Man," he spat out before retreating back into the mansion.

I reached out to grab the invitation, but Bane snatched it first, closing the door once he had the envelope. I caught the young man wink at me right before the door slammed shut on his face.

"Do you think I should get his number? I am on the lookout for a husband," I teased.

"No," he responded assertively, not bothering to look at me as he tore into the envelope.

"Lots of cute girls out there. You could always get one of their numbers," I prodded.

"Bold of you to assume I don't already have them," he mumbled while reading the delicate card he now held.

"What is it?" I asked him when he scrunched up his face in confusion.

"Adonis invited us to something called... a Midnight Menagerie?" he handed me the invitation.

"Dear Sofia and Bane, I do hope this invitation finds you. This address was the only one I had. I hope you can make it. – A," was carefully scrawled at the top in gold ink.

Below the note was an invitation for a party next months in Curiosix, one of the richest areas known for gambling and partying.

"The theme is sexy royalty. Women's cleavage is required and the dress code calls for a minimum spend of ten thousand dollars," I read off and then looked up at my brother, hopeful.

"Angel, no. We don't want to encourage those types of relations with a client." Bane said, disgruntled. "We don't even know what a Midnight Menagerie is."

I stared at my brother with pleading eyes.

"Please Bane, I need to find a husband. This is the perfect chance to look for partners outside of this area."

"I don't know." he looked down at me uncertainly.

"If I marry someone from abroad, it could be a great way to open new markets," I pleaded.

"Take your sister," my father's voice boomed behind me.

I turned to see my father had not wondered off as far as I had thought after the show. He locked eyes with my brother to make him understand it was a command, then turned to walk back to his office.

Bane sighed, "Fine."

9 Months

BANE'S GUNRUNNING BUSINESS RULE NUMBER TEN:

Expect the unexpected.

Be ready for surprises and exploit opportunities when you can.

CHAPTER SEVEN

I spent the next month preparing for the party.

My first task was to design an ostentatious dress fit to my curves and gave it to our family seamstress to produce. Then I quickly booked a phenomenal cosmetologist and arranged for her to meet us at the tiny chateau Bane had rented. Finally, I increased my private English lessons to an excessive degree, determined to be able to hold a conversation with my imagined handsome foreign suitor.

To my surprise, Father met us at our private hangar before we departed for Curiosix.

"Hello Father," Bane grumbled, exasperated with our trip already.

"Hello son," Father mumbled as he looked past my brother to me, pride shimmering in his eyes.

I approached my father, who handed me the transparent box he was holding. Inside was a sparkling round princess crown made with diamonds and accentuated with sapphire.

"Oh, um…, thanks," I said clumsily, puzzled by my father's sudden kindness.

"Remember honey, nobody less than seven figures, OK?" he smiled warmly at me before kissing me on the cheek and disappearing to his car.

After settling in my private bedroom on the plane, I called my tutor for a quick last-minute lesson. We were covering flirting phases when I heard the rasp of knuckles on my door. I ended my lesson quickly, with the promise to call back if I had time, and answered the door. Alexei was leaning in the doorway, one arm propped up, an unreadable expression on his face.

"I was sent back here to check on you," he grumbled.

"I was just practicing some English with my tutor," I explained.

Alexei nodded his head once in satisfaction, then pulled his arm back. To my surprise, he did not walk away, but instead stood awkwardly in the doorway.

"That's a nice pin you have there. I saw you wearing it on one of your first trips," Alexei noted, lifting his hand to brush his fingers of the broach I was wearing. It was shaped like an AK-47 with little diamonds decorating it, a small bejeweled blue flower sticking out of the barrel of the gun.

"Yes, someone left it for me as a gift," I explained, looking down at the beautiful trinket I had come to love.

"Someone?" Alexei asked.

"Yes. I am not sure who. It was just left in a small box in my closet.

Whoever it was must really like me. I had it appraised, and it's real, the diamonds and sapphire. Easily ten thousand dollars," I mused.

"About as much as a raise," Alexei uttered. I looked up into his eyes and they were dark with lust again. His face was close to mine. We had unconsciously leaned in toward each other. His eyes traced down to my lips again, and I felt myself moving in closer to him.

"Angel?" Bane called down the hallway. I jumped back. Alexei stayed where he was, his shoulder leaning into the doorway.

"Yes?" I responded to my brother, still looking at my guard. Alexei's eyes burned with passion. They traced down my body slowly as I heard footsteps coming our way.

"She's just practicing her English," Alexei told Bane, pulling away from the door to make room for my brother.

"Oh, that's excellent!" Bane praised me. "Is that what took you so long? You two were practicing conversing?"

"Yes," Alexei and I said in guilty unison. Bane looked between us for only a moment before brushing past me into my bedroom.

"I have a surprise I want to show you," he told me.

I watched my twin as he walked over to the bookshelf. Then, with a glance back at the door, I noticed Alexei had left. Lust tingled down my spine and then abated. I moved to my bed to wait for the surprise from Bane.

"Remember these?" He said, pulling a book off the shelf and showing me the cover.

Rotten Ryan Second Contact.

I smiled fondly at our favorite childhood book.

"What happened to Rotten Ryan First Contact?" I jest, and Bane and I laugh at our inside joke.

According to the official canon, Ryan was so rotten that he never answered the first alien's attempt to contact the earth. In an endeavor to establish power, he waited for the aliens to make a second contact attempt before answering. In reality, it resulted in a confused fan based who was left wondering "What happened to Rotten Ryan First Contact?"

"My favorite was always Rotten Ryan, Dr. Yes," I mused.

"Really? I thought you would have hated that one," Bane said, grabbing a few more books off the shelf, all of them Rotten Ryans, and placing them on my bed.

"Why?" I asked.

"Because I read it to you after... well, I just always assumed you associated it with..." Bane got uncomfortable mentioning the one and only time my father slapped me.

It was my first- and only time attempting to try drugs. I was fifteen and my boyfriend had talked me into trying cocaine with him. He had secured the drug, and we were staring at a few lines he prepared for us on the table when my father came home.

Father shattered the table, threw my boyfriend across the room, then backhanded me so hard the bruise lasted a week. Bane, hearing the commotion, ran into the room and saved me before worse could happen. My twin locked us in my room and read to me my favorite childhood book while Father cooled down outside.

"I forgot that was the book you were reading to me that night." I said, revisiting the memory. "Father apologized anyway. He promised he would never physically chastise me again," and he never did, despite all the ways I pushed his anger over the last several years.

"What was your favorite Ryan book, Bane?" I asked.

"Rotten Ryan, The Honey Pot, hands down," he beamed at me.

"Ugh, of course you like the worst one!" I playfully threw a pillow at Bane, who caught it with his free hand. He threw it back at me and it softly hit my head.

"Now lay back down, you alien, and let me read this to you." Bane did his best to mimic a cowboy with his Rotten Ryan voice.

I curled up in the bed and Bane laid down next to me, opening the first book he had found and read to me like old times.

We reached Curiosix late in the evening and checked into the rental.

The castle was miniature, with four bedrooms split over two different floors. There was a massive grand salon, that was overshadowed by an upstairs balcony, with an embellished decorative staircase crawling up one side. Near the salon, there was a smaller kitchen with a cute wooden table for conversation while cooking.

I wanted to explore more, but due to the late hour; I claimed my upstairs bedroom and went to bed.

Early the next morning, I was up and full of restless energy. It was going to be a long day, followed by a magical night.

As I was in the kitchen making coffee, Alexei stumbled in. He sat at the small wooden table and mumbled a "Good Morning" through his hands.

I couldn't help but stare, as he had nothing on but tight boxers. Small, dark, curly hair covered most of his body. My eyes roamed up his brawny physique as I felt desire pool within me.

"Angel?" he asked me tiredly. I jumped out of my feverish reprieve and noticed he was peering through his fingers, watching me ogle him.

I quickly returned to making coffee again, burying my embarrassment by pretending I didn't care he was with in the room.

"Angel?" he whispered heavily in my ear. I felt his hands grab my hips. I leaned into him.

His fingers grazed my skin as he moved aside some of my hair, exposing the side of my neck. With utmost tenderness, he pressed his lips against the bare surface, leaving a trail of kisses. His deep scent of amber musk enveloped me, turning me feverishly lustful.

GO-O-O-O-NG.

The castle gong rang out announcing a visitor. I pulled myself away from Alexei quickly.

GO-O-O-O-NG.

The doorbell rang again, heavier this time, and I ran to greet my cosmetologist. As I turned to show her where to take her things, my eyes met Alexei's. He was back at the table again, drinking from a cup of black coffee and staring at me lasciviously. I guided the artist to my room upstairs. Alexei's piercing gaze fallowing me the entire way up.

The rest of the day, I spent commanding Nadia how to do my makeover. I had her sweep up my lengthy hair into a romantic cascading up-do with strings of rhinestones shimmering throughout my curls. My glimmering crown was secured safely on my head. Finally, I asked her to do a drastic glam smokey eye, with a small diamond secured as a Monroe mole.

Bane called from downstairs that the men were ready and my artist collected her tools as I rush to get in my gown.

The floor length sheer dress slipped on and fit heavenly. The dress was incredibly revealing, showing more than hiding. With a deep V-neck to show off my cleavage, it had blocks of gleaming silver fabric strategically placed, covering just enough to not show all of me.

When I stepped out on the top floor balcony, I looked down into the salon to see the three well-dressed men busying themselves, waiting.

Bane was outfitted in a tight green felt suit that had gold ornaments scattered on only one side of his blazer. With no undershirt on, his bare chest was decorated with a thick chain gold necklace, with a lion in the middle. Emerald glimmered from the eye sockets.

Dimiter and Alexei were both fitted into similarly intricate outfits.

Dimiter had on a contoured navy body suit covered in intricate patterns using gold and teal rhinestones. His already broad shoulders were extenuated with extreme and sharp shoulder epaulets.

Alexei was in a similar suit, only his color pairing was black and gold. The suit extended to only his shoulders, but came with a matching overlay blazer that fell to his knees.

Both my men had a crown of golden leaves placed on their heads.

Alexei noticed me first, as he was sitting on the couch eating a croissant. When he saw me, though, he froze, mouth hung open from almost taking a bite. The delectable pastry fell from his hands, hitting the plate with a thud.

Bane looked over at the sound, then followed Alexei's eyes up to me.

"We're going to be having a wedding soon, I see," Bane chuckled to himself as I floated down to the salon stairs.

"Oh, dear Angel," Dimiter rushed over to the bottom of the stairs, grabbing my two hands when I reached his height. "Promise I will be your best man at the wedding," he playfully quipped, before kissing my hands.

"Of course, dear Dimiter," I responded, pretending to faint into his arms. He caught me and carried me to the middle of the room, both of us laughing together.

"Stop fooling around. Adonis is sending over our ride soon," Bane instructed, putting on his flashy shoes.

Dimiter put me down and offered me his arm. I grabbed it and we walked out to the front together to wait for the ride over.

In the middle of the front yard, however, was a massive air balloon. Its basket was tethered to the ground and a man in a vivacious, colorful suit was standing rigidly next to it.

"Bane?" I called into the house toward my brother. "Did you order us a hot-air balloon?" I asked.

"God no, what?" My brother responded, walking out the front door with Alexei. They stopped behind us and gaped up at the balloon. It was purple and gold with a large A and V on it. Bane laughed heartily to himself.

"Adonis sure knows how to throw a party," he mumbled.

The waiting man stepped forward and offered me his hand, which I took. I allowed him to whisk me up into the basket first. My brother and the guards followed, then the man hopped in himself.

It was dark outside, so the only thing we could see in the air were the scintillating lights of the cities below us. As we moved, the lights became scarcer across the landscape. Eventually, the only visible light was that of a few other hot air balloons, matching ours, drifting in the wind.

Adonis's stiff man steered the balloon around a large hilltop, and in the middle of the blackness, a sudden brilliance emerged. The immense castle was spotlighted with indigo lightning. A crowd of people circling the entrance. An abundance of hot air balloons lined stretches of land outside, as other guest were being dropped off.

I felt anticipation rise as we floated closer to the magnificent sight.

We landed thereafter, and Bane made a point to offer me his arm. I took it and allowed him to lead me into the crowded entrance.

"Oh, look!" I exclaimed, motioning at a woman passing by. She had on a long black lace dress that clung to her figure seductively. Over it was a black cage petticoat that stretched out from her hips, enclosing two men in the confine. Fairy lights twirled around the petticoat bars.

"That's the opera singer! She was here last time, fantastic voice," a stranger informed me, overhearing my exclamation.

The castle's interior was immensely decorated with chandeliers, strings of crystals, and bushels of red roses down every hallway. We followed the general flow of the crowd when I found our host standing off to one side, greeting guests.

Adonis had on quite the outfit. He had a tight, low-cut blue and green suit that was heavily jeweled. An immense golden shoulder piece connected with a trailing cape. The cape itself was made from peacock feathers with large sapphires and emeralds scattered throughout. On his head, a large golden crown with matching jewels completed the ensemble.

I pointed Adonis out to Bane and he walked me over to be seen by our host. When he noticed us, Adonis smiled eagerly, pulling me into a hug, and shaking hands with my brother.

"You've come to the wrong party," Adonis said to me, lifting my chin to inspect my face. "Tonight's theme is royalty, not otherworldly," he waved to Bane expectantly, asking him to translate for me. Bane looked at me and we exchanged a smile.

"It's nice to properly meet you, Mr. Valencia," I greeted him in perfect English. Adonis' face light up, his heavily ringed hands touching each cheek in astonishment.

"Well, look who fell from heaven and learned a new language," he playfully pinched my cheek. I beamed back, pleased.

"DONNIE!" a woman with screaming red hair, dramatically pinned up, stumbled over.

The woman's strapless mermaid dress was matching Adonis' suit. The tight silhouette was intricately bejeweled with teal crystals. Then, when the dress started to flair, peacock feathers swept out with more jewels set between them. Her crown was a small and dainty, lost in the sea of red. Every time she moved, her martini glass sloshed liquid about.

"Hey Donnie!" the woman repeated.

"What did I say about calling me Donnie, Cleo?" Adonis responded tightly through gritted teeth.

"I'm bored," she said in her falsetto voice.

"I don't know what you expect me to do about that, princess," Adonis said, annoyed.

"Play with me," she suggested, looking at him seductively.

He chuckled stiffly and moved his arm around her, sweeping her closer to us.

"Here, come meet some of my business acquaintances," he suggested, indicating Bane and me to the woman.

"Hi, I'm Cleo."

The woman raised her hand aimlessly toward us. Bane tried to grab it, but she dropped it before he could. Cleo turned back to our host.

"Ok, I met them. How much longer until midnight?" she demanded.

Adonis laughed another fake, controlled chuckle that barely held his irritation.

"Honey, we still have about an hour. Now this is Bane and Sophia." He tried to turn the redhead back to us. She resisted the movement and took a sip from what was left of her martini.

"Where is Natan?" Adonis sighed heavily, looking around.

"Probably already fucking his way through this party," Cleo went to sip her drink again, only to find it empty. She snapped at someone walking by and handed them her empty glass. The stranger looked down, confused at the offer and clearly not wait-staff. Adonis saw the incident, grabbed at the glass, and dismissed the guest.

"Let me find Natan, my assistant, and he can show you around." Adonis continued his search through the crowd. "Damned if I can't seem to find him," Adonis muttered to himself.

Then something caught his eye, and a dangerous look passed over his face.

"Excuse me, I need to go take care of som-" before finishing his sentence, he charged into the crowd and disappeared.

"Whatever. I'll show you around." Cleo motioned for us to follow her. Bane and I looked at each other, hesitant.

"I don't bite unless you're into that sort of thing." Cleo pointed a finger at Dimiter. "He is, I can tell," she winked. Then she turned to usher us down the hallway, uncaring if we bothered to accept. We followed her without further discussion.

Cleo pushed past guests, a surprising amount of them redheads, to lead us into the grand ballroom. It was breathtaking, with thousands of crystal strings hanging from each wall up to the ceiling. Lights twinkled between the bejeweled cords, casting a soft glow below. Red and black roses adorned every surface of the wall, ceiling, and bar areas. Along the outside of the room, dark leather couches were already occupied with couples caressing each other.

An enormous platform stage protruded from the opposite wall, where a stunning redhead sang into a gilded vintage microphone. She was dressed in a ruby feathered corset, a sheer skirt flowing down from her waist to the stage. Behind her, a small team of sirens adorned in scarlet, sensually moved to her music.

"This is the main dance area for now," Cleo explained when we reached the edge of a dance floor. Several patrons occupied it and were grinding on each other.

"What do you mean, for now?" Bane asked Cleo.

"It's a midnight menagerie," she responded haughtily to Bane, as if that answered the question.

"Right, what's a midnight menagerie?" he asked.

Cleo stared at my brother for several moments. Then realization dawned that we, truly, did not know what 'a midnight menagerie' meant. She giggled wildly, then in her falsetto voice sing-songed, "You'll seeeee."

"We'll see?" Bane's eyebrows shot up in surprise at her giggling.

The redhead ignored him, spotting someone behind us that piqued her interest instead.

"OH Francis, there you are. Hey, you owe me a bump," she ran off, away from our group. I watched her leave before Bane drew my attention back.

"Right, I am going to mingle," my brother said, eyeing a woman across the room from us.

"Good luck with your dating or whatever tonight," he said a bit stiffly, then sauntered off in the direction he was looking.

I stood at the edge of the dance floor, watching the crowd. More people filed into the room, groups of them now chatting on the dance area, too. Apprehension rose in me. Was he here, the man I was going to marry?

"You seem unusually anti-social," Dimiter whispered next to me.

I looked up to my guard, who had moved closer. He was staring out at the dancer as well.

"I'm nervous." I swallowed back the panic rising in me.

"I've never known you to be unsure of yourself," Dimiter tried to encourage me.

"What if he is here?" I asked.

"Who?"

"My... future husband," I flinched slightly at admitting it out loud.

"Then you did what your father asked, and found someone to marry," Dimiter shrugged.

"But what if I am not ready for that kind of commitment?" I said, looking away, my cheeks warming. My guard said nothing to this and continued to let me wallow in my anxiety.

"What about him?" Dimiter gestured across the ballroom to a man in a leather suit that was tied together at the seams, like a corset.

A laugh escaped me before I could stop myself. Dimiter joined soon after, his efforts to cheer me up, by distracting me, worked. I pushed away the thoughts about marriage and focused on having fun tonight.

"I need a drink," I mumbled and suddenly one appeared before me.

It was attached to a very toned man attired in fitted silk underwear. A flashy crown was on his head, tilted slightly to one side. He had aqua green eyes, and a chiseled jawline, with tattoos stretching down the length of his body.

"Good evening, Queen," his deep rumbling voice purred.

I reached out to take the cocktail, enchanted by the newcomer. Instead of giving me the drink, though, the man grabbed my hand and kissed me on the palm.

"You look ravishing, darling," he said as he moved his lips down my wrist, leaving a trail of kisses, before finally letting go and handing me my drink.

"Are you always this forward with women?" I asked him, sipping at the cocktail. It was light and sweet, probably something made from vodka.

"Only the ones who look like you," he winked.

I turned toward Dimiter, but he had suddenly vanished. Looking around, I saw him dragging Alexei away to the bar.

"Tell me, what is a woman in a dress like that seeking tonight?" the man grabbed my chin and commanded my attention back to him. His lips were dangerously close to my own.

"I'll leave that to your imagination," I breathed the words, feeling myself getting turned on by his proximity and confidence.

"Honey, you are leaving a lot out of everyone's imagination," he smiled at me, and I looked down at his delicious lips.

I felt myself getting hot, but pulled back slowly. A sly smile danced across the stranger's face.

"So do you have a name, or should I come up with one of my own, Casanova?" I asked coyly.

"Surly you can do better than that, love," he smiled, and my heart thumped in my chest with excitement.

"Romeo? Don Juan?" I teased.

He purred again, and the sound made me tingle with excitement.

"I do like a well-read woman."

"Natan! Natan!" a blond woman in a navy mermaid gown run up to us. Nathan's face fell a bit as the woman grabbed him by the arm.

"Oh, Natan, this party is just wonderful! Look at how Adonis decorated, and so many people came out! Settle an argument for me. It was at least fifty thousand dollars last year, right? Why did you two decide to lower the dress code price? Are you trying to get more people? You look great. Have you been working out? Prepared for tonight?" The woman blathered on, not bothering to stop and let Natan answer any of the questions.

"Hey Anastasia, did you see that blond man there? He said he could not take his eyes off of you in that dress." Natan finally cut in.

"Oh wow, did he really? I have never seen him before, but he sure is handsome and big, huh? I better go talk to him!" she rushed off, still chattering.

"Natan, I think Adonis was looking for your earlier," I told him, smiling.

"Between us, I hate that woman," he sighed, shaking his head. "As for my employer, he was probably going to tell me to mingle with the guests, and here I am."

"Your employer?" I asked.

"Yes, I am Adonis' assistant. I am also an artist myself, but mostly I create his dream," Natan explained, gesturing around the room.

"Do you get frustrated at not being able to contribute to his vision?" I asked.

"Oh, I contribute, don't you worry."

Natan swept an arm around my waist and led me toward the stage.

"Please come with me, my dear. I must make announcements. Midnight is approaching."

"What happens at midnight?" I asked, allowing him to guide me.

He stopped and turned toward me with a composed face.

"It's a midnight menagerie," he said expectantly. I shrugged, and he laughed wildly.

"You'll find out."

"Why does everyone keep saying that?" I asked.

"Please, please allow me personally to show you around after I am done up there," he pulled me close, then moved us toward the stage again.

We reached the front of the dance floor, and Natan handed me his drink.

"Please hold this, and don't go anywhere," he pointed at me.

"Nowhere," I confirmed.

Natan left for the stage, but then turned back quickly and grabbed me by the neck. He pulled me into a savage kiss. I froze for a moment, then released my inhibitions. His big, soft lips left me dizzy.

Just as quickly as he pulled me in, he withdrew and jumped onto the stage. The singer concluded her song and then everyone, except for Natan, rushed to gather at the back of the platform.

"Hello ladies and gentlemen. As you know, I am your host for the evening!" Natan's voice boomed, the crowd cheered excitedly. A spotlight moved to illuminate my handsome captor more brightly.

"Just wanted to remind everyone that there are party rules. Please see anyone with a glowing red arm band to get the rundown or a refresher... looking at you Maria!" Natan chuckled along with a select few audience members at the inside joke.

"Most importantly, though, we have THE number one rule. Which is-," he leaned the microphone toward the crowd as everyone yelled out, "everyone indulge to the fullest tonight!"

He pulled the microphone back toward himself.

"With that, please allow me to be the first to say for the evening... ♫ *WELCOME TO THE MIDNIGHT MENAGERIE!*" ♫

8 Months

CHAPTER EIGHT

The lights extinguished as soon as the words left Natan's lips. Excited screams rose from the crowd. Fog billowed in quickly as two poles descended on either end of the ballroom, people already posed on them. Silks fluttered to the floor over the dance floor and people in the crowd moved away to make room for the recent additions.

The spotlight changed to beaming red as the pulsing beat of a base rose. Suddenly, the singer cut through the fog, running to the front of the stage with a detached microphone. She was singing loudly, beautifully, and was completely naked. A techno swing song bellowed out as the naked dancers moved in the clouds; their silhouettes just visible through the fog.

Natan emerged in the mist, still on stage, and grabbed the hand of the singer. He twirled her around and dipped her toward the crowd. She held the microphone to her lips and belted out a powerful note. Natan bent over and ran his tongue up her naked body.

I shivered, imagining his tongue on me like that. He pulled the singer back up and made an exit.

"My Queen, may I?" he took his drink back, and offered me a free hand. I took it and he twirled me into his arms.

Looking into the ballroom again, I noticed the party looking starkly different. Almost all guests were nude now. Flashes of light swirled around, illuminating couples on couches engaging in intense acts of intercourse. A chorus of moans swelling louder than the music.

I stopped to watch a couple near the exit. A woman was saddling a man, tenderly bouncing on top of his strong cock. Her head was thrown back with both eyes closed in satisfaction. The man was holding her gingerly. His face was a matching mask of ecstasy.

"Do you see something you like?" Natan's deep voice trembled beside my ear. He kissed down the nape of my neck and I caught a small moan escaping my own lips. Natan moved around to stand in front of me and looked at me with hungry eyes.

"She just seems to be enjoying herself," I murmured, enthralled by the party.

"Indeed, she does," a dark chuckle came from my companion. He grabbed my hand and led me outside. A mesmerizing tunnel constructed from rows of brilliantly lit arches guided us along the way. Cries of orgasmic pleasure met Natan and me before the sights did.

Outside, strings of soft lights were set up to illuminate large, round pillows prepared for lovers. I walked through the couples on the beds, pausing occasionally to watch them engage in sexual acts, most pretty standard. Live peacocks were flocking about, their tails in full bloom. Past the pillows, a large air mattress was already heavily populated by a multitude of nude patrons engaging in exciting carnal acts. Off in a corner, two women were passionately kissing and fondling each other's breasts while men pounded into them. In another area, a brunette woman was sucking vigorously on the clitoris of another redheaded woman. The brunette had a man driving into her from behind while the redhead sucked on another man's cock.

I turned to Natan and smiled in delight.

"A midnight menagerie. Everything becomes hedonic at midnight." I giggled with excitement.

"You can sleep with anyone you want as long as there is consent with all parties involved. Of course, no means no. Not everyone is so voyeuristic, so respect closed doors, and no photos or videos." Natan pulled me into him until his arms circled me.

"And, of course, have as much fun as you want, Queen," he whispered on my lips before his soft mouth collapsed onto mine. As he kissed me, his hands slid down my sides. His fingers grazing the side of my breasts briefly, before continuing down my hips to squeeze my buttocks.

"How would you feel finding a room and losing that dress?" Natan whispered breathlessly, his face inches from my own.

"I would like that," I said, looking up into his golden eyes. Arousal rose in me as I desperately wanted to feel those lips kiss every inch of my body.

Leading me by the hand, Natan tried to pull me into the castle. We passed by another small gathering engaged in sensational play, and I couldn't help but watch in perverted fascination for a few moments. Someone had taken an old majestic Victorian swing frame and added a sex swing in the middle. A ginger man was laid back in the swing, sucking on the balls of a nude gentleman, as a third man penetrated him from the front. A shiver of titillation moved through me as I watched their unrestrained passion. Then Natan tugged on my hand lightly, and I followed his lead back inside.

The party was in full swing now. We traversed hallways, passing hoards of naked people giggling, touching, and moaning as we went. Doors to rooms were often left wide open, showing participants in acts of self-indulgence. Throngs of people were in the rooms too, watching, sometimes even playing with a partner.

Each room was outfitted with different themes. The furniture, chosen for their unmistakable sexual opportunity, matched the motif carefully.

The first room we happened upon was designed as a doctor's office. A woman laid out on an examination table, her feet up in stirrups, holding herself wide open as a man was enthusiastically licking at her sensitive area. Another woman was on her knees, sucking on the man as she played with herself.

"I enjoy seeing what fascinates you. It gives me an idea of how I should please you," Natan whispered in my ear, kissing my cheek softly. I pulled us to the next room, eager to see more.

The room appeared to have mirrors everywhere. The walls and ceiling were all coated in a shiny, clear reflective surface. In the middle of the room stood a large platform bed, where a man was penetrating a woman, while another man penetrated him. The three acted in sync, moving and moaning together. The mirrors multiplied them, giving the appearance of an immense horde all hedonically enjoying themselves.

Back in the hallway, people crowded against the walls, playing with each other. Their hands and mouths were in the most inappropriate of places. One particular stretch of the corridor was remarkably crowded, but at Natan's appearance, the gathering parted to make room for us. The assembly, I eventually noticed, was actually a line into a very specific room. I peeked my head inside to see what had everyone excited. Men and women were formed in a circle of sex, participants penetrating or sucking on their neighbor eagerly. As soon as a member had their desires satisfied, they signaled to leave, and the next person in line eagerly took their place in the rampage.

Natan dragged me past the rooms to a more sensual arena with scenes being played out. Candle wax was being poured and massaged onto someone's back, with hands slipping into intimate places. Another area had a man painting an intricate design on the front of a woman. When he finished, he licked the paint off of her seductively.

"Why is that man licking paint?" I asked Natan as I observed.

"It's edible, my dear," Natan chuckled.

"Seems most areas and rooms have filled up," I mused at my partner. He smiled at me wickedly.

"As host, I keep a secret room all to myself," he winked, then swept me around a corner into a new hallway that was uncharacteristically empty.

"My guests know this room is off limits." Natan grazed the nape of my neck with his lips as we approached a large solid black door. He pushed me up against it and kissed me more aggressively. I giggled with glee until I heard a soft sound at the end of the long, narrow hallway. Glancing over to investigate, I was met with Alexei's brutal stare. He was leaning against the far wall, arms cross, trying his best to look casual.

Natan, unaware we had an audience, moved me away from the door to open it. He tried to pull me into the room after him, but I felt myself freeze. Alexei's dark eyes burned into me, passion lurking deep within them.

"Beautiful?" My host came back out into the hallway, tracing a hand down my back. He followed my gaze, and when he saw Alexei, a small, curt "oh," slipped out. Before any of us could react further, a very naked Cleo ran into the hallway. Someone had carefully painted The Starry Night on her body, with noticeable sections missing from tongue trails among the paint. She stared at Alexei, then followed his glare to Natan and me.

"I didn't take you for the voyeur type. I'll be honest," Cleo informed him. Then she marched down the hallway toward us.

"What do you think you are doing?" Cleo demanded, her full attention on Natan.

"What does it look like I am doing?" Natan shot back, his tone thick with annoyance.

"Looks like you'd rather get your dick wet than get promoted," she huffed back, placing her delicate hands on her hips.

"I am not just 'trying to get my dick wet' as you so crudely put it, but enjoy my evening with this beautiful woman," Natan scolded, enveloping me with an arm.

"Fine," Cleo rolled her eyes, "I'll just go explain to Adonis that you would rather fuck the arms dealer than deal with the situation that's developing."

"What situation?"

Cleo did not answer, but instead tried to move around us toward the exit at the other end of the hall. Natan gripped her arm.

"What situation?" he demanded. Cleo looked over at me, surveying if I was the best audience for this conversation.

"*The Connoisseur* is here," she finally said in a hushed French accent.

Natan's face drained of color as he let go of Cleo's arm.

"Goooooood luuuuuuuck," she sang out and giggled with a fake laugh as she bounded down the hallway and back into the party.

"Wait!" Natan dashed after her, disappearing around the corner. I watched him go as a strange feeling of rejection fell over me. Resisting the urge to look at Alexei again, I looked into the room instead. The door had been left open, and I was taken aback by what I saw.

The space was beautifully illuminated with neon lights. A round bed awaiting sin atop a circular platform, colorful lights glowing along the bottom. What really drew me into the room, however, was the massive one-way mirrored window across from me. I walked into the room to look through it. Below, I saw a new area of sexual activities, one I did not remember passing on the journey here.

Several men stood in a row up on a stage, each one having their privates sucked on by a partner. An assembly had gathered to watch the spectacle, cheering the lewd competition. One man finally climaxed and the redheaded woman who had been sucking on him jumped up in celebration to a loud congratulatory roar from the crowd. She was grabbed immediately and placed gently on her back, still on the stage. The rest of the men crowded around her, stroking their dicks hard in anticipation. She happily busied herself playing with the closest men around her. It was not long before she was moved and straddled onto the cock of a handsome ginger man. Another came up behind her and slide into her back opening. The woman threw her head back in exuberant delight, hitting the chest of the man behind her. He gently grabbed her throat and kissed her gasping lips.

I felt myself grow aroused and slightly jealous of her. Her pleasure burned into my subconscious.

A soft click pulled me from my hot revive. I turned to see Alexei was in the room now. The sound was from him pulling the door shut as he entered. I returned my attentions to the woman and her joy again, ignoring the intruder.

Alexei came up behind me and wrapped me in his vast arms. One of his hands slid down to my hip, while the other moved across my chest. His lips brushed down my neck and I closed my eyes, surrendering to his touch. Alexei moved his lips up to my cheek, then he whirled me around and pulled me into a feverish kiss. Our lips danced with each other as his hands found the zipper of my dress. It slipped down my body to the floor, leaving me naked in his arms. Alexei touched my body greedily. His kiss growing frenzied with desire. He picked me up effortlessly and carried me up to the platform bed. Then he placed me on it, resolute.

8 Months

CHAPTER NINE

As I laid splayed on the bed, I looked up at Alexei, expecting to see a mask of pained constraint. To my surprise, a fiery stare met my own before he traced down my body with his eyes.

My guard undressed himself quickly, but kept the leaf crown on. He stood by the bed, naked with tight muscles, and peered down at me as if I was his prize. My curiosity got the best of me, and I glanced down at his stiff member. The tremendous size sending an exhilarated tingle through me.

Alexei's face softened as he reached out and caressed one of my legs. I twitched under his touch, and he glided his fingers slowly up my inner thigh to my hole, aching to be taken by him. As his fingers slid into me, he groaned deeply as he realized how ready I was.

Alexei moved his thumb to massage my sensitive spot, and I moaned at his touch. A twinkle of pure satisfaction glinted in his eyes, and he took his sweet time at stroking my pearl. Seeing me on the edge of bliss, he removed his fingers from me and trailed them up my body until he found my breasts and grabbed greedily. A boyish joy crossing his face as he played with each of them, fondling the nipples. They became firm to his touch, and I swore his erection grew stiffer.

Alexei jumped on top of me, playfully trapping me under him. He looked up at me with a cocky smirk before he kissed my nipples. I felt his cock on my inner thigh, inches away from where I wanted it to be.

"Oh, Alexei," I mumbled as he sucked on my chest. Electricity coursed through my body, making me feel alive. His touch became overbearing. I yarned for him to take me, to use me for his own pleasure.

"Do anything you want with me," I gasped.

It was all I needed to say. Alexei shoved all of himself into me and we moaned in unison. He moved slowly, taking his time to make sure I felt it all. I groaned each time he slid out of me, knowing he would sink himself deeper with the next thrust.

"Enjoying yourself?" Alexei mused.

"Yes," I breathed, feeling him go in and out of me.

"I've resisted before, but now it's my turn," he growled as he shoved himself into me once again. His movements became faster, building to a steady pace. I closed my eyes, enjoying the sensation of him in me. With each thrust, the closer my climax threatened. Alexei didn't last long, though, and a growl tore out of him as he thrust one final time into me, his seed pouring into me.

"Your constant teasing has had a toll on me," he grunted in my ear once he was finished. Instead of pulling out of me, he pulled me into a rough kiss, which I met back with equal ferocity.

"I see a bathroom door over there. Clean yourself up and come back on your hand and knees," he barked.

"What?" I asked.

"I'm not finished with you," he said, his voice thick with desire.

I did as I was told and returned to the bed on my hands and knees. Alexei moved to align himself behind me, then pushed himself in. I sighed at being filled with him again. He moved his hands to grab my hips, then used them to control me as he pounded into me again and again. Despite his aggression, his movements were still rather gentle, as if he was afraid to break me.

After several thrusts, one of his hands wandered down to my slick clitoris. He rubbed at me with tender force, his finger sliding with ease across my pearl. I responded reflexively by throwing my hips back into him. He grabbed my shoulder with his free hand and leaned me into him as he continued his thrusts. I relaxed onto him, losing myself completely to his control as he concentrated on pleasing me. He kissed my neck as his free hand found its way to my nipple. He worked both together in a stimulating symphony, complimented with a steady thrusting. The effect was overwhelming. My orgasm rose quickly and rocked me violently. The climax rippling in powerful waves as I spasmed in his arms. Finally, I collapsed onto the bed and tried to collect my breath. Once I calmed down, I looked up to see his piercing stare boring down on me, triumphant.

"Open yourself for me," he said in a serious tone. I stared back at him hard. He softened his look and rubbed my cheek with his hand. I smiled back at him and gleefully moved my legs open, inviting him to enter me again. He slid himself back into my slick hole and built up his pace. This time he did not last long again, and after a few quick thrusts, I felt him finish in me once more. He grunted as he came, and I kissed him softly on the cheek as he pulsated into me.

Alexei removed himself from me slowly and flopped down on the bed. He moved his muscular arm around me and pulled me onto his chest. We sighed heavily, satiated by our lovemaking. I leaned into his hard body and we basked together in bliss for several minutes.

A loud bang sounded out in the hallway and I felt Alexei stiffen around me. Neither one of us moved, listening for more noises. A brash knock at the door made my guard jump, but he did not get up. The door handled rattled, but it did not open, as Alexei must have locked it.

"Is anyone in there? We're just looking for a room," Dimiter called into the door, a little out of breath.

"Oh, that's Natan's room. It's off limits. Come on, let's go this way," giggled a woman.

Alexei and I laid frozen as we listened to Dimiter and his companion leave. Silence returned, and I felt Alexei relax around me once more.

"You owe me one," I joked.

He grunted his question.

"You owe me an orgasm," I explained.

Alexei stilled again, then sighed heavily and removed his arm from around me. He turned on his side and propped himself up on his elbow.

"I think this is the only time we will be doing this, Angel," he said, looking down at the bed, unwilling to meet my eyes.

"You should go find a husband," he added, and I felt hope in me shatter. Cold apathy coursed through my veins.

"Do you not…" I stumbled to ask my question, then just stopped. I felt embarrassed.

Of course, it was just sex. He never mentioned anything about dating you, I realized. Big, hot tears welled up and then fell down my cheeks.

"Angel?" Alexei asked. He reached out to wipe away a tear, but I pulled back. He moved toward me, but I scrambled off the bed, away from his grasp.

"Angel, I don't know what to tell you. We got lucky tonight. That chatty blond woman kept Dimiter distracted," he told me, gesturing to the door as if that explained everything.

"Well, glad you got to get your fill. Sorry for confusing you might actually care about me, with all your brutish staring and showing up at my house with books," I spat at him. Before he could respond, I tried to run from the room but fell and tripped over something on the floor. I looked down to see it was my purse.

"Angel?" Alexei had gotten off the bed quickly, concern filled his voice. I couldn't take it and stood up quickly, grabbing my purse along the way. I dashed for the door and managed to unlock it before he could take two steps toward me. Then I darted down the hallway, away from my guard.

Tears fell more freely the further I ran from Alexei. I had dashed into a large crowd to remain hidden while I tried to think. *The group of naked bodies* around me seemed to throb with excitement from the sexual fanfare still ongoing around us. Someone new ran into the crowd, and others moved to make room for them. I was edged out as a result and found myself slung next to an open door leading outside. With one hesitating glance, I dashed through to find myself somewhere near the front of the castle. I veered off to hide in the darkness, and as I ran, crashed into someone strolling in the other direction.

"Hey, careful! Watch where you are running," Cleo protested before catching a glimpse of my face in the dull light.

"Sorry," I muttered and tried to pull away from the redhead and hide.

"Woah, woah, woah. Those tears look real and like someone is not having a sexy time," she commented as she pulled me further into the night.

"I, I, I-" I panted, trying to figure out what to say. "I think I started to have feelings for someone. And I don't think he feels the same about me," I finally confessed.

"Oh, honey," Cleo pulled me into a hug. We were both naked, and she was covered in unknown fluids mixed with edible paint. I let her embrace me, but found the move more awkward than comforting.

"You want to talk about it?" She whispered in my ear as she held me.

"It's complicated," I sighed. She pulled back after a long time and then wiped away the tears from my face.

"There's the beautiful face I met," she said as she pinched me on the nose adorably. I tried to smile at my companion, but felt more tears coming instead.

"Hey, I have an idea!" She exclaimed. "I got invited to a yacht party in Tithal tomorrow. You want to join me? We can find you a new, better someone," she looked at me with an excited expression on her face.

"What?" I asked, surprised.

"I was just about to leave on Donnie's plane. Come with me! We can go shopping together and will find you a great, rich, sexy Tithal man!" Cleo grabbed both my hands and jumped up and down in excitement. "Tithal men are great. They are all deliciously tanned with big, muscular arms. They would worship you. And you deserve to be worshipped," Cleo took on a more stern tone. I stared at her and tried to think of all the reasons I should not go. Then I heard it.

"Angel," the familiar voice called out behind her. I glanced to confirm it was Alexei looking for me. He started in our direction and I snapped.

"Let's go," I grinned at my new friend before adding, "like now." Cleo looked over her shoulder to see who was calling for me. She giggled at seeing Alexei walking in our direction.

"You're bad, I love it," she giggled again. Then, still holding my hand, Cleo ran. Dragging me with her into the night.

8 Months

CHAPTER TEN

"Hello sunshine!" Cleo yelled at the ceiling to floor window of our penthouse hotel room. She was naked and held her arms up, basking in the warm glow that was radiating into the room.

We had outrun my guard last night as Cleo steered us into Adonis's private plane, stashed out, away from the castle. On board, Cleo clawed through the drawers until she found clothes and announced she was going to shower. I fell into a lime green beanbag chair and closed my eyes for what I thought was only a minute. However, I was awoken a couple hours later by Cleo exclaiming loudly we had landed.

"Where do we go first?" She asked me.

"Do you not have a hotel booked?" I asked, hazy from sleep.

"No, I just go with the flow," she ran over to look out of one of the many windows.

I pulled my phone out to see several texts from Dimiter, Alexei, and Bane, but I ignored all of them. Instead, I ordered a car for us to a fancy hotel next to the Golden Mile, the local high-end luxury store center that spanned several blocks. The ride to the hotel was quick and Cleo stuck her face to the window hard, gawking at the glittering lights of the boutiques as we passed.

I demanded the penthouse suite at the hotel, which I knew had two separate bedrooms and a living space. As soon as I opened the door to our room, Cleo stripped naked again and fell onto the sofa in the shared common area. She fell asleep on the spot, so I left her and claimed the larger of the two rooms.

The next morning, I awoke to a gleeful squeal in the living room and rushed out to see Cleo stretching in the sun.

"Let's go get you sexy!" she cheered at seeing me.

The redhead ran into the second bedroom, and it took a minute for her to come running back out. She grabbed at the dress she had thrown off last night.

"Totally forgot I don't have any luggage," she laughed. I watched as energy radiated from her, feeling jealous of her carefree happiness.

When we stepped out of the hotel, Cleo gasped in excitement, pointing to an upscale boutique across the street.

"Let's go there!" she said, then dashed across the road, causing several cars to honk. I cautiously followed and entered the store after her. Given how early we had started, very few people were around. Cleo busied herself talking to an associate about how her boobs had grown in size, so I decided to look around to see if I liked anything.

The place was immaculate. There were rows of tables with swimsuit options laid out methodically. Several live models stood by the tables wearing pieces, so you could get a sense of how they looked on someone. In the center, a large, clear pool was outlined with mirrors, ready for guests to plunge in and evaluate how the suits looked in the water.

I found a gold rack that displayed a selection of bikinis organized by size and color. As I was looking through the options, a jade green one caught my eye. It had emeralds sewn into it and I picked it up to get a better look. That was when my phone chirped loudly in my purse. I dragged it out, ready to ignore the inevitable notification from one of the men in my life.

"You should get the one on the blonde to your right."

I studied the text from Alexei incredulously before looking to my right and seeing the blonde. She had on a plain purple bikini with pink cords strapped around her abdomen. When I saw the outfit, I groaned. That would be something Alexei would pick.

I scanning my surroundings for the man. With very few people in the store, it was easy to determine he was not in there with me. That's when I looked outside the store window, and finally laid sight on them. Alexei and Dimiter, casually sitting at a cafe table across the street. Alexei was on his phone, while his companion was talking to the waitress cheerfully. She set down two tiny cups of espresso in front of them.

I texted him back, "What are you doing here?"

He didn't respond, so I sent him another text. "How did you know where I was?"

"Your father rigged your phone. Had to take the overnight train."

I looked up from my phone and watched the men at the café. They looked tired and disheveled, but had changed into more casual clothes. Dimiter was now happily eating a breakfast pastry, and Alexei sipped from his cup of espresso grumpily.

"Hope you are not too tired. We are going to a yacht party today," I texted Alexei and watched for his reaction. He choked on his coffee and looked over, disgruntled. Satisfied at ruining Alexei's morning, I returned my attention back to finding a suitable swimsuit. I scanned the live models when one of them caught my eye.

A redhead sporting a sheer one-piece outfit with a thick strap of black fabric sewed to barely covering her private areas. The model looked almost exquisitely naked. I walked up to the beautiful woman, and she gestured to the table next to her. Laid out on it was the suit for sale. My phone vibrated again, and I checked it.

"Absolutely not," Alexei had commanded. Cleo ran up to the model with a few suits in her hand.

"Oh my goddess, you are beautiful," she sighed to the stranger who just smiled back at her, gesturing to the table as she did with me.

"I think I am going to go with this one," I said, picking up the sheer suit.

"Yeeeesss!" Cleo hissed in approval before rushing off to another model. This one wearing a pink sheer bikini with red hearts sewed on it.

We stopped for a quick lunch after window shopping all morning. The eatery was quaint, but it seemed we could get a much desired, well-crafted salad. I was also quickly learning this country did not seem to have any

Fleuve de Vie.

"What is Fleuve de Vie?" Cleo asked excitedly after our waiter left.

"It's just bubbly water that's purified and enhanced to help me stay looking young forever," I told her casually while looking over the menu at the different salad options.

"That sounds like a load of crap," she giggled at me.

I looked up at my new friend before laughing myself, "fine, I like it because it's expensive. It's like the iPhone of sparkling water."

This made Cleo snort with laughter, attracting the attention of the people in the restaurant. For the rest of our shopping spree, Cleo went out of her way to ask any clueless food vendor if they carried Fleuve de Vie, just to be disappointed as well.

We arrived at the yacht party late in the afternoon. The festivities started on a long stretch of beach and spanned out to a line of boats anchored nearby. On one side of the beach sat a massive stage, where a popular vocalist serenaded a crowd. Several Hibachi stations were assembled and created a pop-up restaurant for party goers. A larger section was roped off and dedicated to multiple sporting events.

With the sheer suit I had on, and Cleo with her tiny white bikini, we seemed to be greeted by a lot of appraising eyes. Cleo pointed at a spacious bar and we sauntered over to it.

"Fleuve de Vie?" Cleo asked the bartender, who looked at the redhead as if she was crazy.

"It's a water," I explained, then the bartender shook his head a hard no. He pointed to a laminated page on the bar, and we scanned the different drinks they had.

"TWO NAUGHTY NEREIDS!" My friend gasped as soon as she saw the drink on the menu. The bartender looked both of us over, then unenthusiastically turned around to make us the drinks. Cleo immediately started in on her mission and pointed out several potential matches for me. I scanned the crowd with her until my eyes locked with the dark chocolate eyes of Alexei, and time seemed to stop.

He was wearing very short and tight black swim briefs showcasing his tanned muscles. Dark curly hair covered his entire body, giving him away as someone older than the average party goer. I felt myself start to get short of breath at remembering last night.

Alexei stared back at me, his eyes dark and full of a characteristic, protective glare.

"Weren't those guys with you last night?" Cleo asked, pulling my attention away from Alexei. She was now looking at him.

"That's the blond guy that enjoys biting," she added, giggling to herself.

I looked back to Alexei and saw Dimiter towering next to him. Dimiter had on the same short, tight black briefs as well. I smiled, realizing they probably had to get them last minute, which is why they were matching. Dimiter had clasped a hand on his partner's shoulder. He was trying to draw Alexei into a conversation he was having with a group of people. Alexei ignored him while scowling at me.

I turned back to Cleo to respond, but was interrupted by her squealing in glee. Two clear Nautilus-shaped martini glasses were placed in front of us. They were both filled with an ocean blue liquid that had glitter swirling in it. Floating in the drink were frozen pearls. Cleo sipped from her glass eagerly.

"No pearl necklace?" she cooed to the bartender, flashing eyes over her drink. He smirked at her before moving on to the next guest.

"Let's go judge the yachts," I suggested to Cleo, who brightened at the idea. There were about twenty yachts spaced out across the horizon of the ocean. Most of them were modern massive motorboats, but there were a few, more expensive, sail boats among them too.

"I bet whoever owns one of those has Fleuve de Vie," I joked to my friend. I looked to Cleo when she didn't respond and found her ignoring the boats. Instead, she was starting through the crowd of people, looking for someone.

"Who are you looking for?" I asked.

"Ugh, I need to find my plug," she finally admitted.

"Plug?"

"Yeah, he was the one who invited me. I need to find him," she continued to look around, seeing if she could recognize anyone.

"Let's go to the sports arena. He's always there." She said, then dragged me with her over to the roped-off section. As we moved through the chaos, I thought I heard the very familiar sound of a firearm going off. Before I could investigate further, Cleo became very excitable over a new discovery. An enormous crowd was gathering around an inflatable pool as two naked women wrestled with each other. The spectators were pouring bottles of thousand dollar champagne into the makeshift arena.

Cleo downed her drink, handed it off to a stranger, then stripped naked. She jumped into the pool and the two women made room for her to join. The surrounding crowd roared wildly.

I watched the group for a moment, amused, when I heard a firearm go off again. This time my intrigue was too strong to ignore, and I searched around for the source. The definite crack of a Beretta A400 sounded again, and louder. I followed the sound to finally find a smaller gathering shooting clay discs.

A young man stood at the front of the pack, with a gun raised to his shoulder. He was tall and skinny, with a mop of blond curls at the top of his head, the sides shaved. The man fired his gun, then turned to rejoice with his group upon making the shot. He had light green eyes and freckles spotted his nose and cheeks. A bright smile lightened his face as he greeted his friends, then faded slightly when he spotted me. He gave me a once over, then smirked at the drink in my hand. I wandered over to introduce myself.

"Alright?" The stranger greeted me with a thick English accent. His wide smile taking over and lighting up his face again.

"Alright?" I giggled.

"I'm Charles," he introduced himself, stepping closer to me.

"Angel," I told him, looking up through thick eyelashes.

"Yes, you are," he smiled a clever smile, pleased with himself. I pointed to the shotgun in his hand and was about to ask about it when he interrupted me.

"Want me to show you how to shoot?" He asked. I paused for the briefest of moments, then nodded and smiled at him sweetly. Charles took my ridiculous martini and motioned for me to turn around. I followed his command. He came up behind me, but at a respectful distance, and held the shotgun in front, encouraging me to grab hold of it. I clutched the firearm and positioned into the proper form.

"You're leaning too forward," my new friend whispered in my ear. His hands were on my hips as he gently tried to 'correct' my stance. I glanced at him briefly, but allowed him to move me into a new, horrifying stance. Both of his hands slid up my back, then grasped on top of mine on the rifle. He had moved himself much closer, and I was fully in his arms now.

"Good," he whispered, his lips dangerously close to my ear. Satisfied with how I was standing, he reluctantly let go of me and stepped away. Charles moved to my front and indicated he was going to throw a clay disc in the air. I nodded once, then lowered my sight to the proper level, ready to shoot. Instead of seeing a clay disc in my sight, though, I felt the boy's fingers on my chin, trying to lift up.

"Better for aim," he explained.

Does this guy know how to shoot? I thought.

"Thanks," I said, smiling sweetly. Charles smirked at me, then backed away to throw the disc. I got into the recommended, and improper, position again and waited for the throw. It was only a moment later that a moving object registered in my peripheral vision, the disc being sent flying in the air. I pulled the trigger and missed. As the disc fell into the water, I lowered the semiautomatic and looked at my new friend shyly.

"That's ok-" the rest of his words were lost by the sudden blasting of obnoxiously loud music at the station next to us. We busted into laugher together at the poor timing until our hysterics caused our forehead to collide. Charles pulled me close to inspect the damage. He ran a finger across my head gently, then kissed the spot with his soft lips.

As our flirtatious moment subsided, my new friend retrieved five more clay discs for me to try again. I got into his terrible position again, then proceeded to miss every target. Charles used the opportunity to caress me, as he ran a hand up my shoulder in an attempt to be encouraging.

"Show me," I instructed, holding the gun out to my friend. He gladly accepted it with an enormous smile that told me he was eager to show off. As I threw the clay discs out, I studied him. While he hit most of the targets, it became obvious to me that he was not the best shot. I beamed at him with admiration once he was finished anyway, and was met with a dazzling smile.

"Wow, you're impressive," I said.

"I mean, I guess," he tried to brush off the compliment, his smile reducing to a smirk.

"Want to compete?" I asked, purposefully tracing a few fingers across my neckline. The movement pulled his eyes down toward the top of my breast. Charles chuckled dryly, staring openly at my chest for a few moments before recovering and meeting my eyes again.

"Oh, no," he laughed. "I wouldn't feel right humiliating a lovely lady like that." He informed me with another cocky smile on his lips.

"I don't mind. We can make it fun. Want to make a bet?," I suggested, stepping closer to my friend.

"Oh?" He asked as he looped one of his arms around my waist, pulling me into him.

"If you win, what would you want?" I asked him, tracing a finger up his chest. Charles faked a sigh and shrugged.

"How about I... get to take you on a date?" He asked, smiling down at me.

"I like that," I said as I returned his smile. "And if I win?"

Charles laughed at the question.

"What the hell. If you win, I'll give you a bitcoin," he winked at me as he said it. I pulled myself out of his arms and stuck out my hand to shake on it. Charles hesitated for the briefest moment as he stared at my hand, then took it and shook it eagerly.

"Eh, Ladies and Gentlemen. Gather 'round here, we got ourselves a match!" He announced to those around us. People in the immediate area cheered, while others strolled over to join in the excitement. Once he was satisfied he had enough of an audience, he continued.

"Today you get the pleasure of witnessing this beautiful creature standing next to me try out her new hunting skills!" he yelled as he wrapped one arm around me proudly, showing me off while claiming me in one move.

"And a pro like me showing her how to do it with flare," he concluded. The spectators roared in reply.

"You can show me first." I swept my arms open, inviting Charles to commence the game. He walked proudly over to a large table on the side that had rows of shotgun options. Then he replaced the one held in his hands with a new semiautomatic. Sauntering back over to me, he stopped in front of a stack of twenty-five discs.

"Do you want me to throw them?" I asked.

"Oh, don't you lift a pretty finger, love," he replied cheekily and grabbed the top one.

Charles started the game by throwing the disc from behind his back. He took aim and shot right through it. The next three he also threw from behind his back, but in unison. He shot each of them in quick succession before they fell into the ocean.

Pleased with himself, Charles sauntered to fetch three more discs. He stalled only to gesture flirtatiously at me, then turned back into position. The three targets flew out simultaneously again. In a fluid motion, he shot one from his hip, the second from his shoulder, and the last from above his head. The audience gasped slightly when he lifted the firearm in the air, but he got every shot.

Three more points, I noted.

Charles retrieved three more clay disks. He threw them out one at a time, and shot at them while holding the gun above his head. The last target he missed, and the disk glided down into the water. Charles stared out into the ocean, then shrugged, trying to convince the rest of us he didn't care about missing the point.

With a stiffer stroll this time, he went to pick up another two discs. The first he threw out and fired at with his shotgun from behind his back. This time, he hit the target, and Charles' ego made a quick recovery. He quickly threw out the next disk and shot at it with the gun at his shoulder. Again, he hit his target.

"Do you like surf and turf, Angel?" he asked.

"Sorry?"

"Just trying to figure out where to take you to dinner," he teased. I blew him an air kiss and his eagerness to impress exemplified.

Charles gestured towards a random person in the crowd, beckoning them to come and assist. The stranger turned out to be Dimiter, who appeared eager to aid the man. He gave me a sly grin before turning his attention to Charles, listening intently as Charles explained what he needed from my guard next.

Charles knelt down and signaled for Dimiter to toss out five clay discs. He swiftly shot each one with his shotgun, his finger pulling the trigger from beneath his leg. I counted every shot. He didn't miss a single one.

With a swift motion, Charles grabbed Dimiter and forcefully positioned my guard. He shoved his phone into Dimiter's hand and frantically adjusted the camera settings.

"Stay still," he barked, as he moved into position.

Peering through the phone's screen in selfie mode, Charles hurled the disc behind him. Using the phone as a makeshift mirror, he aimed the shotgun at his target and squeezed the trigger with determination. His shot missed, though, causing a collective groan from the crowd as they watched the disc plummet into the depths of the ocean. Charles tried to hide his disappointment, but it was evident on his face. He picked up another disc and attempted the shot once more. This time, he succeeded and the crowd erupted in cheers as he gave me a wink.

"Hold up," Charles called out, stopping Dimiter from returning to the group. He handed my guard the remaining six discs and signaled for everyone to gather closer. Charles walked over to the table and grabbed another shotgun, then got down on the ground. He motioned for Dimiter to throw out the last remaining targets.

With each disc thrown, Charles would do a push-up before shooting it with one of the shotguns. The crowd cheered as he seamlessly moved from one firearm to the next, hitting each target accurately. As he made the final shot and pushed himself back up, the crowd erupted in excitement at his impressive display of skill.

After Charles finished his turn, he gave me a self-satisfied smirk and passed me one of the guns. I politely clapped for my rival and pretended to be awed by his performance. Moving over to the table where all the guns were displayed, I carefully examined then other options. I spotted another semiautomatic with a loose choke, perfect for pulling off tricky stunts. I grabbed it and headed back towards Charles, and asked Dimiter to stick around as help.

"Hold this," I whispered to Dimiter as I handed him something small.

"What?" he started to ask, but I shushed him quickly. He opened his hand to see the one bullet I had given him.

"You'll know," I reassured him, then handed him my purse as well. Dimiter shouldered my purse, and held out his closed hand, ready for further instruction. I studied my guard for a moment, he so carefree and happy. He was looking at me encouragingly as I arranged myself into proper position.

I started by grabbing five clay discs and tossing them into the air simultaneously. With expert precision, I quickly aimed and fired at each one, hitting them all perfectly. Before anyone could even react, I snatched up five more discs and flung them into the air once again. Without even looking down the sights, I shot each disc from my hip.

I turned, my eyes fell on Charles, who stood frozen, his gaze fixed on the empty space where my targets had been. His mouth hung open in shock and confusion. I let out a sharp whistle to snap him out of it, then grabbed five more discs from my stack. With a flick of my wrist, I tossed them into the air, not even bothering to look at the targets. I effortlessly hit each one with precision and speed. Charles's jaw dropped even further as he watched in disbelief.

I threw two more targets over my shoulder to Dimiter, who swiftly hurled them out into the vast ocean. I maintained eye contact with Charles as I aimed and fired at both targets, successfully hitting them. The spectators around us erupted in cheers, and I noticed a smug grin forming on Charles' face.

I grabbed three more clay targets and launched them into the air. As I spun around to face the onlooking crowd, I effortlessly bent backwards and took aim at the first disc. The shotgun steadied in my grip as I leaned even further back and fired at the second target, then quickly shifted my stance lower to hit the third.

I reached for four more discs and tossed them in a smooth, fluid motion. With practiced grace, I spun around and aimed at one disc, firing my gun. Then, without hesitation, I twirled again and shot at another disc. This dance continued until all the targets were eliminated.

With a flick of my wrist, I toss the last disc into the air. My gun was empty, but I lifted it to my shoulder. A deafening click echoed through the air as the crowd gasped in realization.

In one swift motion, I open the chamber and turned to my guard who stared at me in horror. His eyes fell to the shotgun in my hand, its chamber open and waiting for the bullet he holds in his rugged hand.

"Dimiter!" I called out. Understanding flashed across his face and a relaxed smile spreads across it as he tossed the bullet towards me. With lightning reflexes, I caught it midair and load it into the gun. Time seems to stand still as I took aim at the floating disc and fired. The shot rang out, shattering the disc into pieces just before it disappeared into the endless expanse of ocean below. A stunned silence had fallen over the crowd, but it soon gave way to wild cheering and applause. I turned to Charles with a satisfied smile, watching as shock slowly transformed into admiration on his face.

"You hustled me," I read on his lips, the spectators cheering too loud to hear his words. He charged toward me then, and I tossed Dimiter my gun before dashing away from him playfully.

Charles continued to chase me down the beach. Close to the water's edge he managed to catch me. He twirled me around in his arms, then pulled us both down on the beach, pinning me down with his toned body.

"You little trickster," he smiled down at me. My glee bubbled out in giggles, causing my new friend to smile brightly. His lips pressed against mine, igniting a fire within me. The taste of salt lingered on his mouth. I melted into his embrace, lost in the rhythm of our intertwined bodies and the sound of the ocean behind us.

8 Months

CHAPTER ELEVEN

Charles and I walked down the shoreline, holding hands, after our romantic kiss. He insisted, since I had "hustled him," that we call the match even. I allowed him think that but thought of all the ways I'd like for him to make it up to me.

My companion wasted no time in ushering me around, introducing me to people with his hand around my waist, claiming me. We stopped several times to talk to groups of people, and I was usually introduced as "my special friend, Angel." This eventually got shortened a few times to "my Angel," and even once, "my girl, Angel."

Everyone seemed to greet Charles with unusual enthusiasm. His friends rushed to tell me how great he was, trying to distracting me while Charles would disappear suddenly. He would only be gone a few minutes before joining the group again, his arm back around me as soon as he saw me.

We eventually made our way back to the shoreline facing all the yachts as the sun was starting to set, hues of orange coloring the sky. I leaned into Charles, and he pulled me into a kiss.

"Want to go to my yacht?" he asked.

"You have a yacht!?" I responded, thrilled. Originally, I had found Charles to just be adorably cute, if not arrogant. The more I spent time with him though, the more I started to feel as if I might actually like him.

"Yeah, it's over there," he nudged his chin out into the direction of the water and toward the boat right in front of us. It was a massive sailboat with a white outer hull and dark stained wood for framework. I marveled at it for a moment, not believing my luck.

"How do we get on it?" I asked, scanning the water, looking for the answer myself.

"Well, you have to get permission," he grinned down at me.

"Permission?"

"From the owner," he winked at me coyly.

I did my best to look up at him innocently as I ran my finger across his toned chest.

"How would you propose I get permission from *this* owner?" I purred.

"Mmm, I can think of a few ways," he mused. I started to kiss up his neck and felt him shiver under my lips.

"This way," he yanked me toward the long line that was forming for the ferry boats to the yachts. Charles pulled me past the line and into the water where a line of jet-skis where waiting. He flashed a key that was on a chain around his neck and a bouncer in swim trunks indicated one of the watercrafts for us.

"We don't have to wait in line?" I asked looking back.

"Nope. I'm an owner, so we get to cut. I wasn't joking about needing permission though, which is why the line is so long, they are checking with the owners," Charles explained as he hopped on the watercraft and started getting it ready.

I glanced toward the front of the line and noticed a small team on phones, coordinating as they moved guests onto the water taxis. My gaze shifted to the back, where I caught sight of my two watchdogs. Alexei was glaring at me with his arms crossed over his large muscular chest. Dimiter, with my purse still slung around his shoulder, was standing next to him. He was cheerily chatting with a group of people in front of them. I smiled knowing that it would be difficult for them to catch me.

"Coming?" Charles asked, pulling me attention back to him. He was kneeling on the jet ski with a hand outstretched. I took it happily and allowed him to pull me onto the craft. He straddled the seat, and I sat behind him, snaking one of my arms tightly around Charles.

"You might want to hold on tight," he yelled back at me over the sound of the motor roaring to life. I squeezed my arm around him but turned to face Alexei again. With a smirk, I flipped off my guard as the motor of the craft start to roar, driving us away.

Charles raced the craft forward and my hold start to slip. I quickly moved to grab onto him with both arms and pulled myself closer. A small yelp escaped me as he sped up, and he howled excitedly into the wind in full boyish delight.

We whipped across the water quickly, heading out to the larger boats. To my surprise, we passed right by the large sailing yacht and began to curve around another boat next to it. This yacht was the smallest boat, so small I didn't even see it when we were on shore.

As Charles whipped us in a circle around it, I felt my excitement wane. A throng of people already on the boat ran to witness our arrival and screamed in excitement. At our approach I noticed on the side of the boat was large golden letters branding it the "Aussie Kiss." I surveyed the modest yacht, which was light blue and white, and was not impressed.

We pulled into the docking station in the back, and people rushed to greet us. All of them were cheering Charles' name, and the chant spread through the rest of the swarm quickly. Charles helped me off the jet ski and pulled me into his arm. He strolled onto the boat like a king, and the crowd split into two, still chanting his name. I looked over the crowd until I spotted Cleo on the boat, beamed at us chanting "Charles, Charles, Charles."

My attention was drawn to another woman in the front of the crowd. I couldn't take my eyes off her as she gazed back at me, her pupils greatly expanded. I wanted to ask what was the matter, but my words were drowned out by the loud chanting of the crowd. I had slipped out of Charles' embrace to get a closer look at the alien woman. He found me quickly though and I felt his arms wrap around my waist as he planted a kiss on my cheek. Charles motioned for me to follow him as we maneuvered our way through the crowd. We eventually reached a DJ stand that was set up in the middle of the yacht with the mob of people standing where the dance floor should to be. Charles jumped onto the DJ stand and grabbed the microphone, which caused the crowd to die down.

"You lot ready for a do?" he yelled into the microphone and the group roared.

"What is that I can't tell?" he asked, and the crowd wailed louder.

"I've been chatting up this pretty woman o'er here, so I expect you lot to leave me alone as we chin-wag back there," he yelled into the microphone and the crowd responded with a mix of sexual noises. I felt my cheeks burn and cursed Alexei for convincing me to give up learning English slang.

"Remember I better no' catch any o' ya cheeking a stash there is plent' to go around," his English accent started to turn thicker the more he spoke. He turned a knob, and a loud rap song began to blast from speakers behind me. I jumped at the sudden sound and watched as Charles threw what looked like pills into the audience. The people on the dancefloor jumped in excitement, or danced, it was hard to tell, which added to the chaos. Many hands were desperately grabbing at the air for more flying objects.

Satisfied, Charles jumped down, grabbed my hand again and dragged me to the front of the boat. We neared a large mahogany door that he opened and ushered me into. The room was empty, and I felt my anxiety at the scene outside recede. This space was beautifully adorned with large windows that wrapped around the entire room. Heavy dark blue curtains hung over most of them, leaving only the ones facing the front uncovered to let in natural light. A lengthy sofa sat against one wall, its blue fabric matching the patterned floor. On top of a wooden coffee table in the center of the room, a game of chess lay untouched and forgotten.

"Did you not finish your game?" I asked, walking by the board to pick up a Queen. It did not move.

"Oh, no. I don't know how to play. I just like the vibe it gives me, so I glued it down," Charles explained. He had moved across the room to a cabinet on the other side, which held rows of overpriced liquors. I watch him pour out two drinks, then he handed me one of the glasses and pointed at it excitedly.

"It turns the alcohol into a rainbow color," he explained a little too gleefully. I looked down into the glass and confirmed the liquid was shimmering in rainbow hues.

Alexei wouldn't be worried about rainbow glasses. He would play chess with you, then probably sexually punish you for trying to cheat.

I put on a facade of admiration for my host, but I couldn't help picturing Alexei and I in front of a fireplace, lying on a bear rug and making love amidst a field of chess pieces. The thought made me down my drink in one gulp, and I placed the empty glass next to the ridiculous chess set.

"I believe you owe me something," I hummed as I moved closer to the man-child.

"I do?" he asked slyly, looking down at his drink instead of meeting my eye.

"I won a bitcoin," I said as I crossed my arms in pretend indignation.

"Woah, woah now," he started, ready to jump into a lengthy explanation.

"Shh," I placed a finger on his lips, which kept him silent. Then, I removed my swimsuit it in a quick fluid movement.

"I take payment in kind," I whispered seductively. Charles eyes widened in excitement as he ogled the naked woman in front of him. I moved closer to him and rubbed my hands up his chest. He stared at me, breathing heavily, as I pulled him down into a kiss. His tongue moved into my mouth greedily, and he abandoned his drink to a table nearby. Soon, I felt his hands touching my naked body. He groped at to my bare tits first, pinching my nipples between his fingers.

I nibbled Charles' lip and he moaned as I pulled back. The movement jolted him into action, and he scooped me up in his arms, my legs instinctively wrapping around him. He carried me over to the couch and carefully placed us both on it. Our lips met again in a passionate kiss as Charles settled on top of me. He reluctantly broke away from my lips but grabbed at my chest with a rugged roughness. Moving down the length of the couch, he positioned himself between my legs and eagerly dove into me. His tongue moved up and down my slit quickly. It took some time, but he finally found my clitoris and began to gyrate his tongue around it sloppily. I winced at how clumsy he was, the sensation was not nearly as enjoyable as it had been with Alexei.

Eventually, Charles found his rhythm, and a first wave of pleasure began to wash over me. I arched back and moaned in pleasure hoping to encourage my partner. As I did so, looking through the front windows, I found someone was watching us. ♫ *Staring right at me was the dark chocolate eyes of Alexei,* ♫ looking unamused, with arms crossed over his chest. His eyes flickered down my body to where the boy was licking me. The smallest flash of jealousy crossed his face. Then Alexei looked back up and met my eyes again. With a dispassionate head shake of reproach, he walked down the side of the boat, toward the direction of the room door.

"Wait," I shouted, shame wallowing in my stomach.

"What's wrong, babe?" Charles asked as he lifted himself up.

"I need to... I need to step out a moment," I fell off the couch then stood up. Before my partner could say anything, I swiftly left the room.

Alexei was standing next to the door, leaning against the boat. He was staring out into the water.

"What are you doing?" I asked him over the residual sound of techno music wafting our direction from the back of the boat.

"Everyone on this boat is fucked up," Alexei muttered, refusing to look at me.

"Alexei," I sighed, annoyed.

"I'm doing my job. Protecting you. Waiting for you to be done, so I can take you home," he said.

I looked at my guard. He was wet, and the last of the sun made his eyes sparkle in the light as he looked out at the dark blue water. I reached out to touch him, but he pulled away before my fingers made contact. Alexei turned toward me.

"Was he better than me?" he asked in a low grumble.

"I wouldn't exactly expect you to care," I said, anger starting to bubble in me. He ignored my comment and stared into my eyes, deeply, still awaiting an answer.

"How did you get on the boat?" I asked him, accusingly.

"Was he better than me? Was he able to please you as much as I did?" Alexei asked again, his eyes studying me.

"I thought you've already had your fill of me-" I started to retort when the boat rocked to one side, slamming me into the wall behind us. Alexei was also thrown into the wall but was able to recover quickly due to his strength. He pulled me into his arms, and I felt myself come alive with his touch on my naked body.

The door behind us opened and Charles came running out of the room, naked. He gawked at us in shock.

"What the hell have they done to my boat?!" he yelled and tore off toward the back.

I tried to pull myself free from my captor, however, Alexei held onto me tightly. The ship was still tilted and we heard a crowd of people cheering from the opposite side of the boat. A couple ran past us giggling, one of them opening a champaign bottle. "Down with the Aussie Kiss!" the man cheered as the cork sprung loose and popped away.

"WEEE," yelled the girl as she got rid of her top and threw it out into the water. They both ran toward the front of the boat.

"Down with the Aussie Kiss?" Alexei grumbled.

"It's the boat's name," I explained, my body tingling as I realized what was happening.

"Oh, so we're sinking," Alexei muttered as another jolt slammed us against the wall, confirming his suspicions.

"The water police are coming," giggled someone behind Alexei. A beautiful woman passed by us; she paused long enough to eye my guard.

"Hey there sexy," she winked at him, while blatantly ignoring me.

"I'm know how to take care of older men. In case this one is too young for you," She taunted him with an air kiss, before rushing back into the chaos. Jealousy consumed me, and I snuggled into Alexei.

"No, he was not as good as you," I whispered and began to kiss him on his bare chest feverishly.

"Angel, not now," Alexei growled, jerking me in his arms. He dragged me to the front of the boat, and I allowed myself to get carried, feeling safe in his hands. When we reached the front, Alexei carefully looked over the ledge, and into the water. I did my best to try and look as well to see that the boat was definitely tilted to one side. The sea level rising quickly toward us. My protector's grip tightened as he lifted me fully into his arms with a sense of urgency. I smiled up at my hero until I realized that he was preparing to throw me over the boat.

"Don't you da-"

It was too late, next thing I knew, I was airborne screaming and cursing Alexei's name the entire plummet. A look of terror was on his face my entire descent. I landed in the water with a splash, then inky darkness surrounded me. More splashes sounded around me as people started jumping into the water too. Finally, strong, familiar arms found me and pulled me up above the surface.

"You jackass," I yell after pulling in air to my lungs. Alexei was trying his best to keep his hold on me, but I pushed away from him. At first, I was successful and was able to swim away from my guard. Then he managed to grab me and pulled me back into his arms.

"Let me go," I struggled against him, Alexei ignored me and swam toward the beach with one hand. His other was locked around me tightly.

The boat went under the water behind us, causing a wave. Hundreds of people were in the water now, and all of them cheered as the boat drifted out of sight.

I managed to wiggle out of Alexei's grasp again.

"Hey," Alexei shouted as he grabbed for me. We struggled and he accidentally seized my exposed breast. I stopped moving in shock and my guard took the opportunity to pull me toward himself.

"I'm sorry," he apologized stiffly, moving his hand as far as possible any other inappropriate areas.

"I'm not," I whispered into his ear. He grumbled at me, and then started for the beach again. I was dragged along, being held close to his chest.

When we made it to the beach, he picked me up out of the water and carried me to dry land. He placed me down on the sand and held my front to his chest, ensuring he cover my intimate areas with his body. Then he barked an order at someone to get a towel, and soon wrapped me around in it. His movement was tender, and I allowed him to take care of me. When he was satisfied with his feat, he looked down at me with weary eyes.

"It's time to go home," he grumbled. I sighed heavily, the excitement of the day washing over me.

"Where's Dimiter?" I asked, walking past Alexei, and toward the exit.

"Probably still yachts hopping, trying to get onto *the Aussie Kiss*," Alexei grumbled, catching up to me in a rush. "He'll make it home, I'm more worried about you," he added.

I allowed Alexei to take me back to the hotel, where my guards had also managed to book a room. Walking into the massive living room, I realized Cleo was missing.

"What about..." I started to ask, but Alexei dismissed my question with a wave.

"She fell into the water and then got picked up by the water police. She will be fine," Alexei answered. I noticed he remained outside the front door, which was held wide open. His eyes followed me as I walked around the entrance of the luxury hotel room in nothing but a towel.

"Are you going to join me?" I asked him, watching his muscle tighten with willpower.

"I just want to make sure you are safe," he muttered.

I dropped my towel exposing my naked body to him, and his eyes darkened.

"Can't I thank my savior," I asked seductively. Alexei did not move, so I started to walk toward him slowly. Before I could reach the door, he closed it, and my disappointment engulfed me.

Being in the empty hotel room felt incredibly lonely and boring, especially since I did not have my phone. I started going through the TV channels when I heard my door unlocking again. Sitting up on the couch, I watched as Alexei came back, rolling in a cart of food. He positioned it in front of me, then sank into a chair off to the side. I stared at him, and he stared back at me, his face unreadable.

"Eat," he commanded, pointing to the food in front of me when I did not move. I looked at the cart and saw he had brought me my favorite salad. Grilled strips of chicken lined on top of a veggie mix, with raspberries and vinaigrette drizzled over the top of it. Beside the plate was a large clear stained glass water bottle. The clear sections of the glass spelling out in cursive "Fleuve de Vie."

You should go find a husband, Alexei's words echoed in my mind as I studied the water.

What was this man doing to me?

I looked back over to my guard, who was now staring out of the large window, overlooking the city.

"Stay with me tonight," I requested. Alexei held his breath only slightly, before he took a deep heavy sigh.

"Of course," he turned to face me again. "But only if you will eat," he pointed to the food in front of me. I stared down at it again and felt my stomach rumble. This time I listened to Alexei and began to eat my food slowly. After the first bite, however, I realized how famished I felt and ate the rest in earnest.

"Dimiter wants me to give you this," he tossed me my small purse. I sighed in relief at not having lost it.

"Will he miss you tonight if you don't go back?" I asked between bites. A small hard laugh escaped Alexei.

"I like my coworker just fine, but sharing a hotel room is a bit much," he explained.

I felt my cheeks burn a little from embarrassment, but before I could apologize, Alexei motioned for me to continue eating. Once I was done, and not a second sooner, Alexei lifted me into his strong arms and carried me into the bedroom. I snuggled into his embrace, but it did not last long. He laid me on the bed and fell over me. We kissed each other passionately. I felt his engorging cock rising in his pants and, using my legs, pulled him closer. Alexei kissed me carnally for several minutes before rushing to remove his clothes. He laid back on top of me and aligned himself between my legs.

"Angel," he whispered. I knew whatever he was going to say was going to ruin the moment, so I pulled his lips onto mine quickly. He abandoned conversation and instead indulged himself with me. I moaned in delight as I felt his considerable member slide into me. The rest of the night we spent tangled in each other. Fulfilling each other's mutual needs, until we finally fell asleep in each other's arms.

8 Months

FORBIDDEN THING

BANE'S GUNRUNNING BUSINESS RULE NUMBER FIVE:

Never Walk Away with a "No."

No backing down until the deal is sealed.

CHAPTER TWELVE

Heavy banging on the hotel door jolted us awake the next morning. Alexei and I pulled away from each other as the banging sounded again. We climbed out of bed, and one look at Alexei confirmed he was clearly panicking.

"Go see who it is," he whispered to me.

"Me?" I asked.

"Go!" he mouthed, gesturing this time. I walked over to the door and peeked through the peep hole. Bane was on the other side, leaning into the door. I crept swiftly back into the bedroom.

"It's Bane," I hissed at Alexei and watched as his face drained of color.

"Go get rid of him," he instructed, rushing to get dressed.

"How?" I asked.

"I don't know, tell him something. Just don't say anything that will get *me* killed. And most importantly, don't open that door," Alexei whispered as he pulled his shirt over his head. He pushed me out of the bedroom before rushing to gather the rest of his things.

"Angel?" Bane called into the room, having heard movement inside.

"Um, yes. Hey, twin," I responded to my brother. A silence settled between us as Bane waited patiently for me to open the door. When he realized I was not going to, he cleared his throat loudly as if to remind me he was waiting.

"I can't open the door," I exclaimed, a little too excitedly.

"Why not?"

"Because."

"Because?"

"Because I have a man in here," I confessed.

"What?" Bane asked, incredulous. I peeked through the hole to see my twin pulled back from the door, arms crossed across his chest.

"I went to a party with that ginger woman. I met a guy," I told him. Bane did not respond, and the silence between us began to stretch, growing more uncomfortable by the second. "I only have a year to find a husband," I reminded him.

"Well, let me meet the lucky guy, then," Bane finally said, trying to sound supportive.

"Oh, no, *he's* not my future husband. The sex was really bad. His penis had promise, but I found it to not be girthy enough," I called out. Alexei stuck his head out of the bedroom and glowered at me. Outside, Bane chuckled to himself.

"Going into graphic detail about something uncomfortable to me. Are you trying to creep me out enough to leave?" Bane asked through the door.

"No," I shouted back quickly, avoiding Alexei's heated gaze that felt like it was boring holes into me.

"Nice try, sis. I lived in the same mansion as you for eighteen years. You always pulled this stunt when you wanted to scare me off. What's really going on?" Bane called out, his voice tinged with frustration.

"I'm naked," I confessed. Bane went silent.

"And I don't have any clothes, which is why I'm naked," I added, hoping to get him off my back.

"And you're stuck in a hotel room with a guy... with an un-girthy penis," Bane said, letting out a defeated sigh. I couldn't help it—I burst into laughter at his lame, inappropriate joke. Hearing my laughter, Bane's mood lightened, and he started chuckling too.

"Could you please go get me something to wear?" I asked after our shared laughter had subsided.

"ME? Get Alexei or Dimiter to go," Bane dismissed my request immediately.

"Alexei or Dimiter? Go shopping for me? You might as well send me to a nunnery!" I retorted back to my brother. He sighed heavily on the other side of the door.

"Like they would take you," he said under his breath.

"I heard that," I snapped.

"Fine. I'll go shopping for *Daddy's Darling Angel*," my twin mocked, his voice dripping with sarcasm. He used the nickname he reserved for when our father's favoritism toward me got under his skin.

"Thank you, Bane," I called sweetly to my brother and peeked through the door.

"You're welcome, Angel," my twin shot back sarcastically. I peered through the small opening in the door as he turned, clearly irritated, and walked away towards the elevators. Alexei pulled me away from the door by my arm.

"Not girthy enough?" he asked once he had dragged me well into the living room.

"I never said I was talking about you," I smiled at my guard, proud of myself.

"Next time, could you leave my manhood out of it," Alexei grumbled, letting go of me to frame himself with both hands.

"I'm not really wanting to leave your manhood out of anything," I retorted with a wink. Ignoring this, Alexei brushed past me and checked the peep hole to ensure the coast was cleared. He opened the door cautiously and left me, alone, to wait for my twin.

Bane handed me a gift-wrapped present, grinning from ear to ear. I tore off the paper to reveal a baggy, two-piece blue velvety tracksuit. My heart sank as I realized it was at least two sizes too big. Reluctantly, I squeezed into the oversized outfit, the fabric swallowing my figure. I stared at myself in the mirror, stunned into silence for a full minute.

"What the hell, Bane?" I yelled from the bedroom.

"What?" he asked, casually. He was in the living room, on the couch, reading a newspaper he had bought on his shopping trip.

"I look like a 1980's Tithal mobster," I marched into the room to confront my brother. He didn't bother looking up from his paper but continued to skim it.

"Next time remember to bring your own clothes then, or at least have enough to go do your own shopping," he shrugged.

I dramatically yelled in frustration before falling onto the couch next to him, crossing my arms and pouting a bit.

"Speaking of mobsters, I've come to take you with me for a job," Bane stated calmly as he set down his newspaper and gave me a once over. My brother's face lit up with a smug grin as he checked his perfectly styled hair, ensuring it was still in place.

"With who?" I sighed. I didn't sleep much the last two nights, and felt exhausted. Really, I wanted to just go back home.

"The mob," he stated.

"The mob?"

"The mob."

"Like the mafia mob?" I stared at my brother wide eyed.

"Yes, as in THE Tithal Mafia," Bane enunciated his words.

"We *sell* to the mob?" I asked my brother, excitement starting to rise in me.

"Not yet" my brother clarified, folding his newspaper up. He was preparing to leave.

"Why do we not already sell to the mob?" I asked, standing to gather the few items I had brought with me. Bane ignored my question and waited patiently by the door for me as I ran around packing my small purse.

We met Alexei and Dimiter in the lobby. Alexei was half asleep in a chair, but Dimiter became excitable the moment he laid eyes on me.

"Don't," I warned him before he could say anything about my new attire.

"I wasn't going to say anything. Just that I didn't know Louis Vuitton made tracksuits. Is it lined with the trademark red?" He asked, barely containing his amusement.

"Those are *Louboutins*," I explained, crossing my arms in front of me.

Dimiter just smiled as Bane checked us all out. Then my brother ushered us into the hired car he had ordered.

"Right. Today we are going to visit Mr. Dante Adami about starting a contract with us," Bane launched right into business talk as soon as we pulled away from the hotel.

"We are going to go meet the Boss of the Tithal Mafia?" Dimiter looked at us with a boyish elation.

"Yes," Bane confirmed.

"And you are going to allow this... with your sister dressed like that?" Dimiter asked, a twinkle of joy in his eyes. Bane looked over at me and then back to Dimiter.

"Yeah, everything looks covered. We should be fine," he said nonchalantly.

"What does that mean?" I butted into the conversation. Bane took a deep breath then pulled out his phone.

"Well, this trip is a bit of a shot in the dark. I found a contact to the Boss himself by stalking his "family" on-line." Bane explained as he poked around on his phone.

"You contacted the Boss of the most notorious organized crime unit, by stalking him on social media?" I looked at my brother very confused and slightly impressed.

"I'm not sure I would say they are the most notorious..." Bane started to retort.

"Bane."

"Fine. Yes. But really, I found him from his son, Antony Adami, who is our age. He also happens to be very attractive. So, my dear sweet baby sister, for the love of your brother's sanity... do not marry this man," Bane said this as he stared at me with pleading eyes. Then he turned his phone to me and showed me a photo of Antony Adami.

A shirtless, muscular, and carefree man looked at me from the screen. It was a photo. Beautiful hazel eyes captivated me under a mess of dark, wavy, unkept hair. His lips, which looked very soft and kissable, were pouting slightly in the photo.

"Why can't I marry him?" I asked, looking back up to my twin. Bane pulled his phone back and pocketed it.

"If you marry the Boss's son from the Tithal Mafia, I'll have no hope of winning Father's favor ever again," Bane sighed. I laughed at my brother, which was not what he wanted.

"I'm serious, Angel," He smacked me playfully on the leg.

"I know, I know. Don't worry, I'm not interested," I said. Bane turned to face me then. I glanced at him, then to my guards. Dimiter was looking at me a little surprised, but Alexei was fast asleep already after our long night together.

"Is this about your un-girthy stranger this morning?" My twin asked. I didn't say anything for a long time, just struggled to find the right words.

"Yes. No. I don't know," I shrugged.

"Angel?" My brother asked, his voice filled with concern. I felt my cheeks burn with a tinge of embarrassment. Before I asked my next question, I looked over to Alexei to make sure he was asleep.

"How does one know..." I started to ask my question but couldn't seem to get the words out. I sighed heavily then tried again from a different approach.

"I met someone, a man, about a month ago," I started. I felt Bane start to get excited next to me. He held onto his joy though, knowing I was not finished.

"However, I keep getting mixed signals from him," I finally admitted.

"What kind of mixed signals?" Bane asked. I felt his optimism begin to deflate a little behind the question. I thought for a moment before answering.

"I guess, we have not gone on a date or anything. He's been very forward with me though, and he does these things that, to me, seems like he is interested," I explained, massively glossing over the details of Alexei and I's interactions this last month.

"Why has he not taken you on a date? Maybe he is just being friendly?" Bane suggested.

"We've slept together, and he seemed pretty interested in more than friendship during those moments," I added quickly. Bane was quiet for a moment trying to think of how to soften the blow of what he was going to tell me.

"I think..." he started slowly before taking a deep breath. Bane grabbed my hand in a brotherly attentive type of way and twisted to look at me.

"Sis, I don't want to be the one to tell you this, but I will. Men can sometimes only be interested in women for one thing, and you happen to be very attractive..." he started. I pulled my hand away quickly from my twin and glared at him.

"I know how men can be, that's not it," I defended myself.

"It just sound like... I mean if it's been a month and he has not even taken you on a date," he said.

"It's more complicated than that. Just forget I said anything."

Bane grabbed my hand and held it in his brotherly way again.

"As you said this morning, you have less than a year to find a husband. I would recommend UN-complicating things quickly with whoever this guy is," Bane said, pulling my chin his direction until my eyes met his.

"And as your brother, just know, that whoever this man is, if he keeps playing games with you... well, I don't like him for you already," Bane said, smiling encouragingly. I nodded, and he let go of my chin. It was silent in the car for a long time with all of us lost in our own thoughts. Except for Alexei, who was still fast asleep.

"How am I supposed to know," I started to ask, breaking the intense quiet that had settled over us.

"How am I supposed to know who I want to marry? And in less than a year?" I asked Bane, not meeting his eye as I asked the question. He didn't respond immediately, so I braved a look and found my twin staring back at me, concern in his eyes.

"I don't know," he finally admitted. We got quiet again as we stared at each other. It felt like old times when it was just Bane and I in the house. No wars, no guns, no business, just two kids hiding from a father's wrath.

"It's about finding someone you think can complement you. Finding someone you can trust," Dimiter supplied, pulling Bane and I away from a small moment. We both looked at the tall blond guard. He was watching us.

"Complement you?" I asked.

"Like, complement your personality. Someone who has similar philosophies as you, sees the world as you do," Dimiter explained. Bane and I sat with that for a moment, and Dimiter seemed satisfied with himself.

"But what do I know, the longest partner I've ever had is with this handsome devil over here," Dimiter pointed to Alexei, whose mouth had fallen open with sleep.

"ANGEL, WHAT ARE YOU DOING?!" Dimiter shouted suddenly in Alexei's general direction. I felt my stomach lurch, convinced Dimiter had just figured out who I was talking about earlier. Instead, Alexei jolted awake alarmed, his eyes sweeping across the back of the car in a panic. Once he saw I was perfectly fine, Alexei scowled at his partner, annoyed. Bane and I couldn't help ourselves and burst into uproarious laughter together.

"Was that necessary?" Alexei grumbled to Dimiter, eying him with his dark chocolate eyes. Dimiter beamed back, clearly pleased with himself.

"You were snoring," he teased.

"I don't snore," Alexei mumbled, rubbing the weariness from his eyes.

"You keep saying that, but when you get really tired..." Dimiter provoked his partner. Alexei tried not to feed into it, but still half-asleep, he mumbled something barley comprehensible about "sleeping on the train" and "his lower back." Dimiter chuckled to himself.

"You were the one who insisted on taking the first train despite the fact that there were no more beds left. The second train would have arrived only an hour later," Dimiter shot back coolly.

"Oh, don't play coy with me," Alexei snapped, starting to become more awake from his nap. Dimiter responded with a "excuse me" expression on his face.

"You were the one freaking out Spadille ran away," Alexei grumbled through gritted teeth.

"Spadille?" I asked.

"Ace of Spades," Dimiter said, not looking at me but glaring at his partner.

"Trump card," Alexei added his own explanation.

"Death card."

"The highest and most valued card in a deck and... your codename," Alexei finally explained, looking at me for the first time since this morning.

"Oh," I said, and felt my cheeks get hot again. Bane chuckled next me.

"Did Father come up with that?" he asked. Dimiter and Alexei shared a brief glance, but both remained silent, their uneasy expressions hinting at their reluctance to talk about it. Another long pause filled the limo before anyone spoke again.

"Hey Bane, why don't we sell to the mob?" I asked. My twin gave me a sheepish smile.

"I'm not too sure. I just know that when I told Father I found the Boss's contact he ignored me. Then he told me that I can try all I want, but even he has never been able to secure a contract. So, when I got reports that you came here I figured, why not try?" he explained. I smiled brightly at my brother, proud of his courage.

"Oh, stop looking at me like that," he teased.

"We're going to go see the mafia?" Alexei grumbled his question. His head was laid back, eyes closed as if he was asleep.

"Yes," Bane confirmed. Alexei lifted his head slightly and looked at me. A small pleased shiver coursed through me as he eyed my new outfit.

"Is Mr. Adami's son going to be there?" Alexei asked. Bane shrugged back his response.

"Tracksuit was probably a good idea, covers everything up," Alexei mumbled wearily. I glared at him, but he ignored me and closed his eyes again. Bane chuckled and then we were all quiet the rest of the journey.

We pulled up to a gate that was outside of an old and massive gothic two story mansion. A large balcony patio lined the front of the house and was held up by a row of columns. A beautiful woman with large flowing dark hair was standing on the patio drinking a coffee, watching the morning unfold around her. She had on a long flowing sheer green robe with feathers stitched into the ends of it.

"You couldn't have gotten me something like that instead?" I asked Bane, pointing to the beautiful woman. He looked up for only a moment before turning back to his phone.

"Ask her to do your shopping next time," he muttered.

The gates opened for us, and our limo pulled up to the front of the house. An older man with gelled back dark hair stood by the front door. He was outfitted in a cream and white suit. His posture was rigidly straight with both hands clasped behind his back. I noticed he had on a thick gold chain that seemed out of place. On his face was an unimpressed look as we all climbed out of the vehicle.

"We are the Zorics," Bane explained as the man inspected each of us. His eyes lingering on me the longest, clearly unenthusiastic about what I was wearing.

"I am Constantino DeLuco, I am the consigliere to Mr. Adami... and his son," the man stated very stiffly, reluctantly mentioning Antony Adami. Mr. DeLuco side eyed me and my outfit one more time before continuing "Mr. Adami has asked you meet him in his study, please follow me." With this the man turned abruptly and walked into the house. Guards, all in matching black suits, rushed to open the doors for him. Bane and I followed Constantino into the house with Alexei and Dimiter trailing behind us.

The inside of the mansion reminded me of my father's. Both were outfitted in a classic style of interior design, however Adami seemed to prefer more color in his rooms, compared to the drab cream my father always favored.

We were brought up a large winding staircase and down a side hallway that grew darker in style. Mr. DeLuco paused in front of a large set of doors and waited as our group caught up. Then, he led us into a massive office that was twice as large as my father's.

The room was brick with tremendous countryside paintings on the wall. A large antique desk rested in the center of the room, matching my father's. This one, however, was well-organized with careful stacks of paper placed tidily on it. Constantino seated us across from the desk owner's chair, which was immaculate, but empty.

"I will go get Mr. Adami," Mr. DeLuco said before exiting the room from a hidden door I had not noticed. It was between a set of old bookshelves.

"Are you sure we have not sold to the mob before?" I whispered to Bane once we were alone.

"I'm sure, why?" he whispered back.

"Because father seemed to have gotten some of his styling tips from them," I motion around the office.

"This does feel unusually familiar," Bane said, and we chuckled softly together.

The huge black door creaked open, revealing an older man with gray-ing hair. His hair was tousled but styled back with a deep side part. His face was clean but wrinkled, and he wore navy pants paired with a blush pink blazer. Underneath the blazer, a loud purple and blue button-up shirt could be seen, left mostly unbuttoned to reveal his chest hair and several large gold chains hanging from his neck.

As the man took a seat, I noticed he had a couple of golden rings on his fingers, but not quite as many as Adonis. He hooked his hands in front of himself as he rested his elbows on the desk. A permanent frown seemed to sit on his lips as the stranger scrutinized Bane and me. I marveled at his obvious power and intimidation.

"So," the man said in a deep gruff voice, "you come into my house, on the day my daughter is to be married, and you ask me to buy some guns."

Bane and I said nothing for a long time. I looked over to my twin uncertain and a little wide eyed. My brother's face had drained of color and I could see he was trying to figure out how to respond.

"I didn't realize your daughter was getting married today, sir," Bane apologized finally and swallowed loudly.

"I bet it is going to be a beautiful wedding," I added quickly, wondering if the woman I saw earlier was his daughter. The Boss burst into a gleeful laugh, his entire demeanor changing in front of us. He waved his hands in front of himself as he howled with laughter alone. His face turning red at his mirth for the joke we were not in on.

"I don't have a daughter," he finally explained, wiping away tears from his eyes. "I just love saying that to people the first time I meet them." Bane stared at the man, still in shock, but I started to giggle. My joy made the Boss light up with happiness, and we rolled into a strange shared laughter. When we both finally manage to calm down, he reached a hand out to Bane first and introduced himself.

"I am Dante Adami, but please do call me Dante," he said, moving to shake my hand after letting go of Bane's. "You must be Bane and Sophia. I understand you were wanting to reach out about a contract to supply firearms." Bane finally recovered from his unease and sat up straighter in his chair.

"Yes, unfortunately we don't have anything to sample with us, but we do have information on types, prices, and services we can offer. I just wanted to add I do apologize for the last-minute contact, we just happened to be in the area," he stated.

"Yes, yes. That is all good but really, unfortunately for you, I am no longer handling the firearm portion of the business," Dante informed us. I felt my brother become slightly dejected next to me.

"You may or may not have heard but my son, Antony Adami, just became a made man. It's a bit of a well-known secret I am looking to retire one day, soon enough. So, I've decided my son really should be stepping into his role if he is ever going to take my place. His capo says he's been doing fair but keeps getting distracted by women." The boss shrugged at this as if this was a completely justified excuse. "What else are you to expect of a 19-year-old, I guess. Anyways, I gave him some extra responsibilities to bring his head back to the biz, you know?" The boss asked this question to my brother, who didn't know what to say and stumbled out some words before just nodding once.

"So, if you want your contract, you gotta go talk to him about your guns and information," Dante said, shaking his head at us sympathetically.

"Great, where is Antony?" My twin asked enthusiastically.

"CONSTANTINO!" Dante yelled out. The consigliere strolled in with a smooth casual formality from the secret door.

"Sir?" he asked, stepping up next to Dante. His hands grasped behind his back awaiting orders.

"Where is that son of mine?" Dante asked, looking up at Constantino.

"I heard he is down town wasting time at that strip club he bought a few weeks ago. What was the name he decided to call it again? The-" Constantino mused a bit struggling to remember the name, which made Dante laugh.

"The Neon Venus. I told you, pretty women are my son's weakness," Dante laughed to himself, shaking his head a bit before continuing. "You'll have to go to the Neon Venus if you want to talk to him, my men can show you the way."

"Thank you," Bane said, stiff and uncomfortably formal.

The Boss waved a dismissive hand and Bane stood assuming it was meant for us to leave. I stood from my chair as well.

"Hold on a minute, you," Dante pointed at me and I froze. He rose from his chair and walked over to me, taking hold of my hand and spinning me around to get a better look at my outfit.

"You know honey, I think you are the only person I have seen who can look attractive in a tracksuit," he said to me once I was facing him again.

"You're missing just one thing," Dante said before letting go of my hand and unclasped one of the gold chains around his neck. It was of medium thickness and hung very low on his chest. He gestured it to me, and I moved my hair allowing him to put it around my neck.

"Perfetta," Dante enunciated as he gestured a chef's kiss. I looked down at the gold chain which looked bigger on me, given my small frame, and touched it with pride. I stumbled over my own words for a while, trying to process the gift.

"Thank you," I finally stuttered out.

Dante lifted my chin with two fingers and beamed at me.

"Tale bellezza, such beauty. If I ever had a daughter, I would have hoped she would have been like you. You never know, I told you my son's weakness is women. Maybe a firecracker like you could keep in his place," he responded before stepping a respectful distance away from me.

"Firecracker?" I asked. The Boss just waved a hand my direction and winked at me.

"You can just tell," he said simply as he beamed at me. Constantino abruptly broke me away from the moment with a sharp cough. He moved stiffly out of the office, expecting us to follow him back to our limo.

I turned to Bane in the hallway and whispered in our mother tongue, "I was gifted a necklace from the Mafia because you thought you were being funny this morning."

"I don't want to hear it," he mumbled back.

8 Months

CHAPTER THIRTEEN

The Neon Venus loomed over the street like a colossal warehouse, its gaudy neon sign blaring in a kaleidoscope of colors. The logo, an oversized yellow planet with neon purple rings encircling it, glowed arrogantly against the dark sky. As we stepped inside, we were hit with a chaotic scene: an army of toned, young men dressed in sleek business attire hurried alongside scantily clad women in lingerie. Together, they moved furniture around in a seemingly random and disorderly fashion, each member of the team focused on their own task. The atmosphere buzzed with energy and purpose.

One man stood out among the crowd, positioned near the center of the room. His crisp, fitted khakis and sky-blue blazer caught the eye, accented by the lack of an undershirt beneath. The well-muscled bare chest was adorned with a gold necklace that matched the one gifted to me. I recognized him from the photo Bane had shown me earlier in the car.

As soon as he spotted us, he barked something in a foreign tongue, and his companions instantly froze. With piercing eyes locked on me, Antony advanced like a predator stalking its prey. A fiery power seemed to radiate off him with each step.

"English?" my twin called out as the man drew closer to us.

"I said STOP, an Angel has decided to walk in from heaven," Antony repeated in English. Bane was completely disregarded as Antony approached and halted immediately in front of me. Standing so close, I could peer into his captivating hazel eyes, as they trailed down my figure appreciatively.

"I'm sorry darling, but we are closed for auditions," he sneered once he had his fill of checking me out.

"Good thing I am here to sell guns then," I retorted. Antony feigned a look of being offended, before seeing the gold chain around my neck. He picked it up in his fingers.

"My father is sending me a message, I see," A boyish amused smile crossed his lips.

"Antony then, I presume?" I asked. A hard laugh came from him as he dropped my necklace.

"Please, no. Antony is what my father insists on calling me, for you it should be Toni," he explained, then held his hand out for Bane to take. My twin shook his hand, then proceeded to introduce the rest of us to the Boss's son.

"Sophia and Bane Zoric? What is this, a husband-and-wife gun show?" Toni asked, pointing between Bane and me.

"No, no, no, we are brother and sister," Bane corrected quickly.

"Twins, actually," I added.

"Twins, huh? You two don't look related," Toni observed us for a moment before moving on.

"Well, we love family here, that is what we are about. Just ask Giotto "Two Faced" Sivestri up on stage over there," he pointed behind himself.

I looked over his shoulder to see who Toni was referring to. However, a large inflatable obstacle course was being worked on by some of the men, blocking any visibility to a stage.

"Who?" I asked.

"Don't worry about it, Bellissima. What guns are you here to sell?" he asked.

"Well, we are arms dealers from Etristan and we are looking to expand business to this area. Today, we were hoping to set up an ongoing contract with you and your family. We have a very thorough catalog and can supply just about whatever you need," Bane launched into his well prepared business explanation. Toni nodded his head along as he listened to my twin.

"Right, right. The Zorics, I remember you contacting me now. Look, this is great you came out here, but I have tons of associates here who can fulfill contracts for me." Toni stated, I felt Bane start to deflate next to me again.

"That being said, Father clearly approves of princess here, and I can't afford to turn down his blessing. So, I think I'll give you a chance to prove yourself instead," Toni continued, making a point to talk to Bane and Bane alone.

"I like to see how cut-throat my business acquaintances can be, I need sharp people to build contracts with. So here is what we are going to do: we are going to play a little game today, and you all are going to play with us. You win the game; you got a contract. It's as simple as that," He stepped back from us holding out his hand to showcase the strange labyrinth behind him. The men and women in the room had slowly resumed their work on it as he spoke with us.

Bane hesitated beside me. He looked over the mess of tables and chairs trying to calculate if this effort was worth Father's potential favor.

"What's the game?" My twin asked. Toni strode confidently towards a center raised platform with a pole installed on it. We hurried to keep up with him.

"Dumb American," Toni responded as a man rushed up to hand him a beer and a hard seltzer.

"What's the point of the game?" I asked. Toni handed me the hard seltzer and Bane the beer.

"To make Two Face disappear," Toni surprised me by answering my question. He had two more beers handed to him and he gave them to Alexei and Dimiter.

"What did Two Face do?" Dimiter asked, looking at the beer in his hand and nodding an approval at the brand.

"He betrayed the family, and we can't stand that," Toni explained, contemptuous.

"OK, how do you play?" I asked, eager to start. I wanted nothing more than to put this pompous prick in his place.

"Angel. Wait, I am not sure about this," Bane scolded me in our mother tongue.

"What happened to Bane's grand rules of business? Wasn't the first one to appease the client?" I hissed back, also in our language.

"No, the first one was to not sleep with the client, and I already asked you not to marry him, so stop egging him on," he whispered quickly.

"What are you two saying?" Toni had turned on us aggressively, a dangerous look boiled in his eyes.

"He said he is excited to play and show how loyal our family can be to yours," I responded before Bane had a chance to say anything. Toni smirked at me, fully aware that I was lying, but returned his attention back to the game preparation. Our group followed Toni to inspect the room's layout.

At the heart of the room sat the raised platform stage, its shiny surface glimmering under the dim lights. A tall and glistening stripper pole stood proudly in the center, beckoning attention. Surrounding the stage were small containers, each holding a mysterious item of various colors and textures. The entrance to the room was flanked by two long rows of tables and chairs, haphazardly placed in a chaotic line towards the center stage. Upon closer inspection, it became clear that the left side held significantly less furniture than the right, as if purposely unbalanced. Against the walls of the club were circular booths, adorned with mirrors and colorful lights that added depth and visual interest to the space. These nooks seemed like private sanctuaries within the bustling room. The inflatable obstacle course loomed on the opposite side of the platform stage, a colorful and chaotic maze of twists and turns. Tricked ladders jutted out, challenging participants to crawl their way to the top. Two slides snaked down from the highest point, disappearing into the unknown beyond.

"Are there drugs in these?" Alexei asked staring down at the containers on the stage.

"Correct, this is the drug circle, you land here you gotta take a drug. Your pick, of course. On the other side of this balloon thing is two flame throwers. One right in front of Two Face and another one over on Scemo Americano Island. So, you gotta get down there, grab your fire starter, and make Two Face disappear.... get that princess?" Toni looked at me with fierce eyes, clearly testing my taste for competitive violence. I nodded coolly in response.

"Amici!" Toni called out, drawing the group in toward him.

"At the start of the game the ground is to be considered lava, so don't step in it. We will start by chugging a drink. Once you are done, toss it in the lava and rush to the starting places. Make sure to grab a new can," Toni pointed on either side of the entrance where a small circle of beer was on one side and spiked seltzer on the other.

"Men on this side which is called 'Maschilismo Mountains', and women on this side which is called 'Tramp Terra.' And before you try to come join us over on Maschilismo Mountains sweetheart think again, no women allowed," Toni was pointing at me now.

"But this side has more furniture, I clearly start with a disadvantage!" I protested, pointing to the extra tables set up on the right "Tramp Terra" side of the room.

"Tramps start at Tramp Terra, it's not my problem," Toni insisted, making his point with big obnoxious gestures. He prowled towards me, his steps deliberate and menacing until he stood mere inches from my face. Our gazes locked in a fierce confrontation, the air between us crackling with an intense and palpable tension.

"Watch who you are calling a whore," someone muttered dangerously from nearby.

Both of us turned to find Alexei was standing close by, glaring directly at Toni with protective and territorial eyes.

Bane approached my guard and stood next to him, both men crossing their arms as they glared at the Boss's son. I could see my brother's face starting to flush with anger, a trait he clearly inherited from our father.

"It's fine. I've won games with worse odds," I smiled a mocking challenge at Toni, who returned the look.

"Angel, I still don't know about this," Bane tried to reason with me one last time. I ignored him as Toni and I continued to size each other up.

"I am," I declared confidently, popping open the drink and chugging. At my bold move, Toni let out a fierce cry in his native language, eliciting cheers from the surrounding crowd who mirrored my actions. The air was electric with anticipation and excitement as we prepared for the challenge ahead.

Toni and I were the first ones to finish our drinks, we threw them on the ground simultaneously, and dashed to our starting places. I grabbed a seltzer and waited for the next set of instructions.

Everyone followed suit until only one man was left, struggling to finish his drink. He attempted to join Toni and the others but was stopped by Toni.

"Sorry, last one done is the first one out. You are a Dumb American!" he announced, a smug grin on his face. The men standing behind him chuckled at his lame joke, while several girls on my side couldn't help but giggle, their eyes drifting towards Toni with flirtatious smiles.

One of the stunning women, her hair a perfect blend of blonde and brunette in a balayage style, sauntered over to me. She was dressed in deep purple lingerie that hugged her curves, her every movement exuding confidence.

"Hey," she whispered, her voice low and inviting.

"Hey," I whispered back, our eyes locking for a brief moment.

"Shout 'Mamma Mia,'" she giggled quietly, clearly tipsy from the one drink she had.

"What," I asked, confused.

"Do it."

♫ "*MAMMA MIA*," ♫ I shouted out, unsure if I was doing the right thing by blindly following instructions.

The boisterous shouts and whoops of Toni and his men echoed off the walls, their fingers pinched and raised above their heads in unison as if reaching for the ceiling. I couldn't help but laugh at their silliness, but quickly covered my mouth with a hand to stifle the sound.

"Was that you, Sophia?" Toni asked annoyed.

"You just won yourself three spaces," the stripper informed me. I planted a gentle kiss on her cheek, and she let out a playful giggle.

"How did you know to say that?" Toni yelled across the arena. I ignored him and turned to the women around me for guidance. As we surveyed the game in front of me, I weighed my options. The longer and safer route would take me through chairs and tables to reach the drug circle, but there seemed to be a shorter path by taking the booths.

I hopped over to the booth and Toni cackled.

"She went straight to the Bitch Booths," he sneered, his voice dripping with mockery as he commentated to the men. Their cruel laughter echoed, burning my cheeks and making me feel small.

"None of my men are allowed on the booths, do you men understand?" Toni barked.

"Does this game have any actual rules?" Bane asked, still trying to cope with everything.

"Not really," one of the men said and they all laughed again.

"Shut up, shut up!" Toni's voice rang out, sharp and commanding.

"Answer this now: 'From this mafia movie, finish the iconic line: As far back as I can remember I always wanted to be a...'" He held up a hand, fingers spread wide, silencing the room with his intense gaze.

"One, mobster, two, gangster, three, crime boss, four, made man. Hold up the number you think on your forehead Go! Go! Go!" Toni shouted. His eyes darted frantically across our foreheads, shaking his head in disapproval. Then he whipped around, freezing in shock as his gaze landed on someone behind him.

"Correct," he said, a little astonished at the two fingers Alexei held to his forehead. "How could you be the only one?" he shouted, mostly at the rest of his men.

"Superior insight," Alexei mumbled loudly as he stepped over to the booths on his side. He glanced at me, a small, clever smile crossing his face.

The comment flew over Toni's head, who just laughed, prompting his men to join in.

An hour and several confusing plays later, we found ourselves scattered across the front part of the open warehouse. I had inched my way to the end of the booth, only to find myself stuck. The path ahead was a gap of empty space—no platforms, chairs, or tables to bridge the distance to the next part of the obstacle course.

Alexei had advanced several times along the booths on his side, moving silently and methodically. Dimiter was ahead of Toni by just a table, having taken the most direct route to the center circle.

Meanwhile, Bane was the only one close enough to the stage, positioned just a short distance away. When my brother had reached the center, he grabbed a vial that contained an edible inside. He then made his way toward the row of chairs set up around the inflatable leading to the stage. Convincing him to consume the weed took some time; our father had despised drugs and had instilled that disdain in both Bane and me. In the end, the only reason he reluctantly agreed was because Toni told him that refusing to take anything would mean he'd be out of the game.

The rest of the men and women had found places scattered among us, though a large portion had either fallen off or been pushed out of the game.

With the last question, Dimiter and Toni emerged victorious and were given permission to advance. Dimiter was going to have to choose a drug from the circle, and I eagerly watched to see which one he would select. Instead of picking a poison, Dimiter surprised us all by leaping off the final table and grabbing onto a bar attached to the ceiling. The kind typically used for strippers to hoist themselves up during performances. He hung there nonchalantly while Toni laughed at his unexpected move.

"Bold of you to do that. If you fall you will be out," Toni warned.

"If," Dimiter responded coolly and smirked.

As the mocking banter continued, I heard the sharp stomp of a heel. The same woman from earlier was determined to grab my attention. Before I could react, she grabbed a nearby chair and expertly slid it towards me. It stopped right between my booth and the drug circle.

Cheating seemed to be a common occurrence in this game, so long as Toni approved it. So, I climbed up onto the booth and then jumped onto the chair, launching myself toward Dimiter. He let out a small "oh" as I landed on him, adding extra weight to his already struggling form.

Toni laughed heartily at this unexpected turn of events, which I interpreted as his approval. Slowly, I made my way up until I was perched on Dimiter's back, leaning in close to whisper in his ear.

"Don't drop us," I whispered.

"Don't worry, I got this," Dimiter responded, confident.

"Pizza!" Toni announced the category for the next round.

"I don't get this game," Dimiter growled before yelling out "Pepperoni."

I smiled and named a cheese. Toni picked the answer he liked the most and one of his men moved forward.

Alexei, who was clearly over this game, sighed heavily as Toni reminded him that it was his turn now. He asked nonchalantly, "What's my favorite card suite?"

"You can't ask that, who is going to know?" Toni started to rebuff. Without acknowledging him, Alexei began to list the options.

"One, spades, two, hearts, three, diamonds, four, clubs," he recited in a disinterested tone. Alexei surveyed the room to gather all of our responses.

"Dimiter what's your pick?" He called out to his friend.

"Four," Dimiter shouted.

"Toni and Angel, please step forward," Alexei replied wearily. I couldn't help but feel a bit thrilled by his answer. He claimed it was spades, like my family crest and the suite of my codename, apparently.

"I'm going to drop after you jump off, kid," Dimiter whispered to me.

"What? No, please don't," I begged.

"Hey, hey, no worries I want you to win. I'm glad you jumped on, just make it worth it for me, ok?" Dimiter responded.

"Ok."

"Now, jump!" he yelled. I leaped for the inflatable. As Dimiter's heavy footsteps thundered behind me, I felt my heart racing as I desperately reached for the swinging stairs. My fingers grazed the rope just in time and I pulled myself up onto the lower platform of the inflated course, gasping for air. My respite was short-lived as I turned to see Toni snorting yayo from a container with wild abandonment. The drug seemed to ignite a dangerous flame in his eyes as he sauntered over to me, a hungry look in his gaze.

Toni gestured towards the ladder on the other side of the inflatable balloon. "Over there, honey," he said.

"No way, I was here first. It's my call which side I pick," I argued, growing weary of Toni's insistence.

"Fine, you want that side? Take it," said Toni, stepping back a few paces before sprinting and leaping onto the opposite platform of the bouncy castle.

I had strategically chosen the ladder on this side, which lined up with the Maschilismo Mountains region, assuming it would be free of any tricks. Toni's sudden concession made me doubt my decision.

The weight of my competitor's orders to switch sides pressed heavily on my mind as we approached our ladders. I couldn't shake off the feeling of apprehension. My eyes darted to Toni, who was taking off his blazer and tossing it aside.

"Are you ready?" he bellowed, his voice echoing off the walls.

"Just go? No more questions?" I demanded, my heart racing with uncertainty and fear.

My only response was Toni, who began to crawl up the stairs like a crazed animal, clawing at each step with desperation. I cursed under my breath and followed suit, my hands gripping the shaky ladder as it twisted and turned in response to my movements. The cheers behind us grew louder and more frantic, urging us toward the top. We reached the summit simultaneously, and I triumphantly looked ahead, only to realize I had been deceived. My slide was longer than Toni's and sent me careening off the side of the stage.

"Motherfucker," I cried as I plunged down the slide.

"HAHA Scemo Americano!" Toni's mocking laughter echoed through the space as he leapt down his slide, his men joining in with taunting chants.

Landing on a random table off to the side, I quickly took in my surroundings, heart racing as Toni's angry shouts and curses filled the room. A chaotic scene unfolded before me, as a pool table stood between me and the stage, its surface strewn with scattered balls and the holes were sealed shut. On the stage, a menacing flame thrower loomed next to a middle-aged man, bound and gagged in a pinstriped suit. His muffled screams and frantic struggles only intensify as we draw closer, his helplessness palpable as he tries to free himself from the unyielding restraints.

With calculated agility, I catapulted onto the pool table, my shoes slamming against the surface as I raced across it. A final string of profanities echoed in the air as I neared the edge, followed by a loud clank reverberating through the room. Without hesitation, I launched myself onto the stage where Toni's thrower lay abandoned, malfunctioning.

Our eyes locked in a deadly stare as we both lunged for the last remaining weapon on the stage. I pushed my body to its limits, fueled by the seething rage from his misogyny. A primal roar escaped me as I ran, determined to win now I was so close.

I lunged towards the thrower, my body propelled by adrenaline and fear. Toni reacted immediately, mirroring my movements in a desperate attempt to beat me to it. Our bodies collided in a violent tangle next to the machine, his weight crushing down on top of me. With fierce determination, he reached out and snatched the firearm, pulling it closer to our intertwined bodies. I thrashed beneath him, desperately struggling to escape from the weight that pinned me down. With every ounce of strength left in my body, I managed to wrestle one hand free.

As he shifted the gun to aim at the base of the chair, I seized my chance and fumbled for the trigger with my free hand. I found it just as Toni looked down at me with a gleeful cocky face. His eyes twinkled with the expectation that he had just won. I pulled and flames exploded from the nozzle.

Toni's cocky, gleeful expression morphed into a twisted mask of rage and confusion for a flickering moment. As realization set in it was replaced with an unholy lust that sent shivers down my spine.

He studied my face in elated astonishment. With my finger still firmly on the trigger, his hazel eyes traced down to my lips and he leaned in, hunger evident in his move. With a quick instinct, I turned my head to the side, avoiding his kiss that landed wet and awkwardly on my cheek.

Bane and the other men had gathered round the inflatable to watch the conclusion of the game, but I paid them no attention. My eyes scanned past them until they landed on Alexei, who was still standing on one of the booths against the back wall. I met his eyes and saw a fire reflected in them as he watched me reject Toni.

8 Months

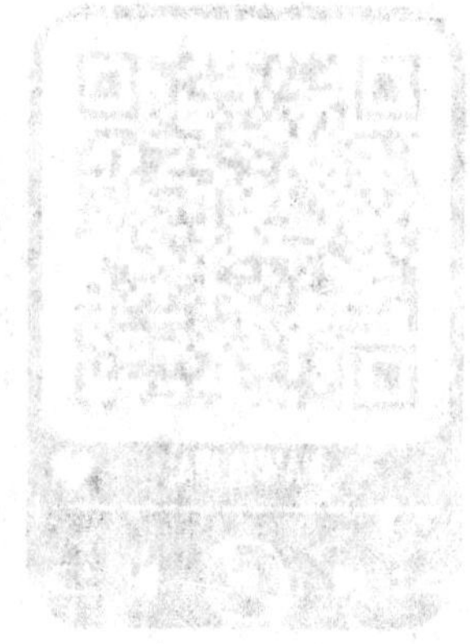

BANE'S GUNRUNNING BUSINESS RULE NUMBER EIGHT:

Beware hidden agendas.

Stay vigilant for underlying motivations; this may affect negotiations and partnerships.

CHAPTER FOURTEEN

"Since you did so well last month with the mafia, Father and I decided we are going to give you an... opportunity," Bane announced, pleased with himself for the use of "Father and I." We were flying to Mystna and discussing the details of the upcoming job at a table on the jet.

"I am going to let you do this deal *alone*," Bane explained. My twin eyed me with a stern expression, attempting to replicate one of the intimidating looks our father often used on others.

Ever since our dealings in Tithal, there had been an unspoken tension building between us. While it was his idea to form a business contract with the Mafia, to my father, I was the one who did everything to secure it. That was all he cared about in the end.

"You will be visiting a monk. His name is Bhante Gan and he has a yearly order of five thousand AK-47s, nothing else. We want you to sell him something *more*," Bane explained to me haughtily.

"Like more guns?" I asked.

"Just more of anything. An add-on to the AK is a good place to start. Otherwise, you seem to know what you are doing, so just eye-fuck your way into a new contract," he growled. I glared at my brother. He knew better, he was just being bitter.

"One more thing, Angel..." Bane added dramatically.

He scrutinized me with intense focus, his breaths coming in short, controlled bursts. After a moment of tense silence, he finally spoke again, his words measured and deliberate.

"Father said if you are able to sell the monk anything extra... he will let you out of the marriage contract."

"What?" I asked, wide eyed with shock. A simple nod is all my twin would give me before he excused himself.

"Bane, wait!" I shouted to my quickly retreating brother. He stopped for a brief moment.

"This is big news, no? Are you not excited for me?" I asked, confused by his rigidity. My twin half turned, he looked at me with an expression-less face.

"Just go sell the extras," he whispered, before disappearing into the long hallway leading to our private bedrooms.

I looked at both of my guards, hoping to catch Alexei's reaction.

"Don't worry Angel, he's excited," Dimiter reassured me with a proud, charming grin. I tried my best to smile back before shifting my gaze to the front of the plane, where Alexei lounged on a couch, looking over his thick, boring book on Mystna ancient history at me. His expression was unreadable. We locked eyes for the briefest moment before he returned to his book.

What a fucking nerd, I thought as I watched him turn a page.

In too short a time we started to descend, and a mix of anxiety and excitement settled over everyone on the plane. Bane had made his way back to the front cabin again.

"Go do... what you do best," he said. My stomach flipped as I stood up to exit the plane. My brother pulled me into a stiff embrace, which I returned half-heartedly. When I left his hold, I walked out with my guards behind me.

It was a bright day out and the landing pad was in a small clearing in the wilderness. The sounds of the jungle greeted me, and I raised a hand up to shade my eyes from the bright light.

In front of me was an elephant, elegantly adorned in rich red colors. On top of it was a canopied howdah and large tassels hung behind the animal's ears. I approached the elephant timidly, looking to see if I could find anyone around. The clearing was empty, except for a small platform erected next to the calm beast.

As we approach, the elephant shifted slightly. I extended my hand and lightly caressed its trunk with my fingers. The elephant responded by inching closer to me, and I continued to stroke its trunk with my hand, feeling the warmth of its skin against mine.

"Use the platform!" someone shouted behind me. I turned to see Bane standing in the doorway of our plane. He was watching me, his hand shielding his eyes from the blinding rays of the sun.

"Good baby," I whispered to the elephant before withdrawing and making my way to the platform. Alexei and Dimiter were already standing next to the ladder, each extending a hand to help me. Ignoring both, I brushed past them and climbed to the top by myself. The howdah door hung open, inviting us in. I stretched over and clambered inside. Once safely seated, I turned to see where my guards were.

Alexei was still on the ladder, glaring up at Dimiter, who had offered him a helping hand. Both men eventually made it into the howdah, though with less grace than I had. We closed the door and sat down, me in the middle with a guard on each side.

"What now?" I asked. Dimiter and Alexei glanced around, searching for further instructions. I turned to look for Bane, but he was already gone, the plane door closed behind him.

A distant whistle echoed through the jungle, causing me to spin around in search of its source. No one was in sight. The elephant beneath us began to fidget, and then another whistle sounded from within the dense trees. This time, the elephant started to move purposefully forward, towards the plane. Just before reaching it, the creature gracefully turned itself around and followed a worn dirt path into the jungle.

After trudging through the thick, humid jungle for what felt like hours, we finally emerged into a small clearing. The elephant slowed as we approached a shimmering platform decorated with vibrant jewels and intricate carvings. We carefully climbed down from the elephant's back onto the luxurious platform with only a bit of fussing from Alexei and

Dimiter.

With a gentle pat on its wrinkled trunk, I expressed my gratitude to the majestic elephant for bringing us safely to our destination. Then, I turned and took in our new surroundings.

"Where now?" Alexei grumbled as he walked up next to me.

"Here I guess," I said gesturing to the temple in front of us.

The magnificent temple before us stood grandeur in every detail. The walls were adorned with intricately crafted gems and tile mosaics, each one glimmering in the sunlight. The towering doors were held open, beckoning us inside with their welcoming presence. It was as if the temple itself was inviting us to experience its sacred beauty. The air was heavy with the scent of burning incense and whispers of prayers could be heard from within.

As we stepped inside, darkness enveloped us. We could hear a low murmur coming from deep within the building. In the far corner of the room, a faint glow beckoned us forward. I took the lead, guiding my guards towards the source of the hushed whispers until we reached a large central room.

The room was filled with a golden glow, emanating from the thousands of lit candles that lined every surface. Ornate statues and religious artifacts adorned the walls, casting shimmering shadows in the dim light. At the center, a monk knelt before a young couple, placing delicate white headpieces on their heads. The couple's attire was a stunning combination of white and gold, intricately decorated with embroidered patterns that showcased careful craftsmanship.

Two elderly couples sat behind the young pair, their faces beaming with joy as they watched the monk in front of them tie a white string delicately to each of the white headpieces.

Alexei leaned in close to me, his voice barely audible as he whispered, "It's a wedding ceremony."

Dimiter and I exchanged a glance, then looked to Alexei. He paid us no mind, his stern brown eyes shimmering in the light as he focused on the ceremony taking place before us.

The monk had finished tying the white thread and stepped in front of the couples. It was hard to see what exactly he was doing from our vantage point at the back of the room.

"He's blessing them by pouring a special water over their hands, then the guest will be able to do the same," Alexei whispered in my ear again. I watched and soon the two older couples stood up and made their way to the front. I felt self-conscious suddenly, witnessing something so intimate. Before anyone could spot us, I glided across the back of the room silently. Alexei and Dimiter quietly followed.

Beyond the grand room where the wedding took place, we encountered a labyrinth. It consisted of long, winding pathways that occasionally branched off in different directions. At the first split, we stopped to consider our options. Down one of the pathways, there was a small table with three palm-sized cups carefully placed on top. We approached with caution, examining the liquid inside each cup.

"What is it?" I asked, as we each picked up a cup and examined them in our own ways.

An overpowering smell of cherries filled my nose as I sniffed the liquid. It smelled delicious and inviting, and without thinking twice, I took a sip. The warm liquid tasted amazing and strangely delicate; I knew I just wanted to finish the cup.

Dimiter commented on the smell of almonds before taking a sip from his cup. Once he swallowed the liquid, he bellowed a hearty laugh.

"It's tea," he beamed, amused.

"And nothing else?" Alexei asked skeptically. I shrugged off his concern and finished the cup in my hand. Dimiter followed suit, and with a heavy sigh, Alexei reluctantly downing his own drink.

We continued down the tract until we came to another split. This divide branched into three different corridors, one of which held another table with small cups, set up exactly as the last one had been. We approached the table and picked up the drinks. This time, an aroma of oranges filled my nose. Taking a sip, I found the drink as complex and satisfying as the previous one, and once again, I was compelled to finish it.

"Does your drink smell like cinnamon?" Dimiter asked us. He took a sip from his cup and appeared to be enjoying the taste.

"No, mine smells like oranges," I explained.

"Mine has more of a smoky undertone, mixed with... something else I can't name. It reminds me of sitting around a fireplace at night," Alexei responded as he drank his tea.

We encountered two more splits, each featuring a table of tea, before anyone finally broke the growing silence among the three of us.

"You ever think we'll end up married...like that couple?" Dimiter asked Alexei suddenly. We both looked at him a bit bewildered; vulnerability was none of our virtues.

"What?" Dimiter defended himself when he was met with nothing but blank, confused stares from Alexei and me.

"You don't seem like someone who would want to get married. You are so... carefree; wouldn't a wife drag you down?" I asked, breaking the growing tension.

"Oh no, not my wife. She's going to be spirited," Dimiter reassured me with a wink. I giggled, realizing just how much he had already thought about this.

"Hard to find a wife when we travel so much for work," Alexei stated monotonously. It wasn't meant as a jab at his job or me, but I couldn't help but feel a bit of a sting at his words. We came across another table of tea and drank from it, and a strange sense of calm began to flood my body.

"Maybe I will be successful today, and then Father will trust me enough to travel without watchdogs," I jested as we ventured down a new hallway. No one reacted, and the growing silence was only disrupted by the soft sound of our shoes trudging along the worn path.

Halfway down the corridor, Alexei mumbled, "You'll still need us." I glared at him, but he refused to meet my eye. Another uncomfortable silence followed before Dimiter spoke up once more.

"So, is that a no on marriage then, Alexei?" he pressed. Alexei sighed heavily, as if he was tired of Dimiter and his questioning, before finally answering.

"Sure. I'd like to think I might get married. We'd have a traditional wedding, wait about two years to enjoy each other before having kids," he explained. We turned a corner, and another divide lay ahead of us. No one spoke as we all drank our respective teas, then we continued down the labyrinth path.

"Kids?" Dimiter urged. Alexei let out a dry, humorless laugh.

"Yeah, I'd like to think if I have a wife, I'd have some kids. Three, to be exact. One boy, one girl, and a wild card. I'd want to be able to provide comfortably enough so my wife could stay at home and raise them. I imagine when I find the right one and things get serious, I'd like to find a job that is a little more stable," he explained. Neither Dimiter nor I knew how to react to this confession, so we remained silent.

"Something that would allow me to come home and help take care of the kids. Then, in our off time, I would worship her for being everything," Alexei continued.

My face heated up with embarrassment as Alexei's words washed over me. I chanced a quick glance at him and saw that he was watching me, his own cheeks tinged with a deep shade of crimson. It dawned on me that he was picturing me in that dream.

Why has he never told me this? If I find the right man, would I also suddenly want a boring, traditional life? I thought. Anxiety started to grow within me, but another crossroad appeared in front of us. I swallowed my fear before it could bloom into full-blown panic.

"Seems a bit conventional," Dimiter noted. Alexei brushed off the remark with a grunt.

We reached the end of the maze. Another table of tea was set out, but standing next to it was a young monk, smiling warmly at us. He presented us with our final teacups and remained silent until we finished our tea. Once we had gulped down the last of the liquid and set our cups on the table, he finally spoke softly.

"We will be asking you control questions until I am satisfied, followed by the security question. Answer correctly, and you may enter," he explained quietly. He gestured behind him to a lush green garden, where a short cobblestone pathway led to another building—this one white, with a red-trimmed roof.

"You will be first," the monk said, his finger pointing gently at me. "What is your greatest fear?"

Before I could think, the words tumbled out of my mouth, the horror of them settling on me only after I'd spoken.

"Becoming someone's nothing wife with no ambitions of my own," I blurted, immediately clasping a hand over my mouth in shock. My face burned with embarrassment, the weight of my confession heavy on my chest. No one said a thing, but the monk smiled reassuringly. The silence was broken by light laughter behind me. I turned to see Dimiter laughing, though his eyes were fixed on the monk with a look of amazement.

"He drugged us! That tea… it gave me a familiar feeling. It's a truth serum," he explained, amusement dancing on his lips. The monk nodded, his smile warm and knowing.

"Yes, we have precautions. The serum is safe, grown here by the most mindful gardeners," the monk explained, then continued his interrogation of me, "Do you have any dealings with the Prime Minister?" he asked calmly.

"Who?" I blurted out before I could stop myself. The monk smiled a full smile at my answer.

"Thank you, now you," he turned to Alexei, "What is your greatest fear?"

"Death," my guard responded quickly, without hesitation. I tried to catch his eye, but Alexei was deliberately avoiding my gaze. The monk eyed him unsure of the answer.

"What do you think your role is in life?" the monk asked, having decided he did not like the answer to the previous question.

"To protect."

"To protect what?" the monk stated quietly. Alexei took a small breath, his dark eyes flickering to me for a brief moment before lowering to the ground.

"Those whom I love," Alexei whispered, barely audible. He leaned in toward the monk as he spoke, hoping his answer wouldn't carry far. No one responded except for a single nod from the monk.

"Do you think you fulfill that role well?" The monk's question caught Alexei off guard. Before he could think, Alexei blurted out his answer in a dejected whisper.

"No."

The monk seemed satisfied with this answer and moved on to his final question.

"Do you have any dealings with the sitting Prime Minister?" he asked.

"No," Alexei grumbled, clearly uncomfortable with the vulnerability the recent questions had exposed. Finally, the monk turned to Dimiter.

"Spiders," Dimiter said before the monk could ask anything. The two men exchanged smiles—Dimiter's was a charming, crooked grin, while the monk's was a tight, unamused one.

"What do you think your role is in life?" the monk asked, observing the tall blond man closely. Dimiter looked down at me with pride.

"To protect," he responded evenly. The monk's smile faded.

"Very well," the monk sighed. "What did you wish you had asked your parents before they died?" he asked. Despite the monk's gentle tone, the question made us all freeze. I watched Dimiter as a range of emotions crossed his face. He had not expected this question, and his characteristic smile had quickly vanished.

"If you know my parents are dead, then you know I'm trained to resist truth serum," he muttered, a slightly deranged look in his eye as he stared down the monk.

"Yes, but what?" the monk pressed. Dimiter sighed and eyed Alexei and me before finally responding.

"I would ask them 'why?'" Dimiter admitted, his eyes staring off to the side, avoiding anyone's glance. I reached out and took his hand, my fingers curling around his with a reassuring grip.

"I didn't know your parents... that you were... I'm sorry," I finally managed to sputter out. Dimiter gently released my hand and pulled me into a side hug.

"Don't you worry, kid. It was a long time ago," he said, offering a reassuring smile. I remained nestled in Dimiter's embrace, looking up at him and wishing I could do more to ease the pain I saw in his eyes.

"Are you two done, or should we give you the room?" Alexei asked icily. Dimiter shot Alexei a look that was more menacing than I had ever seen from him before. It was quickly replaced by a gentle smile down at me, and then our attention shifted back to the monk.

"We will make an exception for the blond one. I have been told to warn you, though: we have your history," the monk cautioned Dimiter. My guard smiled slyly in response, but it was clear he was secretly thrilled.

"Right this way," the monk said, stepping aside with a sweeping hand to invite us into the next section. The doors to the red-and-white building opened, revealing a man in a formal suit standing inside, a tray with mimosas ready for us.

7 Months

# CHAPTER FIFTEEN

We all turned down the mimosas, our newfound mistrust lingering from the drugged tea. The server bowed slightly, then opened the next set of doors.

As we stepped inside, beyond the imposing and weighty entrance, we were immediately hit with a cacophony of yelling and loud music. It was as if we had entered another world entirely.

The building's exterior had given off an air of grandeur and reverence, resembling a temple or palace. However, upon entering, we were greeted with a starkly contrasting scene—an enormous casino that seemed to stretch on endlessly. The vibrant red tables were filled with enthusiastic crowds, their voices blending together in a chaotic symphony.

"Through there," the server instructed, pointing with a white-gloved hand across the casino.

He then added with a sly smile, "Unless you see something you like."

We all stepped inside, and I immediately began scanning the different tables.

The layout of the casino appeared chaotic, with groups of games scattered throughout the space without any clear organization. Men crowded almost every table, their shouts mingling in a chaotic mix of languages. Hands flashed as cash exchanged, moving too quickly for anyone to follow.

As I passed a craps table, a sudden eruption of cheers drew my attention—a seven had been rolled. A winner's triumphant shout signaled a group of women carrying trays of shots to swarm the table. The drinks were quickly downed, followed by the eager slapping of more money onto the felt.

"Let's put some money on two," I joked, grinning at my guards as we approached a roulette table.

"Absolutely not," Alexei growled, arms folded tightly across his chest. His eyes were fixed on the craps table, glaring at those recklessly throwing down stacks of money.

"Oh, lighten up, Great Protector," Dimiter teased, giving his partner a playful nudge. Alexei grumbled something inaudible in response, but Dimiter paid him no mind. Instead, he pulled a thick wad of cash from his wallet and strode confidently to the roulette table. A gap was created for my tall guard as he placed the entire stack on the black two.

"Dimiter!" I exclaimed, horrified by the hefty pile of cash he had stacked on the table. I clutched his arm in protest, but he brushed it off and casually draped his arm around my shoulders. Before I could say much else, the ball was sent spinning around the wheel.

"How much was that? What if you lose it?" I asked, my voice tinged with worry. Dimiter, however, paid no attention to me, his gaze fixed intently on the roulette wheel. A tense silence fell between us as we both watched the ball's laggard descent on the color-coded wheel, which whirled in a dizzying blur. The ball seemed to flirt with each number as it bounced around, gradually slowing down as it settled into its final position. Just as I was about to express concern again, Dimiter opened his mouth to speak, but his words were swallowed by the deafening roar of cheers and shouts erupting from the table around us.

"TWO! TWO!" someone shouted, and more cash changed hands in a blur. The uptight casino dealer next to the wheel began yelling at Dimiter in a foreign language. Dimiter tried to respond in several languages, searching for one they both understood. Frustrated, the dealer eventually retrieved a suitcase made of alligator skin. He stuffed the cash into it, counted it three times, and handed it over to Dimiter. As soon as Dimiter grabbed the handle, the dealer shooed us away from the table.

"You just won me three hundred and fifty thousand dollars and this snazzy alligator suitcase," Dimiter said, flashing a grin. "Some rewards are worth the risk of failure."

Alexei shot him a skeptical look. "The risk of losing ten grand?"

Dimiter shrugged off the comment, striding confidently through the casino and leading us to the other side. I couldn't help but laugh, which only seemed to irritate Alexei further.

"I hope your dreams are bigger than just winning big from gambling," Alexei grumbled, clearly missing the point. I smiled at him and offered my arm. A thrill crossed Alexei's face as he took it. With a nod, we followed Dimiter through the casino.

As we approached, two men dressed in white hurried to open the heavy exit doors. Without missing a beat, we walked through and emerged onto a vast patio overlooking a clear body of water. The moment the doors closed behind us, the sounds of the casino silenced immediately. A flock of seagulls cooed at us as they passed by the railing of the patio.

"I don't think this guy is a monk," I said as I glanced over the edge of the platform. To the left, a set of concrete stairs led down to a long wooden plank extending into the water. At the end of the pier, a lone figure in a bright orange robe stood against the blue expanse behind him.

"We have yet to figure out what he is," Alexei remarked next to me, his gaze fixed on the expansive horizon.

"You could try asking, if there was anyone who could charm it out of him, it would be you," Dimiter encouraged, standing by the stairs and subtly signaling us to move on to the next part of our journey.

"Have you met him?" I asked, approaching the stairs and beginning to descend toward the pier.

"No, but he does continue to be an enigma to your father. Every trip Emilio comes back with nothing good to say. Apparently, he has never taken the same path to the monk twice," Dimiter explained, following me down the stairs. Alexei trailed behind him, and we all walked down the wooden pier together toward the solitary monk. As we approached, the monk bowed slightly and then gestured gracefully to a single kayak waiting by the shore.

"Just Angel," he insisted before we could greet him. I felt Alexei begin to argue but I placed a hand on his biceps, and he hesitated.

"It's okay," I assured him. Alexei glanced at Dimiter, and whatever he saw in Dimiter's expression seemed to convince him to back down. His dark chocolate eyes met mine for a brief moment.

"Good luck," he whispered.

"Thanks."

I let go of Alexei and oriented myself in the kayak, dipping the paddle into the water and pulling it back with a powerful stroke. The cool water splashed against the sides of the kayak as I glided further away from the shore.

"Go be a gun runner," Dimiter called after me. I waved back, grateful for his support.

With no clear destination, I let the tranquil waters guide me as I paddled into the crystal-clear depths. Looking down, I marveled at a vibrant school of fish darting through the blue-green sea beneath my boat.

The further I ventured from the shore, the heavier the paddle grew with each stroke, but I pressed on, driven by determination. The blazing sun beat down relentlessly, its intense rays causing beads of sweat to form on my forehead and trickle down my back. Regret gnawed at me for not asking more questions before setting off from the pier, but deep down, I knew that no answers would have been given anyway.

Alone in the endless expanse of the ocean, I struggled to push thoughts of Alexei's dream wife from my mind. I couldn't help but picture myself with a small child on my hip, waving goodbye to Alexei as he hurried off to work. The thought of being tied down in such a mundane domestic life filled me with a suffocating sense of emptiness.

"Stop it," I yelled at myself and focused on putting more energy into paddling. My arms strained with each powerful stroke, driving me further into the deep blue ocean. The water turned almost opaque, a stunning shade of cobalt as the ocean floor dropped away beneath my boat. Squinting against the blinding sun, I could barely make out a small island in the distance, still miles away despite all the energy I had already expended. The heat was suffocating, closing in on me like a vise as I baked under the blistering sun.

I'm dying of heat out here to sell guns, in order to get out of a marriage contract, to end up with someone who wants me to become nothing more than a domesticated wife, the unsettling thought erupted in my mind, brutally clear and undeniable.

With every ounce of strength left in me, I jabbed the paddle into the choppy water, determined to push past the overwhelming thought threatening to consume me. My efforts were futile as exhaustion took over, leaving my kayak drifting aimlessly in a lethargic circle. Frustration boiled inside me as I mustered up the energy to realign myself. Finally, defeated and drained, I surrendered and let the boat drift freely while I sat hunched over, gasping for air.

The deafening silence enveloped me, pressing against my ears and suffocating my thoughts. I closed my eyes, trying to escape into the darkness, and all I could hear was the frantic beating of my heart in my chest. My body was drenched in sweat and my muscles burned with exhaustion from rowing the boat. As I struggled to catch my breath, a solitary tear traced its way down my cheek, a small crack in my composure. Feeling embarrassed and exposed, I frantically wiped it away, only to realize that there was no one around to shame me for showing emotion in this desolate place.

I am alone, I registered.

As the realization struck me, relief surged through my veins before twisting into a burning rage. My father's and lover's expectations echoed relentlessly in my mind, fueling a fire in my lungs. My brother's cold demeanor, sharpened by our father's sudden favoritism toward me, boiled my blood. With flames building in my throat, I unleashed a scream of pure frustration at the endless expanse of the ocean. The weight of the past several months melted away, mingling with the sweat dripping off my body. The release was fleeting, however, and another primal roar erupted from deep within, this time laced with resolve.

I took deep, deliberate breaths to steady myself, and lifted the paddle high above my head. One last battle cry escaped my lips as an answering call to the challenge.

I am going to do this. I am going to free myself, and then I am going to demand Alexei's honesty about our future, no matter the cost, I promised myself.

A surge of adrenaline coursed through my body, propelling me forward as I plunged the paddle into the water with renewed strength. My arms burned with the effort, but my determination fueled me as I propelled myself toward the distant block of land. In a rhythmic motion—inhale, paddle, switch, exhale, repeat—I moved like a machine, my muscles like iron. The boat sliced through the waves with fierce precision, cutting a straight path toward its target with brutal speed.

As I approached the island, my skin was coated in salt from the perspiration that had evaporated. I quickly leapt out of the boat and waded through the shallow water, carrying my kayak onto land to keep it safe. The island itself was more of a small plot of earth than an actual island, with sparse trees scattered throughout and sand stretching in all directions toward the ocean. In the center stood a wooden platform, where a monk sat perfectly still with his eyes closed. In front of him lay a small yoga mat on the sandy ground, along with several bottles of water.

Sinking onto the rubber yoga mat, I gulped down the cold water from the first bottle until it was gone. Then I poured the second bottle over my head to cool off. Sipping from the third bottle, I observed the monk, who remained completely immobile with his eyes closed. Unsure of what to do next, I let several minutes pass in silence, using the time to catch my breath and ease the soreness in my muscles from the journey to this secluded spot. Weariness began to take over as I sat waiting.

"Bhante Gan?" I finally asked. The monk opened his eyes and looked down at me.

Had he been sleeping?

He smiled and adjusted his sitting position, glancing at the sun to check its position in the sky. Then he turned back to me.

"You may begin," he said, his voice smooth and calming, like the whisper of a breeze through the trees.

"We have the yearly shipment of five thousand AK-47s. The agreed price is one thousand six hundred dollars per unit, which includes a four hundred dollar discount for bulk purchasing and a loyalty discount. All I need to know is what add-ons you want."

"No, I don't believe I need any add-ons at this time," Bhante Gan answered with a calm smile as he looked down at me. I glanced at my hands, blistered from the journey.

"You seem disappointed," he remarked when I didn't say anything.

"Just waiting for you to change your mind," I joked. To my surprise, the monk let out a high, clear laugh.

"I appreciate your dedication to change, but I'll need more than silence to justify buying more," Bhante Gan said with a gentle smile.

"Well, why do you need the guns?" I began, breathing deeply to gather the energy for the negotiations. The monk didn't respond, merely smiling at me.

"It is a beautiful day, is it not?" he asked instead, turning his gaze towards the blue ocean. I nodded in agreement but kept my eyes on him, choosing not to say anything further.

"You are a determined one," he observed. "Why have you really come out here?"

"I'm asking for my freedom," I admitted. The monk tilted his head, intrigued by my response.

"I think I can relate to that, but please clarify," Bhante Gan said as he began moving his body slowly. His movement seemed stiff, as if his body had hardened from basking in the sun all day.

"Clarify why I can't sell you more guns," I countered. The monk simply smiled in amusement, as if he half expected that.

"I suppose the truth serum has run its course," he remarked. I smirked at his response before drinking more of the water in front of me.

"I have a deal with my father. He allowed me into this business, but I have a year to find a husband. Apparently, I have a knack for selling guns, so he's giving me the chance to get out of our deal—only if I can manage to sell you anything extra," I explained, feeling uncomfortably exposed to this stranger.

"A knack for selling guns... I would *almost* say that it might run in the family," the monk said, stretching his arms above himself.

"So, you've met with my father and brother before, and they've never been able to sell you anything more?" I asked, hoping to affirm my suspicion.

"Yes, I've met Emilio and Bane before. No, they've never convinced me to buy more of anything, though they've certainly tried." The monk chuckled to himself, as if laughing at an inside joke I wasn't privy to. "Emilio's thirst for wealth and Bane's desperate need for paternal validation does not interest me," he added with a smile.

With my suspicions confirmed about the impossible task my father had set for me, I sighed heavily into my hands. A fresh layer of fatigue settled onto my shoulders.

"I am running a very covert but well-organized resistance. We are preparing for a regime change in the next several years," the monk surprised me with his honesty. I looked up at him, and he held a finger to his lips, signaling me to keep his truth a secret.

"I want to help, but I have no need for extras for my rifles. Just the rifles," he added slowly, a note of disappointment in his voice.

"If you don't mind me asking, why do you have a routine but limited request from us?" I pressed.

"We are very lean and source guns from many places. The budget we have with you is fixed; all other funds go to other areas that may need them," the monk explained, standing slowly on the platform and beginning to stretch again.

"What is your budget for us?" I asked, and a pleased look crossed the monk's face.

"Now, that is the correct question," he said, looking down at me with a hint of pride before continuing.

"I have half a million left. Any extras I purchase I would want to buy for each firearm," he explained, moving slowly through a yoga flow in the basking sunlight. I did some mental math as he repeated the flow twice more.

"I have these grenade launchers, the GP25s. They usually go for one hundred and twenty dollars each, but I'll offer you a one-time discount of twenty dollars off per unit. So, it would be one hundred dollars per grenade launcher. With five thousand units, that totals half a million," I recited the math.

"Is your father okay with you giving discounts like that?" Bhante Gan asked, opening his arms to the sky and taking a deep breath.

"The task was to sell more; he had no other remarks about how," I responded.

"We both know your father is a man who likes to change the rules, Sophia," the monk replied. Hearing my name from his lips made me freeze and look up at him. He said nothing more as he completed another round of his yoga flow, finally resting in a warrior pose.

"You have a deal," he said simply, so quietly I almost didn't hear him. I finally registered his words and met his gaze. He looked at me with an amused smile.

"May your freedom bring us ours," he added. I wanted to hug Bhante Gan but hesitated, feeling it might be too familiar for his liking.

"We have visitors," the monk said, gracefully falling out of his pose and standing at attention. I turned to see Alexei and Dimiter approaching in boats.

"We heard screaming and made the monk get us kayaks too," Alexei explained as they paddled into earshot. I smiled at the sight of my two men.

"Go to them. I'll take your kayak back; it seems I'll need to gather more cash," Bhante Gan announced. Without a moment's hesitation, I lunged into the water, splashing furiously as I raced toward Alexei and Dimiter, who were lined up waiting for me.

As I approached, Dimiter seized me in a fierce, almost reckless embrace that nearly sent us both crashing into the water. I reached for Alexei next, but his embrace was uncomfortably stiff.

"Hop in," Alexei growled in my ear, his voice edged with an unmistakable demand.

We retraced our steps to the plane, this time with Bhante Gan accompanying us. He stopped frequently to issue gentle commands and requests to those we passed. Just before we boarded the elephant, a new case of money was handed to me, and we exchanged bows with Bhante Gan.

A team of men on all-terrain vehicles pulled up behind the elephant and followed us back. At the plane, I directed our small team on how much to unload, and they worked with the monks to finalize the exchange of goods.

As the teams worked, I skipped up the stairs and boarded the plane, plopping the case of money down in front of Bane as soon as I found him. He was reading a book at a table and glanced at the suitcase with mild disinterest. His eyes shot up to meet mine, questioning. I nodded in confirmation, and I could see my brother's expression shift, growing more tense and cold.

"So, what was it then?" Bane asked, attempting to sound casual as he set aside his book and opened the suitcase.

"The GP25s, one for each AK-47 purchased today," I explained, watching as he began to pull out and flip through the stacks of cash.

"Did he finally tell you why he needed them?" Bane asked without looking up.

"No," I lied. Bane snorted a laugh.

"Of course not, and you still manage to make an extra six hundred thousand," Bane sneered.

"An extra half a million," I corrected. Bane paused in his counting and turned to study me. Slowly, with a hint of condescension, he corrected me.

"The GP25, the grenade launcher for the AK-47, is one hundred and twenty dollars a unit, my dear Angel."

"You told me to sell them extras, not that giving a discount was out of the question," I responded in a tone that matched his. The same pink flush that appears on our father's face when he's angry began to color my twin's face.

"This is gun running; we offer no discounts!" Bane yelled.

"Then why did you have me tell them we give a four hundred dollar discount for each AK-47?" I demanded.

"It's something we say, not something we actually do!" Bane's voice rose to a threatening volume. I noticed Alexei and Dimiter growing tense, their bodies coiling in readiness. I shot a glance at them; both looked ready to pounce at a moment's notice.

"Don't look at them—look at me," my brother commanded. As I met his gaze, Bane stood, towering over me.

"HOW AM I GOING TO EXPLAIN TO FATHER THAT YOU ARE READY WHEN YOU MAKE A ROOKIE MISTAKE LIKE THAT?" He roared.

"WELL WHY DON'T YOU JUST EXPLAIN TO HIM HOW *MY TEACHER* NEVER BOTHERED TO EXPLAIN IT BUT MADE SURE I KNEW NOT TO FUCK THE CLIENTS," I shouted, closing the distance between us until I was nose to nose with my brother. Our chests heaved with rapid breaths as our flaring nostrils filled with hot, seething rage.

"You will not speak to your brother this way," Bane finally responded in a cool, even tone.

"I will speak to you anyway I want. I sold the extras. I am out of the deal," I told him.

"That is for Father to decide," he spat, his eyes blazing with fury as he towered over me. Fueled by a whirlwind of rage, I slammed the suitcase shut and stormed down the hallway toward my private bedroom. Bane tried to block my path, assuming an imposing stance. I barreled past him with such force that he was thrown back into one of the leather seats, his shock evident on his stunned face.

As I approached my door, I heard Dimiter calling out to me, his footsteps echoing in the hallway. He caught up, his alligator-skinned suitcase in hand.

"Want the extra hundred thousand? You won me this money anyway," he said, gesturing to the cash he had won in the illegal casino.

"No, my father will have to accept me as I am," I cried, my voice a bit too loud with the adrenaline still coursing through me. I slammed the door to my private bedroom shut, a thunderous boom echoing as it closed on Dimiter's worried face.

CHAPTER SIXTEEN

The plane landed and my guards confirmed Bane had left before walking me to my car. When I pulled into the front of my house, Alexei was at the front door already, waiting for me. The promise to demand honesty about our future weighed heavily on my mind. I wasn't ready to have that discussion tonight, though.

As soon as I let him inside, we found ourselves naked and in my bed. We spent most of the night making tender and intense love. When exhaustion set in, I drifted off to sleep entwined in his arms.

In the morning, as light filtered through the curtains, I felt Alexei's warm body pressed against mine. I stretched my arms and legs, careful not to wake him from his peaceful slumber. As I shifted, though, he stirred too, his eyes slowly opening to reveal a sleepy yet content smile.

"Hey," I whispered.

"Hey," he whispered, brushing my hair out of my face with a gentle touch. I leaned in and our lips met, igniting a passionate dance as he pulled me on top of him. I reluctantly pulled back, my breath coming in ragged gasps as I locked eyes with him.

"Can we talk?" I asked.

"Sure," he replied, his voice low and rough as he shifted into a sitting position. His sudden movement caused me to slip off his lap, but I quickly sat up next to him, curling my legs against my chest. My heart raced, every nerve on edge, as butterflies erupted in my stomach.

"I don't know what you want from me or from this," I began, my words stumbling over each other. "But I feel like... well, I guess it doesn't matter. It's not like I'm rushing to get married. What I'm trying to say is that I think—no, I know—I want to be with you." My voice wavered as I rambled nervously, unable to meet his eyes. Alexei shifted on his side of the bed, and when I finally looked at him, his gaze was hard, arms crossed over his chest.

Uh oh.

My heart raced as I nervously added, "I mean I don't want to sneak around anymore; I want to announce to the world that you're mine... if you're comfortable with that," I stuttered while he remained silent. I stole another glance at Alexei and saw him lost in thought. A tumultuous storm of emotions washed over his face, most of them negative.

"Say something, please," I begged desperately as the crushing silence ripped me apart from the inside out. My heart fluttered wildly in my chest, each beat a tormenting reminder that I was recklessly headed toward either my dreams realized or my heart completely shattered.

"It's just..." he started softly, then dragged a hand across his face.

"I don't know what to think," he finally admitted. I exhaled deeply, feeling tension in my chest release. Alexei opened his mouth and then shut it a few times, so I stayed quiet, giving him time to gather his words.

"Are you sure your father is just going to let you out of the deal like that? Bane is right—Emilio doesn't deal in discounts," Alexei spat out finally. I stared at him in shock, my heart dropping to my stomach.

I just asked if he wanted to be with me, and he's talking about my father?

"You heard Bane. If I sold anything extra, which I did, then I'm out of the deal," I started, about to ask how this affected us being together when he interrupted.

"Yeah, he told you, but I don't believe anything Bane says until I witness it coming out of Emilio's mouth directly," he exclaimed. I pulled away from Alexei, an audible gasp escaping me.

"You sound like you're nothing more than a guard dog for my father, just waiting for his commands to lap up," I said, feeling suddenly exposed. I reached for a sheet to cover myself.

"Yes, Angel, yes! That's exactly my job—to watch over you. I can't be seen in public with you. I have to protect you!" he said sharply, his voice cutting through the air as he emphasized his point with harsh, frantic gestures.

"You can do both," I whispered, my voice barely audible. I felt my cheeks flush with embarrassment, a lump forming in my throat.

"Both?" Alexei shouted, his voice filled with disbelief. I nodded quickly, tears welling up and threatening to spill over.

"I think we need to stop doing this. I don't want to drag you into a life you don't want," Alexei stated, and my heart fractured.

"What?" I asked, my voice trembling. My vision blurred as the tears started to fall. Alexei let out a heavy sigh.

"You transfix me, Angel. I want to resist you, but I can't help myself. I'm a pathetic man, and you—you yourself admitted that you don't want to be *just a wife*," he said, the last part dripping with mockery. My tears flowed freely now, aching with the sting of his words.

"Well, I thought we could talk about it. Maybe come to a compromise," I admitted softly.

"I'm sure you did," was all Alexei said and then he was up. He threw the covers off and clambered out of my bed.

"What?" I asked again, but the word choked in my throat. Alexei dressed quickly, yanking his shirt on with frustration as he headed for the door. He grabbed his boots and stormed out of my bedroom. I called after him as he rushed down the stairs.

"So I was just a good fuck all this time?" I shouted, trailing behind him and demanding an answer.

"You were just wasting my time?" I challenged. Alexei turned to face me at the bottom of the stairs, his eyes piercing me with a hostile glare.

"How do you expect me to feel? You act so high and mighty, but I see you. I see how you stare daggers at any man who touches me. Why are you fighting this? Why can't you just admit that you might have feelings for me?" I pleaded, my voice breaking with frustration.

Alexei scoffed at my question and sat down on my couch. He began to put on his heavy-duty boots, "Duty, Angel. I have obligations to uphold—for myself and for your family. Just because you don't seem to remember or care doesn't mean I've forgotten them."

"Is it in your duty to fuck me all night too, because I don't remember reading that in your contract!" I screamed at him. The tears had ceased, and anger began to surge in its place.

Alexei ignored me as he finished tying his boots and stood up.

"Stupid and weak—that's what I am. I'm putting both of us in danger, and I can't allow myself to do that anymore," he said, staring at me with dark eyes searching for some sign of understanding on my part.

"I don't understand. Why do you insist on keeping me at arm's length, Alexei?" I pleaded, staring at him in shock and horror at how quickly everything had fallen apart. He ignored my cries and moved to the sliding door. As he slid it open and stepped outside, he paused only briefly at the threshold.

"If you can't understand, then maybe you're too immature for me, Angel. I should have known better," he stated, before slamming the door shut behind him.

It felt as if he had shot me—the sharp, piercing pain left me breathless. A maelstrom of emotions swirled inside me.

I turned and saw the large black suitcase with the money from Mystna. Bane had forgotten to collect it to give to Father, so I had brought it home with me. It had been abandoned hastily last night when Alexei and I had torn each other's clothes off in our frenzy.

I dashed over to it now, grabbing it with desperate urgency.

"YOU FORGOT TO TIP YOUR WHORE!" I yelled, hurling the suitcase through the glass door. The door shattered into millions of tiny, sharp pieces, chaos raining down around the bag of money outside.

Alexei paused only to grab the suitcase before slipping out of sight behind the landscaping along the side of the house.

The front door suddenly burst open as Dimiter rushed in, his gun already drawn and aimed. Overwhelmed by the aftermath of my fight with Alexei, I crumpled to the floor, sobbing uncontrollably.

Dimiter scanned the room, assessing the situation. Realizing I wasn't in immediate danger, he quietly closed the door and holstered his gun.

Without a word, he lifted me into his arms effortlessly and carried me to a couch away from the shattered glass, then gently set me down.

Dimiter pulled me close, letting me sob into his chest. He occasionally kissed my forehead and gently rocked me as I cried out every tear, far more than I ever imagined I could shed over a man. When my weeping finally stopped, Dimiter got up to fetch me some water and tissues. He set them in front of me with care, then settled back on the couch beside me. His arm rested casually along the back of the sofa, but his body hovered close, ready to protect or comfort as needed. After a long and uncomfortable silence, Dimiter finally broke the tension.

"Just so you know, I always tip my whores," he said with a hint of amusement in his voice. I let out a dry laugh and felt my face flush with embarrassment.

"Want to talk about it?" he pried, trying to keep his tone casual.

"Talk about what?" I asked, my anxiety spiking as I wondered if Dimiter was onto Alexei and me—not that it seemed to matter anymore. I grabbed a tissue and began to clean my tear-streaked face.

"Want to talk about what caused you to throw… something… through your back door?" he asked, gesturing toward the mess. He glanced out into the backyard, trying to spot whatever I had hurled. Shimmering fragments of glass littered the ground, both inside and outside of the house.

"No," I replied softly. Dimiter nodded once, instantly dropping the subject.

The weight of everything—Alexei, my father, the business—was crushing me, and I was too exhausted to sift through it all. I didn't want to talk; I wanted to forget, even if just for a moment.

"So, have you talked to Emi-" he starts to say, but before he could finish, I pulled him down to me. Our lips collided in a passionate frenzy, his mouth attacking me with unconstrained desire. Dimiter's hands gripped my body tightly as he moved himself on top of me, his motion rough and urgent. As he towered over me, he pinned my wrists above my head. Our lips continued to move together in a primal rhythm.

"Fuck me," I demanded, panting when our lips finally separated.

"What?" Dimiter breathed, his ocean blue eyes filled with hesitation.

"I want you to fuck me," I repeated, my voice laced with desire and urgency. "Hard and rough."

He stared at me for a moment, still uncertain.

"Please Dimiter," I begged. "I need you inside of me. Unless you don't want to..." My vulnerability made me feel exposed and raw.

"Oh Angel, trust me, I want to," he growled, hungrily devouring my lips as if they were the only sustenance he craved. In one swift motion, he stood and stripped off his clothes. A monstrous erection sprang from his pants and I couldn't help but stare in awe at its size. He caught my gaze and let out a low, guttural chuckle before pouncing on top of me again, his body pulsing with raw hunger and need.

"Do you like them big?" he taunted, his lips tracing a searing path up my throat and jawline.

"Oh, god, yes," I whispered, feeling myself aching for him. He slid into me with his tremendous member, stretching and filling me in ways that left me breathless with desire. A cry of satisfaction escaped my lips as every inch of him slid into me.

Dimiter's hands tightened around my wrists, pinning me down with his brute force. His kisses were rough and demanding, his movements inside of me slow but deliberate. Abruptly, my guard picked up the pace and thrusted into me with an impressive speed. The sound of our naked skin slapping together filled the room along with my uncontrollable moans of pleasure. Dimiter reveled in the noise I made, his own primal groans echoing mine as he plunged deeper and harder into me.

He ravaged me with his monstrous cock, slamming into me with a force that threatened to break me apart. I could feel myself losing control, consumed by the intense pleasure of our rough and wild coupling. Dimiter's grunts echoed in my ears as he fulfilled his promise, fucking me savagely. A powerful orgasm surged through me, threatening to overtake my entire being. My screams grew louder and more desperate, matching the intensity of his movements. With the climax, a sweet and all-consuming euphoria washed over me, eroding away any trace of the terrible morning until all that remained was pure ecstasy coursing through every fiber of my being.

Within seconds, Dimiter let out a primitive grunt and released inside me, his large cock pulsing fiercely before finally quieting. He collapsed on top of me with a satisfied growl, then left a trail of kisses along my neck before reaching my mouth again.

"Fuck, I have not had sex like that in a while," he smiled down at me.

"Me either," I said in a euphoric daze, still riding my orgasmic high. Slowly, the blissful fog began to fade as Dimiter pulled himself out of me with a satisfied sigh.

"Wait. What are you doing here?" I asked, suddenly realizing that Dimiter had rushed into my house unprompted.

"I came to check on you after yesterday," Dimiter explained, flopping down next to me on the couch. "I was a bit worried. I figured I could persuade you to take that extra hundred thousand from me." He looked up at the ceiling, but his hand reached out and gently intertwined with mine.

"How did you get in? Did you knock down the door?" I asked, glancing at my front door, which was still intact and firmly shut.

"Oh, no," Dimiter chuckled. "Your father gave us keys to your place for emergencies. When I heard the glass breaking and you yelling, I let myself in to make sure you were okay."

"Oh," I said, falling silent.

"Are you okay now?" Dimiter asked, giving my hand a soft squeeze.

"Somehow, I'm horny again," I laughed, admiring my own honesty.

"I have that effect on women," Dimiter winked at me. "But you have managed to tire me out."

I looked at Dimiter, truly seeing him for the first time—always supportive, always smiling. Reflecting on how I had mustered the courage to confront Alexei about our relationship, only to end up in a messy breakup, I realized the stark contrast. When I showed my vulnerability to Dimiter, he embraced it with open arms, offering a warmth I hadn't experienced before.

As I lay next to my guard, my phone suddenly chirped, bringing me back to reality. I had left it downstairs with the money, a reminder of the night before when Alexei had whisked me up to my bedroom. A wave of guilt washed over me as I thought about Alexei and found myself facing Dimiter beside me.

"You want to get it?" Dimiter asked, his carefree, happy demeanor easing my guilt.

Alexei made it clear his duty is more important to him than you. It's time to stop caring about someone who called you immature.

I pulled myself up and kissed Dimiter full on the lips, which he reciprocated enthusiastically.

"No, but I will," I said, once I managed to pull away. I found it hard to leave the strong, naked man on my couch, but I walked over to my phone anyway, compelled to see who was trying to reach me.

"Fuck," I shouted, staring at the email I had just received. "I forgot I signed up for this speed dating thing. It's supposed to be tomorrow." I looked up at Dimiter, a twinge of fear rising in me, expecting to find jealousy or possessiveness. Instead, he looked at me with encouragement.

"Why so upset? That sounds fun, and given your situation with your father, it's smart," Dimiter commented, smiling his charming, crooked smile. I stared at him in disbelief for several minutes.

"What do you want from me, Dimiter? I mean, sorry, we just had sex. I just don't want to be strung along again by someone wasting my time," I blurted out without thinking. Dimiter shrugged casually and, to my relief, didn't seem bothered by my question.

"I'm willing to be involved as much as you want," he said simply.

I sighed heavily. As I looked into Dimiter's eyes, I couldn't help but wonder if I was making the same mistake I did with Alexei.

"Just because we had sex doesn't really mean I suddenly own you. I figured you are dating around, waiting to find the most deserving man for you before committing, no?" Dimiter asked, sensing I was upset at his previous answer.

Relief washed over me again. This man was giving me a choice. Somehow that made me crave him more.

"So, what you're saying is you want me to take things at my own pace, especially now that I am out of a deal to get married in a year?" I asked, a smile threatening to break on my face.

"Absolutely. I also don't see the harm in you going to a speed dating event. If anything, it will just prove how I am clearly the best man to be the great Angel of Death's partner," Dimiter beamed at me, a sexy, confident look twinkling in his eye.

"Not sure if that's the nickname I want to stick around," I giggled as I rushed over to Dimiter and jumped into his open arms. I straddled his lap and wrapped my arms around him loosely.

Looking up at him with innocent eyes, I asked, "Will you take me tomorrow? Just you?"

I shuddered at the thought of speed dating in front of Alexei, especially now that he had just dumped me.

"I don't think I have any other choice?" Dimiter responded, though it sounded more like a question.

"What does that mean?" I asked, my cheeks flushing again as I braced for a lecture about how it's *literally his job* to protect me.

"Well, your father is going to Tithal tonight to fulfill your first contract with the Adami family. He's taking Alexei with him, so I'm the one left guarding you. Unless you want Bane to come along too?" Dimiter asked with a playful tone.

"NO!" I exclaimed immediately, my cheeks burning for a different reason now. It seemed my family continued to leave me out of the business and Alexei's failure to mention anything stung with added bitterness.

"Are you okay?" Dimiter asked, lifting my chin to get a better look at me.

"Yes," I whispered, not meeting his gaze.

"I'll call someone to clean up the glass," my guard said as he reached for his clothes, starting to put them back on.

"Wait," I said, looking down at his semi-engorged penis between his legs. "I was wondering if I could thank you in advance for taking me tomorrow."

Dimiter's mouth twisted into a sinister smirk as he stroked himself, his massive cock growing harder and more imposing in his hand. I eagerly positioned myself above him and impaling myself on his stiffness, relishing the sensation of being stretched beyond my limits. The pleasure sent shivers down my spine as I rode him vigorously, lost in the primal urge to merge with him completely.

After our vigorous ♫ *carnal acts*, ♫ I sent Dimiter away with the details of the speed dating event.

The event was designed for individuals "well above their means" to connect with "our own kind." Each participant had to submit an application that included a monthly statement proving they had at least half a million coming in each month and a photo of themselves.

I had applied shortly after my first sale and had forgotten about it until the email reminder arrived.

Dimiter arrived to pick me up on time the next day. He looked incredibly well-dressed, more so than usual, with a pair of mustard work pants and a tight navy polo. He had carefully styled his hair into a clean look instead of the boyish, haggard style he usually went with.

"I'm sorry, I'm waiting for my guard, not whoever you are," I teased the man as I closed my front door and locked it.

"Oh, shush. I'm just trying to fit in, make it less obvious that I'm your guard," Dimiter said, walking with me to his black Lexus and opening the passenger door. I looked up at him, and he smiled down at me expectantly.

"Is your idea of fitting into 'rich people society' to act more uptight like Alexei?" I asked. Dimiter's cheeks burned red.

"No. Look, if I want to open a door for a beautiful woman, I will," he said, stumbling over his words as he rambled a bit more about manners. I watched him with amusement before leaning over and kissing him on the cheek. Dimiter sighed, content, and fell silent.

"Thanks," I said as I got into the car. My guard closed the door behind me and came around to the driver's side.

The ride over was too short. As soon as Dimiter started the car, a greatest hits classic rock CD blasted through the speakers. By the time we arrived at the event, both of us were yelling into imaginary microphones and singing along to the CD. Dimiter pounded on his steering wheel while I played air guitar in the passenger seat. The loud music finally ceased when he turned off the car.

"You ready for this?" he asked.

"No," I admitted, running my fingers across his arm. Dimiter started to respond, but I launched myself onto his lips again. He pulled me close as our mouths collided. The kiss was fierce and consuming, but before it could deepen, I reluctantly tore myself away and stepped out of the car. I walked quickly toward the hotel, not looking back to see if Dimiter had followed.

As soon as I was inside, I dashed to the bathroom.

"It was just sex. That's all I want it to be for now," I told myself as I looked in the mirror. "I need to keep my options open and find the best-fitting partner." My lipstick was smeared from our kiss. I quickly fixed it and tried to catch my breath, still feeling a lingering desire for Dimiter searing within in me.

CARNAL ACTS

CHAPTER SEVENTEEN

The check-in booth for the event was located in the elevator lobby on the fifth floor. After checking in, I was escorted to Room 513, which would be my room for the day. I was informed once more that each woman would stay in her room, while the men would rotate after a buzzer sounded. Each visit was timed to last ten minutes.

Although the event's website never explicitly mentioned that the rooms were intended for privacy, I suspected that this was the case. Couples who hit it off right away could use their remaining time copulating if they chose. I secretly wondered if I could make a man climax from a blowjob in ten minutes or less when I signed up for the event.

As I entered the room, a deep blue light filled the space. Two elegant armchairs were positioned in the center, facing each other. The plush white rug beneath my feet contrasted sharply with the vibrant red and gold carpet it covered. In the corner, there was a small bar with crystal decanters and glasses neatly displayed. I poured myself a drink and settled into the chair facing the door, ready to begin.

The digital clock on the wall ticked away each agonizing second as I sat in the room, my thoughts drifting to taboo fantasies about my guards. Suddenly, the sharp sound of knuckles rapping on the door jolted me back to reality.

A distinguished gentleman, much older than me, strolled into the room with an air of confidence. His electric blue fitted suit shimmered under the lights, highlighting his toned physique—proof that he still hit the gym regularly. Gray streaks adorned his hair, adding a touch of maturity to his otherwise youthful style. With powerful strides, he made his way to the chair opposite mine and settled in, sipping from a delicate glass in his hand.

On the lapel of his suit was a flashy sticker bearing his name: Axel. I raised my eyes to meet Axel's gaze and found him studying me. His eyes lingered on my tits before slowly moving up to my face, almost reluctantly. A cocky smile spread across his lips, knowing he'd been caught ogling my breasts.

"Yes, yes, I can autograph something for you," he started, breaking the charged silence.

"What?" I asked, caught off guard.

"My fans—they usually ask for an autograph," he shrugged nonchalantly.

"Fan? That's awfully presumptuous," I replied.

"I know it can be awkward for some to ask, like *am-I-overstepping-my-bounds-at-a-speed-dating-event* or *man-he's-hot-in-real-life-I-want-to-carry-his-babies.* It can just be awkward, so I want you to know upfront—I'll autograph anything for you," he said, winking at me before taking a sip of his drink.

"Who are you?" I asked.

He stared at me in disbelief for a full minute before gesturing to his name tag as if I was an idiot.

"Uh, it says it right here, honey—Axel," he said slowly, as if I were having trouble understanding.

"Who?" I asked again. The man stared at me for an uncomfortably long time, occasionally mumbling nonsense before returning to his intense stare. Finally, he muttered, "Well, surely you've heard of me. I've been to space!"

"Space?" I asked, still confused.

"Yes, space," he said incredulously.

I nodded, twirling my drink in my cup as I tried to figure out the best way to respond. Axel was staring intently at me, making me feel self-conscious and waiting me out.

"I don't think, uh," I began, unsure of how to respond.

Don't say you have never been to space, that's too obvious, I thought.

"I don't think, uh," I tried again, at a loss for words.

Don't say it! He will think you are dumber than he already assumed!

"I don't think I like space," I finally blurted out, unsure of my true feelings on the subject.

What an idiot.

"DON'T LIKE—WHAT?!" Axel nearly spat out his drink. I studied his face and saw his anger start to surface. Then I realized that from the first moment he sat down, the more I pissed him off, the more aroused I became.

"Yeah, I don't like space!" I said, now more confident.

"Well, what do you know? You're just some dumb little girl," Axel dismissed me with a wave of his hand.

"I know you're old enough to be one of Jesus's disciples," I spat back.

"Excuse me?" The man looked down at me with a mix of shame and horror. I said nothing in response, watching as he slowly tried to recover. We sat in silence for several minutes, avoiding eye contact.

"Is it just me, or is the sexual tension between us thick?" Axel broke the awkward silence. I groaned into my hands. A bell rang loudly in the hallway, signaling that it was time for the men to change rooms.

"Want me to autograph anything?" Axel extended his hand, expecting me to hand him something.

"NO!" I shouted, causing him to jump at my harsh tone. He made a dramatic exit, stalling every few steps and glancing back at me expectantly, clearly hoping I'd say something—anything—to make him stay. As he finally left, I heard him bump into my next guest in the doorway.

The next man walked into the room, and I started to feel more optimistic about my prospects. He was closer to my age, maybe a few years older. His brunette hair was styled in relaxed curls, whimsically yet with the meticulous care of someone who has money. He wore a button-up shirt that didn't quite fit him, expensive jeans, and a casual hoodie jacket. His name tag read "MAVERICK."

Maverick seemed a bit unsure of himself as he took a seat across from me. He respectfully, but shyly looked me over at least twice.

"Do you know how much those cost?" He pointed to the drink in my hand.

"Sorry, no. Why?" I asked.

"Well, it just seems like such a waste of money, right?" he shrugged, pulling out a small flask from his hoodie pocket. "I just bring my own. You really should too; it's where they get you."

He took a sip from his flask and leaned forward, eyes bright with enthusiasm. "You know, if you're really looking to save, it's all about the little things. Like, don't buy their overpriced drinks. I've got a buddy who's a bartender. He told me you can get the same quality stuff for a fraction of the price if you know where to look." He pulled out a crumpled piece of paper from his pocket and unfolded it, revealing a list of discounts and insider tips.

I raised a hand, cutting him off. "Hey, man, look. I don't know how to say this, but this event is for people who bring in at least half a million a month."

"Uh, yes, of course. I mean, I'm technically worth at least two hundred twenty-five million dollars, if I could just remember my passphrase," he mumbled, taking a generous sip from his flask and slumping down in his chair.

"What do you mean, technically? And passphrase?" I asked.

"Well, you know, I bought like five hundred dollars' worth of Bitcoin back when it was five cents," he explained. "Then, when it wasn't going anywhere, I forgot the passphrase to my wallet."

"How did you get into this event, then?" I asked. Maverick shifted uncomfortably, squirming in his seat.

"Well, technically, I also own my own software company, so the income comes from that. It's not quite like the Bitcoin, but it's enough to meet the conditions of this event." He paused, then asked, "What about you? What are you doing here?"

"I made a deal with my father to find a husband within a year in order to join our family business," I said honestly.

Maverick took a deep breath, looking a bit overwhelmed. "Wow, a year? That's not, uh, a lot of time, huh?" he asked, his tone sincere.

"No, it's not. Though a couple of months have already passed, so it's even less time now. I'm not sure if the deal requires me to be married within the year or just engaged. I might have also managed to get out of the arrangement recently, so it's a bit unclear. I probably should figure that out," I mused aloud.

"So, I'm guessing you haven't found anyone yet if you're here," Maverick said, trying to sound sympathetic, but his face was tight with pity.

"Um, not really. I've mostly been fucking my guards," I retorted bitterly, irritated by his expression. He looked at me as if I were a caged animal.

"Oh wow, is this some kind of 'I love him, but my father won't let me be with him' fantasy for you?" he asked.

"No, I just enjoy fucking them. One of them seemed to be growing feelings for me, I think, but he decided to end things recently. I think he's scared my father might kill him. The other just has a big dick," I said casually. Maverick's eyes widened as he absorbed this information.

"Why would he kill him?" Maverick finally managed to ask.

"What?"

"Why would your father kill your guard?"

"Before I made the deal with my father to find a husband, I used to sleep with guards around the house. Whenever he caught us, he would kill them," I explained.

"Of course. Sounds like a stable man, your father," Maverick said, his gaze fixed more on the distance than on me.

"You?" I asked, finally drawing his attention again.

"Honestly, I'm looking for a partner to join me on the vacation island of Ogygia. It's known for older men and their sugar babies, but I'm just hoping for some naked island time together. I'd feel really guilty if it were a sugar baby; it would almost feel like exploiting them," he confessed.

Awkward silence permeated as I ran out of things to say. Maverick seemed to feel the same way, and we just sat there, nodding at each other.

Finally, the bell rang out in the hallway.

"Well, good luck on the sugar baby island," I said, relieved that our encounter was over and eager for him to leave.

"Yeah, thanks, and hey—you too," Maverick replied as he awkwardly stood up. "Good luck with the, uh, big dick guard." He trailed off, clearly uncomfortable, before quickly turning to leave.

A wave of relief washed over me as he departed. It was clear that Maverick would never be comfortable with what I did for a living. I finished my drink, savoring the moment of solitude, then got up to make myself another one.

"Mind making an extra two drinks?" a rich, youthful voice called from the doorway. I turned around, excited to see a young man leaning against the wall. He wore jeans and a loose gray shirt, his curly hair neatly styled with a side part. A pair of glasses added a touch of maturity to his otherwise youthful appearance.

"Of course, but two drinks?" I asked flirtatiously.

"Yeah, sorry," he winced, "but my ex-girlfriend insists on approving my next girlfriend, so she'll be joining us."

"Oh, okay," I said, turning around to make two more drinks. Maybe they'd be open to a three-way at some point. I grabbed the guests' drinks and turned back, only to see the man sitting in his chair—with a human-like sex doll on his lap. I paused for only a moment before handing him both drinks and then retrieved my own from the bar.

"You are?" I asked.

"Oh, sorry, Sofia is probably covering it up. I'm Bruno," he said, fussing over the doll on his lap.

"Sofia? Is that her name?" I pointed to the doll, who was dressed in a miniskirt and corset.

"Yes," Bruno replied, glancing at me.

"That's my name!" I exclaimed excited.

"Oh, no way! Did you hear that, Sofia? Her name is Sophia," he told the doll with such intimacy that I suddenly felt like a third wheel on this date.

"Oh wait, how is it spelled?" I asked.

"What do you mean, how is it spelled?" he shot back, as if I'd asked a ridiculous question. He began running his hand through the doll Sofia's hair.

"You know, like S-o-f-i-a versus S-o-p-h-i-a," I explained. Bruno scoffed at me.

"S-o-f-i-a," he replied. "Who would ever bother spelling it like S-o-p-h-i-a? Too many letters," he rolled his eyes.

I took a long sip from my drink before responding.

"I spell it S-o-p-h-i-a. That's how my name is spelled," I said, locking eyes with him.

He scoffed again, staring down at me. "Well, you spell your name stupid, and Sofia here agrees with me."

"Out," I yelled, pointing a sharp finger at the door of my room.

"What?" Bruno asked, his face turning pale with horror.

"I said out!" I stood up, shouting more forcefully.

"I was told I have ten minutes to talk and... whatever with you, and we are only two minutes in, so I'm staying until I've had my ten minutes," Bruno sat, indignant.

"I'm so tired of men thinking I'm just here to put up with their shit," I muttered, grabbing the doll by her shoulders and yanking her off his lap.

"SOFIA!" Bruno cried as I sprinted toward the door with his toy. He chased after me and caught up just as I flung the stupid doll into the hallway. His horrified gasp echoed as he rushed to retrieve it. I pointed to a guard in the hallway and then at Bruno.

"Watch him. He's not coming back into my suite. Do you understand?" I commanded, staring down the guard.

"I understand," he replied.

As I settled back into my suite, the sound of Bruno's distressed cries echoed through the hallway. I started to pleasure myself, reaching the brink of climax, when another knock on my door interrupted me. I quickly covered myself and sat up as a mature couple slithered into the room.

I studied them warily as the woman began to coo about how beautiful I looked. The man gently ushered her forward, letting her sit in the chair in front of me while he stood behind her.

"Is this like a swinger thing?" I asked the couple.

"No, no, no," the woman replied quickly. "This is about our son, Lars. He needs to find a wife and move out of our house." She pulled a framed photograph from her large purse and handed it to me. "We're looking for a serious bride who can give him the stability he needs. It's become quite a problem—he whores around with different women and comes home at all hours of the night," she explained.

As I examined the framed photo, I realized it wasn't a photograph but a painting of a young man, probably around twenty years old. He wore a smug smile and was dressed in a striking blue and gray suit.

"We do have a questionnaire, if you don't mind filling it out for us?" the woman said, taking back the picture quickly and handing me a stack of stapled papers with a pen. I scanned the questions briefly before starting to answer them.

The couple watched me as I filled out the tedious "Application to Date Lars Augustus III." Once I was done, I handed it back to the woman, who sat with a patient, eager expression. She and her husband scanned the front page.

"Oh, it says here that you are 'in the family business,' but you didn't provide any details. Mind if I ask what that means?" Mr. Augustus inquired, looking at me.

"Yes," I responded, sipping from my drink.

"Yes, what?" asked the mother.

"Yes, I mind," I said, staring at them hard, daring them to press further. The couple exchanged an uneasy glance, shifted uncomfortably, and then returned to the form.

"Oh, wow. Under favorite sexual position you have written 'Anal.' Our son is going to need a baby of his own, so make sure you don't ignore your other... areas," Lar's mother instructed me, her cheeks burning bright red at the comment. I ignored her and stared at the drink in my hand, pondering the absurdity of the situation. If they were going to hand me a four-page application and think I'd take it seriously, the next several pages were going to be quite a surprise to them.

The couple flipped around the document a bit more, then surprised me by closing it. They looked at each other, then at me with bright smiles.

"You're perfect!" the mother exclaimed.

"Uh, what?" I asked.

"Yeah, it's very clear from your response to the essay question 'What does romance mean to you?' where you answered 'Fuck this,' that you're the type of woman who can keep up with our Lars," the man explained eagerly.

"I also saw the note about how you and your father made a deal, so you have to get married in less than a year, which is perfect. We want him out of the house quickly, and if a pretty girl like you can lock him down, that's one less thing we have to worry about!" the mother continued, her smile faltering at the edges.

"Look, sorry, I'm not interested in your son," I said. Both the father and mother stared at me, mortified.

"Well, why not?" the father demanded.

"Our son is perfect, thank you. Maybe a bit of a discipline problem and reckless, but deep down he is, is, is..." the wife started stuttering, struggling to find the right adjective.

"He's also not here. But you are, with an application," I said, glancing down at the paper I had been handed. The back of the last page was showing, where I had given up and drawn a large penis instead of answering. I watched as the parents struggled to come up with a rebuttal, but the bell in the hallway sounded. The father's face turned red with anger at my dismissal of his son.

"Come on, Vivian, we don't want someone lower class rubbing off on our son anyway," he spat before turning to leave the room.

"We all come from the same status! We had to show our income to be here!" I shouted after them.

"We know what 'family business' really means; you had your chance to join us. Consider the chance gone," the woman said, her tone softer but condescending.

"Bye," I waved at the couple as they marched out together.

"Oh, excuse me," came the familiar deep cadence of Dimiter from the doorway before he rounded the entrance to my room.

"Hey, I was wondering when I'd see you. How's it going?" Dimiter sauntered to the chair in the middle of the room and plopped down.

"What do you mean? What are you doing?" I asked, my curiosity piqued.

"Oh this," he twirled his finger in the air.

"What do you mean, this?"

"The speed dating," Dimiter said, jumping up to check out the bar. He helped himself to some of the food and made a drink.

"Do we really pay you half a million a month?" I asked, excitement rising as I hoped this could be a way to appease my father's demands.

"Oh no, I just photoshopped your statement with my name and changed a few numbers. Can't pass up on an opportunity to find a sugar mama. Maybe I could retire early, go be a beach bum or something," he said, returning to his chair.

"How's it going for you?" he asked again.

"Take off your pants," I demanded.

"That well, huh?"

"Take off your pants."

Dimiter did as I commanded and I kneeled in front of him, his large member twitching with eagerness for my touch. I stroked a finger down his length and he took a deep breath.

"Angel," he murmured my name seductively.

"I want to know if I can make a man come from a blow job in less then ten minutes," I whispered. Then I kissed the tip of his penis before swallowing him in my mouth. He groaned as I took him in and began sucking on him hard. As I looked up at Dimiter, hoping to make eye contact with him, I noticed he was pretending to ignored me instead. My guard looked around the room casually, occasionally taking sips from his drink. His face showed no signs of noticing me working on his prize between his legs. The neglect turned me on, and I became desperate to get a rise out of him. Changing my tactics, I began to suck on him slowly and sloppily. This caused only the smallest of smirks to form on his lips. The small encouragement fueled my desperate desire to please him.

With each passing moment, our time together seemed to elongate into an eternity. I relentlessly took Dimiter in, pushing deeper and harder, his face barely contorting with strain and pleasure. My own desire grew until I couldn't resist the urge to touch myself, adding to the already intense experience. Just as I was starting to reach my peak, the bell outside the door rang, signaling the end of our allotted ten minutes.

"That was the best blowjob I have ever gotten," Dimiter spoke quietly, removing himself from my lips and putting his pants back on.

"But I didn't make you climax," I pouted, still kneeling in front of him.

"That's because you did a number on me yesterday," he grabbed my chin and lifted it until I met his eyes. He traced my lips with his thumb softly. "Besides, I couldn't let you "win," thinking you can make me orgasm in ten minutes," he murmur with a smirk. Dimiter swiftly left, abandoning me a lustful mess on the floor, still kneeling in the center of the room.

"Oh wow, someone looks ready for me," the next man remarked as he walked in, looking down at where I was kneeling on the floor. I quickly stood up and returned to my chair, taking liberal sips of my drink to steady myself. My mind was still stuck on Dimiter and his dick.

"I'm Cameron," the newcomer introduced himself, settling into his chair.

"Sophia," I replied into my drink, eyeing him. He wasn't terribly attractive, but he was younger than most of the other men I'd seen today. Dressed in black sweats, a black tank top, and black sandals, his appearance was as unkempt as his long hair. A large yin-yang pendant hung around his neck.

"I know what you're thinking," Cameron said with a grin.

"Oh?" I responded, raising an eyebrow.

"You see, I'm a psychic, and I'm picking up on some strong sexual energy in this room. I think you want me as much as I want you," he smiled confidently, and I cringed.

"I was blowing the guy before you," I explained, hoping to wipe the self-satisfied arrogance off his face.

"Consider that a warmup," he insisted, his smug grin stretching into something meant to be a smile, but it only came across as creepy. "With me, I'll hypnotize you. I don't just mean that with my dick, I mean I will really hypnotize you to follow my commands."

"I'm good," I said.

"Have you ever been sexually hypnotized? Like consensually of course," he giggled awkwardly to himself and continued before I could respond. "It's mind blowing... so I have been told. The girls I pleased were so loud in their orgasmic pleasure that my mom had to soundproof the basement."

"Um, what?" I asked.

"My mom had to soundproof the basement because I make women come so hard when they are hypnotized," he reiterated, making sure to emphasize the part about how he pleases women, as if I hadn't heard him the first time.

"Sure, sure. So, why do you live with your mom?"

"Why not? Mom's the best. She even makes my favorite dish when I'm a good boy for her," he replied, flashing that unsettling smile again.

"When you say your mom, do you mean your actual mom?" I pressed, feeling a bit puzzled.

"Yeah, why?" he asked, looking genuinely confused.

"It's just the way you said 'good boy'..." I began, searching for the right words.

"Oh no, no, not like that!" he quickly clarified, waving his hand dismissively. "I mean, when I do something nice for my mom—non-sexual, of course," he added, pulling out a stack of cards and starting to shuffle them.

"What are you doing?" I asked as I watched him shuffle and reshuffle.

"Asking the Tarot if you will be my bride," he stacked the cards and presented them out to me.

"Are you going to spend most of our relationship referring to your Tarot over asking me?" I looked down at the stack of cards but didn't touch them.

"You don't know what you want. The spirits that guide us know better," he urged me again to shuffle the cards. Instead, I just stared at them, then up at Cameron with a sharp expression. The look took some of his original enthusiasm, and he cut the deck before flipping over one.

"Oh wow, the Lion. I told you, sexual energy," he mumbled, then flipped another card. He glanced up at me with guarded eyes before looking back at the card. I leaned forward to see it myself.

"What does the Jackal mean?" I asked, looking back at Cameron to find him staring at me, looking mortified.

"What?" I pressed.

"The spirits, they whisper," he said softly, then jumped out of his chair and dashed to the door.

"THEY WHISPER WHAT?!" I yelled after Cameron. Instead of an answer, I heard the bell in the hallway and the fading sounds of him running away.

The last date of the day was the most frustrating. The young and attractive man who walked in had a nervous energy about him. He was well-dressed and groomed, tall but skinny. A large smile stretched across his face from the moment he entered the room.

"Hello, I am Enrique from Ange," he said slowly in English.

"Hello, I am Sophia from Etristan," I responded back slowly, inviting him to sit across from me. He did.

"I am Enrique from Ange," he said again with a smile.

"Yes, I know. I'm Sophia," I repeated, a bit annoyed.

Enrique and I sat staring at each other in silence for a moment.

"You do anything for fun? Do you like Tarot?" I asked.

"I am Enrique," he replied with a smile. After a beat, he added, "from Ange."

"Do you know English?" I asked, hoping to determine his level of understanding. Enrique smiled broadly and nodded yes. I smiled back tightly, beginning to suspect he might not actually understand.

"Do you want a drink?" I decided to test my theory.

"Enrique," he said, pointing to himself.

"Right, from Ange," I said with him.

We spent most of the remaining time together, with Enrique repeating that he was "Enrique from Ange" in response to every question I asked.

After what felt like an eternity, a loud thud echoed from the doorway of my hotel room, and a woman burst in. She was curvy and beautiful, with large, cascading black curls framing a stunning face. Her body was very fit, though a noticeable bump showed under her dress.

Enrique stood as if he recognized the woman, and they walked toward each other, their eyes drinking in every detail of the other. I thought they were going to kiss, but to my surprise, the woman backhanded Enrique and began to yell at him in another language.

Enrique recovered quickly and started to argue back, speaking in the same language with equal passion. I watched as they quarreled, the woman pointing accusatorily at me multiple times. Just when I thought I might need to call a guard, Enrique grabbed the nape of the woman's neck and pulled her into a kiss.

The kiss seemed to slow the woman down, and she responded with equal intensity. Their hands quickly found each other's clothes, starting to remove them as their lips remained locked. Enrique pulled her further into the room, his hand groping for a surface to lay her down on while he continued to kiss her neck and shoulders.

A flash of Alexei's lust from our last encounter crossed my mind, and I quietly and unobtrusively removed myself from the scene.

As I left, I stopped by the booth to retrieve my calling card. Each man who showed interest in me had the opportunity to leave their number, and if I was interested, I could call them. Flipping the card over, I saw that only Axel and Dimiter had left their numbers. I discarded the card on my way out.

CHAPTER EIGHTEEN

I t was very late at night, several days later, when his phone call came in. I found I couldn't sleep and had called the family chef to prepare a midnight snack. Although it was well past midnight, my father paid his staff well. Despite a slight grumble, the woman arrived fifteen minutes later with a basket full of ingredients.

My phone was hooked up to the house's stereo, blasting a new playlist I had created. When the call came in, the house shook with the sound of my loud ringtone. I looked down to see his name illuminated in big, bright letters: Alexei.

"Hello?" I answered cautiously, disconnecting my phone from the Bluetooth system for a more private conversation. A grumble came through, followed by a gasp on the other end.

"Hello?" I asked again.

"Your boyfriend misses you," Alexei's voice came through clearly, though it was tinged with irritation.

"Boyfriend?" I replied, slightly breathless. A dark chuckle echoed down the line in response.

"The Adami kid had some choice words about what he'd like to do to you. You should have seen your father. I haven't seen Emilio that red since Arousal," Alexei mumbled, his words slurring slightly.

"Not sure if Daddy was proud of his little Angel for capturing the mob's attention, or disgusted by what some man-child thought he could do to his daughter," Alexei continued, his voice thick and muddled.

"Have you been drinking?" I asked.

"Have I been? Do you know what I'd like to do to that little prick, Angel? To hear him talk about you like that," Alexei rambled on, the clink of ice punctuating his words as he sipped on something.

"Alexei, you said—" I began, preparing to confront him about our fight. He interrupted before I could say anything more.

"Angel. What a strange nickname we've all given you. I get it—your beauty is something to behold, but calling you an Angel doesn't do justice to how gorgeous you really are," Alexei mused aloud. I remained silent at this admission, my breath caught in my throat.

What is he saying? I thought.

"That Adami *fuck* could never make you feel pleasure like I can," he added after a long silence, the jingle of ice cubes clinking in the background. It was rare for Alexei to curse, and I was both shocked and confused by what he was telling me.

"Alexei, you called this off," I finally accused him.

"*Alexei, you called this off*," Alexei mocked, his tone suggesting frustration with himself more than with me. I heard a grunt on the other end, followed by the subtle sound of liquid hitting his glass.

"Where are you? Are you safe?" I asked. I was met with another sip, then the sound of Alexei collapsing into a chair.

"I'm in a hotel room in Tithal. It's not as nice as the one we—"

"Alexei."

A boyish laugh came through the line, and my guard sounded pleased with himself.

"So, you do think of it then, think of me still," he whispered.

"It's only been half a week, idiot," I shot back. Alexei didn't respond right away. Instead, I heard a faint mumble and some grunting.

"I'm naked," he finally admitted, "I miss you." I closed my eyes at his words, unsure of how to feel.

Should I just hang up?

"I... How am I supposed to take this? One moment you're hot with me, and the next you're cold. What do you want from me?" I asked.

"If I close my eyes I can see you, naked and breathtaking. Happily, greedily, sliding on my cock," he breathed. It dawned on me he was probably touching himself, imagining me there with him.

"Alexei."

"Angel."

I stayed silent, listening intently. He moaned my nickname a few more times, interspersed with other sounds of pleasure. His breath quickened until, finally, I heard him release himself. I imagined, sadly, that he spilled into his hand, his phone held to his face between his shoulder and cheek.

"That Adami boy should worship you. Who else could defeat him at his own game?" Alexei finally spoke again. I heard him moving around, presumably cleaning himself up.

"Your snack is ready," the cook announced from behind me. I turned to acknowledge her and then waved a hand to dismiss her. She placed a plate of food on the kitchen counter before starting the process of cleaning up.

"I want to worship you," Alexei mumbled, followed by a grunt as if he had stumbled and fallen into a piece of furniture.

"Is that an invitation, then, for when you come back?" I asked, feeling a bit breathless as I spoke. There was no response for several minutes. I pulled my phone away from my face and saw that the call had ended. He had hung up.

"Your snack, ma'am," the cook reminded me as I stood up from my chair. I looked at the plate of food and suddenly felt a wave of disgust. Without hesitation, I grabbed the plate and hurled it across the kitchen. It struck the gray tiled wall with a sharp smack, shattering into a dozen glittering pieces. The food scattered on the floor with a heavy thud.

The cook froze in her cleaning, staring at me with tired eyes.

A few days later, as I descended the stairs into my living room, a glint caught my eye. A silver platter sat on the dark brown coffee table, perfectly positioned under the overhead lights, as if a spotlight were shining on it. Curious, I walked over to examine it.

In the center of the silver platter, a long-stemmed red rose lay elegantly across a deep purple pillow. The soft fabric cradled a large diamond attached to the end of a butt plug. It caught the light, sending sparkling reflections across the room. In front of the pillow, a single notecard rested, its edges trimmed in gold, with elegant calligraphy spelling out "An Invitation" at the top. I reached for the card, turning it over in my hands. The only details were a date for tomorrow night and an address. I thought back to my question to Alexei the other night.

Is that an invitation, then, for when you come back?

I stared down at the card, debating whether I should go. Eventually, I decided against it and placed the invitation back beside the pillow.

For the rest of the day, I left the setup untouched. Each time I passed by, I would pause, staring at the large butt plug. It did look enticing. Then I would glimpse my sliding door again and decide against it.

"Let's just try it on, see how it feels," I murmured to myself, feeling a reluctant pull as I passed the pillow setup once more. The seductive glimmer of the enormous butt plug taunted me, luring me in with a promise of pleasure. With cautious movements, I inserted the toy and felt it slowly expand within me, stretching me to my limits. Memories flooded back to when I would proudly ride my dildos around my Father's mansion. Then there was that first time, when I caught Alexei's ravenous gaze fixated on my breasts, fueling a fire within me that never truly died down.

"It's not like I have anything sexy to match it," I said aloud to no one. Walking into my closet room, my new toy still inside me, I approached the closet wall and shuffled through my lingerie, finding nothing that would suit.

Then I approached the full-length mirror and tapped it twice. An image of me appeared, accompanied by a list of clothing categories ranging from "sex kitten" to "girl you take to meet your mother." After flipping through the options in the "diamonds" category, I sighed in defeat.

"Connect to the web?" a button appeared over the image of me. I stood in front of the closet computer, hesitant.

"It's not like I can find something that will arrive by tomorrow," I told myself, then clicked on the button, unlocking the new feature in my smart closet. A new selection of lingerie appeared for me to browse. I skimmed through the options until I found a simple black crotchless teddy, intricately laced with diamonds carefully stitched into the fabric. I clicked on it, and it appeared on the computer image of myself. The picture of me twirled in a stiff circle, showing how the piece would fit.

Not bad, and it would go with the plug, I thought.

I clicked on "More Information," and the hefty price along with other details appeared on my mirror computer. I scrolled quickly through the information until I froze, a bitter laugh escaping my lips.

There, in big letters on the screen, was the arrival date: tomorrow before noon. It would indeed arrive on time. I stared at the screen for a long time, feeling the effect of the butt plug stretching me out. My resolve weakened, and desire surged until I finally pushed the buttons, confirmed my address, and purchased the overpriced set.

"He better worship me," I muttered as I reached for one of my many dildos and went to go release some frustration.

CHAPTER NINETEEN

s evening approached the next day, I pulled up to a small, single-story house and sat anxiously in my car. The diamond encrusted crotch-less teddy graced my body, along with the butt plug, of course. The sight of the modest house brought one thought to mind: I should talk to my father about getting raises for my guards.

I got out of the car and grabbed the bottle of wine I'd brought, then started up the path. Anticipation built within me as I reached out and pressed the doorbell. It rang out loudly, followed by a brief silence. Then, I heard the sound of a hushed conversation and the rushed shuffling of people inside. The door finally opened, revealing Dimiter in nothing but his boxers and an annoyed look on his face.

"Can I help you?" He asked, irritated, his words trailing off when he noticed it was me standing in his doorway.

"Dimiter?" I asked, stunned.

"A-Angel?" he stammered as he pervertedly appraised me in my bare-ly-there lingerie.

"I received this invitation," I explained, holding up the elaborate card with the address on it.

"Yeah, that was me. But Angel, that was an invitation for last night," Dimiter said, looking at me with hurt clear in his eyes.

"It is actually for today," I corrected, holding out the card for him to inspect. He took it and examined it closely, then glanced at his watch.

"Shit," he muttered. "I thought you stood me up. I'm sorry, Angel." An apologetic grin spread across Dimiter's face. He glanced back into his house for a moment before turning back to me.

"Um, can you give me a minute? I have to take care of someo-, some-thing, and then I can let you in." Before I could respond, he slammed the door shut in my face. I waited patiently, listening to muffled voices and clattering sounds coming from the other side. It was only a minute before the door opened again. This time, I was staring right at my own face.

A woman who looked startlingly like me, but a bit older, was staring back in alarm. Dimiter, clearly trying to hurry his guest along, noticed they had stopped moving. He attempted to gently push her forward and out of the doorway.

"Wow, Dimiter," the woman said in an accent I couldn't place. "Are you replacing me? I can't blame you; she looks so much more like her." I gawked at the woman, confused.

"No, no. This is just my friend," Dimiter said quickly, trying once more to push the woman out the door.

"Oh, well, do you like making money, honey?" the woman asked, ignoring Dimiter's gentle attempts to usher her outside.

"I'm sorry, what?" I responded, confused.

"You look just like that Zoric girl too! Let me tell you, men love to fuck her. I get bookings all night and they all tell me the same thing; they picked me because of who I look like."

"They do?" I asked, unsure of how to feel knowing people hire sex workers in my image.

"Oh yeah, she got spotted at one of those sex parties a few months back. Let me tell you, business was spectacular for weeks. Let me get you my agency's Instagram handle. You can reach out to Tiffany, that's not her real name, but she can help you get more information."

The woman finally stepped through the threshold as she rummaged through her purse. Her hand searched around in the deep black bag as she smiled up at Dimiter, who had a sheepish look on his face. She eventually found what she was searching for and handed me a purple and blue business card adorned with a large crescent moon. The card featured an Instagram, Snapchat, phone number, and OnlyFans, all listed under a large, italicized, fancy name.

"Roxxxy Angel," I read her name out loud.

"Yes, nice to meet you," She held out a hand, which I shook.

"Seriously, reach out to me and I can help show you the ropes. I'll even share all my OnlyFans marketing tips," she said, winking at me encouragingly. Then she turned to walk to her car. As Roxxxy passed me, she gave me a playful slap on the ass and whispered, "Have fun," before continuing on her way.

"My god," she exclaimed when she saw my car in the driveway. "What do you do, hardcore porn or something?"

"Yeah, porn or something," I responded absentmindedly, pausing for a brief moment before asking, "Hey, how many men a week, if you had to guess, use your services specifically because you look like Sophia Zoric?"

"Honey, so many that I get to be choosy about who I respond to. The rest I direct to my OnlyFans," she replied.

"So why Dimiter?" I called out, catching her before she got into her modest car.

"With how you're dressed, I think you know why, babe. Plus, he always tips generously," she said, giving me a final once-over before loading into her car. My body ignited as I remembered the sensation of Dimiter's massive member inside me, filling me with raw pleasure.

An uncomfortable cough caught my attention, and I turned to see Dimiter holding the door open a little wider than before, motioning for me to come in. I stepped inside, and as soon as the door closed behind him, I burst into uncontrollable laughter.

"If you must know, since you asked before, I did tip. I even gave her extra tonight, despite us being... interrupted," he said, turning to me with a red face, his embarrassment evident despite his cocky tone.

"She looks just like me!" I exclaimed, excited, and strangely titillated.

"I watched you fuck some of the largest dildos ever, for like *months*. What did you expect? You make a man go crazy Angel!" He rushed to justify himself, running a hand through his hair in a surprisingly boyish gesture. We smiled at each other, and neither of us moved for a few moments. Dimiter cleared his throat again, clearly feeling uncomfortable.

"You brought wine!" He finally said, reaching out to grab the bottle. Dimiter wandered off into the kitchen, and I took the opportunity to look around his house.

As I stepped inside, my feet sank into soft carpet. To my left was a sparsely furnished dining room with a heavy, dark wooden table surrounded by mismatched chairs. The table was cluttered with papers, mail, and various trinkets stacked in haphazard piles.

To the right was a cozy living room, dominated by a large U-shaped couch upholstered in deep red fabric. It was massive and looked plush and inviting. On either side of the couch were small tables adorned with carefully arranged coasters. A striking piece of abstract art hung on the wall above the couch, surrounded by dark curtains that blocked out the sun.

Opposite the couch was a flat-screen TV perched atop a cabinet filled with action figures and photos of Dimiter with unfamiliar people.

I was examining his collection of figures when he walked back into the room with two glasses of wine.

"It's not as big or nice as your place, but it's home," he said, handing me a glass, which I took. Dimiter walked over to the couch and sat down, indicating that I should join him.

"You sounded surprised to see me when I opened the door," he said, skipping over any further explanation of the woman he'd just sent away. I felt myself stiffen slightly as I sat down next to him.

"You thought... someone else left the present, didn't you?" he asked lightly, trying not to sound too bothered.

"I don't know what you mean," I murmured into my wine.

"Sure," Dimiter replied, sipping from his own glass. He threw an arm around me casually, and a strange silence settled between us.

"It's just that I thought I was being obvious," Dimiter said, breaking the silence. "Given the gun brooch."

"What?" I asked, shocked.

"Well, I left both items under floodlights. I wanted it to be like a sign.

Like a calling card, but with gifts for my girl," Dimiter explained, smiling down at me.

"You left me the gun pendant?" I asked, my mouth still open in disbelief. I tried to close it, only to have it fall open again as I struggled to process this new information.

"Yeah, who did you think left it for you? Alexei?" Dimiter scoffed a little at his own joke. I felt myself blush, looking down at my glass of wine in embarrassment.

"Wait, really?" he asked when I didn't respond.

"He said it cost as much as a promotional bonus, as if he would know..." I rushed to defend myself, causing Dimiter to chuckle as he realized what Alexei had done.

"That man is so cheap," Dimiter said with a touch of anger in his tone. "He'd rather waste energy defending the thoughtfulness of a poem as a romantic gesture than spend money to truly impress his 'future perfect wife.'"

I reached out to touch Dimiter, but he seemed lost in thought, staring straight ahead at the TV. I watched him carefully as his anger slowly subsided, his arm slipping from around the couch as he pulled me in closer.

"I hope I wasn't a disappointment for tonight," Dimiter said, finally turning to look down at me.

"The only thing I am disappointed in is not knowing what you planned on doing with Ms. Roxxxy Angel here tonight. Roxxxy with three X's," I smiled up at the man holding me close.

A big jolly laugh shook us both and Dimiter pulled my legs up into his lap.

"Oh no. I'm not going to fall for that," he said, shaking a finger my direction.

"Fall for what?" I asked innocently, willingly moving myself closer into the arms of my handsome guard.

"Don't think you can just look at me with some little, innocent 'fuck-me' eyes and I will just spill all my fantasies," he explained as he kissed me on the cheek.

"Those were barely 'fuck-me' eyes. Besides I don't want to simply hear about what your fantasies. I want you to describe them to me, in intimate detail. Then I want you to do them to me." I said, looking up at Dimiter with actual pleading "fuck-me" eyes.

Dimiter choked on his wine and took a moment to recover. A cocky smile danced on his lips as he absorbed the look I was giving him. Then, Dimiter lifted me into his arms until our lips met.

"It's easier to just show you," he breathed. His free hand brushed down the side of my body. He grabbed my buttocks, then slowly traced a finger down until it brushed against the toy nestled between my cheeks. Dimiter groaned in lust, bringing his forehead to mine, closing his eyes. He moved his finger away from the gem and traced it up my thigh softly until he caressed past the crotchless underwear, and into me. He slipped his fingers in effortlessly, and I can't help but let out a loud moan.

At the sound, Dimiter's large ocean blue eyes opened, brimming with desire. I locked eyes with him as he begins to tease me with one finger inside of me, the other stimulating my clitoris.

"I want you," I whispered. It was all I needed to say. He took the wine glass from my hand and moved it safely away. Then his lips fell onto mine again as he laid me out on his huge couch. Towering over me, he moved his lips to caress down my sprawled body, then pulled himself off me to remove his boxers. As soon as he was naked, his hands found my body again, running up the sides of my abdomen.

"Is this expensive?" he asked, caressing the delicate fabric of the lingerie.

"Yes."

I barely managed to get the word out before his strong hands ripped the fabric from my body. I let out a lascivious moan, surprised by how much this savage act aroused me. My body writhed beneath his hands, begging for more, but he suddenly pulled away. I was left panting and wanting. Dimiter sat back on his couch and pointed at his large erection, ready for me.

"Come girl," he demanded in a deep, commanding voice. His eyes twinkling with a dark lust. I removed myself from the tattered lingerie and straddled him, my opening finding his cock with ease. Dimiter grabbed my hips, his fingers digging into my hips as I took my time sliding down his cock. The feeling of him stretching me out once again, along with the pressure of the butt plug induced an overwhelming euphoria.

"Fuck, Dimiter," I breathed, then wailed with pleasure as I rode the entire way down his cock again.

"Is it big enough for you, Angel?" Dimiter asked, watching me ride his manhood.

"You are enormous," I confessed, reaching the bottom of his shaft again.

"I take it Alexei's cock doesn't fill you up quite the same way, does it?" He kissed the corner of my mouth and smiled.

"I don't... I don't... I don't know... what you're talking about," I struggled to get out, moaning between each attempt, drunk on the pleasure Dimiter was stirring in me. With both hands tight on my hips, he thrust me up and down himself again, then settled me down fully on his massive member. A dark chuckle escaped Dimiter before he kissed my face and neck. His hands traced up to my breasts and started to play gently with my nipples.

"Don't play coy. You showed up at my doorstep ready to fuck him," Dimiter accused lightly. Before I could respond, my guard's fingers pinched my nipples, and my body flooded with rapture at the mixture of pain and pleasure.

"I bet Alexei is quite sweet on you. He doesn't understand you like I do. A power-hungry girl like you Angel, you like it rough!" Dimiter barked the last word next to my ear as he thrust into me with his mighty organ. His hands glided back down to my hips, and he seized me again. His fingers digging tightly into my buttocks as he thrusted himself into me roughly. A cry of ecstasy escaped me as Dimiter bounced me on his cock. He was seated back drinking up the view. His arrogant smile twisting into a delighted smirk, as if he was entertained at how much I was enjoying myself on his shaft.

His enormous cock was hitting me in all the places I wanted, and I threw my head back ready to climax. Dimiter halted his movements, knowingly and I cried out in exasperation.

"Oh no- I was too nice to you the other day Angel," Dimiter chuckled darkly, holding me down to prevent me from squirming on his penis. He brought his mouth to my breasts as he held onto me, nibbling at my erect nipples. I gasped, frustrated as my satisfaction settled without releasing.

Dimiter ran his tongue around my nipple then up my breast. He moved to my ear and whispered, "Go bend over my dining room table."

"Where?" I breathed, desperate and willing to please. My body was frantic for an orgasmic release.

"Let me show you," he whispered, then slapped me on my butt. Dimiter slowly removed me from his cock, and I let out an annoyed groan as I slipped off. He chuckled and grabbed my hand to drag me over to his dining room. Then with one big sweep he pushed off half of the table's contents onto the floor. Dimiter pulled me into a violent kiss before shoving me face down onto the table.

"Hope none of that was important," I said breathless. I felt Dimiter behind me, lining himself up to thrust inside. He slipped into my aching hole easily and held me on his dick again.

"Right now, you are the only important thing," he snarled before building up into a frenzied rhythm, thrusting into me frantically. A delighted moan came from me, encouraging his brutal pounding. He spanked me once and continued his work.

My moans crescendoed into desperate cries as Dimiter's rough thrusts invaded every inch of me, sending waves of pleasure. He spanked me hard several times, leaving stinging red marks in its wake, as he ravaged me with his powerful penetrations. Too soon I felt him slow down, savoring each agonizingly slow thrust into me. I heard him breathing heavy breaths and I realized that I was tiring him out.

To make up for losing momentum, Dimiter relentlessly spanked me with increasing force. I bit down on my lip to stifle a cry as the fiery sting of his palm scorched my buttocks. Each slap from Dimiter's hand felt like a branding iron searing into my flesh, leaving behind a trail of blistering heat. My guards satisfied chuckle only added fuel to the flames, as he rubbed the raw and tender area he had just spanked.

His hand caressed around to the front of me as he thrusted into me at an agonizingly slow pace. Then his fingers found my swollen and throbbing clit and begin to work it in small, torturous circles. The intense pleasure caused me to gasp and writhe under him.

"You will only come when I grant you permission," Dimiter instructed, playing with my pearl aggressively. A loud, sexual moan escaped my lips as I ignored his command. The sensations of an orgasm was threatening. I pushed my hips back and swallowed up his cock with my wet, desperate hole. He understood immediately what I was trying to do and grasped onto my hips, restraining me from from taking any more pleasure from him. An anguished cry came from me as I struggled on him. I was on the fringe of exploding.

"Please, please, please. I understand, I come only when you want me to. Please, oh god, Dimiter, please, give it to me," I begged, whimpering and giving him what he wanted to hear. "I'll be good for you all night, please just let me have it," I continued, aching for him to move inside me again and drive me off the edge of ecstasy. Dimiter didn't move, and I spasmed my muscles around his cock. The movement caused him to spank me, licking me right where I was already sore.

I ignored the jolt of pain and continued with my pleas. Dimiter moved his fingers slowly down to my sensitive area again. His other hand pulled on the back of my neck, lifting me up until his mouth was by my ear.

"Good girl," he whispered seductively, his fingers teasing around my clitoris again.

"You may come now, you slut," he said as he started slowly thrusting again, his fingers gliding across my pearl freely.

A scream of rapture tore out as the orgasm spasmed through me. Waves of gratification crashed over me with each of my guard's deep thrusts. My full body succumbed to the pleasure and I continued to scream as I rode out the orgasm on the gigantic cock penetrating me.

When I finished, I collapsed onto the table, a limp pathetic mess.

Dimiter slid out of me and pulled my hair back until he could kiss me on my neck.

"You still want me to do to you what I was going to do with to Ms. Roxxxy Angel?" Dimiter asked in a low voice that rumbled in my ear.

"Yes," I barely managed to whisper.

"Good."

We had to allow several minutes for me to recover before I could find myself on his dick again. I enthusiastically sucked on his cock while we waited. Dimiter's powerful hands finding their way into my hair and, grabbing at the base, he aggressively drove my mouth along his shaft. I felt myself becoming aroused again as I allowed him to be rough with me.

The rest of the night was a befuddled blur of orgasmic haze as Dimiter used my body thoroughly. He indulged greedily in his own pleasures, while making me feel new ones I did not know were possible. With each touch, I felt a mix of pain and pleasure that left me panting for more. I had to ask for permission every time before giving in to the release that would build inside me, making the experience even more intense. We lost count after six orgasms, each one leaving us both breathless and craving more of each other.

I finally laid ruined in Dimiter's bed, naked and sticky with sweat and sex. He had allowed me to come one final time, then he dropped me onto his bed to unload on my breasts. My guard eyed me as we both caught our breath. His face was illuminated with triumph at the sight of me.

Without explanation, he ran off and when he came back, he had a wet and dry cloth in his hands. I reached out for them, but he pushed me back down. Then gently, almost intimately, he began to clean up his mess on me. His mild movements a strange stark contrast to how he had treated me the rest of the night. I felt myself becoming aroused once more somehow. As soon as he was done, he threw the towels into a hamper, turned off his lights, and curled up in the bed next to me.

"Goodnight, Angel," he whispered, pulling me into a cuddly spooning position and planting a kiss on my cheek. I couldn't help but giggle at the absurd and drastic change in Dimiter.

"You fuck me ragged all night, then gently clean me up, cuddle me, and tell me good night?" I asked as Dimiter pulled me closer into him, his large body wrapped around me like a protective shell.

"I'm a complicated man, baby," was the only response I received. Within seconds of him saying it, Dimiter quietly started to snore next to me.

BANE'S GUNRUNNING BUSINESS RULE NUMBER TWO:

Trust is nothing, money is everything.

This is just Father's motto to life.

CHAPTER TWENTY

It was late the next morning when I woke up to ♫ _Dimiter's bright smile_. ♫ He was naked and standing in the doorway with a tray with a plate of food, coffee, and a small vase with a single flower.

"Wow, is this the same service you give Ms. Roxxxy Angel as well?" I teased Dimiter as he gently set the tray in front of me.

"Yes, minus the flower—that's just for special guests," Dimiter replied with a dazzling smile before kissing me softly on the lips. He dashed out of the room, then returned with an identical tray of food for himself, setting up next to me.

"I love breakfast in bed," Dimiter sighed contentedly, then added, "Food and a sexy, naked woman in my bed... young me would be so proud." He chuckled to himself, a boyish amusement in his eyes. I went straight for the cup of coffee and purred in delight after a sizable sip.

"I recently got a fancy coffee maker and have been learning all these different ways to make coffee in my free time," Dimiter explained as he took a bite of the food on his plate.

"Have you been learning to cook as well?" I asked, glancing at the delectable spread he had placed in front of me.

"That's just leftover from growing up. I've always been interested in the culinary arts. Food fuels us, and if you want to look as good as I do, you have to eat properly," he lectured. I nodded along as I cut into my food.

We chatted through breakfast about trivial matters. Once we had finished eating, Dimiter cleared away our plates and crawled back into bed with me.

I wanted to thank my host for his hospitality and countless orgasms. As I caressed a hand down his body to his shaft, I watched it stiffen. As soon as it was wrapped in my hand, his member solidified immediately. I kissed Dimiter before moving down to his cock and licking slowly up his shaft.

"Angel," he moaned my name softly. I tongued down to his balls and sucked on them, one hand still roughly playing with his outstanding member.

Dimiter reacted just as I wanted him to and I rewarded him by swallowing his penis whole in my mouth. This caused his hips to buck under me. With quick movements, I sucked hard on his cock the best I could. Each lick had me wondering if I ever had to struggle this hard before as I devoured his whole erection in my mouth.

A long string of familiar chirping rang from a phone and pulled my attention away from my partner.

"I found your phone in the living room this morning and decided to charge it for you. I guess it just woke up," Dimiter explained.

I pulled away, apologized, and went to check the notifications on the shelf where he had plugged in my phone. Apparently, I had missed several calls and texts from my brother while I was busy getting fucked out of my mind last night. The latest text was from my father, though, so I decided to read that one first.

"Angel, come by for lunch – Father."

My father was not known for his texting abilities and rarely used that method to communicate with me. Fear began to spread across my chest; whatever my father wanted, I doubted it would be good, especially given the number of times Bane had tried to contact me without a response.

I quickly typed out a confirmation to my father and then sent a similar message to Bane, letting him know I was alive.

"What is it?" Dimiter asked, noticing the panic in my eyes.

"My father just texted me; he wants to see me for lunch," I explained. Dimiter nodded, immediately understanding.

"Here, kid," Dimiter said, getting up and retrieving a large, old shirt that he tossed in my direction. The shirt swallowed me and could have easily been a dress. I delighted in its scent, which still carried Dimiter's smell. I quickly grabbed the rest of my things and headed for the front door.

"Hey, don't worry. I'll be there too, to keep you safe," he said, then pulled me into a deep kiss. I melted into his arms, but he pulled away sooner than I wanted. Still dazed and undoubtedly satiated from last night, I walked out the door to my car. As I settled behind the wheel, my phone chirped again, bringing me back to reality. I peeled out of the neighborhood, remembering I needed to hurry.

I pulled into the mansion driveway thirty minutes before lunch. As soon as I stepped out of my car, Bane grabbed me firmly on the arm and dragged me toward the mansion.

"There you are," he sneered. "Where have you been?"

"Let go! I'm prepared to deal with Father myself today," I said, pulling away from my twin.

"Angel, he's found you someone to marry," Bane hissed. I looked at my brother in shock, finally understanding why he had been urgently trying to reach me last night.

"Who?" was all I could manage to ask.

"I don't know, but I'm supposed to fly you out tomorrow to meet him. That's what Father wants to tell you today." Bane glared at me, a dangerous look in his eyes.

An agonizing stretch of silence passed between my brother and me.

"Bane, he said that if I sold—" I began.

"He doesn't care, Angel," he cut me off. "I think Father won't stop until he sees you married off to the most 'strategic ally,' which would probably be aging troglodytes." Bane glared at me, his anger still burning. As I looked at my twin, it dawned on me that, for the first time in a long while, most of his anger was directed at our father again.

Bane and I sat waiting at the massive dining table, an array of food spread out before us, but neither of us touched it. The tension in the room was palpable. I stared at the feast, my stomach churning with anxiety after the recent news. Bane's glare at me was constant, as if I were somehow responsible for the delay. The silence that hung between us was thick with unspoken words. As lunchtime dragged on with no sign of my father, each passing minute felt like a lead weight in my stomach. My nerves were starting to fray.

Twenty more minutes dragged on until, finally, my father bustled in casually, staring at an electronic tablet in his hand as he bounded to his usual seat at the head of the table. Only after he sat down did he set the tablet aside and look up to see Bane and me. He acted startled, as if he had forgotten he had commanded us to join him today.

"Oh, yes," he mumbled, then proceeded to fill his plate with food and began to eat. Bane and I remained still, despite Father's urging for us to follow suit and pile up our plates.

"Father," I started to say, but he hushed me with a wave. He pointed at the food in front of me, commanding me to serve myself. Reluctantly, I began to pile some of it onto my plate until it looked passably filled. Bane followed suit, slowly adding food to his plate and nibbling at it. I picked at my food, occasionally chewing a piece but mostly just moving it around.

"Angel, honey, stop messing with your food and eat," my father's voice cut through the silence.

"I had a big breakfast before I got your text, Father," I mumbled into my plate.

"Well, that's a shame. If you're done, then let's move to my study to talk," my father said as he stood up. Bane and I exchanged a look before rising to follow him to his office. He settled behind his large desk and, with another commanding gesture, invited Bane and me to sit across from him.

"Sophia," my father began, notably using my real name to start the conversation.

Fuck, I'm really in trouble.

"We are coming up a little under half a year since our deal. How close are you to finding a husband?"

My mind flickered back to being on top of Dimiter last night and under Alexei just the week before.

"I... I... I've met a few men, but you said if I sold the monk extras, and I did," my voice trailed off weakly under my father's intense gaze. He studied me over his glasses, a tight, unimpressed look on his face.

"Meeting people is not going to get you married. I, on the other hand, have been searching for a suitor in case you fail to find someone by the agreement date," he stated matter-of-factly, a hint of pride in his voice. Bane and I remained silent, and our lack of reaction seemed to disappoint my father.

"You are to meet him," my father continued. "He knows about our deal and understands that the guarantee of marriage is not promised. But he has asked to see you, as he is eager at the prospects of making you his wife."

"But you said..." I tried to challenge my father again. He waved his hand dismissively.

"I say a lot of things," Father shrugged off before staring at me intensely, his eyes daring me to challenge him further. I looked at Bane before turning back to my father, feeling slightly defeated.

"Who is it? Do I know him already?" Bane asked.

"His name is Mikhail Volkov, and no, I do not believe you know him. Both of you will meet me at the plane tomorrow morning," he ordered, then dismissed us with a wave of his hand. Bane and I remained seated, staring at our father. I was still in shock, while Bane seemed to be deciding whether or not to say something.

"I said I will meet both of you at the plane tomorrow morning," Father growled when he noticed neither of us had moved. Bane and I jumped to our feet and left his office together. As soon as the door was closed, I turned on my twin.

"Bane, what did you tell him about the deal?" I demanded.

Bane shrugged off my question.

"What does that mean?" I pressed.

"It means I will see you tomorrow morning. At the plane," he said, his tone emotionless. Then my brother trudged off down the hallway, not inviting any more conversation.

The next morning, I pulled up to the plane and saw my father, brother, and a few guards scattered around. Father was on the phone, so I approached Bane, looking around at the men.

"Where are Alexei and Dimiter?" I asked, not seeing them among us.

"They were given the day off. Father wanted to bring his own men," Bane said, patting my shoulder in a feeble attempt at comfort. Father finished his call and walked over to us, handing me a large black duffel bag.

"Change into this on the plane. It looks like I won't be able to join you today, as some business elsewhere needs my attention. Bane will accompany you, and I'll leave two of my guards with you as well. There's also a hairstylist on the plane who will get you cleaned up," my father instructed.

He whistled loudly once and stalked off in the opposite direction, most of the guards following him, leaving Bane and me behind.

We boarded the plane, and I retreated to one of the private bedrooms to examine my father's gift. Opening the duffel bag revealed an intricate dress that cascaded to the ground. It featured a strapless bodice made of shimmering gold fabric, adorned with ornate patterns of jewel-encrusted flowers that twinkled in the light. The dress was stunning but felt far too formal for a meeting with a potential husband.

On top of the dress, nestled carefully in the bag, laid a note in my father's handwriting: "He bought this for you and specifically instructed that you wear it today. - Father."

I got a sinking feeling that I wasn't going to like this man if he was deciding how I should dress before even meeting me.

Before I had a chance to put on the outfit, a sharp woman entered the room holding a robe. With a tone that suggested she was not in the mood for any arguments, she commanded me to put on the robe and sit in the vanity chair. As soon as I was seated, she began working on my hair. I attempted several times to make conversation as she pulled at my head, but her responses were short and uninviting. It didn't take long for me to give up on small talk and let her do her job in silence.

Several hours passed before I was turned around and allowed to see myself in the mirror. When I first glimpsed my reflection, I stared wide-eyed in shock. The stylist had carefully curled my hair, pinning it back into a stunning cascade of ringlets. Interwoven among the spirals were pearls and matching jeweled flower hairpins that complemented the dress. I gaped at the result, and the stylist smiled, clearly pleased with her work.

"Go get dressed, then I'll touch up your makeup," she instructed. I did as I was told, and once everything was in place, I gawked at myself in the mirror.

My brother, who had spent most of the flight ignoring me, opened my bedroom door to say something. Instead, his mouth dropped in surprise.

"You look like a doll," he said, walking around to examine me from different angles.

"I look like I'm being dressed up and presented as a gift. Do we have any ribbon to tie a bow on?" I replied, still staring at my reflection and uncomfortably tugging at the formal dress.

"You have a suit as well; it's in the other bedroom," the stylist informed my brother, then went to fix a part of my hair, adding hairspray liberally.

We landed shortly after I was made up. My stomach lurched as the plane touched down. I had grown apprehensive about meeting the man who was already demanding so much of me before truly getting to know me.

My brother, now dressed in an elaborately embellished gold traditional Kaftan, looked out of the window and gasped loudly.

"What?" I asked, frightened.

"Mikhail Volkov is, uh," my brother stumbled over his words. "We've landed at his private airport... which is apparently right next to his castle!"

I rushed to a window and opened it to see a lavish garden stretched out before me, with a massive castle in the near distance. Before I had a chance to take in the whole scene properly, the plane door opened. In walked a tall, handsome young man with dark, perfectly styled hair and twinkling brown eyes. He was dressed in a crisp, stylish black suit that fit him impeccably.

"Hello, Bane, Sophia," the man greeted us, speaking sharply, clearly, and very politely as he bowed. "I was so excited to meet you that I wanted to come down to the landing pad myself. I apologize if it's considered rude to barge into your plane. I just really wanted to meet—" The man broke off mid-sentence, his eyes flickering to me. Neither Bane nor I moved, and I had to remind myself how to breathe.

"My name is Mikhail," the man continued. A sense of tension began to release upon hearing his name. Standing up straight, I approached Mikhail.

"It is nice to meet you," I said, extending my hand. Mikhail took it and brought it to his lips for a kiss as I curtsied in my dress. I felt like a fairytale princess meeting the handsome prince she was destined to marry.

And they lived happily ever after, I thought as Mikhail looked up at me again, his eyes dancing with excitement and a genuine, warm smile on his face. Mikhail extended his arm for me to take, which I did, and he proceeded to lead me down the plane stairs and through the garden to the castle.

I was captivated by my suitor almost immediately. He kept a playful smile on his lips but had a serious, intimidating gaze. As we walked, with Mikhail leading the way, I caught him stealing many glances my way.

Perhaps my father is not so bad at being a matchmaker.

"Do you like the gardens?" Mikhail's voice interrupted my fantasy of what our future might look like. I nodded in response.

"I cultivate them myself. I've had an interest in botany since I was young. Come, follow me, and I'll show you my pride," Mikhail said, guiding me down a different pathway, away from the castle.

"Here, I grow some of the rarest flowers," my host explained, still holding my arm as we walked quickly through rows of beautiful vegetation. He stopped in front of a particular area and gently released his hold on me. Mikhail approached a delicate pink flower, picked a few from the shrub, and returned with them. He secured the flowers into one of my hairpins and lifted my chin to admire his work.

"Rhododendron Schlippenbachii, the royal azalea, one of my favorite flowers. A rare beauty for a rare beauty like you," he explained, a playful twinkle in his eyes and a coy smile on his lips.

"Okay," I giggled like a teenager who had just been called beautiful by a boy for the first time. My cheeks burned with a mix of embarrassment from my awkward response and joy at my suitor's compliment.

Mikhail extended his arm again, which I took, and we continued to walk deeper into the gardens. Rows of vibrant colors lined our path, and I was so captivated by the sights and smells that I almost missed noticing we had entered what seemed to be a small village. The bustling sounds of people drew my attention, and I looked around to see men, women, and children dressed in old-fashioned village garb, engaged in play-acting lively activities of a quaint, busy town.

"Are we going to watch a play?" I asked, my curiosity piqued. A soft, musical chuckle escaped my companion's lips as he shook his head.

"No, we're actually in your village," he explained. I stared at him, wide-eyed and confused. A wistful, sad smile crossed his face as he continued, "This used to belong to my mother, but with the marriage, you would inherit it. It is the only place on the entire grounds where you will be left alone. It is an exact replica of the Hameau de la Reine that was built for Marie Antoinette, with a few additions to expand on the Hamlet."

"The—what?" I asked.

"The Hameau de la Reine," Mikhail explained. "My mother was obsessed with Marie Antoinette, so my father had this built for her as a wedding present. The people here are employed to dress and interact with you as you see fit," Mikhail finished, gesturing into the village.

I turned to look and noticed that everyone had stopped moving. Instead, they had filed into a neat line, staring right at me, waiting for instruction. I looked out at the group, stunned. Among their ranks, I could see a baker, cook, carpenter, librarian, painter, florist, farmer, barista, and couturier. Mikhail pulled me forward to introduce me to the group.

"What do you think?" Mikhail asked.

"I don't know," I replied, still stunned by what I was seeing.

He spoke to the group in his native tongue, and they scattered again, resuming their tasks. A baker soon brought me a *Le Pain au Chocolat* on a small, delicate plate. I thanked him, and Mikhail led me to an area set up to look like a quaint outdoor café. Moments later, a small cup of coffee was placed in front of me.

"Stay right there," Mikhail gently instructed as I sipped the delectable drink. He hurried off to speak with one of the workers—the painter—who followed him closely with supplies.

"He's going to paint you, so try not to move too much," Mikhail explained as the painter set up next to the table. The artist sat down on a stool and began observing me intently, taking in every detail.

"How long is that going to take?" I asked, watching as the painter started to outline his work.

"Not long, don't worry, you can relax," Mikhail chuckled, then sat down across from me at the café. I turned to look at Bane, who stood behind me with a displeased expression. I wanted to ask him why he was in such a mood, but the painter began to grumble in another language.

"He says please look back toward him; he wants to capture your angelic features," Mikhail translated. I looked back at the painter, who did not seem like one to compliment his subject, and tried my best to sit still.

The longer I sat for the painting, the more people seemed to flock around us. Several would stroll by in groups, staring openly before hurrying off into a sea of whispers. Those who owned shops or trades would stop by to show off their work. From food to textiles to jewelry, each trade showcased their collection, leaving us with a small gift at my table. Every worker took pride in their craft, eager to discuss their work in intimate detail, only to be hurried along by the grumpy painter if they lingered too long.

"What happened to your mother?" I asked several hours later, after the initial excitement of my arrival had worn off and the village had returned to its usual bustling.

"She... died," Mikhail replied with a deep sigh. I could sense from his tone and the way he spoke that they had been very close.

"I'm sorry to hear that; mine is dead as well," I said, reaching across the café table to take his hand. "But I wasn't as close to her as it sounds like you were to yours," I added. Behind me, Bane grunted loudly enough for me to hear, but I chose to ignore him. Mikhail looked at me with sorrowful eyes as he placed his other hand on top of mine.

The painter started to lecture me again, and I shot him a sharp glare, irritated that he was ruining the intimate moment with my future husband. He stopped speaking immediately, a fleeting look of fear crossing his face before he quickly masked it with annoyance. Returning to his painting, he made no further attempts to snap at me. I turned my attention back to Mikhail.

"Are you hungry? It's getting late, and we should probably head in for our meal," Mikhail said wistfully, withdrawing his hands and checking his expensive watch. Seeing the time, he jumped up immediately and grabbed my hand.

"Actually, we're late—we must go in immediately!" he insisted, pulling me after him and shouting something back to the painter.

"What do you mean, late?" I asked, but Mikhail didn't respond as he practically ran, pulling me with him. I glanced back at my twin, who followed behind, equally confused by the sudden rush.

The castle grew larger and more impressive as we hurried towards it. I tried to take in its grandeur amid the rush. The exterior had a rounded, almost whimsical appearance, adorned with numerous balconies. Decorated columns supported expansive sections of the building, and the walls were white with dome roofs in faded hues of red, blue, and green.

As we entered through the grand front doors, the contrast between the exterior and interior was striking. While the outside blended modern renovations with classical charm, the inside was a stark contrast—dusty, dark, and gothic.

An intricately sculpted vaulted ceiling loomed above us, illuminated by electronic light fixtures designed to resemble clusters of candelabras. In front of us, a dry fountain stood as a grand centerpiece, its marble basin intricate but empty. Flanking the fountain were two grand staircases, elegantly winding upward from either side, leading to the upper levels of the palace.

"Please excuse me. I must get my father. Please follow Ivan, our servant here, to the grand dining room." Mikhail bowed, and Bane repeated the gesture while I curtsied in return. With a final glance, Mikhail ascended one of the grand staircases with quick, purposeful steps.

A well-dressed, older, balding man emerged from a side hallway as Mikhail left. He nodded slightly and gestured for us to follow him.

"Follow me, please," Ivan instructed, turning on his heel and walking stiffly down the hallway from which he had just appeared.

Bane, still not thrilled about the day, made a point to offer his own arm to me. I took it, and we followed the servant through several winding, ornate hallways. Each turn revealed an even more elaborately decorated space. Old paintings of angels and demons adorned the walls, their vivid and loud colors making a bold statement.

The ceilings were masterpieces in their own right, with intricate murals that revealed more detail the longer you stared. Everything was framed with ornate carvings painted in bright gold. The palace's grandeur explained the ostentatious dress.

"You'll need a special GPS just to get around here," Bane joked, breaking the growing tension between us. I stopped walking beside him and began to laugh quietly. Eventually, I couldn't contain it anymore, and fits of laughter escaped me. The stress of the day seemed to fall away in waves of giggles. Ivan, the servant, stopped and stared at me disapprovingly.

"I'm sorry, it's just that this is all so strange to me—the dress, the village," I managed to say, glancing at Bane, whose smile had also grown until we both burst into hysterics. Our laughter echoed through the grand hallways, amplifying in the vast, ornate space.

We eventually quieted down, the impassive and unimpressed servant still watching us with a stern expression.

"Finished?" Ivan asked impatiently.

"Is this some kind of fetish for your lord? He seems pretty young to want such a traditional-looking castle or wife," I asked. Ivan looked me over with disdain and didn't respond. Instead, he turned on his heel and began walking down the hall again.

I brushed at my gown, took Bane's outstretched arm once more, and we continued to follow Ivan down the hallway.

Ivan brought us into a grand room with a long table. On closer inspection, only five place settings were laid out, all around the large red and gold chair at the head of the table. Bane escorted me to the seat on the right side of the chair and helped me into it before taking his own seat next to me, muttering something unfavorable under his breath.

I was about to ask him what he had said when the sound of Mikhail entering the room cut me off. His footsteps echoed through the expansive, mostly empty space as he made his way toward us.

"Father will join us shortly," Mikhail explained as he got closer, walking around the table and sitting down right across from me. I smiled at him politely, but tilted my head in confusion.

"Sorry, but will you not be sitting at the head of the table?" I leaned in to whisper my question.

"No, why would I?" he whispered back, looking surprised by the inquiry. I glanced at Bane, who mirrored my confusion.

"I'm sorry, are you not Mikhail Volkov?" I asked, louder this time, a hint of alarm creeping into my voice.

"My child and namesake," a commanding voice boomed through the room. We all turned to see a brutish older man standing in the doorway. He exuded an authoritarian presence, his posture rigid and his air decidedly aristocratic.

His maroon suit, adorned with a gold and red design on the collar and cuffs, starkly contrasted with his son's more fitted and understated black ensemble. The man was bald, with thick gray eyebrows that nearly met in the center, and a hard face that never seemed to smile.

We all stood as he began to make his way over to the table.

"I am Mikhail Volkov," he declared, his voice carrying an undeniable authority. "Your father informs me that you are prepared to be my bride."

6 Months

CHAPTER TWENTY-ONE

Mr. Mikhail Volkov, Sr. extended his hand, which I took before starting to curtsy. He interrupted the formal greeting, pulling me away from the table.

"I don't care about your formality, silly girl," he growled, slowly walking around and inspecting me. After completing his examination, he stood rigidly in front of me, scrutinizing my face closely.

"We need to do something about that face. You also need to lose about twenty pounds. Burn off some of that baby fat hiding those striking cheekbones," Mr. Volkov mused aloud. He ran a finger across my cheek, and I tried not to flinch.

His eyes flashed to the flowers placed in my hair by his son. He glared at them for a moment, then his gaze darted to his grown child, unamused. He reached up and removed the azaleas from my hair, crumbling them in his hand. Having seemingly lost interest in me, he moved to take his seat at the head of the table. I felt myself release the breath I had been holding and rejoined the group, looking at Bane with panic.

The lunch was mostly quiet, with only the clanking of utensils echoing in the room as we ate. As I took a few bites of the small meal placed in front of me, I felt Mr. Volkov's glowering gaze. Eventually, he broke the silence by looking at me earnestly and saying, "If you finish the plate, you'll pop out of the dress I bought you."

I paused and looked at my host; his eyes dared me to take another bite. With as much composure as I could muster, I suppressed any outburst and took my last mouthful. Slowly, I lowered the fork and placed all the utensils on my plate, signaling that I was finished. The small plate, still mostly filled with food, was whisked away immediately by a servant.

I sat at the table, dejected, and watched the men finish their food, scowling at them and trying to keep my empty stomach from growling. Bane leered at our host and ate his food with more aggression than I thought he possessed.

At the conclusion of the meal, our host stood abruptly and dismissed his son with a wave of his hand. The son began to object, but one sharp look from his father had him storming out of the room in silence, disappearing into the castle.

"Let us go for a walk; it will help your sister burn off that entire meal," Mr. Volkov scoffed.

I waited for him, expecting my suitor to offer his hand or arm. Instead, he walked away from the table and toward one of the many doors in the room. When he reached it, he paused, scowling at Bane and me expectantly. We hurried from the table to catch up with him, and the door led us out onto one of the many balconies.

Mr. Volkov stopped once we had stepped outside. He leaned on the terrace, surveying his vast land stretched out and basking below in the hot sun.

"I assume my son showed you *his* garden; he is quite proud of it," he sneered. I nodded in response, but he did not see it until he turned his head in my direction, sending me a sharp glare.

"Speak, girl!" he bellowed.

"Yes... yes, sir," I responded quickly. "And the village," I added as an afterthought.

"Of course," he growled. "Did he insist on having your picture painted?" He spat the question as he asked it.

"Yes."

"Well, let's see it," he insisted to a nearby guard, who, in turn, nodded to another guard. The second guard dashed off at the unspoken command and returned shortly with a large painted canvas.

Mr. Volkov examined the painting of me carefully. It depicted a close-up of my face, poised gracefully in the café setting. A small, mischievous smile tugged at the corner of my mouth. I barely recognized myself, as the portrait was done in a very classical and historical style.

"The painter did a good enough job considering the subject he had to deal with," Mr. Volkov sniped before handing the painting off to Bane.

"You don't want it?" I asked, surprised.

"Why would I want a painting of you as you are now? No, I'll have a much larger one commissioned once we are wed and you've shed that weight," he said, looking me over again. "I take it my son did not show you the zoo?" he added, turning back to stare out at the vast yard.

"No, sir," I responded quickly, not wanting to provoke another outburst.

"It was not a question," he replied tersely. Mr. Volkov slowly turned away from his land and offered me an outstretched hand. I looked at it, confused and unsure of how to interpret the only formal gesture I had received from my host.

My suitor sighed impatiently. "You're a dumb one, aren't you? I know your father's reputation. It's a shame he hasn't been able to teach you better manners."

I looked up at Mr. Volkov, dumbfounded by his words.

"Don't just stare at it—grab it," he snapped. He grabbed my hand with force and yanked me to his side. We began to descend the steps and into the flourishing greenery of the garden.

The walk was quiet, with no one daring to say a word. Bane followed behind us, and Mr. Volkov's guards trailed behind Bane. An uncomfortable aura encircled us, and no one dared to disturb it. The crunch of our footfalls on the small gravel paths was the only sound until a loud roar tore through the air. I gasped in surprise and stopped walking when I heard it. My host, clearly annoyed by my response, dragged me along anyway.

"No need to fear. That was simply Kitten, my tiger," Mikhail explained.

I heard the animals before I saw them. We turned around a neatly trimmed corner and encountered the first cage, large and containing a variety of colorful birds. About half of the birds were flying around, while the others sat on branches, chirping happily. I was in awe of the sight and was grateful that Mikhail allowed me a moment to pause instead of yanking me along. After several long minutes, I looked at my host in amazement, and he seemed pleased with my reaction.

"Every animal you see here is rare. I have spent more money than you can imagine on this collection," he explained. I felt him watching me as I studied all the colorful birds in the cage. Then, Mikhail surprised me by lifting our clasped hands to his lips and kissing the back of my hand in an oddly tender gesture before gently leading me to the next cage. I allowed him to guide me, still dazed by the unexpected tenderness.

We passed many other cages filled with smaller animals. Despite a few objections on my part, he rushed us past them, seemingly eager to show me his prized possession.

When we stepped up to the tiger's cage, Kitten growled loudly at the sight of us. The cat laid out in the middle of a magnificent, enclosed area, panting in the sun with its front paws crossed lazily. My host let go of my hand and pulled me close to him, wrapping one arm around my waist. He moved us to a railing and pinned me to it, wanting to force me to watch the tiger. The closeness was uncomfortable, but I did not resist the movement.

"It is nearly feeding time, my dear," Mikhail whispered in my ear as I stared at the beast. "Kitten here is my most treasured animal. She was, unfortunately, named by my idiot son, but do not be deceived. She is quite a specimen."

I heard a delicate chiming sound and glanced at my host.

"As I said, feeding time," a sardonic smile spread across his face as he answered the question I hadn't asked. Mikhail didn't bother to look at me but instead watched his animal with feverish excitement. At the sound of the chime, the tiger pulled herself up, clearly conditioned by the tone. All was silent for a breath, then a faint grunt and squeal could be heard somewhere behind several bushes.

Kitten caught the smell and began to crouch, staring into the brush where the sounds came from. Suddenly, a boar burst through and, after spotting the tiger, began to growl. The tiger did not stall in its attack; it ran after the wild animal with such ferocity that I felt sorry for the poor creature living life in a cage.

The two animals danced in battle, but it did not take long for Kitten to claim her prize. Catching the boar, the tiger began to tear into the animal with zest, eventually pulling away her bloody muzzle with chunks of meat that she began to swallow.

"Does power like that intimidate you?" Mikhail whispered in my ear with zeal, assuming the gore would terrify me. I realized this display was meant for my benefit but chose not to react. My host laughed with a dark and cold chuckle. We stood watching the tiger devour its prey for several minutes. Only when Mikhail was satisfied, in his own mind, that I was properly horrified, did he drag me away to another part of the zoo.

He moved us over to a medium-sized cage next. This one held a troop of marmoset monkeys playing around. I watched gleefully as most of them ran around the cage, chasing each other.

One of the marmosets climbed down to our eye level as we arrived, and I giggled at it. The little monkey cocked its head at us and made faces at me. I made a face back, which seemed to excite the monkey. It gave me a cheesy smile, twisting its face delightfully, before pulling on the tail of one of its friends. The pair ran up the tree in the cage, chasing each other playfully. I laughed again at the sight but noticed my host remained impassive.

"Yes, the monkeys are quite charming with the guests," he informed me. A strange smile began to form on Mikhail's lips at my joy. A small understanding almost passed between us. However, the sweet moment came to a crashing halt when a streak of brown flew through the air. Mr. Volkov looked down to see that dung had landed on the upper thigh of his pants.

We both looked up at the cage together. The same monkey as before was back down at eye level again. Now, however, it was taunting us by making faces, chattering loudly, and waving its tiny arms. It seemed to revel in the attention as it performed exaggerated movements. Nothing was said, but a simple look from Mikhail to his guards sent them into action.

"What are you going to do?!" I grabbed Mikhail's arm, panic rising in me. "It's only an animal. He doesn't know any better," I argued.

A guard appeared with a dart gun, which he handed to my host. I tried to grab it from him, resulting in a brief tug-of-war until he pushed me hard enough that I fell into the dirt path. I watched in horror as he got the gun into position and aimed it right at the small animal. He pulled the trigger, the shot hitting its target dead-on. The creature fell to the ground with a thud, its little body twitching as the sedative began to take effect.

I stared up at my host furiously. He smiled sadistically as he turned to face me.

"What do you think I should have done to him, my dear? Have him stuffed? It wouldn't be the first time I've had my taxidermist start the process while the animal was still alive," a cruel, entertaining pleasure seemed to cross my host's face as he considered the possibility.

"What a weak man you are for your fragile ego to be shattered by a little critter like that," I spat. My insult washed away my host's amusement and was replaced by a murderous rage.

"And you are an insolent brat," he snapped, throwing the rifle at his closest guard. He marched over to the cage and reached inside carefully, lifting the paralyzed monkey out of it.

"What are you going to do?" I demanded to know. Mikhail ignored me and started to walk back to the tiger's cage. I quickly pulled myself up and gave chase.

"Do you really get off on hurting those around you?" I asked as I caught up, trying to grab the animal from his hands. Mikhail pushed me away with a strong hand and continued his march toward his beloved Kitten.

"You are one to talk, from what I have heard from your father," he mumbled as we reached the cage. Mikhail stalled, determining the best way to toss the limp animal into the arena. It was just long enough for me to snatch the monkey away from his grip. I pulled the dart out and held the creature in my palms. This angered my host, and he grabbed tightly onto my shoulders, bringing his face right up to mine.

"You obnoxious child, if you do not give me back my tiger's dessert, I am going to have to feed you to Kitten instead!" he yelled into my face.

Bane was suddenly next to me, desperately trying to pry Mikhail's hands off me. When my host's hand did not budge, Bane smacked us with the portrait of me until it broke in half.

Everyone started yelling in a storm of chaos. Mikhail listed out all the ways he would enjoy killing such an evil girl like me. I screamed back at Mikhail with a list of profanities of my own.

Bane was now fighting off Mikhail's guards, who had caught up to him, while still trying to get the monster to release my shoulders.

"LET ME GO," I screeched just as one of the guards managed to pull my twin away from us. Still holding the monkey in one hand, I punched upward with the other, putting all my strength behind the blow.

The hit made contact with the bottom of his jaw, and the crack of the punch echoed around us. Everyone stopped moving in shock, except for Mikhail, who grabbed at his jaw. His hands finally freeing me.

I grabbed the train of my dress and ran as fast as I could in a direction I hoped was toward the plane. Tears of hatred ran down my face, and I felt my makeup start to run with the tears. Bane yelled something behind me as I took off, but I ignored him, racing through the twists and turns of the vast lawn with the monkey's limp form still in my hand.

Keep running; I am not going to die by that man's hand. The thought kept circulating in my mind as I sprinted through the wild, lush greenery.

After several turns, I slammed into someone deep in the maze. While untangling myself from the stranger, I dropped the poor animal I had carried with me during my escape. The monkey landed on the dirt path with a thud before running off into the brush, having apparently recovered from the tranquilizer.

I prepared to hit my assailant before realizing it was my twin. Bane had been running too, looking for me when we collided. He grabbed my hand with a worried look and pulled me in a different direction than I had been running.

"This way," he whispered as he yanked me.

Bane held my hand as he led me the entire way back to the plane. We didn't stop running, even dashing up the plane's stairs. As we reached the door, I heard a scream from one of the edges of the garden.

"YOU BRING THAT WHORE SISTER OF YOURS BACK, SHE WAS PROMISED TO ME!"

I slammed the plane door shut behind me and fell into a tight embrace with my twin.

"Go!" Bane yelled at the pilot as he wrapped his arms around me. We sank to the floor together. I laid in his arms as we took off, crying fresh tears. Bane kissed my hair softly and rocked me in his arms well into our journey back home.

When the tears stopped flowing, I remained in Bane's arms, frozen from shock. My twin tried to get me up and back into my bedroom, but I couldn't move. Eventually, he picked me up and carried me. As he gingerly sat me on the bed, I snapped back to reality and violently started tearing off the dress I was wearing. I didn't stop until I was left in just my underwear. The vile dress laid in a pile of threads on the floor, and I spat at it. Bane chuckled humorlessly, then tossed me a PJ set from one of the many cabinets.

"It looked tacky on you anyway," he reassured me.

I began to gently take down my hair as Bane walked out of the room with purpose. As soon as the last hairpin was out, I curled up in the bed, feeling myself settling back into shock again.

Fifteen minutes later, Bane bustled in with a tray of food for me. He placed it on my bed, but I ignored it.

"Angel, please eat," he pleaded. I remained unresponsive, feeling too tired to move, much less eat. Bane slid the tray of food over and laid down right in front of me. His green eyes were full of concern as he watched me.

"Will you please eat something for me?" he asked, caressing my cheek as he tucked a stray strand of hair behind my ear. When I still didn't respond, he pulled the food closer to himself again. Bane broke off a piece of something on the tray and held it up to my mouth.

"Open up," he demanded gently. I glared at him.

"Please," he pleaded again. I obliged and opened my mouth. He fed me whatever he had in his hand, and an explosion of lemon and sugar hit my tongue. I smiled slightly. It was a piece of lemon tart, my favorite dessert.

To Bane's relief, I sat up slowly and pulled the tray closer to myself. Without much more prompting, I began to eat the food he brought me, which also included a big bottle of Fleuve de Vie.

"Thank God. I thought I was going to have to hand-feed you the entire thing," he mused aloud.

It was dark outside by the time we returned. Bane and I had fallen asleep on the bed at some point and didn't realize we were home. Dimiter and Alexei woke us up, having boarded the plane when we did not exit upon landing.

Alexei's dark eyes, staring down at me coldly, were the first thing I saw as I woke up. I stared up at him lazily in a haze of sleepy confusion, followed by the sudden recollection of the day's events.

"Your father is waiting," one of my men said before both left the room. I grabbed the clothes I had brought with me this morning and changed. Bane stretched and then moved to the front of the plane to wait for me.

My twin held out his hand as I walked through the cabin toward him. I clasped it, and we stared at each other anxiously, mentally preparing for the inevitable confrontation with my father. We turned and left the plane together.

Our father stood at the bottom of the stairs, his arms crossed, his gaze sharp and calculating. He observed us with a cold intensity as Bane and I descended in unison, still gripping each other tightly. I was prepared for a screaming match to erupt at a moment's notice. Instead, the air was thick with tension, and the silence was oppressive. It seemed to stretch on, heavy and unyielding.

Eventually, I took a deep breath and opened my mouth to apologize when Bane cut me off.

"He spent all day calling her fat and stupid. He was cruel, and any marriage would end in the guaranteed death of your daughter! You cannot marry her off to him, and you know it," Bane said loudly and defensively. I had never seen my brother yell at our father like that before. Father's eyes flashed with anger at Bane's outburst, but he remained silent.

"I would hope you are not that cruel," Bane said, his voice softer this time but still tinged with anger.

"Mikhail Volkov has been a long-time business partner of mine," my father began, his voice level, which surprised me.

"A business partner because we both understand that we cannot hold hard feelings over each other," my father concluded. Bane and I twitched slightly under his intense stare, unsure of where he was going with this.

"Several years ago, there was a rumor that he fed his wife to that tiger of his simply because she did not wear a necklace he liked. Most of the traders stopped working with him after that act of cruelty. I even halted trades temporarily, but Mikhail is powerful and a reliable supplier of arms. Not to mention a dependable source for rare firearms, so I decided to continue to work with him." My father paused, letting the words sink in. He then walked toward us slowly.

"I would never marry off my only daughter to such a monster; you are correct about that, Bane." Father stopped right before me now, his eyes boring into me alone.

"I was simply teaching a lesson. Of what kind of future you could have." My father's hand shot up and grabbed my jaw, pulling me toward him so that I was standing only by his grip. A small gasp of surprise and pain slipped out of me as I struggled to meet his gaze. He waited until I finally made eye contact.

"Never undersell me again," he growled. His face began to blur as tears formed in my eyes from his tight grip.

"DO YOU UNDERSTAND?" he roared, and I nodded as best I could.

"Good," he said, then shoved me roughly toward Bane. My brother caught me and wrapped a protective arm around me, his face a mask of unreadable emotion.

"You could have had an easy, good life, but you insisted on being in this business. I do not make concessions for my children; I expect them to be *better*. Just because you are a woman doesn't make you immune to the brutality of the life of a gun runner. You are just an easier target to punish," Father said as he backed away from us, his gaze still fixed on me.

"I am serious about you finding a husband, Angel. Just know that I am a powerful man, and your future is in my hands. I may have allowed you your tantrums, but there are ways I can always make your life worse," my father warned, then turned and walked away. Heat rushed to my cheeks at his words.

Alexei refused to look me in the eye, guilt coloring his face as he stared down in shame. Dimiter seemed ready to rush to my side, but Bane pulled me closer into his chest, trying to physically shield me from our father's aggression.

Overwhelmed, I shoved Bane, struggling to escape his grasp. It took three attempts before he finally let go, and I ran straight to my car.

I peeled out of the parking lot and drove home as quickly as I could. My phone lit up with calls and texts, but I ignored them all. I pulled into my driveway and dashed straight into the shower, shedding clothes in my wake.

The hot water scorched my skin as I jumped in. I scrubbed myself raw, desperate to wash away everywhere that monster had touched me and to erase the Zoric name from my skin. Fresh tears mixed with the water as I tried to cleanse myself.

Once I was dried off and dressed in a pair of shorts and a crop top, I collapsed onto my bed. I scrolled through the onslaught of messages on my phone, ignoring most of them.

I paused at a message Alexei had sent earlier in the day: "Come over tonight" along with an address. I tapped on the message and replied:

"I thought you were done fucking me."

His response came swiftly: "I can't stop thinking about you."

I stared at the text for a long time, unsure how to reply.

"Come over tonight, I'll show you how a man should really treat you," he sent when I didn't respond.

"Please," he added after a moment. I locked my phone and stared up at the ceiling. It dinged again.

"I owe you an orgasm," Alexei's last text read.

"Tomorrow," I responded.

I could use the stress relief, I thought. Then I threw my phone to the side. It bounced off the bed and landed on the bedroom floor. I ignored the impulse to pick it up. Lying clean in my bed, I felt the full weight of my father's expectations crushing down on me. His demands for me to marry felt suffocating. All I wanted was to prove that I belonged in the family business—his business. For the first time in my struggle with him, I felt utterly powerless.

Sleep eluded me as I lay there, trying to sort through the chaos of my life. I was tangled in a mess—unable to find a man I liked, my guards distracting me with their fun but unhelpful advances, and my brother fluctuating between supportive and indifferent. As the sun began to rise, light trickled into my room, but it brought no clarity. I stared at the ceiling, desperate to form a plan to reclaim control in my life.

6 Months

CHAPTER TWENTY-TWO

My phone had been chiming and ringing all morning, but the effort of getting out of bed felt overwhelming. I let it continue to chirp on the bedroom floor until the battery finally died. Not long after, I heard keys jingle at the front door. Heavy footsteps made their way upstairs and approached my bedroom. I turned toward the doorway and saw Bane standing there, his expression one of surprise at finding me so easily.

"Hey," he said casually. I grunted in response.

"I tried calling this morning, but you didn't answer, so I got worried and—" He trailed off when he noticed my phone lying on the floor between us. He walked over to it cautiously, picked it up, and then moved to my nightstand to plug it in.

"This family has some real issues with boundaries," I blurted out to no one in particular. Bane didn't really respond; he just stood by my bed awkwardly.

"So, what did he do to you?" I finally asked.

"Hmm?" Bane feigned confusion.

"That man we call our father threatened to marry me off to a man who feeds his wives to a tiger. Let's stop pretending we don't both know I'm the favorite. What did he do to you?" I asked calmly.

"He shot me."

"Where?" I asked, turning my head to look at him fully. My twin was staring blankly at the ground. He didn't answer, but his hand instinctively went to his left shoulder.

"It was shortly after I started to get involved. Father was particularly annoyed about catching you sleeping with one of his men. It was at the start... he just would not shut up about it on the ride over. Anyway, as we were getting off the plane, he handed me a gun and told me to be careful with it. He mentioned that this might be a tough negotiation and wanted us to be prepared. That's all he told me," Bane said, still staring at the floor as he recounted the story. His fingers continued to rub at something invisible on his shoulder.

"That's all he warned me about. The client ended up pulling a gun and pointing it directly at our father, and I panicked. I grabbed my gun and pulled the trigger without thinking. I just remember thinking, 'Whoa, that man's head disappeared,'" Bane said quietly, his eyes taking on a distant, far-off look. I waited patiently for him to continue.

"Father got really upset. After we managed to run back to the plane, he started yelling at me about gun safety. He went on about how sometimes clients pull stunts like that to scare us into better prices." Finally, Bane looked at me, as if he were talking to me again.

"I was so confused. He kept calling me all sorts of names and told me, 'I needed to learn how to look down the barrel of a gun like a man.' Then he pulled out his gun and shot me. Right in the shoulder. I felt scared, like I was going to die, but then he brought out a first aid kit and taught me how to patch myself up. 'There,' he told me, 'Now you know how to handle a threat.' Then he just left me there. I think he gave you money to redecorate the plane afterward. He told you it was a side project to keep you busy, but really, he just wanted to cover up the blood," Bane finished telling me his story, his eyes watering a bit.

"We should really nominate that man for Father of the Year, huh?" I asked sarcastically. Bane laughed dryly.

"Bane?" I began.

"Hmm?"

"How does Father track me?" I asked.

Just then, my phone chimed to life, with notifications from when it had been dead coming in all at once. Bane glanced at my phone, then quickly looked away, a guilty expression on his face.

"Oh," I said, remembering Alexei had mentioned something similar a while ago. "How does it work?" I asked.

"How does what work?" Bane pretended not to know what I was asking.

"Bane," I scolded. He sighed.

"It's a smart app, hidden in the background. It lets us know when you leave the house and when Alexei or Dimiter is near you. That way, if you're in the vicinity of one of them, we all know you're safe in case of emergencies."

"Who is 'us'?" I asked.

Bane winced. "Alexei, Dimiter, and I."

"What happens if I go over to, say, your houses?" I asked, thinking about the other day when I was at Dimiter's house and wondering if anyone knew.

"Well, when you leave here, Alexei and Dimiter are alerted and expected to respond. However, when you get into a safe vicinity of any of our phones, they're notified that they don't need to come because you're around someone who can keep you safe."

"Why is Father so concerned about keeping me safe?" I mused aloud. Bane remained quiet where he stood. Then he mumbled something so softly I couldn't hear him. I stared at my brother with a questioning look until he repeated himself louder.

"Because you are his Angel."

That he is willing to gift to cruel men in an expensive golden dress, I thought.

"Uninstall it," I instructed Bane. My twin didn't move. He stared at me with uncertain eyes, clearly debating internally.

"No," he finally said.

"Uninstall it," I commanded again.

"Or what? You're going to throw something through the window at me?" he asked, growing agitated.

"What do you know about that?"

"Nothing."

Bane and I locked eyes and scowled at each other. Luckily for me, Bane was never good at using silence as a negotiation tactic.

"Phone numbers that are unregistered in our system, and show up at this location, get reported to us, too. The app also does a quick search using AI and provides us with background information on the person. Someone for glass repair was here a couple of weeks ago. I asked Dimiter and Alexei if they knew what happened, but they're pretending they don't know," he explained.

I looked up at the ceiling again, as a long, tense silence stretched between us. Anger rose in my chest before being washed away into the sea of indifference growing inside me.

"Why did you need your glass repaired? Are you ok?" Bane asked me. I disregarded his questioning.

"Uninstall it," I demanded through gritted teeth. My twin swallowed hard but was determined not to give in to me.

"Angel, you underestimate—" he began in a condescending tone, preparing to lecture me. I sprang off my bed and grabbed the secret gun I keep hidden in my nightstand. Bane backed away when he saw what was in my hand. I took the opportunity to slam into him and throw my twin against the bedroom wall. My hand found his balls, and I squeezed them hard, causing him to yelp in pain. I pointed the gun at his left shoulder and got so close to his face that our noses were almost touching. The only thing in my vision was Bane's panicking green eyes. Red-hot anger nearly blinded me as I roared in his face.

"You underestimate ME."

I squeezed his balls just a bit tighter in my palm. Bane's eyes screamed in silent pain. He held his hands up on either side of himself, indicating that he meant no harm.

"Something I don't think you or Father ever understand is that I have this insatiable hunger for more. You may choose to continue wallowing in Father's shadow, but I intend to crawl out of it, even if it's only one inch at a time. Fuck being *just a wife*. Fuck an easy, stupid, pointless, forgettable life. I'm willing to bring destruction upon every one of us to get my way, even if it takes my last dying breath. Do you understand?" I barked.

Bane swallowed hard and opened his mouth to say something, but then he blinked a few times and closed it again.

"Uninstall it," I commanded again, twisting Bane's balls in my hand. He quivered in my grip, his face red from pain and his lips trembling as he tried to speak.

"Okay," he managed to squeak out before I released my grip. He collapsed to the ground, curling into a ball. His body shook as he breathed deeply, trying to catch his breath. I walked back to my bed and sat down, holding the gun in my lap with one hand.

Bane recovered slowly and stood up again, watching me like I was a dangerous cat ready to pounce. He limped over to my phone and unplugged it gently. With a trembling hand, he held it out to me to unlock. I scrolled through the missed calls— all from Bane— and cleared them before handing the phone back to him.

"Do you screen my calls and texts too?" I asked casually.

"No," Bane responded quickly as he maneuvered through my phone. I snapped the safety off my gun.

"I said no. I mean it," my twin said, holding his hands out in a calming gesture. He had a wild, frantic look in his eyes. I clicked the safety back on, and he began to breathe normally again. He gingerly returned to pressing things on my phone screen, both hands shaking. Once he finished removing the app, he handed the phone back to me.

"Now leave," I exclaimed as soon as I had my phone back.

"What are you going to do?" he asked.

"Call a locksmith for starters."

"Sophia," Bane cried, a touch of condescension creeping back into his voice.

"I SAID OUT!" I screamed, crawling off the bed toward him. Bane scrambled back but didn't leave my room. I pointed the gun at him again, and he darted out into the hallway. Aiming at my wall, I pulled the trigger three times. Each shot echoed loudly, causing Bane to drop to the floor. I slammed my bedroom door shut, locking him out in the hall.

"I came over to tell you we have a new deal coming up," Bane's voice mumbled through the doorway.

"Good. I'll see you then," I shouted back.

"It's a new client," he yelled.

"Good. I'll see you then!"

I listened carefully at the door for several minutes, hearing nothing. Then my twin sighed, and I waited to hear his departure. Bane slammed the front door hard behind him as he left, and I waited a few more minutes to ensure he was truly gone. Once I was sure, I put my gun back in the drawer and began calling different service providers.

The locksmith and the security system vendor arrived at the same time. I managed to get the locksmith started on changing the locks right away, but the security system vendor seemed unclear about what I needed.

"Okay, what exactly do you claim to have?" he asked, pinching his nose.

"Look, my family rigged the house. I don't have a security system, so go ahead and pull out any strange-looking tracking technology," I instructed him for the third time. He looked at me warily, trying to decide if he believed me.

"How old are you? Shouldn't we, like... contact the police?" he asked. I sighed heavily and went to grab some cash. A couple of thousand dollars later, he stopped asking questions and started checking my house. I laid on my couch while the men worked, reading a book.

It took only half an hour before the security man threw a strange tangle of wires onto the coffee table in front of me. I looked up to see him, clearly bothered that I was right, staring at the wires with a look of sick revulsion on his face.

"Sure we shouldn't call the police?" he asked, finally able to meet my eyes after proving me right.

"Find any cameras?" I asked instead of answering. The man shook his head 'no' quickly.

"Any wiretaps or other communication or visual taping devices?" I pressed. He shook his head 'no' again, though he hesitated for a moment.

"I mean, not unless that's anything. I've never really seen anything like it. It seems to be a home job. This is just the start; it leads back to a tangle of wires I still need to pull out," the security man mumbled his thoughts aloud.

"Then what are we waiting for? I hired you to rip it out. Let's go rip it all out!" I said, smiling encouragingly at the man. He stared at me for a brief moment before scurrying off quickly.

The locksmith stood still at the door, staring at the pile of wires on the table. When he realized I had caught him looking, he quickly returned to his work, pretending to be uninterested in the strange altercation between me and the security vendor.

Going to have to tip him extra to keep his mouth shut, I thought, then returned to my book.

The locksmith finished first and pretended not to be interested in the ever-growing pile of wires on the coffee table. After I gave him an extra few thousand dollars as a tip, he became more convincing in his pretense of not caring about the wires. As I walked him out the door with my new lock, of which I had the only key, my power went out.

I heard cursing and the sound of someone frustratedly pulling apart something unseen. It took only ten seconds before the power was restored, and out walked the security man holding a microprocessor board. Wires, still connected to the board, dangled from his hand, with some having wrapped around his body. I was witnessing the aftermath of a fight between the security man and my father's technology.

"Well, this is at the core of whatever you had," the man said as he placed it gingerly on the coffee table. My phone chimed nearby, and I went to check it. A text from Bane flashed on the screen.

"Sophia, seriously. How are you going to explain this to Father?"

The security vendor was slowly trying to disentangle himself from the wires. I approached him as sweetly as possible for my next request.

"Can you check my phone for me too? Do a sweep for any questionable technologies?" I asked, trying to sound as innocent as I could. The security man, still shaken from discovering the tracer technology in my house, agreed and examined my phone. Once he confirmed that nothing else was on it, he returned it to me.

"I want to do one final sweep of the house, if you don't mind. I want to make sure I got everything," he explained. Then the security man began his final inspection.

I need to pick something slutty to wear for tonight, I thought and sauntered upstairs to my closet.

One side of my closet room had slowly been growing to house all of my sex-related outfit and toys. I started in that section when the glint of an onyx heart shaped butt plug pulled at the corner of my mind with a memory.

I was riding a dildo in the library when Alexei came in and watched me. He groaned when he saw my butt plug, but then Dimiter had walked in on us. *What if he didn't? What would Alexei have ended up doing with me that day?* I wondered.

I grabbed the plug and some lube, then worked my toy into its proper place. Once it was in, I covered myself with a thin crop top, and a very short skirt that barely fell past my butt cheek.

"Hello, Miss?" I heard called out from the living room.

The security guard was standing by the coffee table again, clearly surprised by my dramatic change into something so promiscuous. He averted his eyes and never looked directly at me as we concluded our deal. Although he initially did not want to charge me, I kept handing over a grand in cash each time he begged me to call the police. Eventually, he stopped asking and charged me an arbitrary amount.

"No cameras or wiretaps," he confirmed once more, and I quickly shoved him out the door.

I glanced at the time and realized I was late. Cursing, I texted Alexei to explain the delay. He responded with instructions on how to find his hide-a-key and enter his house. I grabbed my car keys and left. As I drove over, I was acutely aware that this would be the first time no one really knew where I was.

6 Months

CHAPTER TWENTY-THREE

I walked into Alexei's house using the spare key. It was dark as I let myself in.

"I'm here for my orgasm!" I yelled into the house. There was no response except for the muffled noise of a television coming from another room. Assuming Alexei hadn't heard me, I headed in the direction of the sound.

"I said—" I started to announce as I walked into his living room, but I paused when I registered the voice coming from the TV.

"I take it Alexei's cock doesn't fill you up quite the same way, does it?"

I froze, my eyes locked on Alexei, searching for any reaction. He was slouched on a large leather chair across from the TV, his hair unusually disheveled. Ignoring me, he stared at the TV with bloodshot eyes and an unreadable expression on his face.

Leaning to one side, he rested his head against his arm, which held a small crystal glass of light brown liquid. Occasionally, he took a slow, deliberate sip as he continued to watch the scene unfold on the screen.

"I bet Alexei is quite sweet on you. He doesn't understand you like I do. A power-hungry girl like you Angel, you like it rough!"

As soon as Dimiter barked "rough" on the screen, Alexei slowly raised the remote and froze the video. I watched him intently, trying to decipher his reaction. When his eyes finally met mine, they were wild and intense.

"I didn't realize I was being too soft on you," he said, his voice cracking slightly.

"Alexei, I—" I began, but he raised two fingers toward me, cutting me off. I hesitated, then moved toward him and slowly knelt in front of him.

"I didn't realize he recorded us. It wasn't my intention to hurt you. I don't expect you to watch me... with anyone else," I rambled. His fingers brushed across my lips, silencing me.

I could smell the alcohol on him as he leaned in closer.

"*Angel*, I know... What I didn't know was that you wanted me to be rough," he whispered, his voice edged with danger. Alexei's fingers caressed my cheeks before tangling themselves in my hair. He pulled back my head, as he gazed into my eyes with a dangerous intensity. My guard stood up and began to unfasten his pants, a wild look still burned in his gaze as he held me in place. His pants fell to the ground and his erection sprang out, it drew my attention as I watched him sit back down in his leather chair.

"Suck on it," he ordered. I raised my gaze to meet his, hesitating to proceed with his demand, knowing that doing so would only fuel this madness—but also aware that deep down, I craved it.

"SUCK ON IT!" he shoved my face toward his member. I starting by licking up his shaft.

"Good bunny," he muttered before grabbing his remote and hitting several buttons.

The sound of Dimiter's voice filled the room as I heard him ravage my lingerie on screen, then commanded me to straddle his massive cock. My lips wrapped tightly around Alexei's dick, sucking with an intensity matched only by the explicit footage playing behind me. My body pulsated with raw desire, the arousal between my legs dripping as I took in the electrifying situation that had unfolded since my arrival.

I couldn't tear my eyes away from Alexei as he lounged in his chair, completely ignoring me as I eagerly sucked on him. His gaze was fixed on the television screen dissecting my every move as I delighted in his coworker's massive tool. My own screams of ecstasy echoed through the room, a symphony of pleasure that only fueled Alexei's intense focus on the screen.

As Dimiter granted me my first orgasm on camera, Alexei's grip on my hair tightened to the point of pain. Without warning, he began to thrust his throbbing member in and out of my mouth aggressively, using my hair as a handle. The roughness of his actions sent a shockwave of arousal through me, surprising me with its intensity. This was a side of Alexei I had never seen before, and it excited me.

I sucked Alexei's cock powerfully, desperate to reward him. Finally, when video Angel had impaled herself onto Dimiter's dick again, he spasmed into my mouth. I swallowed his gift and pulled back to breathe.

For the first time since I started sucking his cock, Alexei looked down at me. He traced his fingers along my lips before moving down and lifting up my skirt. A finger slipped inside me, and he smirked sinfully as he realized how wet I was.

"Good bunny" he said, then sucked on his fingers to clean them off. The sound of me orgasming again on the television answered.

"I have something for you," he whispered, his hand tucking my hair behind my ear. Gradually, his fingers moved to the nape of my neck. He grabbed me harshly and lifted me up with him.

Alexei's warm breath tickled my ear as he whispered behind me, "I spent all day putting it together." His lips then trailed down to my neck, while his hand expertly found its way under my shirt and cupped my breast. He gently pushed on my neck and led me towards a red and black bench in the corner of the room.

"You see, I've been watching that video since it arrived yesterday and have been thinking about how you like it rough" he continued in a low rumbled tone. A deep chuckle reverberated from him, and he playfully licked my cheek. This was not the composed Alexei I knew; he seemed to be unraveling at the seams, turning into an absolute mess in front of me.

"Strip and assume the position for me," he growled, throwing me towards the new bench. I hesitated, trying to process this new, unfamiliar side of Alexei. It was a moment too long for my companion, as he produced a paddle and smacked my across my buttock hard, leaving a stinging mark. A twitch of a smile pulled on my lips.

"Get naked and assume the position!" he barked. This time, I complied with the demand, removing what little clothing I had on and climbed onto the whipping bench. I felt oddly exposed in my position on the post.

Alexei chuckled as he noticed the butt plug I had slipped into myself earlier, just for him.

"That will not save you tonight," he said brushing a hand up my back side before delivering more sharp blows with the paddle again, leaving behind more biting marks.

Alexei circled around the bench to face me and lift my chin to meet his gaze. A mix of unreadable emotions passed behind his dark eyes. He pried open my lips and then jammed his shaft into my mouth again. I started to suck on it, feeling it expand to its full length.

My guard let out a satisfied grunt before his hands began to fiddle with something. I glanced up and saw he was manipulating rope, tying a few secure knots. When he finished, he gently removed his manhood from my mouth and leaned over to fasten me securely to the bench. I cooperated with minimal resistance and he rewarded me with a series of gentle kisses along my spine and shoulder before tilting my head up for a kiss on the lips.

His kiss began with a fierce urgency, his teeth biting down on my lip before his tongue plunged into my mouth, ravaging me as if trying to consume me. When he finally pulled away, his eyes locked onto mine with a hungry gaze. He chuckled darkly and said, "This is payback for years of torturing me with your irresistible temptations."

He came up behind me and covered my eyes with a blindfold. I took deep breaths, filled with anticipation, when the first crack of the paddle hit my exposed buttock. My moans mixed with the stinging sensation left on my rear as he continued to deliver rhythmic smacks. Each one harder than the last, leaving prickling marks on my skin. Heat radiated from my buttock as blood rushed to the areas where the paddle had made contact. I couldn't help but squirm under his blows, which only seemed to encourage him to spank me more.

He focused on each cheek until they both throbbed with a constant stinging sensation. Just when I thought I couldn't take any more, one final hard blow left my bottom tingling and then I heard the paddle drop to the ground. Alexei ran his fingers lightly over my sensitive butt cheeks, causing a quiet moan to escape from between my lips.

A finger briefly entered my wet and slippery sex before quickly withdrawing. Alexei positioned himself at my entrance and gradually eased the tip of his member inside me. I moan, craving more of him. Alexei didn't move, and I whimpered with anticipation. In response, my guard gave me a sharp spank on my already sore bottom. I whined again, and this time he slid an inch deeper inside me. Growing impatient, I tried to push back against him, only to have him pull out and deliver another forceful smack to my behind.

"Naughty girl," Alexei scolded, but his harsh tone only turned me on more. Once again, he positioned himself behind me and slowly slid an inch or two of his hard length inside. I stayed still this time, and he rewarded me by sliding in another inch gradually. Alexei repeated this process of thrusting into me at an excruciatingly slow pace. Each time, he steadily moved another inch deeper into me, sending shivers of pleasure through my body.

When he pulled out again, leaving only the tip of his member inside of me, I couldn't help but moan in frustration. Instead of giving in to my pleas for more, he focused on caressing and admiring the butt plug nestled between my warm, red cheeks.

A low groan escaped his lips as he pushed himself fully inside of me. It took me by surprise and I howled in pleasure at the sudden sensation of being filled by him. He wasted no time, moving his hips forcefully against mine, thrusting deep into me. His hands roamed over my sensitive skin, eliciting tingles wherever they touched. He then gripped onto my hips and began a rough rhythm, grunting with each powerful thrust. My body responded to his intense movements and I instinctively grabbed onto the rope that bound me to the bench, arching my back in response.

He gave me another playful slap on my rear before shoving his cock into me and leaving it deep inside. His hands traveled up my back to the front of my body, caressing my breasts and gently squeezing them. He kissed my upper back slowly as he began to play with my chest, teasing and pinching at my sensitive nipples. Initially, I squirmed in pleasure, but soon the pain became too much, and I couldn't help but squeal as I pushed my hips back against him.

"That's it," he chuckled, his fingers still pinching my breast when he resumed his movements inside me. He emitted an animalistic growl as he unleashed years of frustration on my body with each savage thrust. His hands roamed all over, gripping and pulling at various parts of me. The mix of pain and pleasure was overwhelming. When he returned to pinching my nipples, I felt myself starting to reach my peak. A small whimper escaped my lips.

"LOUDER!" Alexei roared, intensifying his movements within me. I parted my lips and with each thrust, a louder moan escaped from me as my climax approached. Eventually, the overwhelming sensation burst through, and I could no longer hold back; I screamed in ecstasy, my body convulsing in the awkward position I was restrained in.

"OH, OH, OH, MY GOD" I shrieked.

Alexei slowed down as my climax came to an exceptional end. He let out a deep chuckle and tenderly kissed my back before whispering in my ear, "what a good little slut."

My guard withdrew himself from inside me, leaving me feeling empty. His fingers traced up my sore buttock to the heart-shaped butt plug. Slowly, he pulled it out, causing a small gasp to escape my lips. I knew what was coming next. He replaced the butt plug with his slick, wet dick, easily sliding into my anus that was already stretched from the plug. He eagerly grabbed onto my hips and began thrusting slowly, reveling in the pleasure of this illicit experience.

Alexei didn't continue the leisurely thrusting for very long, and soon began riding me with the same roughness as before. I was still buzzing from my first orgasm, so the added sensation around my anus only heightened my pleasure. I couldn't help but moan in ecstasy as Alexei pushed himself to climax with a loud grunt. After he pulled out of, I could hear him moving around behind me.

"That was the first time I have ever done anal," I admitted.

Alexei laughed "I seriously doubt that Angel, I've seen your sexual exploits before."

"I swear, Alexei, that was my first time... and I can't think of anyone else I would have rather shared it with," I whispered. My guard gently brushed his fingers against my lips before wrapping his hands around my neck. His mouth met mine in a passionate kiss that borderlined on roughness.

"I'm not done with you yet," he growled after breaking the kiss. I could hear him fumbling with something before he removed the blindfold covering my eyes. My vision was met with the sight of the largest purple dildo I had ever seen, and I couldn't help but feel a little intimidated. Alexei looked down at me with a mischievous smile on his face, a glint of menace in his eye. As scary as this new side of him was, it also made me desire him even more and I felt myself getting wet once again.

Without checking to see if I needed any help, my partner grabbed some lube and began to coat the toy with it.

He has no idea what he is doing to me, I thought as my sex ached with the promise of more pleasure.

Alexei moved behind me and massaged excess lube around my entrance. He slipped his fingers into me and another small snicker escaped his lips.

"Little whore is excited already again, I see," he muttered, removing his fingers from me. Alexei inserted the dildo into me, gradually and gently as before. Once it was fully inside, he withdrew it, only to then slowly penetrate me again, inch by inch. I was lost to euphoric bliss.

On the third repetition, I started to feel a strange tingling sensation around my vulva lips.

I let out a breathy question, "Alexei? What type of lube did you use?" as he slid the dildo out of me. He remained silent but pushed the toy back into me at a slow pace. Once it was fully inserted, he leaned down to kiss my cheek.

"Cold sensation," he responded. I moaned with pleasure as the lubricant began to tingle inside of me. This time, Alexei left the dildo inside and picked up his paddle once again. He alternated between spanking me and sliding the toy in and out of me, creating a deliciously conflicting mix of hot and cold sensations. I felt as if I was drowning in ecstasy.

Eventually, Alexei set down his paddle and walked away, leaving me tied down with the large dildo still inside me. I protested loudly, feeling vulnerable in such a compromising position.

"I have to clean my dick, little whore," was all I heard as an answer from another room. I squeezed the toy inside of me to stimulate myself while I waited.

It was only a minute before Alexei came back. His pleasurable penis rigidly hard again.

"I want you to sit on me and ride me, like with Dimiter," Alexei explained. He leaned over and untied the bounds that were holding me down to the bench. Then, he removed the purple dildo and walked over to his chair. As soon as he sat down, he immediately began stroking his member, watching me with his piercing dark chocolate eyes. I stood up, feeling sore and stiff, and stretched my limbs before walking over to him at a leisurely pace. His chair was spacious enough for both of us, and as I straddled him, I slowly eased myself onto his eager and waiting member.

As soon as I slide down to the base of him, Alexei reached out and pulled me closer. His lips met mine in a slow, sensual kiss. He moved his hips beneath me, drawing me in, while his hand traced down my back.

"Alexei," I whispered against his lips. That was all it took. His face contorted in pleasure and I felt his member throbbing in me, pouring his seed.

We cleaned up together, then Alexei and I sat on the couch curled into each other. Something felt different since the start of the night. In his embrace, I felt connected to him in a new way; secure and content. We sat in silence for a while, both absorbing what had just occurred.

Eventually, Alexei broke the silence between us.

"I... I still don't think it's a good idea for us to..." He left the rest of the words unsaid. I felt them hanging in the air between us, creating distance once again.

I sighed deeply and began to remove his arms from around me.

"Angel?" he asked.

I grunted in response.

"Where are you going?" he asked.

"We had our fuck, you said your piece. We've done this so many times now I know the script by heart," I said, indifferent. I grabbed my clothes and threw them on quickly.

"Angel, please don't be like this," Alexei scolded.

"I don't know how you expect me to be. Don't worry, you won't get any argument from me anymore. You've made it very clear what you want from me... and what you don't," I said, heading for the front door.

"Angel, this is for the best," he followed me into the dark front room.

"Again, no argument from me," I said. He snapped on a light, revealing the room in absolute chaos, with stacks of bills and papers scattered everywhere. I ignored the mess but turned around to see a perplexed look on Alexei's face.

I ran up and grabbed him by the chin, pulling him down to my lips to kiss him. He pulled me into an intimate embrace and kissed me back. When I pulled away, his lips were red from mine.

"I'll see you at the next gig," I said, then walked out the front door to my car. As I climbed in and took off, I saw Alexei standing naked at his front door, arms crossed and a hard look on his face.

6 Months

4 Mortis

BANE'S GUNRUNNING BUSINESS RULE NUMBER ONE:

Never sleep with the client.

Maintaining professional boundaries is what sets us apart from other gunrunners.

CHAPTER TWENTY-FOUR

I had packed a bag for the trip to Cliuz Plyae, following the details Bane had texted me since our fight. My brother greeted me shortly after I parked at our private hanger, by grabbing my bag out of my car.

"This is going to be more of a sale than a delivery. As I mentioned, it's a new customer, so he's not sure what he wants yet," my twin said, acting as if nothing had happened between us.

"Do we know anything about this new client?" I asked.

"Some new warlord who just overthrew the government with his rebel army. He wants to spend a whole day 'exploring' our catalog before deciding—whatever that means. We're loading our usual amount to bring with us. I'm really hoping this is a one-time stop with occasional visits to replenish," he explained, casually pointing to the back of the plane, where it was being loaded with guns, ammo, and more.

I caught sight of my two guards waiting on either side of the stairs leading up to the plane. There was an air of tension between them, but neither said a word. As soon as Bane looked away, both of them ogled me. I tried my best to ignore their stares and followed my brother into the plane's cabin.

Bane moved my bag to my bedroom while I sat down at the table next to the plane's bar, the spot that my brother and I often favored. I signaled the bartender for a drink and then reached into a small carry-on I had brought with me. One by one, I pulled out a stack of erotica novels I had found and placed them on the table. Dimiter and Alexei watched me passively as they set up their own sleeping areas, feigning disinterest.

Unbeknownst to all men on the plane, I had arrived with a vibrating Bluetooth dildo and butt plug carefully inserted into me already. I pulled out my phone and texted the dildo app to Alexei, and the butt plug app to Dimiter. Both men looked at their phone, then each other. The tension in the plane became thick.

I propped my legs up on the seat across from me and grabbed the top novel to begin. I was only a few pages in when Bane sat down on the opposite side of the table.

"Can we talk about... the disagreement?" he began.

"I think I said everything I needed to," I replied, not looking up from my book. Bane sighed and covered his face with his hands for a moment.

"Just promise me that you'll call if you need anything or feel threatened. I won't ask any questions unless you want me to. Just please promise me," Bane pleaded.

I glanced at him briefly, then muttered a "fine" and went back to reading.

A long stretch of silence followed, with neither of us saying a word. I assumed my twin was done talking, but he surprised me by commenting on my book.

"Nice reading material. Woman gets kidnapped by a mob boss," Bane said, grabbing my stack and flipping through the titles.

"Erotica. Of course," he laughed dryly.

"They're in English. I'm practicing," I pointed out, still not looking up from my book.

He sighed again. "You should let Toni know you're into this. He'd probably let you play out any fantasies with him," he teased.

"It surprises me to hear you're suddenly encouraging a relationship with him," I retorted seriously.

"I think you made it clear enough that I don't exactly have a say," Bane mumbled, then reached out to grab one of my hands. I looked at my brother sincerely this time, and he held my gaze with an intense stare.

"Let's not do this again, Angel," Bane said in a tone that felt familiar. I stared at him, perplexed, for a moment.

"What?" I asked.

"Let's not fight, okay?" he said, squeezing my hand slightly with a sorrowful smile on his lips.

Suddenly, Dimiter's Bluetooth connected to my butt plug. I jolted as he started to play with the vibration frequency. Forcing a tight smile, I carefully looked back at my brother, trying hard to act normal. Alexei's phone connected only seconds later and he began to play with me too.

"You should read the Sleeping Beauty one. It's excellent," Bane suggested, shoving the pile of books back toward me. He got up and, to my relief, went back into his bedroom.

My guards stared intently at their phones, only looking up to watch me react to the vibrations. I leaned back, enjoying the sensations as they toyed with me, then opened my book again and continued reading.

No one spoke for the rest of the night. When I grew tired, I walked back to my bedroom without acknowledging either man. As soon as I had gone behind the bar their devices were out of range and both toys turned off.

I pulled the vibrators out of me and climbed into bed. Neither had been able to make me climax, and I was hot with desire. I thought about asking them to join me in my bedroom tonight, but decided to it was too risky with Bane across the hall. Instead, I put on a thin silk pajama set and fell into bed to sleep.

The next day, I woke to a loud voice coming from the plane's cabin. Sleepily, I walked into the room and found my twin talking to a god.

The stranger was a tall, shirtless, and muscular man, with a scar on his upper left chest that resembled claw marks. His hair was styled in a messy Mohawk fade, and his jeans hung very low, revealing well-toned abs and a pronounced V-cut. A long gun was haphazardly tucked into the front of his belt.

The stranger stared at me with fire in his eyes and whistled. "And who is this peach? Does she cost extra to come naked?" he asked without humor.

"That is my twin sister, and she's not for sale," Bane said incredulously, glaring at the man.

The man stared at my twin for an uncomfortable amount of time before a small chuckle escaped his lips.

"Of course, sister. Not for sale, duh," he said, playfully smacking his head with his palm before gawking at me again. A new, deeper lust seemed to twinkle in his eyes now knowing I was *the twin sister*.

Alexei, who had been standing off to the side, shifted slightly to block the man's glare. The shirtless man sized up my guard before turning his attention back to Bane. My brother crossed his arms, trying to look more menacing and protective. The man merely sneered and walked off the plane.

"Come, come. The Jackal will show you his kingdom now," he said, waving his hand at my brother to follow. Bane turned toward me to give instructions.

"Hurry and go change, please. I'd recommend shorts; it's fucking hot today."

Still trying to recover from the sight of the tanned, toned god, I hurried to get changed. In my rush, I skipped putting on a bra and quickly pulled on a tank top and shorts.

I ran down the plane's stairs to catch up with my group, who waited for me at the bottom. As I bounded down, I noticed the tanned god staring openly at my breasts. My brother also saw this and moved slightly to position himself between the man and me as I approached.

"Sofia, this is Vasco Zavala, the new president," he reluctantly introduced us.

I held out my hand, which Vasco grabbed quickly before slowly bringing it to his lips. He caressed and kissed it softly, his eyes boring into me.

"The pleasure is all mine, Ricura," Vasco said with a smile, then released my hand. We stared at each other, drinking each other in, until my brother coughed. Vasco slowly tore his eyes away from me and reluctantly turned his attention back to Bane.

"But please, call me ♪ _The Jackal_. ♪ No need for formalities here," Vasco told my brother.

"The Jackal?" Bane asked.

The man nodded. "Why The Jackal?" my twin asked.

"Because long ago I got into a fight with a jackal and survived, so everyone calls me The Jackal," Vasco said, cackling at the end. He then began to howl into the sky. All around the wooded encampment where we had landed, men started howling back in a similar manner.

"Were you all trying to sound like a bunch of jackals howling?" I asked once the howls had died down. The Jackal stared at me intensely, sizing me up.

"Yeah, was it? Because you all sounded like a pack of wolves. Are you sure you weren't attacked by one of those?" Bane added.

The man turned to my brother with a much harder stare. We all looked at each other awkwardly, waiting for someone to break the tension. Eventually, The Jackal smiled at Bane and then began to walk away from the plane and into a dense grouping of trees. We followed him.

"Why don't we try some of the toys you've brought me?" The Jackal said cheerfully. He pulled the shotgun from his belt and fired it haphazardly twice into the air. The entire landing area came alive with movement as The Jackal's men carried out unspoken orders.

"Sorry, but it was an overnight flight. Can't we start with some breakfast first?" my brother asked, running up to The Jackal. The man fired the rifle into the air once more, and everyone around us stopped moving.

"Breakfast? BREAKFAST?!" Vasco exclaimed indignantly. "You come all the way to MY POOR COUNTRY, in the throes of freedom from an oppressive dictator, in this fancy plane that you own, and ask for some fucking flapjacks?!" The tanned god stared at my brother with wide eyes.

"Why have this thing if you're going to ask me for breakfast?" The Jackal gestured to the plane behind us.

Bane stared at the man, a hint of fear showing on his face as he worried about having already offended our new potential buyer. Unsure of what to say, my twin froze momentarily. The Jackal leaned in, mocking him. "Sorry, but what was that? I can't hear you."

Bane opened his mouth slightly before closing it again, unsure of how to react. Fortunately, that was when The Jackal began to laugh hysterically, seemingly at nothing. Bane looked back at me, clearly lost, and I shrugged in response. After a while, Vasco finally stopped laughing.

"It's okay. I'll get you a banana for the ride up there," he said, firing two more shots into the air. "Come," he added, putting his arm around my brother, "let's get you some food so you can concentrate on selling me shit."

We walked together into a thicket of trees, the low sound of a helicopter starting up in the direction we were headed. We followed the sounds and discovered an old military helicopter being prepared for us. The doors in the middle section were missing, and a fresh coat of neon spray paint decorated the exterior. On the back, in a street art style, were the words ♫ _Azteca Kings_. ♫

The Jackal and Bane lifted one of the many boxes we'd brought into the middle section of the helicopter. As both men climbed in, they each extended a hand to help me up. I ignored their offers and pulled myself up, then settled off to one side.

"No, no, no," Vasco protested as Alexei and Dimiter tried to follow me onto the helicopter.

"They are for my sister; they're her guards," my brother shouted over the whirling rotor of the craft.

"Why, does your sister bite or something?" our host asked. Bane shot him a look of restrained annoyance, his jaw tightening and eyes narrowing.

"Here, take this. It's for the jeep over there. This craft has a weight capacity, and you two look too fat. Meet us here," The Jackal said, tossing Dimiter a pair of keys. He then pulled a map, caked in dried blood, from his back pocket. A man handed him a pen, and he marked a large X on the map before handing it to Alexei. With a flick of his fingers and a whistle, he signaled that it was time for us to go.

The helicopter began a slow ascent as The Jackal whistled at someone still on the ground. He caught a yellowish-green object that the person had thrown up to him. I watched his back muscles ripple as he moved to tear off a piece of the prize. A moment later, he extended his hand to offer something to my brother. In his hand was a solitary banana. My brother looked down at the fruit, unamused, but took it with a sigh.

Vasco turned to me with a pleased expression, tore off another banana, and tossed it in my direction. I caught it and smiled with amusement at The Jackal, who winked at me in return.

I glanced at my brother, who had wandered over to one of the boxes of arms we'd brought, engrossed in eating his own fruit. Turning back to the warlord, I peeled my banana and ate it suggestively, returning his wink.

As the helicopter rose above the treetops, I gazed out at the landscape as we flew to our unknown destination. The area was heavily forested with occasional clearings, and I could see a beach in the distance. After an hour, the helicopter came to a stop and descended slightly, hovering above a large, flat, circular clearing.

I tried to point out the beach to my brother, but he just waved me off and continued detailing the specifications of the gun he was holding to our potential buyer.

"Why are you so rude to your sister?" The Jackal interrupted my brother's rambling with the question. "She has a good eye for the beauty of this place, but you just ignore her," he said, looking past Bane and toward me with appreciation.

Bane stared at the warlord, agape, for a long moment before responding carefully, "I'm trying to sell you guns so you can continue to enjoy the beauty of this place." Vasco burst into laughter as if he'd just heard the best joke ever. He quickly recovered, waving away my brother's comment.

"I don't care about these details; I need to know how it shoots," The Jackal said. He grabbed the gun from my brother's hand and waved to someone down below.

I stared down into the clearing, waiting to see what would happen, but nothing did. Just as I was about to look back at my companions, a man was thrown into the bare patch of land from the thicket of trees. He was completely naked, with his hands bound and a gag in his mouth. He glanced around, confused, before looking up and seeing us. His eyes widened in fear as he started to try to run out of the clearing.

BANG!

The gun fired beside us. Bane and I turned to see The Jackal. He was laughing maniacally, gun in hand, firing round after round into the clearing. Glancing back at the clearing, I saw that the naked man was now lifeless on the ground, surrounded by a pool of blood.

When he was finished discharging, two of The Jackal's men dragged the body away. However, The Jackal shouted down at them, ordering them to leave it.

"Who was that?" Bane asked, his voice tight with surprise.

"Oh, don't worry about him," The Jackal said, waving the gun at the dead man. "That was the previous president. This gun is good, but I want something more. A more powerful gun means fewer bullets, which saves my country money. I've got to start thinking more like a president now." He handed the gun back to my brother, who stared at it in shock for a moment before putting it away and selecting another piece.

The next gun Bane pulled out was larger. He decided to start showing the warlord the automatic options. The Jackal eagerly reached for the new weapon and waved his hand below, signaling his men.

This time, two teenage boys were thrown into the clearing, both naked. They glanced at the dead man and immediately panicked, running in opposite directions. The sound of Vasco's laughter filled the air as he showered bullets below. Soon, both bodies were splayed out in the clearing, bullet holes scattered across their forms. The Jackal let out a war cry, which was echoed by his men below.

"More! More!" he exclaimed, tossing the gun to my brother and extending his hand for a new one.

The rest of the afternoon was filled with the same routine. Bane would hand The Jackal a fresh firearm, which would be used to gun down another naked individual who had been tossed into the clearing. A triumphant cheer erupted after each kill, and then my brother would place a new weapon in The Jackal's hands once more.

Out of the twenty kills of the day, only one nearly escaped the chaotic scene in the clearing below. As the exercise neared its end, and after hearing gunshots all day, the naked prisoner began running the moment he was thrown into the clearing. He darted into a thicket of bushes as soon as he could and then tried to carefully make his way around to the other side of the clearing, seeking a path to freedom.

The Jackal laughed gleefully at the sight and went off on a tangent about the cowardice of the man.

"Come out and die like a man!" he screamed below, shaking his head in mock disappointment. Then he glanced at Bane and me, and an idea struck him.

"Do you want to shoot?" he asked.

"Oh no, no, thank you though," Bane replied quickly. The Jackal's glare shifted to him, silencing my brother immediately.

"I wasn't asking you, fool, but your sister. You can see the bloodlust in her eyes," he said, moving closer to me.

"She doesn't—" my twin started, but I cut him off as I walked toward The Jackal. The warlord positioned me in front of him and handed me the rifle. He placed both hands on my hips and whispered in my ear seductively, "That was the president's adviser and my best friend. He used to feed me information about my enemies' movements. I should thank him, but, in the end, I cannot trust a rat." He mimed the shape of a gun with his hand and made a gesture to shoot him.

I nodded and brought the gun up to firing position, waiting for the captive to be recaptured by The Jackal's men. The Jackal, still behind me, moved his hands slowly up my body, caressing me and occasionally adjusting my stance.

"She already knows how to shoot," Bane said, grabbing Vasco's hand before it could slide further up my side to graze my tits. Both The Jackal and I turned to stare at Bane, who quickly let go. My brother sneered at me before reluctantly stepping back.

I stared down and patiently waited. After what felt like ages, I saw the Azteca Kings hauling the escaped prisoner back into the open space. I quickly straightened into the position, ready to take action again.

"Do you have a shot?" The Jackal asked, his warm breath tickling my neck.

"Yes," I said, as my sight lined on the naked man.

"Then shoot," The Jackal instructed, kissing my neck.

I exhaled and pulled the trigger. Blood splattered where the man's head had been, and I was knocked back from the force of the gunshot, into The Jackal's arms.

"Oh, Reina," he cried, staring down at the shot I took. "You didn't even take out one of my men," he said, smiling at me like a perverse, proud father. His face was tantalizingly close to mine, and he wrapped his arms tighter around me as his eyes flickered to my lips.

Bane yanked the gun out of my hand, pulling me sharply back to reality.

"What?" I mouthed at him. My twin ignored me and glared at The Jackal.

At the conclusion of the day, The Jackal insisted that we stay and witness his men stacking up all the bodies in the center of the clearing. Once they were all piled, he asked Bane to pass him the bazooka we had brought along. With a triumphant shout, he aimed and fired at the pile. We stood and watched as the bodies burned for what felt like an eternity; Bane clearly ready to leave a long time ago.

It was only when the sun was starting to set that The Jackal allowed us to return to the helicopter pad. Once we had landed and disembarked, The Jackal pulled my brother into an awkward, stiff embrace.

"It was good of you to share this afternoon with me. I hope we have a long and lasting partnership," he said, holding my brother close. Bane didn't return the hug, only tapping Vasco on the back in a detached and uncommitted gesture. I watched gleefully, enjoying the cunning power struggle between the two men.

After pulling away from the hug, The Jackal laughed wildly and exclaimed, "I will take everything, all you have brought today! Men, pay this man and his pretty sister!" He ordered, then grabbed the bazooka—clearly his favorite—and walked toward a glass mansion visible in the distance.

Alexei and Dimiter were already waiting for us at the helicopter pad. Alexei was clearly in a foul mood, while Dimiter remained carefree.

"Where were you two?" Bane growled as we regrouped and followed The Jackal toward his house.

"Lost," Alexei muttered.

"The map we were given was faulty," Dimiter explained. "Then we started hearing gunfire and thought it best to head back before we got ourselves killed."

Bane tried to talk us out of staying the night, but The Jackal insisted.

"I mean, I was so rude not to serve you breakfast this morning; let me make it up to you with dinner instead," was all The Jackal would say when Bane tried to protest.

Dinner was a chaotic affair, with food sloppily prepared and served on a long table in the kitchen without any pomp or circumstance. Bane seated us in the middle of the table, mistakenly assuming Vasco would prefer to sit at the head to assert authority. Instead, The Jackal took a seat directly across from me. Throughout the meal, his eyes studied me—and my breasts—the entire time.

The air was tense as soon as The Jackal settled near me. Alexei and Bane had claimed the seats on either side of me, and neither was welcoming toward the stranger who was openly sexual with me. After catching The Jackal eye-fucking me once again, Bane finally broke the silence by asking about the glass castle we were dining in.

"This mansion belonged to that former president until our recent revolution," The Jackal explained to my brother as the food began to be set on the table. "We rounded up his entire family and captured his loyal followers. We turned this place into HQ, deciding to keep the mansion as a spoil of war."

He gestured toward a dark hallway. "You see that bedroom there? That's my bedroom, the master bedroom. It's the largest I've ever owned. It allows me to more thoroughly please women." The Jackal smiled to himself and glanced at me, waiting for a reaction. I did my best to remain composed, but every time I felt his gaze on me, I was starting to become undone.

Bane chuckled dryly, which pulled me out of my hot revive.

"Don't worry, amigo," The Jackal said, pointing in the opposite direction from his room. "I set you and your sister up over there." Bane glanced at the indicated area and seemed satisfied with the distance from our host's quarters.

Empty plates were set in front of us by one of the many Azteca Kings tasked with serving the impromptu dinner. As soon as a gold plate was placed in front of me, The Jackal started to fuss immediately. The man who had set the table stood stiffly behind me while his boss berated him loudly in their native language. Once Vasco finished his tirade, the man grabbed my plate and walked off with it.

"Do I not get to eat?" I asked, panic rising, as I glanced at the tanned god, my mind flashing back to my trip with Mikhail.

"Shh, of course you get to eat, Reina. I just sent him to prepare your plate. I can't have you tasting anything from my country that you won't like," The Jackal said sincerely, before turning to pile food onto his own plate. Moments later, my golden plate was set down in front of me, brimming with delicious-smelling cuisine.

"What about me?" Bane asked, noticing the Azteca King goon walking away without taking his plate as well. Vasco fixed my twin with a hard stare, and the table fell silent, waiting to see who would speak next.

"Are your hands broken? Do I need to baby you?" The Jackal mocked. Bane looked to me for help, but I was already distracted, savoring the delectable flavors exploding in my mouth. Finally, Bane mumbled a "no" and served himself dejectedly.

"The rest of my men sleep wherever they like," The Jackal explained as we ate. "I've asked them to clear that hallway for my guests, but if you wake up and see a bunch of men sleeping out here, it's just how we are."

By the time evening rolled around, most of the men were lounging in the kitchen and dining area. Plates and trays of food were shared among everyone. A group of women also wandered around the mansion, most of them naked.

A particularly beautiful woman with an ample bust walked over to Vasco and planted a kiss on his cheek, leaving behind a mark from her cherry red lipstick. The Jackal motioned for the woman to crawl under the table, and she complied without hesitation. The sound of his jeans unzipping was barely audible over the chatter and laughter around us. I became deliriously jealous, overwhelmed by a dangerous longing I had never experienced before. The Jackal noticed my reaction and his piercing gaze dared me to give in to my desire and take the woman's place.

"What's with the women?" Alexei asked, breaking the growing tension between Vasco and me. The Jackal acted completely unfazed by what was being done to him under the table as he answered.

"We bought the local brothel, paid off those who wanted to leave and brought anyone willing to join us here. These women are ours to enjoy, whenever we want. We feed and protect them. It's a paradise you might say," the Jackal explained, saying the last line while locking eyes with me in particular.

As it grew later in the evening, groups of people began to engage in sexual activities openly around the house. Having been teased the last twenty-four hours by my guards and then The Jackal, I felt myself grow hot with lust each scene I witnessed.

Our party went to bed early, as instructed by Bane. Alexei and Dimiter dragged chairs into the hallway leading to our bedrooms, preparing to sit, sleep, and guard throughout the night. As I entered my bedroom, I overheard Bane telling them that no one was to go into my room. I glanced back at my brother before closing the door. He was watching The Jackal warily, who was still at the dining table, laughing boisterously with his men.

5 Months

CHAPTER TWENTY-FIVE

Despite my exhaustion, sleep evaded me thanks to the constant teasing I had endured since the plane ride. The sounds and scents of sexual activity coming from just outside my door only added to my restlessness. The burning desire to be ravished consumed me like a fever. Desperately, I pleasured myself while moans of ecstasy echoed down the hallway, but it only intensified my longing for a partner.

I listened intently as the noises of pleasure gradually faded away in the late hours of the night. Soon, an eerie calm settled as people fell asleep. I quietly stood up and gently opened my door. Alexei was slumped over in his chair, fast asleep. However, Dimiter was still awake and sitting up, with a noticeable bulge in his pants.

I signaled to my guard to stay quiet, indicating I was just getting some water. Dimiter began to rise to join me, but I dismissed him with a wave.

I made my way into the open kitchen area, stepping carefully over several Azteca Kings sprawled across the floor, fast asleep, many with their arms wrapped around women dozing beside them. When I entered the kitchen, a woman's moan caught my attention. Drawn by the sound, I followed it through the massive living room, stopping in front of a large door that was slightly ajar.

Looking in, I saw the Jackal driving into the same gorgeous woman as before, her moans growing louder with each thrust. The tan god held her legs to his chest as he plunged into her. His eyes were closed with his head tilted back, seemingly relishing his desire.

I moved a hand down my body as I watched them and slowly pressed a finger into my own very slick, wet hole. A guttural moan slipped out involuntarily when I realized how much I was dripping with lust. The sound reached The Jackal and his head snapped up. His eyes bore into me as he continued his mating.

Vasco stared at me through the narrow opening in the door for a long time. His eyes steadily traced every inch of my body with a predatory hunger. A sinister chuckle escaped him as he thrusted into the woman one final time and pulled away. She groaned at being suddenly empty of him, but he slapped her buttocks and whispered aggressively, "shut the fuck up, we have company."

He moved around the bed and opened the door wider, revealing me standing there, watching them.

"Lost, Sugar?" he whispered to me, a mischievous twinkle in his eyes. I did my best to keep my eyes locked on his, fighting the urge to look down at his thick erect cock that was hovering inches away from me. A piercing sticking out the end of it.

The Jackal bent down until his face was inches from mine, his mouth almost brushing against my own but never truly touching.

"It's ok, you can watch," he breathed against my lips. To my frustration, he pulled away, and I felt myself sway ever-so into the room.

The Jackal turned around and strutted back to the opposite side of the bed. He smacked the woman on her hip, ordering her onto all fours. She obeyed without hesitation, and he took a handful of her hair. His eyes never left mine as he penetrated her from behind. My body flushed with heat, and I entered the room, closing the door softly behind me.

As The Jackal intensified his thrusting with the woman, I removed my top. He smirked and focused intensely as each tit bounced free from my shirt.

"I appreciate a woman who goes without a bra," he commented, his eyes fixed on my chest as he increased the pace of his thrusting. I seductively removed my shorts and discarded them off to the side. The Jackal pulled on the woman's hair, and she yelped in pain.

I felt his powerful gaze on me as I ran my hands down my body, teasingly cupping at a breast. Vasco licked his lips as I moved a hand to my slit and withdrew it, revealing just how drenched I was with desire. With a sultry smile, I licked myself off of my fingers as I eyed my conquest. Aggressive, primal lust twisted across his face as he watched me.

I glided over to the couple and positioned myself in front of the alluring woman. Lifting her face to mine, I planted a gentle kiss on her nose, causing her to smile invitingly. Encouraged, I deepened the kiss and toyed with her voluptuous breasts. She moaned softly as I teased her nipples, so I continued to apply pressure for a while longer.

Kinky.

"Eat me out," I whispered to her, and she nodded, eager to please. As soon as I positioned my wet slit in her face, she moaned into it. I placed my hand over The Jackal's and he released his grip on her hair. Then I seized a handful of my own, prepared to take control.

"I told you to eat it," I said firmly as I pushed her face deeper between my legs. The woman eagerly began licking and sucking at my sensitive area, her enthusiasm evident in the way she devoured me. The Jackal gave her a sharp smack on the butt, urging her on even faster as she mixed her saliva with my already wet juices.

Vasco and I locked eyes over the back of the woman.

I struggled to hold back any moans as she simulated my sensitive pearl. The Jackal appeared to be fighting his climax, prolonging the inevitable. Soon enough, though, I saw the telltale glint in his eyes. He was on the verge of release.

I yanked the woman's hair forcefully, pulling her off of his cock before he could reach completion. She let out a squeal from the rough handling, gripping onto my hands in her hair for support. The Jackal let out a groan of frustration as I removed our mutual companion from the bed by force.

"Thank you for your services but go make one of the men out there happy," I whispered to the woman, pinching her nipples a few times on the way out. She whimpered at my touch, but allowed me to throw her out of the room. I closed the door behind me.

Vasco studied me with fascination as I approached him on his side of the bed. I stood tall beneath his gaze, just as close as he had been to me in the doorway.

"Lay down," I commanded.

"What makes you think I will listen to you," he asked amused. I grabbed his chin firmly and leaned in until our faces were inches apart.

"Because you are a warlord. Allow me do the work to satisfy you," I responded with an innocent smile. The Jackal smiled wickedly and pulled me into a sloppy, groping kiss, which I returned feverishly.

I playfully pushed against him, hoping to topple him onto the bed, but he barely budged. The Jackal's grin grew wider as he purposely shifted himself and reclined on the bed. He nonchalantly placed both hands behind his head and gestured towards his fully aroused member, eagerly waiting for me.

"Well, well, well, I think I've just found my favorite gun vendor. I don't think this kind of customer service can be matched," Vasco whispered as I straddled him, positioning his thick penis at the entrance of my very slick, aching pussy. I had intended to glide down his length, but my eagerness had left me dripping wet. Instead, I slipped down his cock and pleasure exploded in me the moment I fell onto him. A moan of deep gratification escaped my lips.

The Jackal withdrew his hand from behind his head and began to tease my nipples with playful fingers. A look of amusement danced on his lips as I started to ride him fervently.

I writhed on his throbbing cock, lost in the intoxicating pleasure of our union. My body was slick with sweat as I enjoyed every inch of him for several long minutes. Suddenly, the door creaked open and my eyes widened at the sight of one of the Azteca Kings, fully naked and stroking his cock with greedy urgency.

"Oh, I heard noises and assumed, sorry-" the man said. He stared down at me riding his boss and started to stroke his member a little faster.

"Sometimes my men join me in my sexual exploits," Vasco explained, before dismissing the man with a small wave.

"Wait," I exclaimed as the man turned for the door. The Azteca King stalled, and I faced the Jackal, pausing my movements.

"There has been something I've been wanting to try…" I whispered, biting my lip, feeling strangely shy.

A slow, seductive smile spread across Vasco's face, filled with knowing intent. He grabbed me by the nape of my neck and pulled me towards him, pressing his lips onto mine in a fervent kiss. I responded with equal passion, feeling his teeth lightly nip at my lips before he released me.

The Jackal looked over and jerked his head my direction. I heard the man come up behind me, then felt as his hands caress down my back. A shiver of feverish anticipation slid down my spine.

Vasco tenderly pulled me closer, his strong grip digging into my hips as he presented my other empty hole to his man. My body trembled with excitement as I felt the tip of the stranger's cock threatening to enter. I squeezed my eyes shut, bracing for the rapturous sensation that was about to consume me.

I was so sloppily wet that with one swift motion, the man plunged himself inside of me, filling me completely. His rough hands cupped my breast insatiably. A primal moan of pleasure escaped my lips as they filled both my holes, sending shivers of ecstasy through my body. The two men took turns ravaging me, each thrust feeling like a magnificent animalic blow to my body. I struggled to adjust at first, but then I surrendered to the relentless pounding. Allowing myself to be consumed by the carnal rhythm of their strong bodies.

The Jackal caressed a finger across my face, forcing me to focus on the man beneath me.

"There is a rumor about you among my men," he whispered, his hand finding its way down my body.

"I didn't believe it at first, but seeing you here makes me think it could be true," he said. The relentless thrusting of both men continued, their bodies slamming into me with primal urgency. With a twisted glint in his eye, Vasco reached behind the pillow he had been resting his head on.

"They gossiped about the raven-haired Angel of Death who would fuck her family's guards until Daddy would catch them," The Jackal spoke without missing a beat in delightfully annihilating my body. I remained silent, only biting my lip to fight a loud pleasing moan from escaping.

"They say you got off on getting men killed. Is that true?" he asked seductively.

My body trembled with pleasure as the man behind me thrusted rabidly. The sensation of being shared between the two men leading me close to the edge of ecstasy. A wild moan escaped, but The Jackal silenced me with one finger, brushing it across my lips in a gentle gesture.

"*I think* you get off on danger, and risky affairs," The Jackal murmured, maintaining grave eye contact with me. "but why don't we find out together," he sang, taking his fill of pumping into me.

With slow, calculated movements, he withdrew his hand from under the pillow, revealing a gleaming six-shot revolver. My heart raced as I tried to maintain composure and focus on the men pleasing me, but my eyes kept wondering to the weapon. Each thrust sent adrenaline coursing through my veins and, secretly, I knew I wanted to ride out this dangerous game until the very end.

"Let's make a deal," The Jackal continued, his eyes still watching me with an unmatched concentration. Goosebumps prickled my skin as the intensity of his focus sent a chill through my body.

"We'll play Ostraria Roulette, while my man and I continue to fuck you. I'll go first, then it's your turn, and finally Diego behind you. If I can make you climax with my little game, I'll triple what I bought from your family today," a depraved and seductive smile lit up The Jackal's face.

"And if the gun goes off?" I managed to ask.

"That's part of the thrill, darling. Your brother, your guards, and half of the house will come running in here to see you milking my cock. Based on how they looked at me today, I don't think they'd approve, do you?" he whispered. A strange and dangerous thrill filled me at the thought of what he was proposing. I fought to suppress a moan that threatened to escape. This only fueled the twisted glee that had spread across the Jackal's face into a godless grin.

"And if I don't orgasm," I asked in hushed tones, feeling myself on the brink of ecstasy anyways.

"Well, then, I guess I'll just have to stick with what I bought today, and keep fucking the women we have here, instead of fully enjoying the ravishing monster that is taking my dick right now," The Jackal said, lazily pinching my nipples in his free hand. My body trembled with arousal as a wave of pleasure threatened to overtake me then and there. I fought against it, agreeing to his game, his touch leaving me gasping for air and begging for more.

The Jackal delighted in my response. He opened the chamber of the gun and, with a movement so imperceptibly smooth, loaded a single bullet. With a flick of his wrist, he spun the chamber and locked it back into place, taunting me with the uncertainty of our reckless game.

"Ready, Princess?" he whispered, as he slowly raised the gun until the barrel pointed directly at his own head. Panic coursed through me at the sight of the weapon aimed at his own face. The Jackal's hand, however, remained steady and determined.

"Look at me," he requested, and I locked eyes with my lover. Panic seized me as I come to the horrifying realization that one of us could be moments away from death. My breaths came in quickened successions, every nerve in my body on edge. I watched with rapt attention, trembling in suspense, as he pulled the trigger.

Click.

The chamber was empty. A malevolent smile stretched across his face as endorphin flooded my veins.

"I guess I live to see another day," he hissed, his eyes twinkling as they studied me, searching for any signs of my inevitable rapture.

My eyes widen in apprehension as I watch him slowly raise the gun. The cold metal of the barrel pressed against my temple, sending a jolt of fear and adrenaline coursing through my body. With my senses heightened, every nerve was on edge as I braced myself for what was to come.

With both men thrusting into me, the pleasure mingled with the terror and caused me to tremble uncontrollably. The overwhelming sensations nearly brought me to climax that instant.

"Don't worry, you have an eighty percent chance of surviving," Vasco said sardonically. My heart pounded violently in my chest as I fixed my gaze on the gun in his hand. My mind was racing, frantically searching for a way to convince myself to stop this gamble with fate. Time slowed to a screeching stop as I waited for my destiny to be revealed.

"Look at me," his words caressed me. I forcefully tore my gaze away from the horrifying sight and looked deep into The Jackal's dilated pupils.

"I don't want to die," I whispered, a lone tear escaping from my eye and landing onto his chest.

"I know, Baby," he spoke softly, cupping my face in his hand as we shared a final moment. I closed my eyes and savored the sensation of being filled by both men one last time.

"Angel, Baby." The Jackal's voice pierced through the thick haze. I opened my eyes to face my fate.

Click.

Another chamber empty.

I pressed my lips gently against the Jackal's hand, feeling the roughness of his calluses. As I pulled away, he gave a small, almost imperceptible kiss in return, causing a flutter in my stomach.

Abruptly, the man behind me let out a groan that reverberated through my body. I felt him pulsating inside me, violently releasing himself as I shared an intimate moment with The Jackal.

"That does not excuse you from the game," The Jackal's voice was cold as he turned the gun swiftly toward Diego. With the six-shot revolver inches away from my ear, he pulled the trigger without hesitation. The sound of a harsh, metallic clank rang out sharply, echoing with the mechanical finality of the hammer striking an empty chamber.

Click.

Massive waves of amplified pleasure consumed me, causing my body to spasms uncontrollably as my orgasm drowned me. The Jackal collapsed back onto the bed, a triumphant grin on his face, as he watched me writhe on top of him. His arms were spread wide, one hand still lazily holding the gun, as he reveled in claiming his victory over me. An astounded glint in his eyes conveyed his sadistic pleasure at bringing me to this state of blissful submission.

The man behind me withdrew slowly, adding to the pleasurable sensation that was still building inside of me like wildfire. My climax tore through me like a vicious storm and I barely registered Diego leaving, careful to close the door behind himself.

A violent scream of hedonistic joy spilled from my lips and The Jackal lunged towards me and gripped my face in his rough hands, smothering my cries with a crushing force.

"Shhhh, Princess or you will wake the house," he warned. I bit into his fingers, but he paid no attention as he continued to forcefully pump into me, encouraging the orgasm. As the climax peaked, wild and barbaric, I closed my eyes and lost my mind to the rapture until I no longer felt myself exist anymore. When I crashed back down to my senses, I collapsed off of The Jackal and onto the bed, gasping for air.

Vasco let out a deep, appreciative chuckle as his fingers traced up my leg. He took control and eagerly positioned himself above me, easing back inside of me. I was still riding the aftermath of my previous climax, but another wave of rapture crashed over me as he entered me again. Tears of ecstasy streamed down my cheeks, which Vasco tenderly kissed away as he thrusted into me harder and faster. I wrapped my legs around him and pulled him closer, meeting his passionate movements with equal fervor. It wasn't long before he gave one final powerful thrust and pumped his seed into me. Then all went still.

The Jackal and I refused to move. His cock remaining inside of me as we held onto each other tightly. My lover's face hovered over mine, his eyes holding a serious look for the first time all day. Vasco pushed my hair aside to get a better look at me, then he savagely began kissing me.

We continued to kiss each other with barbaric force long into the night. Only when the sky outside began to threaten us with the first hues of sunrise did he pull back reluctantly. The Jackal looked down at me with an intensely serious expression.

"Never figured I was the marrying type, but woman, I'm going to marry you," he whispered insistently. I laughed softly, and he kissed me again.

"Mark my words," he said against my lips, then pulled away, slowly removing himself from me.

I rolled off the bed and stood up. My body ached, and semen was leaking out of me. The Jackal came up behind me and kissed my back, his arms wrapping around me. I relaxed into his embrace as he feathered more kisses up to my cheek.

"I've got something for you," he whispered in my ear. One of his hands held up a single bullet right in front of my face.

"What's this?" I asked, grabbing the object and twirling it in my hand a few times.

"The gun wasn't loaded," The Jackal murmured, his devilish eyes looked at me, wildly entertained. My mouth dropped in shock as I started to stutter at least five different questions at once. The Jackal placed a hand on my lips to silence me.

"I would never risk your life. No, you are too rare," he whispered, his eyes holding me captivated under his gaze. The Jackal kissed me vigorously, the unfired round slipping from my fingers and landing on the ground with a small clink. Vasco's hands found my tits again, and he broke the kiss reluctantly.

"Let's go get you cleaned up, my magnificent little devil, before brother wakes up and starts demanding breakfast again," he whispered. Then The Jackal led me to a connecting bathroom with a standing glass shower.

My lover carefully tended to my body, surprising me with his gentle touch. Despite being turned on by his actions, I couldn't ignore the soreness in my vagina and anus. To show my appreciation, I playfully pushed him into the water and gave him a slow blowjob while the warm water rained down his face and back.

"When you are my wife, I will fuck you however you want and with whoever you want. I will make you come like that every night," he told me. His eyes were shut, savoring the feeling of my lips on him. He rested his hands on my head but let me satisfy him at my own pace. It wasn't long before he climaxed in my mouth, and I eagerly swallowed every drop.

I was still kneeling in front of him when he dropped down to my level and lifted my chin, holding my gaze on him.

"You're beautiful, Reina," he whispered.

"Thank you," I said dismissively, having grown used to the compliment.

"No, no," he waved his finger in front of my face, then moved it to my heart. "In here, in your soul." This time, I blushed deeply, overwhelmed by a wave of emotion. For the first time in my life, I felt I had bared my naked soul, and he embraced it without hesitation. My defenses crumbled, leaving me speechless and in awe of his acceptance.

"How do you know I'll marry you?" I whispered, smiling at the Jackal, my heart warming a little.

"Tell me, do you know anyone else who relishes giving you such a severe strategic thrill?" he asked. My mind flitted to Dimiter for a moment, and I wondered if he would have simulated such a daring game. Just as I settled on the answer "no," The Jackal continued.

"I get the impression you intimidate a lot of people. You'll never have to worry about that with me. Our spirits are evenly matched." I thought about that for another moment, then leaned in to find his lips with mine.

The Jackal, however, pulled back slightly and waited until he caught my full attention.

"You let me know when you are ready," he said, playfully poking me on the nose. "And not a minute sooner. Now, let's get you back to your room, Mi Corazón."

I grabbed my clothes and threw them on in a rush. My hair was still wet, but there was little I could do about that. The Jackal kissed me powerfully one more time before I left him at his door.

Navigating back to my room, I moved carefully to avoid waking anyone. As I turned down the hallway, anxiety surged within me; I had been gone all night.

At the end of the hallway, Alexei and Dimiter were slumped in their chairs, fast asleep. I sighed in relief, realizing that Dimiter must have fallen asleep after I went out for water. I slipped into my room, closed the door silently, and climbed into bed. As soon as my head hit the pillow, I fell into a deep sleep.

5 Months

CHAPTER TWENTY-SIX

I woke up with a start. Loud noises and yelling echoed from across the hall where Bane had slept. I scrambled out of bed and hurried into the hallway. Rushing to Bane's doorway, I arrived just in time to see my brother grabbing The Jackal and pulling him into a real embrace.

I stopped and watched the two men in disbelief. When I first heard the yelling, I was certain I'd find them fighting. Instead, I saw them hugging, and I allowed myself a breath of relief.

Later, on the plane ride back, Bane told me he had woken up early that morning to the sun. At the foot of his bed, sitting cross-legged in just his boxers, was The Jackal, peeling a banana. Initially annoyed, Bane was about to ask Vasco to leave until the man started going off on a tangent about how charismatic and strong-willed his twin sister was.

Jackal then told my brother that he saw me in the kitchen late last night, and we started talking. Our conversation, supposedly, shifted to his vision for his empire here in Cliuz Plyae. That's when I surprised him by laying out a very aggressive dual front-and-back-end strategy that really impressed him. He hadn't expected me to be capable of such brutality at first glance. Apparently, we spent the rest of the night collaborating, refining a proposal that guaranteed his success.

After walking Bane through fifteen more minutes of cleverly concealed double entendres mixed with business buzzwords, he finally concluded with, "I'm sure your sister wanted to tell you herself, but I figured she wouldn't mind. I want to quadruple my order from yesterday."

When Bane didn't believe him, Jackal continued.

"I'm going to need the firepower and ammo for Sophia and my future plans. Clearly, the Zorics are the best vendors out there, and I personally appreciate such a dynamic customer relationship approach."

Once Bane recovered from the shock and started believing him, he mentally did the math. When he realized how much we had just made, he started yelling in excitement, which woke me up across the hall.

Bane was still embracing The Jackal when he saw me and pulled away. He ran over, scooped me up into a hug, and twirled me around the room.

"The Jackal just told me he wants to quadruple his order!" Bane exclaimed as he spun me around.

"Woah, woah, woah. Who is this fucking Jackal person you're talking about?" Vasco asked, making Bane pause in his excitement. My twin put me down and stared at the tanned god, mouth agape in confusion.

"You... you are?" Bane stammered.

"What, me? No. I am The Lion!" The Lion answered, winking in my direction.

"You introduced yourself as The Jackal yesterday?" Bane asked, still unsure. He looked to me for help, but I just shrugged and tried to hide a knowing smile.

"No, no. The Lion," Vasco insisted.

Bane gawked at The Lion, clearly confused. It took my twin a few seconds to fully recover.

"Why... why The Lion?" he asked.

"Did you not listen yesterday? I was attacked by a lion and survived," The Lion said, pointing to the claw mark scars on his chest.

Bane said nothing but continued staring at The Lion before finally asking, "Are lions even in this region of the world?"

Vasco just stared at Bane, the tension between the two men becoming palpable. My twin eventually broke the staring contest and turned to me.

"Angel?" he asked, seeking support.

"What? He's The Lion," I shrugged in response.

Bane gaped, and The Lion eyed me with a wicked smile, a dark glimmer shining in his sinful eyes. He shoved past my brother on his way out of the room, turning around only to give Bane one last command.

"Bring her back when you deliver the rest of my fucking order!"

The Lion saw us off. Bane had already contacted Father to coordinate the delivery of the rest of the shipment and provided an estimated turn-around time of a few weeks.

This pleased The Lion greatly, and he paid Bane for the goods we were leaving with him. Vasco then turned to me and handed over the rest of the money he had.

"This is the first half of what you sold me. You earned it," he purred, his fingers caressing my hand slyly as the money exchanged between us.

"I gave you a little extra. Maybe we can revisit that strategy when you come back. Find areas to add tertiary or quaternary players if it would please you," he said, his eyes locked onto mine with knowing intent.

"Mi Corazón," he added in a whisper so low no one else could hear. I felt myself grow hot again. His enthusiasm to bring out such sexual savagery in me made my body ache for him. His fingers brushed my ring finger intimately during the exchange.

"I have a deal with my father," I started to whisper to him. The Lion shushed me immediately, placing a finger gently on my lips.

"I said when *you* are ready," he said, poking my nose in the same manner he had in the shower. Then he stepped back and away from me in the most formal manner I had ever witnessed from him.

"Angel," Bane called from halfway up the stairs of our plane. I looked up at him, then back at The Lion. I fought the urge to run over and kiss him one last time and instead just stood there, looking at him blankly. In the smallest, almost imperceptible moment, Vasco moved his lips, blowing me a small kiss. With that, I bounded up the stairs and greeted my twin with a smile and wads of cash in my hand.

5 Months

BANE'S GUNRUNNING BUSINESS RULE NUMBER NINE:

Choose your partners wisely.

You wouldn't want to work with an unreliable supplier, now would you?

CHAPTER TWENTY-SEVEN

I pulled up to Dimiter's house, excitement bubbling inside me. My guard greeted me at the door wearing just a blue robe that left nothing to the imagination. His erect member was clearly visible between his thighs, and he made no attempt to hide it.

As soon as he pulled me through his front door, Dimiter ordered me to get strip.

"Take my clothes off yourself," I said provocatively, hoping he would rip my short dress off of me. Dimiter did no such ripping and instead just crossed his arms and looked down with a domineering glare.

I obeyed his command and undressed, attempting to put on a performance for him. He feigned disinterest until I was completely naked, then he swept me up into his arms. As Dimiter dragged me further into his house, he kissed my lips, neck, and finally made his way down to suck on my nipples.

"Stay here. I've got something for you," he insisted, after setting me down in his living room. My guard disappeared into his room and returned a moment later with a dark purple leather-like strap in his hands. He placed the gift in my hand, and I inspected it.

The present was an O-ring month gag, with the letters "WH" on one side of the ring and "RE" on the other, to spell out *whore*. I smiled in delight and felt myself getting excited as I put on the new toy.

After checking the placement of the gag, Dimiter removed his robe belt and moved behind me. He tightly bound my hands together behind my back, then began to caress my skin with his fingers, gently kissing my shoulders and neck as he made his way up to my ear.

"I saw you in Cliuz Plyae. Not exactly negotiation tactics you'd want to explain to your brother," he chuckled before kissing my ear. I jerked around to face him, shock and panic flooding through me.

I attempted to ask, "How?" but the gag in my mouth muffled my words and they came out jumbled. Dimiter chuckled and smiled a devilish smile.

"There's a reason your father keeps me employed, Angel. The big, tall, and clumsy bodyguard is usually not a spy. But between you and me, I've perfected the art of knowing everything about everyone," Dimiter whispered the last part quickly, a dark, sinister twinkle in his eye. His hands glided over my bared skin as he confessed to me.

"Alexei and you were actually pretty good at sneaking around. Just not good enough for someone as trained as I am in gathering information.

Don't worry, I didn't tell Daddy. I have my own secrets to hide," he casually added, fondling my breast. I groaned into the gag as a response to his enjoyable groping.

"You tried to be quiet, but I'm a light sleeper," he explained further. "It was curious, since you hadn't come back. Then I peeked through a door where the most delicious sounds were coming from, and you know what I saw?" Dimiter bent closer to my ear and whispered, "two men pounding into you at the same time." My hair stood on end and I shivered as his breath caressed my ear, sending tingles down my spine.

"I find it to be very, very erotic, my dear Angel," Dimiter continued as he pulled back. His fingers trailed down the curves of my body before firmly gripping my hips and pulling me closer to him.

"The Ostraria Roulette was a bit much." I felt my face flush at the memory.

"But once I realized The Lion had palmed the bullet, I couldn't help but jerk myself off as I watched you," he admitted with a strange, demented, yet proud look on his face.

"When you finally orgasm, it was such a treat. I had to make a mad dash to clean up and hide from that Azteca King as he left," Dimiter kissed me on my cheek.

"Now it's my turn with you, though."

My guard dragged me to his plush couch. He made himself comfortable on it, spreading his robe away from himself. Then he grabbed his massive dick and stared at me with lustful, bright eyes.

"Sit on me while facing the TV. I have something for us to watch," he commanded.

Following his instructions, I straddled him and positioned myself on top. His confession had aroused me, making it easy for me to slide onto his large shaft. As soon as he was fully inside of me, a sigh of relief threatened to escape. I began to slide back up his length, but Dimiter firmly gripped my hips and pulled me down onto him with force.

"Oh no, you are going to be my little dick warmer while we watch this. Do not move or even try to satisfy yourself." my guard commanded. He removed one hand from my hips and began clicking away at the remote pointed at the flat-screen TV I was facing.

"This came in before we left. I didn't get to watch much of it yet, so we will be enjoying it together," he explained. The screen turned on, revealing Alexei sitting in a dark room, illuminated only by his own TV. Between his legs was me, sucking on his dick. I groaned as I realized what we were about to watch. Alexei must have recorded us the other day and sent the footage to Dimiter.

Men and their egos, I thought.

Dimiter's hand landed on my rear with an excited smack. He then reached around, his fingers moving slowly until he found my sensitive spot and began rubbing it in an enjoyable, rhythmic motion.

On the screen, my mouth was still wrapped around Alexei's member as he watched his own TV with a stoic expression. Every now and then, he would thrust into my mouth forcefully, causing Dimiter to chuckle and increased his stimulation on my clitoris vigorously.

As we watched, I squirmed and shifted in an attempt to stimulate myself to climax. Dimiter's impressive member kept me on the brink of pleasure, and my body begged for release. Every time I moved, though, he would hold me down firmly on his cock, denying me my ecstasy. The sexual frustration almost became unbearable, and I couldn't help but moan through the gag, exasperated.

Once Alexei had finished into my mouth on camera, Dimiter took hold of my hips and glided me up and down on his considerable manhood for several seconds. The sensation electrifying to my already titillated body.

"You swallowed quite a load there, my good little whore," he said before impaling me once more on his substantial dick and holding me down again. I struggled to keep moving, but he held me firmly in place and delivered a few harsh slaps to my buttocks. I retaliated by tightening my lips around his organ, causing him to release his grip on my hips. He moved his hands up to fondle my nipples gently.

"I like this, you being my personal little sex toy while I watch porn," he said as he pinched one of my nipples. I didn't respond, being gagged and all, but I found I was enjoying myself just as much.

The scene on the screen showed Alexei placing me on the whipping bench and starting to spank my buttock.

"My comment about him not being rough really bothered him, huh, Angel?" Dimiter laughed as he watched Alexei smack me until my butt was bright red.

As Alexei thrusted into me vigorously from behind, Dimiter's hand found my clitoris once again. On the screen, I could hear Alexei urging me to scream louder as I started to reach climax. On Dimiter's cock, a different type of pleasure was building up as he roughly stimulated my pearl with his fingers. He circled my sensitive area easily, his touch slick from my juices.

On-screen Angel moaned in ecstasy, almost triggering my own climax. Just as I was about to reach the peak, Dimiter abruptly pulled his fingers away and grabbed onto my hips. The frustration of not being able to release built up, replacing any pleasure I could have felt. In a fit of sexual tension, I tried to move on his cock again, hoping to reach that elusive high. Dimiter was one step ahead, restraining me firmly on his massive member. My muffled cries and squirming only seemed to amuse him more.

"Not so fast, my dear," he teased as I surrendered, unable to move under his strong grip. I yearned for release, my body begged for it.

Dimiter's hand returned to my nipples, causing me to shudder with pleasure. He lazily thrusted in and out of me, knowing just when to slow down to prevent my intense climax.

On the screen, Alexei was pulling out the onyx butt plug from between my cheeks. The image then showed him slowly entering my exposed rear with his cock. A moan escaped his lips as he entered me completely.

Behind me, Dimiter slid a finger into my buttock as he watched Alexei savoring his time inside me.

"Naughty, naughty," he whispered inching his finger into my buttocks a little more. Suddenly, Dimiter removed his finger from me and thrusted his immense shaft into me, eliciting a series of moans from me in delight. After several forceful pumps into me, he held me down onto again and warned me not to move.

I couldn't tear my eyes away from the television screen as I watched myself tenderly riding Alexei on his couch. Dimiter's fingers were once again exploring my anus, but this time coated in lube. With a click, he turned off the final moments of the tape and directed me to get on all fours. My wrists were released from their restraints, allowing me to comply with his demand. I got into position and waited for further instructions.

I could feel Dimiter's massive member slowly penetrating my buttocks, and a small wave of panic washed over me. Most men wouldn't be cause for concern, but his size was inordinate. The lube he applied helped ease him in, and the fear quickly turned into excitement as my hole opened up to accommodate him. He glided in and out, gradually increasing his speed until his naked body made a loud smacking sound against mine. Then he gripped my hips tightly, pulling me onto him as he grunted with each thrust.

My other poor, neglected hole twitched with aching desire now that it was empty of Dimiter's massive manhood. With each thrust into me, my body craved another cock, and my thoughts drifted to The Lion for the briefest of moments.

I could tell by the grunting noises that Dimiter was reaching his climax. With one last powerful thrust, he released himself inside me, pushing his entire length into my rear.

"Don't move," he instructed as he removed himself from my opening. I stayed locked in place until Dimiter returned. He gently placed a blindfold over my eyes, and I remained frozen on all fours as I heard him move around the room, almost drunkenly.

I waited for what felt like forever. Finally, I felt his hands on me again, guiding me to stand up. Dimiter placed something around my neck, then kissed my cheek. I started to reach up to feel the necklace, but my hands were caught and tied behind my back once more with the robe tie.

Carefully, Dimiter moved me around his house, giving the occasional instruction as I fumbled about, blind to my surroundings. We made our way outside, and I could feel the cool air lick my naked body. I tried to ask where we were going, but the gag was still in my mouth, making it difficult to speak.

"Don't worry, Angel, it's dark, so no one can see you," he tried to comfort me as he continued to guide me outside. Eventually, he gave up, frustrated by how slow we were moving, and picked me up to place me in what felt like a car. Dimiter made sure to strap me in with a seat belt, so I mentally confirmed I was probably in a vehicle.

The car started to move and Dimiter's hand found its way between my legs again. He slid a few fingers into me, teasing my opening and keeping me on the verge of climax but never quite letting me reach it.

Shortly, the car came to a halt, but the engine continued to hum. Dimiter got out and assisted me, holding me up and preparing to lead me once again. He planted a kiss on my lips through the gag before inserting his fingers back inside of me. Then he dragged me along in the desired direction.

We finally stopped, and he positioned me to stand straight, my arms still tied behind my back. I heard the sound of his knuckles knocking hard on a door, and then... nothing.

Dimiter's car started to sound further away when the hinges on the door finally moaned as it opened. A deep, tired sigh escaped someone's lips, and then my blindfold was ripped off by the unknown person.

There, in the doorframe of his own house, stood Alexei, his eyes aflame and cutting into me.

My gaze drifted downwards to my exposed form, adorned only with a flash drive strung around my neck on a makeshift twine necklace. Dimiter had apparently chosen me to be the messenger in this twisted game between my men.

My pent-up sexual frustration reached its boiling point when Alexei forcefully pulled me into his house, gripping my arm tightly. He carelessly discarded the rope and USB drive that were dangling from my neck. Then he carefully untied the knot restraining my hands and released the gag that had silenced me.

After everything was gone, I collapsed onto Alexei, wrapping my arms around his neck and pulling him in for a kiss. At first, his lips were firm but then he started to return the kiss hesitantly.

"Fuck me, please," I begged, moaning on his lips. I was starving for release.

Alexei said nothing, but picked me up in his arms. He carried me to his bedroom and laid me out on his bed. I stretched as he took off his clothes then hopped on top of me.

My mouth found his quickly and we kissed feverishly. With our lips locked, he slipped into my wet opening, and I groaned in rapture. I felt sore with frustration as he moved into me slowly and shivered under him. The sensation of an orgasm rose almost immediately, but Alexei took his time.

"Alexei," I begged, but he continued to slowly thrust into me.

"Roll over," he commanded, pulling out of me abruptly. I let out a low growl of annoyance.

"Now," he barked, looking at me with hard eyes. Following instructions, I flipped onto my stomach and felt a soft trail of kisses on my neck. They slowly made their way up to my cheek, causing shivers to run down my spine. Alexei intertwined his fingers with mine, heightening the intimate moment. I turned slightly toward him and met his passionate gaze.

As Alexei's lips touched my cheek, I could feel him ease back into me once more. This time, his movements brought me to the brink of orgasm, and with one final thrust, I was overwhelmed with intense pleasure. My body shook as wave after wave of ecstasy coursed through me, and I let out a cry of pure bliss.

Despite my climax, Alexei remained inside me, feeling every pulse and tremor around him. The sensation seemed to last for an eternity before finally subsiding, and Alexei resumed his movements inside me once again. He settled into a steady rhythm, our fingers still interlaced. Then he brought our intertwined hands close to his lips and kissed each of my fingertips one by one, then my palm. His climax came without warning, and I could feel him release inside me as he groaned above me. As soon as he finished, he withdrew and pulled me into his arms, holding me in a tight embrace.

Alexei held me for a long time. Anytime I tried to speak, he would hush me with a gentle touch of his finger against my lips. As exhaustion started to overtake me, I felt myself sinking into a relaxed state, drifting closer and closer to sleep. Despite the haze of unconsciousness, I could have sworn I heard a barely audible whisper in my ear:

"I love you, Angel."

4 Months

CHAPTER TWENTY-EIGHT

The next morning, I drifted awake, blissful. The sun filtered through the window and onto the bed. I felt around and realized I was alone. Disappointed, I pushed myself up to look around the bedroom. Alexei was nowhere to be found.

I threw on one of his many shirts that had been left on the floor and wandered down the hallway, listening for any signs of my guard. The house felt unusually still and quiet.

I stumbled through the modest house and eventually reached the kitchen, where I found Alexei. He was seated at the dining table, both elbows resting on the surface, with his hands clasped in front of his mouth.

On the table before him were two cups of coffee and the USB drive from the night before. Alexei stared intently at the drive, his expression deeply pensive. He remained motionless as I took a seat across from him.

"Did you watch it?" I asked casually, grabbing one of the cups of coffee and taking a sip. Alexei continued to stare at the drive on the table, not responding. He closed his eyes slowly and sat there for a few breaths.

"No."

He spoke so softly I could hardly hear him. I looked up from my coffee and met Alexei's gaze. A deep sadness consumed his face.

"Angel, I... I can't do this anymore," he sighed.

"Do what?" I asked, bracing myself for the same old song and dance.

"I can't do *this*." He picked up the USB drive and turned it over in his hand a few times. Then, he suddenly got up and threw the drive in the garbage.

"I don't think I understand," I said, watching his movements. Alexei sighed and returned to his seat across from me.

"I kept pushing you away so you could find someone who could support your lifestyle," he said, his voice condescending and sharp. "Not because I don't have feelings for you. Of course, I have feelings for you!"

His confession settled between us, and I stared at him in shock.

"I thought you only wanted sex since—" I began to defend myself, but something in Alexei seemed to snap.

"I wanted you to find someone you could marry, without having to worry about how I felt. At least, that's what I told myself. I know I can't afford to marry you. I can't *support you*—not in the way you're used to, that's for sure," Alexei barked, not meeting my gaze. I didn't respond; the weight of his words left me stunned, my mind racing in disbelief.

"I didn't expect you to go and fuck half the guard staff again!" he roared. The outburst echoed in the room, leaving me momentarily paralyzed. I stared at him, speechless, as the silence between us stretched, heavy and charged.

"Why have you never told me any of this before?" I finally whispered, my voice breaking. His accusation cutting through me, stinging deeply.

"I didn't think I had to. Your father made it clear: you have a year to find someone to marry. Surely you weren't just going to date someone like me and hope for the best after a year," he started to lecture, his voice laced with frustration.

I shrugged and looked at him. "I was allowed to marry who I wanted, and I guess I always assumed I'd find someone I could truly love. I wasn't fixated on whether they had the means, uh... money," I stammered, barely managing to get the last word out. Before I could finish, Alexei leaped from his seat and began pacing agitatedly behind his chair.

"You didn't think about that, did you? No, of course not. Not little princess Angel, who can kill and destroy whomever she wants. Don't worry—Daddy bankrolls her life. And her guards? They'll just be sent in to clean up her messes!" He began muttering hysterically as he paced.

"Typical!" he yelled, stopping behind the chair he had just vacated. He placed his hands on the back of the chair, his knuckles turning white from gripping it so hard.

"That's just typical coming from you. That's why this has all been another game to you. I was concerned for you. I worried you'd take this all too seriously—especially with how clingy you were at the beginning. But no! No!" Alexei threw his chair aside and began slamming his hand on the kitchen table. My coffee cup bounced as his hand struck the surface. "NO! In fact, you barely took me seriously at all, not when you could just go jump on Dimiter's enormous cock!"

His voice kept rising, and I felt tears streaming down my cheeks as he screamed at me.

"I did care about you," I whined. "I asked you to be my boyfriend!"

"NO, ANGEL! I CARED ABOUT YOU, BUT TO YOU, I WAS JUST ANOTHER DICK TO BE USED!" he screeched, pointing aggressively at me.

My cheeks grew hot with frustration, and the room became blurry as the tears poured from my eyes. Alexei was glaring at me with a bile expression.

"I asked you to be my boyfriend. I wanted us to go public!" I managed to sputter, the words falling lamely between us.

"Why, thank you. But have you forgotten that I WOULD GET SHOT BY YOUR FATHER!" Alexei screeched at me, his condescending, hateful gaze making me feel stupid. It became clear to me in that moment that, to Alexei, I was nothing more than a spoiled, good-for-nothing little girl. His dreams of molding me into the ideal housewife had shattered.

I began to panic; my breaths came in short, frantic gasps. The room felt like it was closing in on me, with the walls pressing tighter and tighter until I felt I would suffocate. I stumbled away from the table and ran down the hallway, my feet barely touching the ground.

There was no need for the rush—Alexei didn't bother chasing me. When I reached his bedroom, I slammed the door shut with a deafening thud and fumbled with the lock, my hands trembling uncontrollably. As I scanned the room, my eyes locked on Alexei's cell phone, still hooked up to the charger. I snatched it up and dialed the number I needed.

Bane answered on the third ring.

"What is it?"

I began to cry harder at the sound of my brother's voice.

"Bane?" I sobbed into the phone.

"Angel?" Bane's tone shifted to one of warmth and concern, far different from his initial response.

"Can you come pick me up, please?" I asked. "You said if I needed anything, if I was in trouble, I could call you and you would be there and not ask any questions. Right?"

My twin didn't respond immediately. I could hear him breathing heavily on the other end of the line.

"Please, Bane, please," I pleaded with him.

"Angel, are you hurt?" he asked.

"No," I bawled into the phone.

"Then why are you crying?" he asked, his tone growing harsher.

"Please," I begged.

I heard a defeated sigh on the other end. "Yeah... yes, where are you?"

It took twenty minutes before I heard the sound of a car pulling up in the driveway. I had stayed in the locked bedroom the entire time, Alexei not bothering to engage with me again. When the car arrived, though, a pounding started on the bedroom door.

"YOU CALLED YOUR BROTHER?!" Alexei yelled. "What exactly is your plan here, Angel? What are you going to tell him?"

I said nothing in return.

The doorbell rang, and Alexei went to answer it, knowing better than to ignore his employer's son.

"I can explain," I heard Alexei say.

"Where is Angel?" my brother demanded through gritted teeth.

"She's fine, but please, Bane, let me—" Alexei was cut off by what sounded like a shove.

"I don't care. I said, where is she?" Bane barked into the house, his temper starting to boil over.

I cautiously opened the bedroom door and walked toward the front of the house. Bane had made his way deep inside, clearly having barreled through Alexei to get in. I ran into my brother's arms, fresh tears slipping down my face.

"Thank you," I whispered in Bane's ear.

"I want to ask..." my twin gritted out, still seething with anger.

"You promised you wouldn't," I said, pulling away from his embrace to look him in the eye. Bane stared down at me for a moment before shaking his head in reluctant agreement. He moved a hand to wipe away my tears, then clasped my hand and led me to the front door.

I didn't look at Alexei as I left the house, but once I was safely in my brother's car, I stole a glance back. My guard was posted in his doorway, his face a mix of anger and shock.

"Am I still not allowed to ask now that we are no longer within earshot of Alexei? Because it sure does look like there was a relationship that is not allowed to happen... happening," Bane threw out the accusation flatly.

"No questions," I responded, prompting my twin to sigh heavily.

"Can I at least ask as a loving brother? I'm not exactly thrilled that my sister called me from some guy's house, using a phone that's not hers, wearing only a t-shirt and what seems to be little else," Bane ranted, glancing over to confirm my apparel choice.

"And I'm really NOT happy to be doing all that, especially when she's crying her eyes out," he added, his tone now filled with brotherly concern.

"Please, no questions," I said, staring out the car window. A comforting numbness began to envelop me, swallowing up the hurt and pain from this morning, turning the remnants of my heart to ice.

Bane pulled up to my house and got out of the car.

"I want to be alone," I said as I walked toward the front door.

"No," my twin demanded, stepping in front of me to unlock the door with his key. He tried to insert it into the lock, but it wouldn't fit. Remembering our argument from the other day, he turned to me, his face flushed with fresh anger.

I approached my new electronic lock and discreetly entered my passcode. The door unlocked, and we walked into the house together, but I pointedly ignored my brother. Instead, I moved straight to the bathroom, removing the shirt I had on and tossing it in the trash along the way.

The shower I took was hot, and I scrubbed every inch of myself, feeling an indifference that was growing inside of me. When I got out, I put on a comfortable old set of pajamas and crawled into bed. My brother was already sitting in a chair in the corner of the room, but I continued to ignore him.

He cleared his throat to get my attention and then said stiffly, "Dimiter called…"

I didn't respond.

"Apparently, Alexei started calling your phone after we pulled away. So, I have Dimiter driving your car and cell phone over."

I looked at my brother for a moment and then returned to staring at the wall, ignoring him again.

Bane cleared his throat once more, his tone on the edge of losing its cool.

"Hey, Angel. Why is your car and cell phone with Dimiter?" he asked harshly.

"No... questions..." I responded slowly.

It took a while for Dimiter to drive over, and during that time, Bane and I remained very still and silent. I kept replaying the fight in my mind, Alexei's words echoing over and over: *I didn't expect you to go and fuck half the guard staff again!*

When Dimiter arrived, Bane went to greet him at the door as I refused to get out of bed. I heard their voices downstairs as they spoke softly, followed by their footsteps coming up to my bedroom. Both men entered with concern etched on their faces.

"Angel, Dimiter wanted to see you. He's worried about you," Bane said softly.

I disregarded them, mostly annoyed by the presence of so many people when I just wanted to be left alone. My brother returned to his chair, and Dimiter knelt beside the bed, bringing his face to my level.

"What happened, Angel?" Dimiter whispered.

I closed my eyes as a fresh wave of tears threatened to overwhelm me. I felt Dimiter's hand gently caress my face.

"It's okay if you don't want to talk about it, but are you hurt? Did he hurt you?" he asked.

"No," I whispered, opening my eyes again to look at Dimiter. He nodded, then reached into his pocket and set my phone in front of me on the bed. I looked at it for a minute before going back to ignoring both men. Dimiter stood, crossing his arms and sighing, clearly upset with my lack of reaction to anything. He walked over to the wall behind Bane and leaned against it, waiting.

My phone started to vibrate on the bed, chiming my ringtone loudly. I glanced to see Alexei's name pop up with a photo I had taken of us recently. It was a rare moment when he let his guard down, and I had managed to snap a selfie of us together.

I grabbed my phone and threw it across the room. It hit the wall with a loud smack, then slid down, crashing to the floor. The screen was black and shattered, and the phone itself was no longer vibrating.

"Don't worry—Daddy bankrolls her life. And her guards? They'll just be sent in to clean up her messes!" rang through my head, and a blanket of guilt washed over me.

I curled myself into a ball and allowed the sadness to engulf me. Tears poured out in large, unrestrained waves. Dimiter and Bane were at my side in an instant, each sitting on opposite sides of the bed to offer comfort.

Before either man could say or ask anything, my brother's phone rang. He checked it and stiffened at the caller ID.

"Hello, Father."

"Mmhmm."

"I'm with her. Yeah."

"And Dimiter."

"Umm, I think it's best we just go alone."

"No, no, everything is fine. Just think it would be better to go smaller given the assignment. I'm not even sure Dimiter should—"

"Yeah, yeah. No problem."

"Bye."

Bane pulled the phone away from his ear and hung up. He let out a deep sigh before turning to us.

"So, you remember that man you were supposed to marry? And how we ran away from him and might have insulted him a couple of dozen times during our stay?" Bane asked casually.

"Did you really just ask me if I remember that?" I responded, stoic.

"Yeah, well, he's now refusing to sell us guns anymore," Bane continued. I snorted softly at that predictable twist of fate.

"And you might also remember that you just sold a warlord four times his original order," Bane added when he realized I wasn't going to say anything.

"Where are you going with this?" I asked, eyeing my twin.

"Well, since Mr. Volkov is no longer supplying guns to us, and your new boyfriend just quadrupled his order, we need to find a new vendor," my twin said with a tight smile. I didn't bother responding, so my brother continued.

"That was Father, and luckily, he has one lined up for us. However, he's insisting we go 'since you two idiots got us into this mess!' His words, not mine," Bane concluded, using air quotes around my father's words.

"No," I said simply. Bane just smiled tightly down at me.

"I don't think this is negotiable," Bane pressed.

"Father tried to marry me off to him. His fault," I asserted.

"You're going," my brother insisted.

"No."

"Angel."

"I'm not going."

Bane pinched the bridge of his nose, struggling to keep his temper in check. His face flushed pink, mirroring our father's expression when frustration began to overtake him.

"I'll promise to keep my mouth shut about what I saw this morning, but you have to come with us on this trip to the vendor," Bane finally stated, trying to sound as calm as possible.

"Whose 'us'?" I asked.

"Dimiter and me. Apparently, this guy isn't one for large crowds, so I managed to keep Alexei away from us for this trip, at least," Bane said, his voice betraying his growing irritation.

I took a deep breath and finally conceded.

"When?"

"Like now," Bane winced as he answered. Without further prompting, I crawled out of bed, to my brother's relief, and got ready for the trip.

Bane boarded the plane first and claimed our usual table. I walked past him toward my bedroom.

"Hey, where are you going?" Bane called after me, grabbing my arm to turn me around.

"To the bedroom," I stated, then jerked my arm out of his grasp.

"What? You don't want to hear about the man we're meeting, or what we should expect and plan like we usually do?" my twin asked as he followed me down the back hallway. I paid no heed to his question and reached my favorite private room, locking the door quickly before Bane could barge in.

"Angel! Unlock this door and come out here. At least, run through the brief with me!" he called into the room, slamming his hand against the door.

I flopped onto the bed, grabbed the TV remote, and turned on the TV to whatever was streaming first. As the sounds from the television filled the room, Bane's banging on the door grew louder and more insistent.

"ANGEL, WE ALWAYS GO OVER THE DEAL. IT'S A RE-QUIREMENT! IT'S RULE NUMBER THREE OF MY BUSINESS TIPS FOR GUN RUNNING!" he yelled, pounding the door with a heavy fist. I responded by turning up the TV volume to an uncomfortable level, but it was enough to drown out my brother's yelling.

Eventually, Bane gave up and left me alone to sulk in my room.

4 Months

BANE'S GUNRUNNING BUSINESS RULE NUMBER THREE:

Don't bring a knife to a gun fight.

This means we do a thorough briefing before every deal. It's non-negotiable.

CHAPTER TWENTY-NINE

The plane landed several hours later, and I moved into the cabin of the aircraft to disembark with my brother and guard.

"Where are we?" I asked casually, not actually caring.

"You would know if you had spent time going over the details with me," Bane snapped.

"Fine, don't tell me," I responded and moved past him quickly to open the plane door. The shining sun met me, blindingly bright. The heat weighed down on me before I even disembarked. The air felt thick, and sweat trickled down my face almost immediately. I put on a pair of big black sunglasses I had stored away before making my way down the stairs to the flat, deserted land.

Within the vicinity of our plane was a massive army tank, in light camouflage beige, resting and appearing abandoned. I approached the unit and walked around it slowly, looking for signs of life. On closer inspection, it looked as if something had been rigged together on the top commander's hatch, with wires springing out chaotically.

I turned to my brother, unamused.

"What is this?" I asked.

Bane shrugged before pulling out his phone to check a text message.

"Father said we need to provide a password before our contact will reveal himself," Bane said, skimming his phone to read what little information Father had provided us.

"He's in the tank, isn't he?" I guessed.

"Hmmm?" Bane responded, glancing up at me briefly before returning to his phone. "I kill people when you need me to, I am not accepted and sometimes illegal, I need to be refilled from time to time, and I can harm my owner. What am I?" Bane read aloud instead of answering my question.

"Angel!" Dimiter chimed in enthusiastically, pointing in my general direction. Bane and I turned to stare at him, neither of us amused.

"Sorry," he apologized quickly, then walked up next to me to inspect the tank.

"I kill people when you need me to," Bane began reading slowly behind me, pacing slightly as he tried to think. I ignored my brother and instead started climbing up to the top of the tank.

"Angel!" Bane chastised, his attention drawn to my efforts.

"No, I already suggested that," Dimiter repeated his joke. My twin approached the tank while I continued climbing to the top.

"What are you doing?" Bane shouted up at me.

"I don't have time for this," I said, grabbing the hatch handle and trying to pull it open. The small door didn't budge.

Beep.

I jumped at the sound and tried to locate its source. That's when I saw, at the end of all the wires, a small electronic clock slowly counting down from five minutes. I grabbed the unit and traced the wires with my eyes. They all disappeared at the base of the gun cannon, which I then realized was aimed directly at our plane.

"Bane, what's the password?!" I yelled to my brother.

"What do you mean 'what's the password'? I was trying to figure that out!" he yelled back, only then noticing the small electronic device in my hands.

"What's that?" he demanded, panic rising in his voice.

"This is counting down from five minutes and is wired to this gun that's pointed at our plane," I explained quickly.

"Goddammit, this is exactly why we should have gone over the briefing on the plane," Bane started to lecture me.

"When has a briefing ever prepared us for any of our visits?" I shot back immediately, clawing through all the wires in search of a specific one.

"Why didn't you at least listen to me before climbing up there and setting it off?" my twin shouted back.

"Hey, don't you think we should be figuring out a password right about now?" Dimiter interjected, interrupting our argument. Bane went back to his pacing, muttering parts of the riddle to himself slowly.

"An assassin?" I asked, checking the clock as it reached three minutes.

"No, no, I am not accepted and sometimes illegal..." he mused.

"Poison? Coffee?" Dimiter started guessing wildly.

The clock quickly ticked down to two minutes.

"Bane, hurry, we have two minutes!" I shouted, still searching for one specific wire.

"Hurry? Hurry? If you hadn't messed with that thing in the first place, we wouldn't be in this mess!" my brother shouted back. I didn't respond as I was busy rifling through the tangle of wires.

"What are you doing?" Bane barked up at me.

"I can't find the pink wire!" I announced, panicking.

"Pink wire? Pink wire! This isn't a fucking Rotten Ryan novel!" My twin roared.

The argument escalated quickly. Bane's face turned red with anger as he threw his hands up in frustration. "You're so reckless! Why don't you think anything through?"

Beep.

"Reckless?" I shot back, my voice rising. "At least I'm up here trying to stop this thing! What the hell are you doing? Just standing around and yelling at me!"

Beep.

"Father is going to fucking kill us because of your negligence!" Bane snapped, his tone dripping with self-righteous indignation.

Beep.

"Stop being so completely fucking useless!" I retorted, my fists clenching around several wires as I desperately searched for the right one.

Beep.

The countdown dropped to one minute.

"AGH, I DON'T HAVE TIME FOR THESE GAMES, DO YOU HEAR ME IN THERE?" I pounded on the hatch with my palm. The banging reverberated through the tank, but no other movement could be heard inside. Bane continued shouting at me about how I'd gotten us into this mess.

Beep.

"FINE, HOW ABOUT THIS FOR A PASSWORD?!" I yelled, grabbing a fistful of wires and yanking them out of the clock.

Beep.

Beep.

Be...

The unit froze in my hands with twenty-five seconds left on the countdown. Bane, Dimiter, and I stood frozen, waiting for any indication that the gun on the tank might fire. To my relief, I heard a small clatter as the hatch unlocked next to me. The door lifted up and was pushed to the side.

Out popped the bald head of a fifty-year-old man, his face partially obscured by large steel reflective aviators. He wore a brightly colored tropical shirt and had dog tags hanging around his neck. He was chewing on a toothpick.

"Well, it ain't the password, or the correct way to diffuse a bomb, but I'll take it," the stranger grumbled roughly in my direction.

"Were you testing us?" I asked angrily, narrowing my eyes at him.

"You learn a lot about someone if you put them under pressure," he said, twisting the toothpick in his lips without using his hands. I just stared at him, dumbfounded.

"By the way, I love Rotten Ryan. *Goodbye, Mrs. Doomsdame* is by far the best one," he added when I didn't respond. "Come on in; we've got a bit of a ride ahead of us," the stranger instructed before climbing down into the tank.

We made our way into the cramped interior of the tank, which felt even more confined with the four of us inside. Bane introduced us to the man, who didn't return Bane's handshake but simply stared at it with an untrusting gaze.

"Moniker: Cockroach," was all the stranger offered by way of introduction. I snorted in laughter.

"Are you not going to tell us your real name?" I asked.

"Wouldn't you like to know that information, Diva? Who's paying you to ask? The army? SEALs? KGB?" Cockroach eyed me suspiciously.

"None of those," I said, irritated.

"Why Cockroach then?" my twin asked.

"Some claim I'm a so-called 'doomsday prepper,' but really, I know the war is coming," he said, as if that explained everything.

"What war?" Bane asked.

"THE NUCLEAR WAR, YOU FOOL!" Cockroach shouted at Bane.

"Oh, I get it! Cockroaches are supposed to survive nuclear blasts," Dimiter explained.

"Finally! The smart one of the bunch," the strange man said with a nod of reassurance toward my guard. "Buckle in; it's going to be a bit of a drive," Cockroach instructed before heading to the front of the tank.

"Hey, you weren't really going to shoot our plane, were you?" Bane called after him. Cockroach barely acknowledged the question, responding with a vague grunt. None of us pressed him further.

The three of us took a seat inside the tank and settled in for the ride. An hour passed in silence. My thoughts kept drifting back to my fight with Alexei, no matter how hard I tried to push his harsh words out of my mind. Eventually, restlessness got the better of me, and I called out to the front of the tank.

"Cockroach, how long is this trip going to take?" I asked.

"Oh, about... another four hours, if I had to guess," he called back.

"FOUR HOURS?!" I sputtered loudly.

"Why the hell is it going to take four more hours?!" I yelled, my voice growing louder with frustration.

"Angel!" Bane scolded.

"Why did you make us land so far away?" I demanded, ignoring my brother's presence.

"I can't reveal my exact location. Do you have any idea how much people would pay for that information?!" Cockroach shouted back, as if I were being unreasonable.

My twin stood up and crossed his arms, clearly gearing up to reprimand me. Only when I gave him my full attention did he start his lecture.

"What the hell has gotten into you today? You are never this impatient with clients," Bane chastised.

"We are the clients!" I exclaimed.

"It doesn't matter. Father expects professionalism in this business!" Bane retorted.

"Who the hell do you think you are, lecturing me like this and in front of a 'client'?" I asked him.

"Have you forgotten that *you're* supposed to be shadowing *me*?" Bane's voice rose in frustration.

"Oh really? And how's that going? Because the last time I checked, *I* was the one who secured the contract with the Tithal mob. *I* was the one who sold The Lion four times his original request. *I WAS THE ONLY ONE IN THIS FAMILY WHO GOT BHANTE GAN TO BUY ANYTHING MORE THAN HIS USUAL ORDER*," I retorted, my voice rising to match my twin's pitch.

"Oh yeah? And how exactly did you get 'The Lion' to buy four times his original request? Can you explain that? Because the two of you got really vague about the plan you sold him on, and you seemed uncomfortably close the next day!" Bane began to openly yell at me. I had never seen him so emotional in front of a stranger before.

"What are you accusing me of?" I hissed. My twin didn't respond but glared down at me from where he stood, his lips pressed tight as he loomed over me.

"JUST SAY IT!" I screamed at him.

"I believe he's accusing you of sleeping with this Lion person," Cockroach contributed from the front of the tank. Bane and I didn't say anything but glowered at each other. "Just from what I've gathered from the context of your... little squabble," the vendor added when no one said anything for several minutes.

"And what about Alexei?" Bane threw the accusation at me.

"AND WHAT ABOUT ALEXEI?" I shouted, my voice echoing off the sides of the tank wall.

"Well, from what I thought I saw—" Bane began, but I cut him off.

"What do you think you saw, huh, Bane?" I glared at my brother, indignant.

"WHY WERE YOU IN ONLY HIS SHIRT? Why were you there to start with?" My twin demanded.

"What does it even matter?" I shouted back.

"Do I really need to remind you that Father made a sport of killing the guards you slept with before your little arrangement? What makes you think it would magically be okay to sleep with the staff now?" Bane asked, exasperated.

"AND HAVE ALL OF YOU FORGOTTEN THAT I GET TO PICK WHO I MARRY WITHOUT FATHER'S APPROVAL? That was part of the deal!" I roared.

"Angel, please. We all know that Father would never allow that to happen. He is always going to have the final say in who you marry," Bane dismissed my outburst.

Cockroach piped up from the front of the tank again. "Oh yeah, Zoric's daughter. I've heard of you," he called back.

"How?" I snapped.

"About a year or two ago, your dad was looking to make a deal with me for a special kind of gun he needed. He didn't like my terms of payment—I deal exclusively in NFTs—so he tried to negotiate other things. One of his offerings was your hand in marriage," the vendor explained.

I turned to stare at Bane, making my point. My twin avoided meeting my eyes.

"I get to pick who I want to be with—not you, not Father, not Alexei or Dimiter. Me! That's all I wanted, not to be sold off to be fed to a tiger or to live here in the middle of nowhere with—" My voice began to crack, and I felt a fresh wave of tears threatening to rise.

"You do understand that dating Alexei is a liability for us, right? He's hired to protect you, and if his self-interest in being involved with you overshadowed a critical decision to save any of our lives... it's a conflict of interest. I mean, you have the whole world, Angel. Why him?" Bane asked sincerely.

I took a deep breath to fight back the tears before answering.

"It's not him. I mean, we are not dating. Nothing happened," I lied to my brother.

"Angel." Pain cracked in my twin's voice.

"This is hard, Bane. It's impossible to find someone to date, much less get married in a year. Do you realize what we do? I travel all the time and have two men following me wherever I go! Let's face it—who would want to marry me? Besides us, who else do you know is willing to be sucked into this world?" I looked at my twin with pleading eyes. Bane's breath steadied, then he stepped back slowly and plopped down into one of the seats directly across from me.

"And even then, we were born into it," Bane sighed, looking down at his hands.

"You were born into it; I was unwittingly groomed to be traded off," I murmured. Bane took a heavy breath before responding.

"Of course I know what it's like. Dating, that is. You don't think you're the only one interested in finding a partner, do you?" My twin confessed quietly. Bane's statement caused me to stall, and I felt a sliver of my anger start to evaporate. He looked so sad as he studied his hands.

"Bane, I thought, I mean, since you moved out of the house so quickly... Well, I thought you were looking for privacy to..." I bumbled along, trying to find the right words.

"Sure, sure. I mean, at first it was fun—finding someone new and easy for a night or two. Having money sure does help with getting laid. It's just that lately, I've been wanting something more. Someone to connect with... long-term. This life can get awfully lonely with the travel, and it's not like I have anyone to talk to about... stuff," my brother admitted, glancing up at me with sorrowful eyes. As a small tear escaped, I moved to sit next to my twin. He quickly wiped away the wetness with the palm of his hand in shame.

"I've tried speed dating, parties, menageries—nothing seems to stick.

I only have a few more months left," I said softly. Bane grabbed my hand, our fingers entwined, and he sniffled slightly.

"You said a little while ago that I was stuck in Father's shadow," Bane chuckled dryly. "He's told me he wants me to take over the business, and I feel like I am stuck trying to figure out how I can contribute to it. And then, of course, you come in—super charismatic. You know what you want, and you just go for it and get it. Sure, I can manage to contact the mafia, but if you weren't with me, Toni never would have listened to anything past 'Hi, I'm Bane Zoric and I want to sell you some guns.' I'm just... still figuring out who I am and where I fit into everything too," Bane confided.

"These last several months, though, with you along for the ride, have been the best months of this job for me. I feel a lot less lonely, like someone else in the world understands... Father and Father's wrath. Someone to share the small moments of insanity and the demands of gun running. I really feel like we could build a vision together and take this someplace as partners." Bane squeezed my hand, and my cold heart melted hearing him say this.

"I also felt like we were getting closer again too, like when we were kids," Bane added, looking down at our entwined fingers.

"I know you're not dumb enough to sleep with The Lion. I just felt... betrayed. I want to trust my business partner, and I thought we had each other's backs. Then I discover you might be keeping secrets from me, and Alexei and Dimiter might be in on it," my twin continued sorrowfully, gesturing toward my guard as he mentioned him. Dimiter was sitting casually, being very quiet as Bane and I talked.

"I'm sorry," I whispered, squeezing his hand. "I am not trying to keep secrets from you," I added.

"I know. I know. Just please understand that, at the end of the day, I do care about my little sister and want her to be safe. I hate to see you cry. It makes me feel like I failed to protect you," Bane said, meeting my eyes with a sad smile on his lips.

"We're twins, Bane. I'm not your little sister," I chuckled. Bane's smile became more genuine. He let go of my hand and draped his arm around my shoulder, pulling me closer to him.

"I know," he whispered, kissing me tenderly on the forehead before loosening his grip. His arm remained protectively around me. No one said anything else for a long time. Finally, our vendor broke the silence.

"You two done fighting? Not that I don't like to hear what sounds like fun family drama, but your yelling is distracting," Cockroach called back to us, his tone surprisingly void of any sarcasm.

"I think they are done fighting now, Cockroach," Dimiter called up to the front. He sat across from us, smiling at Bane and me with a look of approval, like a proud father.

"Good," Cockroach muttered toward the front. Bane and I giggled together.

A loud clank hit the top of the tank, followed by several smaller ones. Our driver didn't acknowledge the noise or seem to care; he simply continued driving.

"What's making that noise?" I eventually asked, growing concerned as the sounds persisted.

"Oh, that? It's just the local Yowie. He doesn't like the tank, so he throws stuff at it whenever he sees it. Pay no attention to it," he called back, still painfully focused on the nonexistent road ahead.

Dimiter, Bane, and I exchanged glances. It was clear we were all thinking the same thing.

Who was this guy Father sent us to deal with?

4 Months

CHAPTER THIRTY

As promised, we finally arrived four hours later. This wasn't announced to us in any formal way; Cockroach simply stopped the tank and got out.

"Were we supposed to follow him?" I asked when he did not return.

"Are you kids coming or not?" he answered from the hatch door.

We all climbed out as the sun was setting. The drive in the tank had taken most of the day, and it was much cooler now, starting to get cold.

I looked around and found that, despite traveling quite a distance, the landscape remained the same. It was flat, bathed in the orange glow of the setting sun, with dead foliage scattered about. In the middle of the barren desert stood the smallest red brick building I had ever seen, with a white, unmarked door.

Cockroach approached the building, and we followed. He turned on a single external light that buzzed with life.

"What is this place?" I asked.

"You sure do ask a lot of questions for someone claiming not to sell information to any government agencies," was the only answer I got from the vendor. He opened the door and ushered us onto a small lift that occupied the entire building. Once we were all on, Cockroach pressed a huge red button, and the lift started to move, though shakily, downward.

The ride down lasted a full, long minute. When we disembarked, it was into a dimly lit room that felt surprisingly spacious. To one side was an uncomfortable-looking bed that seemed to be painstakingly made every morning. Beside the mattress was a corkboard with a large map pinned to it. Various pins and different-colored yarn littered the map, while several newspaper clippings in different languages surrounded it.

To the other side was an older computer with a vintage radio next to it. Everything felt dusty, but it was clear that the area was carefully cleaned on a rotating basis.

"What is 'cannot-smoke-the-roach-dot-com'?" I asked, noticing the name on a document near the computer.

"It's my vlog," Cockroach replied. "It's how I communicate with my fellow roach nests. I share survival tips, signs of the impending war, and other important updates. I have a good following and host several forums to foster discussions on topics like saving more people, preparing for nuclear winter, and post-doomsday government planning." He then pulled a newspaper clipping from his pocket and walked over to pin it on his board.

"Occasionally, I have some anti-drug people find me because of the name. Apparently, there's noise about a new drug empire ruthlessly taking out its competition—some Daddy Death asshole making his way up the ranks. It can get annoying when they hijack a forum with their straight-edge talk, but then again, any traffic is good traffic. It's important to get information about the coming war out there so people can prepare.

"It's actually how your father found me. He has some strong opinions on drug trafficking for someone whose business is arms dealing," Cockroach continued as he moved over to a large security panel on the wall next to his bed. He started pressing a series of buttons.

"I'd love to see what Emilio was trying to search that landed him on your site," Dimiter chuckled to himself. Bane stifled a laugh as well. Cockroach paid no mind to the two men as he began flipping a row of light switches above the security panel.

Several dingy overhead lights illuminated the largest underground bunker I had ever seen. Shelves lined the walls, stocked with every kind of preserved food imaginable. A large section was dedicated to first aid supplies and water.

Handy benches and tables were scattered about, each with projects half-abandoned. Tool and wiring kits were laid out neatly next to them, ready to be picked up again. Across the massive layout from us was a door leading to another section of the bunker.

"What is this place?" Bane asked, his eyes widening.

"That's my business," Cockroach muttered.

"What is your business?" I pressed, gawking at the room.

"Arms and secrets, woman. Thought you would have figured it out by now. Cannot smoke the roach because I'm wanted in a dozen countries!" Cockroach exclaimed, pointing a finger at his head to indicate that I should think. He walked over to the other door, opened it, and urged us to follow him.

Walking through the door triggered the next set of lights to turn on automatically. We found ourselves in a long hallway stretching far into the distance. Hanging along the walls, and illuminated as if on display, were rare guns from every country in the world. Bane and I stared openly in wonder at the sight.

Cockroach continued walking down the hall, seemingly indifferent to the display. He only stopped when he noticed we were not following him. Bane and I were ogling the rare finds, stopping to point out different firearms as we tried—and failed—to keep up with our leader.

"Come on, kids! We don't have all night, and this hallway is long!" Cockroach yelled down to us. Bane and I rushed to where the vendor was standing, and he stalked off down the hallway again.

Our group went through another door, which led to a large room similar to the first. As we entered, the lights switched on automatically, revealing shelves lining the walls. This time, instead of food and supplies, the shelves were filled with an extensive collection of firearms and their corresponding ammunition. Each was meticulously categorized by country, make, model, size, and type.

"Your father sent me a list and the NTFs already. I have the boxes here, but we need to pack them," Cockroach explained as he walked into the middle of the room where a small table stood with a couple of lists on it. Six large steel boxes stood open next to it, ready to be packed.

"Seriously, what is this place?" Bane asked again, looking over the shelves of goods.

"You kids ever hear of the Cold War?" Cockroach asked.

"Of course," I responded.

"Well, it's a lie! They sold the public this idea of two world powers in great technological tension. People ate it up and got behind the vision. All that money went into outdoing each other's technology, but they never told you the real reason. It was a joint agreement so we could advance quickly. The two great world powers knew a war was coming!" Cockroach told this story with such conviction that it was as if he truly believed it.

"Yeah, the nuclear war," Dimiter said matter-of-factly.

"No, you fool! The alien war!" Cockroach snapped at my guard.

We all just stared at him, dumbfounded.

"We had been contacted! They were going to attack! We fought to get to the moon, and guess what? We put a defense system up there too!" Cockroach lectured us as if we were all grossly uneducated. Bane, Dimiter, and I were at a loss for words.

"Northern Mineva might have landed on the moon and done the work, but they also claimed it. Sold it back in the '90s to Ximon, though. Damned outsourcing of work," he added when none of us responded.

"Sorry, what?" I asked.

"They have to maintain the technology up there," he said, as if that was the only explanation needed.

"So, you're saying there are people on the moon, right now, maintaining a collaborative defense system put in place during the Cold War?" Bane asked slowly. Cockroach nodded in response.

"What does that have to do with this bunker again?" Bane asked.

"Right! This bunker was an abandoned underground secret base where they conducted experiments during that time. I got it for cheap as a favor from the army for my involvement in MK ULTRA," Cockroach explained.

"The drug experiments in the '50s and '60s?" Dimiter asked, scrutinizing the vendor, trying to gauge his age.

"They told you it was just the '50s and '60s, but they only got better at covering it up." At the end of this explanation, he began to handle some of the guns with a strange tenderness.

Bane, Dimiter, and I moved over to the list and reviewed it, then began helping Cockroach pack the boxes. The process was long and laborious, with little conversation. Occasionally, Cockroach would stop one of us for "doing something wrong" and launch into a lengthy explanation about why we were all fools. I began to wonder why my father hadn't worked with him before, as they seemed like they would get along swimmingly.

Hours passed, and we had finished about half the boxes before Cockroach allowed us to take a small break.

"Think you could spare a couple of those water bottles from the supply room?" Bane asked as we sat, worn out. Cockroach looked us over a few times before rolling his eyes and conceding.

"Do you have Fleuve de Vie?" I asked, figuring it couldn't hurt to ask.

"Do I have what?" Cockroach looked at me in disgust. Bane nudged me hard in the side.

"Don't worry about her, just give us whatever you have," my twin said before I could say anything else. Cockroach grunted and then grabbed Dimiter to help him carry water back.

My guard handed me the water bottle with an amused look on his face. His eyes flickered between me and the bottle he was extending, pressing me to look at the label. I followed his gaze.

"Moon Water," the bottle read. I stifled a giggle, which almost made Dimiter lose himself to laughter as well. He sat next to me, and we smiled at each other as Bane glared at us for acting like fools.

"So, Cockroach," Dimiter began casually.

"Yes?" the man replied, eyeing my guard, clearly not in the mood for conversation.

"How do you feel about... I mean, is the earth..." Dimiter struggled to get the words out and instead mimed a flat line in the air.

"Oh no, you don't!" Cockroach yelled.

"Don't what?" Bane asked.

"He thinks I'm one of those nutjob conspiracy theorists who claim the earth is flat!" Cockroach threw the accusation at Dimiter, who smiled wickedly into his water before sipping.

"Wait, the earth isn't flat?" I asked as sincerely as possible. Cockroach turned to me with a flash of hatred in his eyes.

"You seemed smarter than that, young missy. But just in case, no! How else would they explain the tunnels?" he said matter-of-factly. Bane choked on the sip of water he was taking.

"Sorry, what tunnels?" Bane asked hoarsely after recovering. Cockroach looked pointedly at each of us for a minute before answering.

"The tunnels to the hollowed-out core of the earth, where all the old alien technology is hiding. It's why they came back in the '60s and why we had to build a defense system. They wanted their technology," Cockroach explained this carefully, then waited for a response.

"Wait, if we have their technology, why did we have to build up our own?" I asked. Cockroach sighed in an exaggerated manner.

"Because it didn't integrate with our technology back then! We studied it and used that knowledge for our own good. I'm pretty sure this bunker was an abandoned attempt to connect to one of those tunnels, you know, so they could bring up the instruments and tear them apart. Just can't seem to find the connection yet," he admitted. None of us said anything for a long time.

"I think I learned a lot today," I offered.

"Good. It'll do you good to become a free thinker," the vendor said, cheering his water bottle in my direction before gulping down the rest. "Now come on, we've got the rest of the boxes to pack," he insisted, prompting all of us to groan in unison.

"Just a few more minutes? Please?" I asked.

Cockroach ignored my request and went to work. Dimiter and Bane followed shortly after, and I joined in, though begrudgingly.

The rest of the packing took less time than the first half, as we all got into a groove while moving around the bunker. By the end, we had six full boxes ready for The Lion. I smiled in satisfaction at our work.

"There's a cargo elevator down a bit. You three start moving these boxes down that hallway, and I'll go refuel the tank," Cockroach explained, pointing at a larger door across from the one we had entered.

"Wait, what?" I asked, startled.

"What?" Cockroach asked back.

"We're taking the tank back? No way. There has to be a faster way!" I stared at the vendor indignantly.

"It's all I have, my tank," Cockroach shrugged.

"My sister does have a point—where are we going to store all of this?" Bane asked, looking at the six large boxes.

"My baby has the best towing capacity," Cockroach said simply before slipping out of the room.

"UGH, no, Bane!" I yelled in frustration at my brother.

"I don't know what to tell you, Angel," he shrugged, continuing to figure out the best way to move the boxes.

"Bane, with towing a whole other vehicle and all this crap, it's going to take even longer to get back!" I followed him around the room as he coordinated with Dimiter on moving the loaded guns.

"Look, just stay over there. Dimiter and I got this," Bane instructed me as he worked on opening the large door leading to the cargo elevator.

They moved the boxes silently, and every time I tried to help, both men would yell at me. I eventually gave up and sat to the side, watching my guard carefully. His muscles rippled with each movement, turning me on. I felt guilty for being upset over Alexei with Dimiter right in front of me. My tall, handsome blond guard seemed to care about me just as much, if not more. He never yelled at me or called me selfish. If anything, he's always been supportive and encouraging, whether it's about gun running or dating, pushing me to go for what I want.

Dimiter doesn't seem to think his life is in danger by being with me. Does that make him brave or just more reckless? Would my father actually shoot them? I wondered.

"Let's go," Bane interrupted my thoughts. They had just moved the last box out of the room and into the elevator. He closed the door behind us, and we rode up together.

When we reached the surface, we found ourselves in a warehouse, far larger than the small one-room red brick building we had entered to access the bunker. Dimiter and Cockroach had already loaded the other five boxes onto a large towing trailer connected to the tank.

"What if the Yowie sees us? Will he leave the cargo alone?" I asked.

"Oh, don't fret about the Yowie. The sun will rise in an hour, so he'll be closer to the city. There's a higher chance he can catch something to feed on over there," Cockroach dismissed my concern as he and Bane loaded the last box into the trailer.

We all climbed back into the tank, and I felt exhaustion fall over me. The ride back was quiet for the longest time. Dimiter had passed out immediately, snoring softly. Bane sat right next to me, and I felt the weight of his head on my shoulder occasionally, my brother trying his hardest to fight sleep. I spent the remaining five hours, silent and watching my man and my twin sleep. A small, fractured sense of hope washed over me, a tentative reassurance that maybe things would work out. I whispered to myself reassuringly, "I'm going to be fine."

4 Months

CHAPTER THIRTY-ONE

I was jolted awake by the plane touching down on our private runway at home. Bane and I had decided to stay in the cabin with Dimiter for a while on the flight back. We had planned to discuss the strange theories Cockroach had shared with us, but we ended up falling asleep in our seats. I got up and stretched, feeling stiff from sleeping in the leather chairs. They were comfortable, but not as cozy as a bed.

"When are we taking this shipment to Cliuz Plyae?" I asked, yawning.

"Mmmm?" Bane mumbled, also stretching. "Eager to see your boyfriend?" he teased. I smiled but didn't respond.

As we headed towards the front of the plane, the door opened and

Father bustled in, followed by a reluctant Alexei.

"Did you get the guns?" Father asked.

"Yes, they're loaded below," Bane replied flatly, glaring at Alexei standing behind Father.

"Excellent. Let's prepare for takeoff," Father said, then walked past us and settled comfortably at the table Bane and I preferred during our flights.

"Where?" I asked, following my father to the back of the plane. Dimiter stepped between Alexei and me as soon as I passed him. Alexei seemed to have made a conscious decision to remain at the front of the plane.

"To *The Lion*," Father chuckled to himself after saying Vasco's name out loud.

"Right now?" Bane asked, exasperated, joining me as I stood next to the table.

"Yes, right now. He's reported some issues with freedom fighters and has offered to pay us a ridiculous amount of money to rush this shipment to him," Father stated, casually pulling out a newspaper and opening it.

"And you're coming with us?" I asked, noticing the plane beginning to move for takeoff.

"Yes. I want to meet this man. He seems like quite the character. He also had plenty of nice things to say about you, Sophia," Father said, looking over his newspaper at me. Sophia, not Angel. Bane and I exchanged a glance.

"Are the four of you going to settle down so we can leave, or am I missing something?" Father asked curtly. Bane and I quickly sat down next to him.

I noticed Alexei chose to sit as far away as possible, taking one of the front seats of the plane, shifting uncomfortably. He kept looking at me, almost openly staring with a mix of anger and concern. Dimiter sat closer, positioning himself between Alexei and me. His demeanor was much sterner than usual, shooting death glares at Alexei but smiling softly whenever he caught my eye.

As we took off, the atmosphere grew quiet, thick with discomfort that seemed to smother us all. The silence became almost unbearable, making the cabin feel impossibly small. The weight of every moment lingered, charging the atmosphere with crackling tension.

Bane found the unease too much to bear and decided to busy himself. He jumped up anxiously and made his way to the fancy cappuccino machine we kept behind the bar.

Acting as if everything was normal, he hummed to himself while making drinks. A few minutes later, he bustled over with two cups of coffee, setting them down in front of Father and me. Then he returned to the machine to make his own cup. Reluctantly, he sat down next to me, clearly hoping to have killed more time.

We all sat in silence. I sipped at the coffee Bane had made, barely tasting it. Eventually, Father looked up from his paper, surveying the airplane cabin.

"You're all so quiet," Father observed, folding up his paper and tossing it aside. "What's wrong?" he asked pointedly. Bane shifted uncomfortably in his seat as Father took a sip of his coffee.

"We're all just tired," I said wearily, and Bane nodded beside me.

"How was that doomsday man?" Father asked.

"Strange," Bane replied thoughtfully.

"Did you really pay him in NTFs?" I asked, recalling the vendor's comment.

"Yes," Father responded curtly.

"How?" I pressed. Father looked at me sternly.

"It's a good thing we have an art aficionado as a client. Adonis seemed more than happy to help us out. He's been looking to get into NTFs himself, so we collaborated," Father explained.

"You collaborated with Adonis?" Bane was pointing at Father, conveying our combined surprise.

"Yes," Father confirmed, as if the question was absurd.

"How was he?" I asked.

"Throwing a desk out of a window over a woman," Father replied with an air of finality. My mouth gaped open, but my father waved his hand as if to indicate he would no longer entertain questions about Adonis.

No one said anything else for several minutes. Bane, Dimiter, and I were visibly exhausted. Alexei's presence was making the men uneasy, putting them on edge. My father's eyes swept over the plane several times, taking his time to scrutinize each member of the party, as if expecting one of us to break and confess to some unknown sin.

"Seriously, you're all so quiet," Father said again, looking between Bane and me.

"As I said, we're drained. We had quite the journey," I repeated. Father looked over both Bane and me, carefully inspecting us. I held his gaze, but Bane couldn't stay still under our father's intense survey.

"Fine," Father finally said. "Tired. Why don't you go to the back to your private bedroom and get some sleep, Angel?" he suggested.

"Yes, Father," I replied, relieved to have an excuse to escape. I got up and walked toward the back to my bedroom.

"Oh yes, I almost forgot. Angel?" I paused, hearing my father's voice again, then turned to face him.

"Speaking of rest, make sure you rest well in the next several weeks. I've set up a couple of meetings to help you find a husband in your last few months. Bane will take you shopping once we get back to prepare you for your new social calendar. I think it's time you meet someone of your own ...caliber," he finished, taking a sip of his coffee and locking eyes with me as he said the word "caliber."

"How does that sound?" Father asked after a brief pause. I looked around at the other men in the cabin. Each one actively avoided my gaze and sat very still.

"I think it sounds wonderful," I finally managed to say, trying to inject some excitement into my voice as I stared at Bane. My brother looked up at me and relaxed into a warm smile at my response, which I returned.

"Good," Father said shortly, almost as if he were disappointed by how agreeable I was being.

While feeling a weight of anxiety growing in the pit of my stomach, I headed back to the bedroom, aware of all the men's eyes on me as I walked.

This time, I was woken by my father telling me we had arrived. I moved slowly out of bed and realized that I felt surprisingly good. It was the first time I had felt so spirited since Alexei ended things. Excitement tingled in me at the prospect of seeing The Lion again. I made my way to the cabin of the plane and saw that everyone else was already standing and ready to depart.

The cabin door flew open, and a tall man stormed in, a gun dangling prominently from a tactical vest.

The instant he crossed the threshold, a series of metallic clicks echoed through the plane as each man swiftly drew and cocked their concealed handguns. Their eyes narrowed with instinctive readiness, all firearms trained on the intruder.

The man immediately raised his hands and froze.

"The Panther sent me!" he exclaimed, a slight tremor in his voice.

"Why did you think it was a good idea to charge in here with a gun out in the open like that, son?" my father asked, annoyance evident but keeping the man in his sights.

"Sorry, it's just that we've heard some activity to the east, and I was sent to protect the woman," the man explained, his hand shaking slightly as he pointed a trembling finger at me. All eyes turned toward me. Alexei and Bane wore expressions of mild annoyance, my father looked at me with confusion, and Dimiter sported a cheeky grin.

"Fine," my father finally said, lowering his gun and putting it back into its concealed location. The rest of the men on the plane followed suit. I moved past everyone toward the front.

Alexei was already standing halfway into the aisle. As I passed him, I shoved him roughly, hitting his shoulder with mine on my way to reach the armed stranger.

"Show me the way to my client," I said with a smile.

We descended the plane stairs and gathered in a group at the bottom.

"The house is just this way," the tall man said, pointing toward a patch of trees. "I've instructed the men here to unload the merchandise while you talk to—" The sound of distant gunfire cut him off.

Everyone ducked at the noise. The man spun toward a group of soldiers, barking orders in his native tongue and pointing in the direction of the shots.

"Sorry about that. The Azteca Kings will handle it. Just a few pests left to squeeze out," he explained. "It's perfectly safe, though; the Panther will make sure nothing happens to you while you're here."

He paused, inspecting each of us to ensure we were unhurt. Satisfied, he nodded and added, "Let's go."

The stranger moved into the trees, both hands on his gun. I exchanged a quick glance with Bane before we followed him, the rest of the party trailing behind us. The Lion stood at the door of the house, his gaze fixed on the trees where the gunshots had come from moments earlier.

He was wearing a pair of ripped jeans, hanging low to reveal his cuts, and no shirt. A tan straw cowboy hat sat atop his head, and a pair of aviators obscured his eyes. With his hands on his hips and a frown on his face, he seemed oblivious to our approach as he studied the underbrush from which the gunfire had originated.

Someone stepped on a twig, snapping it, and finally, Vasco's head shot in our direction.

"Mi Reina!" he exclaimed, jumping down the porch stairs. As soon as he reached the bottom, he ran over and picked me up in a hug. I melted in his arms once more.

"Mi Corazón," I corrected him softly in his ear, a giggle escaping. He held me for a long time before finally letting me go, keeping one arm casually wrapped around my shoulders.

The Lion dragged me forward with him as he approached my father. Extending his free hand, he introduced himself confidently, "I am The Panther, el presidente of this area, and a big fan of your guns and family." The Panther flirted his eyebrows at the last part, his gaze lingering on me with a smoldering intensity.

My father's expression darkened as he took in the sight of the arm draped possessively around me. His eyes, filled with irritation, locked onto mine as the sides of his face began to tint a deep red. He remained silent, his jaw clenched, clearly displeased with how quickly this man had become so familiar with his precious daughter.

A discomfort settled over the group as my father stood there, grappling with the casual audacity of the man.

"I've heard the great Zoric was always introverted, but I didn't expect this," The Panther teased with a smirk. He waved his hand in front of my father, who glared back, his face flushed a deep red with rage.

"Oh yes!" The Panther snapped his fingers with dramatic flair. "I know what language you speak. Allow me." With a fluid motion, he removed his arm from around me and reached into his back pocket, producing a thick wad of cash. The cash was rolled tightly, and as The Panther tossed it to my father, the tension in the air shifted breathtakingly fast. My father's eyes widened with excitement, and an unconditional acceptance softened his expression as he took the money. Suddenly, my father seemed much more at ease with the shirtless man's presence. The Panther, unfazed, slid his arm back around me with a satisfied grin.

"Nice to meet you, Panther," my father said, flipping through the bills. "Where is this Lion person I have heard so much about, though?" he asked.

"Lion?" The Panther said, shaking his head in confusion. "I don't know anyone named The Lion. Do you know anyone by that name?" The Panther looked down at me. I shook my head no.

"I see we've moved on to cat-themed nicknames," Bane snorted at his own joke. The Panther regarded my brother with an expressionless stare.

"I don't know what you mean. You see, I got my nickname because I got in a fight with a panther," Vasco began.

"And you won, which is how you got your scars," Bane finished for him.

"Ah, so you've been paying attention. Good. Seems a shame you keep forgetting my name then," The Panther said with a wily smile at my brother before turning his attention back to my father. "Come on, there's more cash for you in the house."

Still dragging me under his arm, Vasco turned, and we moved up and into the house together.

The inside of the glass mansion had started to look as if fifty men lived in it. The large table, which I remembered being more extravagant, now had writing etched into all its surfaces. It appeared to have been recently cleaned, though, as it was the only surface without clutter.

The Panther insisted everyone sit down around the table, including Dimiter and Alexei. He guided me to a seat next to him, positioning himself to the right of the seat of honor. His gesture clearly signaled to my father that this place of prominence was his. Bane quickly moved to sit on the other side of me, and my father seemed pleased as he settled into his chair at the head of the table. Dimiter and Alexei shifted uncomfortably, trying to figure out where to sit, before finally settling across from Vasco and me.

Men everywhere had started to bustle the moment The Panther walked in, and drinks were set in front of us immediately. Each drink was the same frozen cocktail, but adorned with different colored straws and a cute little umbrella on top.

"What is this?" my father boasted, looking down at his drink.

"Something to cool us down. It is hot outside, no?" Vasco asked, moving his drink closer to himself and taking a sip from the looped crazy straw.

I looked down at the drink placed in front of me and started to pull it closer.

"Wait!" The Panther stopped me. "This is not what I asked for!" he yelled as he picked up my drink and stood up. "I said the fucking heart one! What is this? You insult me like this in front of Mi Corazón?" he chastised the two men who had served the drinks. They stared at him, petrified, and said nothing. After several tense moments, The Panther began to laugh—a cheerful, light laugh. His laughter grew, and his men started to look at each other in confusion.

"I'm just kidding. I got you; you were so scared," Vasco said, amused. Both Azteca Kings relaxed, with one starting to laugh along with The Panther.

"Sorry, sir, just a misunderstanding," the laughing man said with an uncertain, tight smile.

"A misunderstanding, of course. I won't kill you over a crazy straw," Vasco said, still amused.

The man reached out for the drink still in The Panther's hand, but The Panther threw it across the room with force. The drink smacked into one of the large glass windows, shattering into pieces, with the frozen concoction dripping down slowly.

"FIX IT," he demanded, a demented look replacing his cheerful demeanor.

Every one of The Panther's men went very stiff before springing into action, rushing in different directions.

It was only a matter of seconds before a new cocktail was placed in front of me. A pink crazy straw, shaped like a heart, stuck out from the glass, and it was decorated with a matching pink umbrella. I smiled at The Panther, who seemed pleased to see me happy.

My father, having witnessed the entire interaction, chose not to press the issue about his own drink but didn't bother drinking it either.

As we sipped our cocktails, the conversation flowed more freely. The Panther leaned forward, his eyes bright with enthusiasm as he recounted a harrowing tale from his recent ventures.

My father listened intently, nodding in agreement as The Panther said, "Being in charge isn't always as glamorous as it seems. The real challenge is keeping everyone in line. I've had to kill five of my own men this very week!"

"It is a challenge," my father replied. "People are so hard-headed. You lay down the law, but it's like they forget. You'll probably have to remind seven more by the end of this week, with their own demise."

I stared in disbelief at their growing bond as their voices mingled, exchanging stories and strategies about maintaining tight control. Each man's face lit up with a shared understanding of the burdens they bore.

I glanced over at Bane, who was staring down at his drink with a frown. His straw, yellow and looped in a circle, had a small plastic banana perched at the top. Alexei was also eyeing his cocktail with evident distaste, not even bothering to take a sip.

Dimiter, however, was the only one to finish his frozen drink and promptly asked for another. His second cocktail arrived with a straw adorned with a small plastic penis, and Dimiter smiled gleefully. He then locked eyes with me and winked as he eagerly started on his second drink.

"Ugh," my twin groaned beside me. I turned to see him staring at his drink, his face contorted in a mix of disgust and annoyance.

"What's wrong?" I asked my brother in a low tone.

"It's ♬ _banana-flavored_," ♬ Bane whispered back.

I couldn't help but burst into laughter, drawing the attention of the rest of the men.

"What is it, Mi Amor?" The Panther slid his arm around me once more, pulling me close.

"Nothing, it's just that you have quite the sense of humor," I said between fits of laughter.

"Yes, of course," Vasco said, kissing me on the cheek before removing his arm to reengage in conversation with my father. I flushed from the alcohol and his affection, but Father did not seem to mind.

The Panther then began shouting into the house in his native language. At the end, he added, "And bring this man a real drink! You insult him with this crap!" while pointing to the cocktail in front of my father.

In a flash, a briefcase and a glass of brown liquid appeared before my father. He took a big swig from the glass, glad to finally have a 'proper drink,' and popped open the case. Then he began to mentally count the stacks of money inside.

"Looks to all be there," my father confirmed, then closed the briefcase and hid it under the table.

"Of course, the Panther lives up to his word," Vasco smiled at my father. "Hey, you know, for rushing this order, I think I can offer you a little extra," The Panther added after a sip of his cool drink. My father studied the warlord, untrusting.

"You already gave us extra," Father said.

"Yeah, but we found these things on the property, and I don't know what to do with them. You want a goat?" Vasco asked. Father considered the question for a moment.

"What kind of goat?" Father finally asked.

"Just a goat."

"Is it worth anything?" Father pressed.

"Absolutely nothing," Vasco said with enthusiasm. He allowed Father to finish the brown liquid in his glass before adding, "but we named it Angel."

Father raised his empty glass in the air, expecting someone to rush over and refill it. The Azteca King server glanced at The Panther with his question. Vasco gave a barely noticeable nod, and Father's drink was quickly refilled. With a new glass in front of him, Father finally responded.

"Yeah, I'll take a goat."

Vasco stood up immediately and pointed to two of his goons across the room.

"Get this man his goat," he ordered, and the two men ran from the house. Moments later, they returned, an animal in tow by a rope.

The goat was small, covered in a luxurious black coat with striking blue eyes. It bleated at my father as he was handed the rope.

"Oh, my. Angel, it looks just like you!" Father cooed at his new pet in a way I had never seen before. I gawked at my father as he whispered affectionately to the little animal.

"You won't leave me and rip out all of my technology to make sure you're protected, will you, little guy? I'll let you stay in the front yard and munch on those damned flowers my wife planted years ago that the gardener refuses to tear out," Father murmured in a high-pitched baby voice. I went rigid at the mention of my recent clash with his surveillance technology. Thankfully, The Panther swiftly whisked my father into another conversation about money and power.

As the afternoon wore on, it became clear to everyone that The Panther and my father were growing closer. Laughter frequently erupted from their corner of the table, punctuated by clinks of glasses as they toasted each other's audacity. With each drink, my father's stories grew more animated, his hands gesticulating wildly as he recounted his tales of daring and ruthlessness.

The Panther leaned in, his laughter rich and deep, clearly savoring every word. Occasionally, he would place a reassuring hand on my father's shoulder, as if sharing a private joke that only they understood. My father's speech grew more slurred, his eyes glazing over with the warmth of alcohol. Then, with a heavy sigh and a sentimental slur, he raised his glass and said, "But you know, my daughter, she's always impressed me with her tenacity."

I stared at my father in shock; I had never heard this before.

"Has she ever told you how many men she killed just to be here with us?" he slurred, his eyes gleaming with joy as he pointed at me with his drink. A wave of heat flushed my cheeks, ignited by the fierce pride in his voice.

"Oh, don't turn red now, dear daughter. I was proud of what you did. It showed me you'd do anything for our family business," he said, his smile broadening as he looked at me with burning admiration.

He reached for another sip of his drink and found it empty. Snapping his fingers at the nearest man, he commanded, "Fill this up again." The man hurried over, eager to comply, while my father's gaze remained fixed on me, radiating a fierce, possessive glint.

"This man right here is exactly who I always imagined you would end up with. This is a great man for you, sweetie," he said, pointing to The Panther. The Panther looked at my father with a pleased smile.

Suddenly, Bane jumped up from the table and tried to grab the drink away from my father's hand. "I think that's enough drinking," he instructed. Father slapped my brother's hand and pushed him away.

"Angel, this man knows true power. He knows how to keep these men in line. He is willing to do whatever it takes. Just like you, baby girl," my father slurred in my direction. "And he is very clearly taken by you and wants to keep you happy." He looked at me with sincere eyes.

"This man can keep you happy," my father enunciated each word as he pointed to The Panther, his eyes boring into Alexei. I turned to look at my guard, who remained silent and still. His head was hung in shame, and he was taking deep breaths, struggling to keep his composure.

"Alexei?" I uttered softly. My guard did nothing to acknowledge he even heard me.

"I forgot to mention, you got a marriage proposal this week, darling," my father chuckled into his drink. "But don't worry, I turned him down for you. No need to be dragged into poverty."

The words hit Alexei like a slap. His face darkened, and with a surge of anger, he stood abruptly and stormed out the front door. I rose to follow him, but Bane caught my arm. Then The Panther's hand shot out and seized my brother's arm in a vice-like grip. Vasco's eyes pinned my twin with a fiery glare.

"Let her go," The Panther said dangerously. My brother released me, and I ran out the front door.

As I left, I overheard the Panther telling my father, "Poor girl feels sorry for him."

I found Alexei on the porch, staring out into the small clearing in front of the house.

"Alexei, what did you do?" I reached out to touch his arm, hoping he would finally look at me.

He didn't respond to my touch, so I moved to stand in front of him and gently pulled his face down to meet mine. He grabbed my wrists, holding them firmly, while his gaze remained fixed over my shoulder.

"Alexei," I pleaded, my voice trembling as tears began to well up in my eyes, "you didn't have to go to my father. You could have talked to me directly. We could have given 'us' a real try. It's not about the money for me—I can earn my own. Look, I'm working now. Can't you see that I've wanted to try and make 'us' work since the beginning?" My voice cracked as tears fell. I tried desperately to meet his gaze.

Alexei did not respond, his grip on my wrists remaining firm and unyielding as he held my arms to my sides.

"I'm not sure about marriage just yet, but we can figure it out," I continued, my voice steadying as I spoke. "Let's try a real relationship first. Why didn't you tell me how you felt or that you were planning to ask my father for my hand?" I asked, my eyes searching his face. Alexei remained unmoving and impassive.

"Alexei, do you hear me?" I urged, my voice rising with desperation. "Alexei! Do you want me to say it? Do you want me to tell you that I love you? Is that what you need to hear, that I love you? I don't know for sure, but maybe I've fallen in love with you. I keep coming back to you—doesn't that mean something? If we just tried a relationship, don't you think we'd get there? I'm sorry. I'm sorry if I've hurt you, but please, just talk to me." I found myself rambling, my words tumbling out in a flood of emotion.

"Alexei, did you hear me?" I cried out, desperation washing over me.

"I did," Alexei responded tightly, "but I don't think it matters anymore, Angel."

Tears streamed harder down my cheeks, my breaths coming in ragged gasps.

"Why, Alexei? Is it because of Dimiter?" I choked out, panic gripping my chest.

"No, it's because we're in danger," he replied, his voice stiff, his face a mask of stoicism.

"Because of my father?" I scoffed, my heart pounding as I desperately sought his gaze.

"No. Because of them," he said, his eyes darting toward the front lawn.

I whirled around to look.

In front of us stood rigid rows of militia men, their eyes cold and unyielding. One stepped forward, his voice cutting through the air with chilling authority. "We are here for the Lion. Surrender him to us, and we will spare you."

4 Months

BANANA

BANE'S GUNRUNNING BUSINESS RULE NUMBER SEVEN:

Know your product.

Real pros know their products inside and out.

CHAPTER THIRTY-TWO

"It's The Panther," Alexei and I exclaimed in unison. Alexei wrapped his arms around me protectively as I turned to face the men in the yard.

"What?" the man who stepped forward asked.

"His name isn't The Lion; it's The Panther," I clarified.

The front door was suddenly kicked open, and The Panther emerged from the house, casually holding his frozen drink.

"Hello, boys," he greeted the militia men with a nonchalant tone. Then he took a sip from the drink's crazy straw and looked at the man in front of him with a satisfied smirk.

The front man stepped closer and shouted with more conviction as he focused on his target.

"Vasco! Vasco 'The Li—The Panther' Zavala, we are here to arrest-" he stumbled mid-sentence, watching as The Panther waved his finger in the air.

"No, no," The Panther corrected, "It's The Bear."

The militia man blinked rapidly in irritation.

"Well... they said it was The Panther," he said, pointing to Alexei and me.

The Bear turned to look at me, hurt in his eyes.

"Mi Corazón, you told them I was The Panther," he said.

"I'm sorry, I've had a lot to drink," I apologized.

"Well," he turned back to the man, "you try to impress your woman by telling her how you wrestled with a bear and won, which is how you got these scars. But she drinks too much." The Bear shrugged.

"Are there... are there bears here in Cliuz Plyae?" the front man asked before remembering their purpose. "WE ARE TRYING TO ARREST YOU!" he screamed.

"Oh yes, of course. Why not start at the beginning?" The Bear suggested, taking another sip from his glass.

"Vasco 'The Bear' Zavala, we are here to arrest you for your crimes against this land and its—" he trailed off again, staring dumbly at The Bear. I followed the man's gaze and saw The Bear, with a bored expression, lazily waved his hand, urging the man to hurry up, all while continuing to sip from his drink.

The man's confidence began to wane. He turned to seek guidance from his army. None of them moved, but someone in the front gave a slight shrug.

Alexei whispered in my ear, "This fucker is crazy and going to get us all shot."

The man standing out front cleared his throat again and tried once more, his voice sounding even less confident this time.

"Vasco, we are here to arrest you..." he began. The Bear held up a finger, which stopped the man from speaking. Vasco continued sipping from his crazy straw until all the liquid in the glass was gone.

"One moment, and then you can arrest me. I just need to get something first," The Bear said, tossing his empty glass onto the porch, where it shattered. He turned and disappeared back into the house.

Alexei and I stood frozen on the porch, staring at the army. The tension in the air was palpable, the heat of the moment intensifying as we awaited the next move.

Loud clanking sounds emanated from inside the house for several long minutes, as if Vasco was throwing objects around. Then The Bear emerged, walking out with a rocket launcher on his shoulder, aimed directly at the man in front.

"No se mueva!" The Bear sang out and pulled the trigger.

♫ *Two things happened simultaneously: the man in front disappeared in an explosion of fire, and from all sides of the house and woods, The Bear's men appeared, armed to the teeth.* ♫

Alexei, The Bear, and I crouched down on the porch as bullets began to fly.

"Get out through the back of the house!" The Bear yelled at Alexei, pulling out a gun he had stashed on the porch. The gunfire was growing as more men joined the fighting.

"Out the back door and to your left is your plane. It should be a clear run. We will occupy these idiots here," he shouted.

"And I swear to God, if you get her killed or hurt, I will find you and—" The rest of The Bear's threat was lost in an explosion out front, but his hand gestures left little doubt about his meaning.

In a strange moment of tenderness, The Bear locked eyes with me. He brushed some hair behind my ear and murmured, "I will find you; I promise." Then The Bear cocked his gun, snapping me back to the chaos around us.

Alexei and I stayed frozen on the porch, our minds struggling to process the dramatic shift in the day's events.

"RUN!" The Bear roared at us, his voice cutting through the chaos.

Alexei sprang into action, grabbing my hand and yanking me into the house. I barely registered his urgency as I stared at The Bear. The tan god blew me a kiss, his eyes fiercely locked on mine for a fleeting, tender moment before he turned away. He charged down the stairs, firing at enemies with fierce determination as he plunged into the maelstrom of battle.

Alexei reached my father first, urgently pulling him toward the back of the house as the sounds of gunfire and explosions filled the air.

"Where are we going?" my father demanded, his voice thick with annoyance and alcohol. "What's going on?"

"The freedom fighters arrived!" I shouted, desperation cutting through my voice as I moved to help Alexei drag my father toward the back door. "We have to leave this way!" I yelled just as a stray bullet shattered a front window, sending glass scattering across the floor.

Bane and Dimiter drew their weapons, their faces tense as they scanned the front entryway for any immediate threats.

"Come on, Father, it's time to go!" I yelled, sliding under one of his arms and helping him to his feet. The roar of gunfire and the chaos of the battlefield surged around us, heightening the necessity of our escape.

Alexei and I managed to get Father to the exit. Bane charged ahead, stepping out first with his gun raised, his eyes scanning for any immediate threats. When he saw it was clear, he signaled for us to follow. We dragged Father along, but his heavy, wriggling form made our progress slow and awkward.

"Where's the money?!" Father slurred, his voice barely audible over the uproar of battle.

I glanced back and saw Dimiter clutching the briefcase tightly in his hand.

"Dimiter has it, let's go!" I hissed, my voice strained as I struggled to push my father through the door.

"No, Angel!" he exclaimed, his hand shooting back toward the table in a frantic motion.

"I'm right here, Father," I said, trying to calm him as I assumed he was confused.

"My goat," he drunkenly sighed, his voice tinged with distress.

I exchanged a quick, exasperated glance with Alexei, who hoisted my father onto his shoulder as I sprinted back to the gifted animal. Angel The Goat was bleating wildly, clearly terrified by the barrage of gunfire out front. I grabbed her and bolted to the back door. Dimiter held it open, waiting for me, and slammed it shut as soon as I made it out.

With everyone now out of the house, we dashed into the trees to our right, the crackle of gunfire and the roar of explosions echoing behind us.

More gunfire erupted behind us and from far out to the side once we were covered by the dense foliage. We scanned our surroundings, trying to determine the best escape route. Alexei took charge, pointing toward a direction deeper into the forest.

"This way. We need to clear the battle and get to the plane. Quickly," he ordered.

Alexei led the way, dragging my father through the thick underbrush as our group followed. Bane and Dimiter stayed close by, and I carried Angel The Goat in my arms.

My guard led us deeper into the trees, his pace relentless and determined despite the burden of my father's weight. The sound of gunfire gradually faded as we pressed on, offering some relief. We ran through the forest endlessly, the only sounds were our rustling in the underbrush and the occasional snap of branches. No one spoke, as we remained on high alert, eyes scanning for any signs of an ambush.

Eventually, we emerged at the edge of a war-torn town. The streets were in disarray, and the buildings in shambles from a recent battle. Everywhere, dead bodies littered the ground, pools of blood collecting from the massacre.

"Well, it's not the plane, but it's not an active war zone either," Bane muttered, daring to move ahead of the group as he cautiously stepped into the desolate town to scout around.

Alexei remained near the tree line with my father, his "instincts" telling him it wasn't safe yet. I set Angel The Goat down next to my father, pressing the rope leash into his hand. He immediately began sweetly reassuring the animal, his voice oddly gentle as Angel The Goat looked up and bleated softly.

I moved ahead with Dimiter, starting to take stock of our surroundings. Buildings stood abandoned, their windows shattered, and many had entire walls blasted away. It was a struggle to navigate through the clutter of bodies, guns, and debris strewn across the street. I peered into some of the buildings, searching for anything useful.

Dimiter and Bane crouched over a lifeless body, their faces set in concentration. Dimiter pointed to the wounds. "Thirty minutes ago," he said.

Bane frowned, then shook his head and pointed to something on the ground. "That has to be from at least three hours ago. We should be relatively safe."

Dimiter stood, still staring intently at whatever Bane was pointing at. "That was like an hour ago, max," he insisted.

"Let go of me!" my father's voice rang out, and we all turned to see him struggling to pull away from Alexei. He started stumbling toward us, with Angel The Goat trailing behind on her leash.

"Oh, an Uzi. We really should be collecting these guns," my father mused, picking up an abandoned firearm and making his way over to us. His drunken stagger made him unsteady, and he stumbled a few times as he walked. Bane moved toward my father to offer assistance when a loud shot cracked through the air.

"GET DOWN!" Alexei shouted, sprinting toward Father and Bane. Dimiter threw himself on top of me, and we both hit the ground as the air erupted with gunfire. Scrambling to his feet, Dimiter quickly dragged me behind a large concrete slab that had once been part of a building's wall. Bullets ricocheted off the other side as we huddled behind it for cover.

"ANGEL!" I heard my brother scream from within the building next to us.

"Yes?" I called back.

"Just wanted to make sure you're alive," Bane answered.

"How is Father?" I asked. The only reply I heard was the relentless crackle of bullets peppering the other side of the concrete slab.

"I'm going to be honest. Not well. A random bullet hit him as we ran into the building for cover," Bane finally admitted, his voice laced with frustration.

The sound of his argument with someone inside was barely audible as our enemies' bullets died down. After a beat, he added reluctantly, "The goat is safe. Father wanted you to know."

I glanced at Dimiter, who was intensely scanning the area for any sign of our opposition.

"I think there are only a few of them," he said, his voice steady but urgent. "Stragglers from whatever conflict happened here."

"Which way to the plane?" I asked.

"On the other side of whoever is shooting at us, I think," Dimiter sighed, exasperated.

"Of fucking course," I muttered, catching sight of Bane frantically waving at me through the window of the building next door.

"Father is getting worse," Bane shouted over to us, his voice carrying a note of desperation.

"We need a way to get past those men, and quickly," I informed my twin, then turned to Dimiter. He met my gaze and we shared a concerned look before my guard ducked down in front of us. Dimiter started sorting through the scattered guns left from the last fight, picking out ones that still seemed usable.

I dared a glance from around our concrete haven.

Across from us, three injured men were barely clinging to life. They were covered in blood and dirt, one of them missing an arm. The other two were reloading their guns, their movements slow and labored.

Dimiter stood up, having found a suitable gun, and began shooting in the general direction of the men. His shots rang out with fierce intensity, hitting one of the three, but the other two quickly retreated behind a low brick wall, their movements sharp and desperate.

Soon, Dimiter's gun ran out of bullets. He cursed under his breath as he ducked back behind our cover. I glanced over at Bane while also cowering behind the wall. My brother's eyes were wide in shock as he stared down at our father.

"BANE?" I called out, my voice trembling as I saw the look on his face. Slowly, he turned to look at me, his eyes pleading and powerless. It was then I realized the full extent of my father's injuries, the gravity of his condition hitting me like a punch to the gut. *He's going to die if we don't do anything.*

I dared another look over the concrete slab and spotted what I needed.

"Cover me!" I shouted to Dimiter, my voice sharp and urgent.

"What?" he asked, his concern clear at whatever idea involved him "covering me."

"SHOOT AT THEM!" I commanded with a confidence in my voice that startled even me. Dimiter stopped asking questions and immediately started firing around the brick wall. With the gunfire providing a diversion, I sprinted around the slab and dove toward my target, adrenaline fueling every movement.

The artillery cannon looked functional, with a crank wheel attached to aim the mortar. As I slid behind the unit, Dimiter ran out of bullets and hid behind the wall. I ducked behind the cannon, curling into a ball on the ground to make myself as small a target as possible.

The two men fired at the concrete slab I was now in front of, causing a shower of dust to cascade over me from the bullets impacting the wall. Luckily, their focus remained on the slab, as they were drawn by

Dimiter's gunfire.

When they ran out of bullets, Dimiter switched to a new gun and resumed shooting at the enemy immediately. I uncurled myself and grabbed the hand crank. The cannon creaked initially but started to move in the direction I wanted. As I lined up the shot with the opposition's brick wall, I glanced down and realized the cannon was not loaded.

"Fuck," I whispered, spinning to frantically scan the immediate area.

The first click of Dimiter's empty gun echoed ominously, and I hit the ground hard, bracing for the inevitable return of fire. Bullets hammered the concrete slab just as I collapsed. I rolled back behind the cannon, catching my breath from the close call.

As the onslaught of bullets continued, I cautiously began peeking at the bodies scattered around me.

That's when I saw it.

A dead man laid right in front of me, clutching the artillery's projectile missile. He appeared to have been in the process of loading the shell when he was shot and fell backward.

I reached for the missile and yanked it toward me, but it wouldn't budge. Growling in frustration, I pulled harder, yet the projectile remained stubbornly in place.

Just then, Dimiter started firing again, and I heard someone sliding toward me. Alexei appeared at my side in a flash, his expression grim but determined. Together, we heaved the missile toward the cannon.

As the projectile inched closer, Dimiter's gun ran out of bullets, the only warning being a few empty clicks and a small curse. Enemy bullets began raining down on us in a sudden bombardment. Alexei pulled me into his arms, and we ducked together, hugging the missile between us.

"KEEP SHOOTING AT THEM, DIMITER!" I screamed, my voice

barely audible over the roar of gunfire and the dust raining down.

"I keep running out of bullets! Most of these guns are partially used already!" Dimiter's frustrated shout cut through the chaos.

"Find more than one gun at a time then!" I snapped back.

The enemy's gunfire momentarily subsided, and Dimiter resumed shooting immediately.

Alexei and I worked in frantic coordination. He hoisted the missile with determined effort, positioning it at the cannon's opening. I joined him in pushing the projectile into place, using all my strength. Once it was securely lodged, I impulsively reached for the trigger.

Time and space froze to a startling crawl as I yanked the lever to fire the cannon, my body coursing with adrenaline as I desperately tried to save my father, my twin, and my lovers.

"NO, ANGEL, NOT WHILE BEHIND IT! THE RECOIL!" Alexei shouted as I launched the unit. Confused by his urgent cries, I started to turn toward him when a searing pain erupted in my stomach. I felt myself being hurled through the air, then crashed hard against the concrete slab wall and collapsed to the ground. Pain radiated through every inch of my body, making movement nearly impossible. My head throbbed violently where it had struck the wall with a sickening crack.

"ANGEL!" Alexei pulled me up into his arms, gently smacking my face to wake me up.

"Ow," I murmured, looking up to see his handsome, worried face.

"Angel," I saw him mouth, his words starting to fade as blackness surrounded me.

I closed my eyes as I felt myself being lifted.

Where are we? I thought before losing the fight and slipping into unconsciousness.

4 Months

CHAPTER THIRTY-THREE

When I opened my eyes, it was dark. I groaned, still feeling hazy, and my body ached all over.

"Angel," someone whispered, followed by the soft click of a light being flicked on, illuminating my childhood bedroom. I looked over and saw Dimiter sitting on the edge of my bed, deep concern etched in his face.

"Dimiter," I smiled at seeing him. "What happened?" I asked, trying to remember how I ended up in this bed.

"What do you remember?" he asked, tucking some of my black hair behind my ear.

"We just came back from the deal with The Lion. Why am I in my old bedroom?" I looked around at what was left. The only things remaining were the bed I was on and a shelf full of trinkets lining the wall across from me. Everything else I had taken with me when I moved out.

"Angel..." Dimiter's voice trembled, and he swallowed hard before continuing, "Your father... he didn't make it."

His face was etched with sorrow as he reached down for my hand, intertwining his fingers with mine.

"Didn't make what?" I asked, staring out into the room, still very confused as to why I was here. Dimiter cocked his head and eyed me suspiciously.

"When you say you're back from visiting The Lion, do you mean The Lion or The Panther?" he asked, his face growing very serious.

"What do you mean? The Lion! He was named The Jackal, and then he said it's The Lion," I said, my head feeling fuzzy.

"He changed it again, to The Panther," Dimiter explained.

"Okay, he changed it again, but the last time I saw him, he went by The Lion," I insisted.

"Angel, I think you have some memory loss. We went back—" Dimiter started, but I waved him off.

"No, no. We only went the one time. He bought a bunch of stuff," a drunken giggle escaped me at the memory. The hand Dimiter was not holding onto fell to my lips in a lazy "sh" gesture before I continued, "I slept with him; we had this mind-blowing intimate moment." Dimiter smiled down at me, a small shimmer of entertainment in his eyes despite the grief on his face.

"He sort of reminds me of you. You fuck me hard and rough. I never told you this, but I love it when you do," I said, feeling buzzed on painkillers as the words tumbled out with another little giggle. Dimiter's mouth shifted into a small, bemused smile as I tried to poke his nose with my free hand. My guard caught my hand in his and entwined our fingers.

"But I won. I won the challenge. He bought more guns from us. We are going back," I stated all of this as fact and started to sit up slowly.

"Angel, we dropped off all of that shipment already. The—whatever—had some issues with local militia or something. We dropped off the rest of his order after getting it from this conspiracy theory vendor. I guess it was a good thing for him that you won your challenge," Dimiter told me, his voice sweet. He freed one of his hands to caress my cheek.

"We got caught in some crossfire trying to leave, and your father got shot," he said, watching me carefully to gauge my reaction. I shook my head in defiance and pulled my knees up to my chest. Moving hurt as pain jolted through me with every shift; it felt as though every muscle and joint was stiff and achy.

"Then you came in like a fucking hero, firing that cannon at the men shooting at us," Dimiter continued, a sad smile touching his lips. His bright eyes sparkled with admiration, as if I were a legend in his eyes. The admiration quickly faded, replaced by a deeper sorrow.

"Your father... he didn't make it. According to Bane, shortly after you ran out to load the artillery, Emilio Zoric passed away." Dimiter's voice trembled as he used my father's full name, grief evident in his expression.

I studied Dimiter's face closely as he watched me, looking for any signs of understanding of the harsh realities he had just delivered.

"You're lying," I concluded, another intoxicated titter escaping my lips.

"Angel, the funeral was today." Dimiter ran a frustrated hand through his hair, ruffling it slightly. "Alexei and I have been watching over you while you were recovering. He went to pay his respects, but I stayed here... just in case you woke up." His eyes softened as he spoke, revealing a depth of care I had never seen before.

I leaned in towards Dimiter and kissed him softly on the lips. He gently grasped my shoulders and held me at a respectful distance from himself.

"Angel," he chastised, though his tone was only partially serious.

"Fuck me," I whispered.

My guard shook his head in disbelief. "You've been in a coma, and I don't think the first thing we should do is have sex."

"Of course it is. Besides, you're turning me on by calling me a hero. I love when you praise me. Keep going." I wriggled out of his grasp, attempting to look up at him with big, pleading "fuck-me" eyes. "Don't just make love to me. Take me like you know you want to. Rough."

As I slid the covers off, I discovered that I was already naked. Moving slowly, I inched my way closer to Dimiter, guiding his arms around my body and encouraging him to hold me as I straddled his lap.

Dimiter did not resist as I guided him. I leaned in to kiss him again, and as our lips met, he responded eagerly, his arms pulling me closer and wrapping tightly around my waist. I attempted to move his hand towards my chest, hoping to encourage his lust. He surprised me instead by suddenly breaking away from our kiss. His forehead rested against mine for several seconds, his eyes remaining closed, as both of us breathed heavily.

"Angel," he whispered so softly I could barely hear him. Something wet fell onto me, and I looked to see my guard with tears in his eyes. I moved a hand up and wiped away one of the tears rolling down his cheek.

"What's wrong?" I asked, worried.

Dimiter wrapped his arms around me more tightly, pulling me into a firm, comfortable hug. A small chuckle shook his body, followed by a deep, dejected sigh.

"This is the wrong time and the wrong place to tell you this, but—" He swallowed hard. "I genuinely believe I'm falling in love with you," he finally admitted.

His confession lingered in the air between us. I slowly eased out of our embrace to look at him. He was staring at me with profound sadness.

"Don't try to say it back. Please," he said, placing a finger on my lips before I could respond. "I know that Alexei is upset about us, but it's too late. I want to be with you too. You're strong and brave, and I love how difficult and playful you can be, how *we* are when we are together." Dimiter cupped the back of my head, looking into me as if he could see into my soul.

"I won't make this a grand ultimatum, but I can't promise Alexei won't," he said, his voice steady but intense. "I just want you to think about it. And when you decide... know that I'll be right here, waiting." His finger lingered on my lips, and his gaze was soft, as if he were on the verge of kissing me.

I nodded slowly, though confusion clouded my thoughts.

"Why would Alexei be upset? He watched us. That tape—you sent him that tape," I said, struggling to understand.

Dimiter looked at me with deep sadness and a touch of relief before he replied, "You don't remember it, then."

"Remember what?" I asked.

"The fight," was all he said.

I strained to recall details but came up empty. My eyes locked with Dimiter's ocean-blue stare, and a feeling of comfort and security washed over me.

"I'm tired of fighting with Alexei," I confessed, a weight lifted off my shoulders with the admission. "I'm tired of crying over him. I'm tired of trying to figure out what I mean to him. Why do I always feel like I am the bad guy when it comes to Alexei?" I asked. Dimiter's surprise was evident as he listened to me ramble.

"I am tired of being told I'm not good enough or that I have to find a husband. I don't want a husband; I want a partner. I want time to explore what I like and to find someone who will treat me right. I want... I want... Dimiter—" I didn't get a chance to finish my thought before Dimiter's lips were on mine. He kissed me fiercely, his embrace tightening possessively.

As he whispered on my lips, "I'll have to be gentle with you, darling. You are injured," Dimiter carefully guided me back onto my bed and removed his shirt. He climbed on top of me, but the slightest pressure from his body caused me to gasp in pain.

"Let me be on top," I said a little breathless. Dimiter stood up and fumbled with the button and zipper of his pants, his movements eager and a little clumsy. Then he climbed onto the bed, his impressive erection already at attention, waiting for me.

I pounced on him with a fierce hunger, impaling myself onto his engorged erection with ease. The sensation of his swollen cock inside me sent immediate waves of pleasure coursing through my body. Dimiter's hands greedily gripped onto my hips, guiding me in a gentle rhythm as we moved as one. Our moans mingled together in a symphony of ecstasy.

My body ignited with pure pleasure coursing through me. It had been a while since I had felt this level of rapture, and I couldn't handle it any longer. A fierce orgasm threatened to break free, pulsing through me with such force that I arched my back in uncontrollable bliss. My body shook with orgasmic elation as the first flood of fulfillment began to ravage me, but my joy was quickly interrupted as a pair of rough hands grabbed my shoulders from behind.

My frenzy came to a brutal halt as I was viciously ripped off of Dimiter's large cock and hurled across the room. The impact of my body against the carpeted floor sent pain shooting through me, but I barely registered it as my eyes snapped up to see Alexei's enraged face. His usually polished features were twisted in disgust as he glared at the naked form of Dimiter.

"HOW DARE YOU TAKE ADVANTAGE OF MY WOMAN LIKE THAT!" Alexei roared as he lunged at Dimiter, his hands gripping the man's throat.

I stared in shock at the confrontation before rushing to Alexei's side, my fists pounding against his back in a desperate attempt to intervene.

"Stop it! We weren't doing anything you didn't know about! What are you doing?!" I shouted, grabbing at the sleeve of Alexei's black formal suit, desperately trying to pry his hands away from Dimiter's throat.

"She doesn't remember," I heard Dimiter choke out, his hands gripping Alexei's wrist with a tight, knuckle-white grip.

When Alexei refused to let go, Dimiter curled his legs up to his chest. With a fierce thrust, he kicked Alexei hard in the stomach, sending him stumbling backward into the trinket shelves across from the bed. The impact was violent, causing the shelving unit to crack and collapse. Alexei hit the shelves with a deafening crack before sinking to the floor, one hand clutching his head as debris rained down around him.

I had been thrown back as well, landing roughly in the spot where Alexei had originally thrown me. My eyes darted frantically between the two men as my heart beat wildly in my chest. The air grew thick with hatred, and I couldn't help but feel as if I was balancing on a knife's edge.

Dimiter took deep, ragged breaths, his eyes shooting daggers at Alexei as he collected himself.

"The choice is Angel's, not yours. Just because you make a scene doesn't mean she suddenly belongs to you," Dimiter seethed at Alexei, his voice sharp and cutting.

Alexei struggled to his feet, unsteady and disheveled, brushing off the debris with a rough, angry motion.

"I am going to marry her," Alexei declared, his voice vibrating with indignation as he glared at the naked Dimiter on the bed. His gaze then shifted to me, revealing a tumultuous mix of love and hatred burning in his eyes.

"Don't you remember?" he asked, his voice breaking with emotion.

I shook my head, lost and bewildered. "You proposed to me?" I asked softly, my voice trembling with confusion.

"No. He asked your father, who told him no. Then he threw a fit," Dimiter breathed heavily, still wheezing for air.

Alexei's eyes locked onto mine, desperation etched into his features. "You told me you loved me. You accepted my proposal. On the porch—you must not remember." His voice was pleading, his gaze studying me for any signs of recollection.

"I don't rem—" I barely got the words out before Dimiter shot across the room. In a swift, powerful motion, he grabbed Alexei by the chest of his suit and lifted him off the ground. With a fierce growl, he roared, "Like hell you will marry her!"

"DIMITER!" I cried, but my voice was drowned out by the sharp smack of Alexei's punch. The blow landed hard on Dimiter's cheek, forcing him to release Alexei. Dimiter stumbled back, clutching his face in pain, and tripping over a scattered trinket. He crashed down onto the floor near where I sat, his expression one of shock, his eyes wide as he fell.

Alexei didn't hesitate. He lunged at Dimiter, aiming a brutal kick toward his ribs. Just as the kick was about to connect, Dimiter reacted with lightning speed, grabbing Alexei's raised leg and shoving it away with all his strength. Alexei stumbled back and crashed onto the floor, sprawling out with the rest of us.

The air crackled with fury as the two men glared at each other. Their heavy breathing was loud and intense, eyes locked in a deadly stare that seemed to set the very room ablaze with their anger.

"She gets a choice in this! You do not get to decide for her!" Dimiter roared, his voice filled with raw emotion. The two men sprang into action simultaneously, both scrambling to be the first to rise and continue their violent confrontation.

"Stop!" I begged, my voice breaking as tears streamed down my face, blurring my vision. "Stop!" I cried out desperately. I struggled to rise from the floor, my limbs heavy and uncooperative due to the lingering effects of the drugs and my injuries. As I stumbled toward them, my efforts were futile.

Dimiter was the first to his feet and seized the advantage over Alexei, who was still struggling to regain his footing. With a powerful surge of strength, Dimiter grabbed Alexei and hurled him over his head. Alexei flew through the air, crashing hard onto the ground on the other side of Dimiter, the bone-jarring thud echoing through the room.

By this time, I had managed to rise to my feet and stumbled over to the still-naked Dimiter. My hands weakly grasped his arms, trying to pull him away from the chaos.

"Please stop! I can choose—just please stop fighting!" I begged, my voice trembling with desperation as tears streamed down my face.

Suddenly, a sharp crack resonated through the room. Dimiter let out a pained grunt and turned to see Alexei had hurled one of my hanging picture frames at his back. The glass shattered into a million glittering fragments.

Dimiter growled, his voice edged with fury. "I love you, Angel, but this is more than just about us. It's about his entitled fucking attitude."

In a frantic attempt to distract him, I pulled Dimiter into a desperate kiss, my lips moving feverishly against his. Dimiter pulled away roughly, his eyes blazing with hatred as he turned to face Alexei.

Alexei, still seething with fury, backed out of the room. He held up his hand, making a taunting gesture as he beckoned Dimiter to follow him into the hallway.

Dimiter stalked over to my front door, his movements deliberate and tense. I gasped when I saw the small shards of glass embedded in his back from the picture frame Alexei had thrown.

Suddenly, the hallway was filled with the violent crash of bodies slamming together, the walls trembling with each impact. The chaotic sound of their struggle echoed down every corridor.

I screamed in terror and dashed out of my bedroom, my heart hammering uncontrollably as I ran after my men.

They pushed, punched, and kicked their way down the hallway, each blow crackling with raw power. Dimiter and Alexei were locked in the brutal struggle, equally matched and relentless. Dimiter shoved Alexei against the wall once more, gripping his lapel and snarling inches from his face. In response, Alexci grabbed one of my father's vases and smashed it over Dimiter's head. The ceramic shattered with a sharp, explosive crack, sending shards flying. Alexei used the momentary distraction to shove Dimiter away with a vicious kick. Dimiter was hurled across the hall, slamming hard into the wall with a painful groan. The impact was brutal with glass pieces embedding into his skin adding to his agony.

Alexei started to run down the hall, but Dimiter's hand shot out, grabbing him violently by the arm. With a powerful twist, Dimiter spun Alexei around, flinging him into the library with a forceful swing.

Alexei crashed into a chair in the room, his face flushed with rage. Dimiter, blood trickling down his back from the shards of glass, followed with a deliberate and menacing stride.

Seizing the chance to prevent further violence, I rushed forward and positioned myself between them, one trembling hand held out in each direction.

"Please stop!" I yelled, my voice overflowing with desperation. Both men ignored me, their eyes locked on each other with burning hatred.

Alexei managed to stand and approached me with unsettling calm. Without meeting my gaze, his fingers brushed softly up my arm, a chilling contrast to the fury in the room. Then, with a sudden, harsh grip, he seized my elbow and yanked me out of the way. I stumbled backward, disoriented, as he lunged aggressively at Dimiter once more.

Bang.

Bang.

The sound of two rapid gunshots shattered through the air, each shot exploding with a deafening crack. The high-pitched ringing that followed was piercing and unceasing, drowning out all other sounds.

Time seemed to stretch into endlessness. Then, Alexei and Dimiter collapsed simultaneously, their bodies crashing to the floor in a grotesque, tangled heap. Both men laid motionless and eerily silent, their once fierce gazes now vacant.

I screamed, a raw, desperate cry echoing through the air as I stared down at my men, lifeless. Their blood had splattered onto me, and the sight of it made my legs buckle.

The reality of the massacre was unbearable, tearing through my soul. Agony erupted from my core, a piercing, gut-wrenching pain that made me cry out as my heart shattered. The relentless, high-pitched ringing persisted, acting as a harsh, unyielding cover for my nightmarish shriek.

Somehow, I managed to look up.

In the doorway stood my twin, Bane, his hand trembling as he held a handgun extended and aimed at the men at my feet. His cold, enraged eyes were locked onto the horrific scene before him. I stared at my brother in stunned disbelief, wailing louder as his face blurred through the torrent of fat tears streaming down my cheeks.

Bane spoke, but his words were drowned out by the constant ringing and my desperate screams. He set the gun down on a side table and rushed toward me, his eyes softening with concern.

A rush of emotions overwhelmed me, and I felt my head growing light. As Bane's hand touched my arm, darkness closed in once more, and I collapsed, fading away into oblivion.

4 Months...?

BANE'S SECRET GUNRUNNING BUSINESS RULE:

Always keep the upper hand.

Never show all your cards—keep an ace up your sleeve.

CHAPTER THIRTY-FOUR

I woke with a jolt, my whole body lurching. A small cry escaped me.

Bane was lying next to me, reading a tattered copy of *Rotten Ryan*. As soon as I was awake, he set the book aside and wrapped his arms around me.

"It's okay, it's okay," he said soothingly, pulling me closer.

I gathered myself and began taking slow, deep breaths.

"There you go," my brother said, noticing that I had calmed down a little.

He kissed my forehead, then pulled back to look me in the eyes. A gentle smile appeared on his face as he pushed my hair back.

I looked up at him, terrified, with the memory replaying in my mind—the blood, the lifeless bodies of my men before me.

Bane stared down at me with an intense expression. He took a deep breath and was about to speak, but the words never came. I watched as he studied my face, his eyes taking me in as if seeing me for the first time.

Then, slowly and to my horror, he leaned in and kissed me fully on the lips.

I immediately began hitting my twin's chest, trying to push him away. He complied, and I scrambled to get out of the bed, realizing only then that I was naked. I grabbed the bed sheets and wrapped them around myself as I moved hurriedly away.

"WHAT THE FUCK, BANE?" I yelled as I wrapped the sheet around myself several times.

"Angel, babe, please be careful. You went into shock, and I'm concerned about that terrible head injury. I'm not sure those idiots allowed you to heal properly," Bane said with concern.

"Babe?" I sputtered, ignoring the rest of what he was saying as I wiped at my lips bitterly.

"Just get back into bed, please, before you hurt yourself more," Bane instructed, holding out a welcoming arm for me to lay into.

I paced around the bed, realizing I was now in Bane's childhood room.

"What was that, trying to kiss me? I'm your twin sister!" I stopped moving to yell at him but resumed pacing, trying my best not to get too overwhelmed or grossed out.

"Actually, you're not," Bane responded calmly. I halted and turned toward him slowly.

"You're adopted," he said casually, shrugging his shoulder as if it were no big deal.

The room seemed to shrink, and the air grew stiflingly hot. I snatched the nearest object—an old book—and began fanning myself frantically.

"W... wh... what?" I stammered, my legs growing weak again, as if they might give way at any moment.

Bane's hand was firm yet gentle as he grasped mine and guided me back down onto the bed.

"Look, I want to talk to you about this—about everything. But you just woke up from fainting right after coming out of a coma from a head wound. So let's take things slow, okay?" Bane lifted my chin and smiled at me. I tried to smile back, but it came out stiff, and I could tell he wasn't convinced.

"Let's go get some food in you," he suggested.

"Please don't try to kiss me again," I requested.

"Of course," he said simply.

I glanced down at myself, noticing that someone had cleaned me up, as there was no blood remaining. I went into Bane's closet, picked out an old band shirt, and put it on. When I came out, Bane was waiting patiently, his hand extended toward mine.

I froze, studying him warily, unsure whether to trust this unfamiliar man who had ripped my heart out. Seeing my hesitation, Bane chuckled softly and walked over to me, gently taking both of my hands. "Here," he said, guiding me slowly toward the door. He paused to show me that he had retrieved my house slippers, which were ready for me. I started to put them on, but he stopped me.

"I've got it," he said, bending down to slip my bright pink, fluffy slippers onto my feet.

Bane guided me through the mansion, one hand firmly gripping mine while his other rested on my shoulder, urging me forward.

"I'm not disabled," I started to say as we neared the dining room. The words faltered, though, as I realized we had arrived right outside the library. I stopped in my tracks, my eyes drawn to the room with morbid curiosity. It was empty. No bodies, no blood—nothing to indicate the horrors that had occurred. It was as if the scene of my nightmares had been wiped clean.

Bane watched me intently, and I struggled to keep my composure. I turned my face away as a tear betrayed me, slipping silently down my cheek.

"No more tears for men who don't deserve you," Bane said coldly.

I glanced back into the room and lingered, as I sensed Bane's growing impatience to move along. He tugged on my hand, urging me forward. Weakness overtook me, and I collapsed. My stepbrother caught me and lifted me into his arms with ease.

Bane carried me the rest of the way to the dining room and seated me next to the head of the table before taking the seat of honor for himself. The table was already set with an abundance of food, far more than two people could eat in one sitting. My stepbrother filled my plate for me, but I only picked at the food while he ate his meal.

"Please eat," he said, placing a hand on top of mine on the table. "I will tell you everything if you eat for me," he implored.

I nodded sullenly and ate what I could from the food in front of me.

Bane snapped at one of the servers standing ready in the room, "Fetch me a Fleuve de Vie."

The drink appeared next to my plate, but I stared at it, my mind drifting back to Alexei in Tithal, and my appetite vanished.

When Bane decided I was probably not going to eat much more, he pushed back his seat and began to stand up.

"Let's go to Father's... I mean my office," he corrected, gesturing for the staff to clear the table.

I looked at my adopted brother, meeting his eyes for the first time since I saw the cleaned library.

"So it was true. He's dead," I whispered.

Bane searched my face for a reaction before simply saying, "Please, my office. I *will* explain everything."

Bane settled me into my usual chair, directly across the desk from where my father normally sat. Then, my stepbrother took our father's seat and reached into the desk to withdraw a piece of paper.

I surveyed Bane in Father's chair, smiling to myself slightly. He seemed to take up only half the space. Bane leaned forward, placing his elbows on the desk, and began to read the document in his hands to me.

"Here on this day, Emilio Zoric declares his intention to adopt this girl, Sophia Boiko, as his daughter, Sophia Zoric..." Bane continued reading until he grew bored with the legalistic details and then placed the document in front of me.

I glanced down at it, confirmed what he had read, and then looked up at Bane with a shrug.

"Do you remember what happened the second time we were dropping off the shipment to The... Panther?" he asked.

I closed my eyes and concentrated. A rush of memories surged through me.

I will find you, I promise, echoed in my mind.

Opening my eyes, I nodded softly.

"Good," Bane said sternly. "Father had obviously had too much to drink and ended up taking a bullet before we could get to cover. As we were being fired upon, he started rambling to me. At some point, he waved me closer and said he had a secret for me." Bane paused to make sure I was paying attention. I nodded, which encouraged him to continue.

"He told me that my twin sister wasn't my sister at all—that she was adopted and that he had the papers to prove it in this desk. Then he told me, 'Take care of her.' He said you were his precious stolen Angel who had saved him in more ways than she could ever imagine."

I looked down, feeling the weight of Bane's intense, possessive stare as he relayed this.

"He died shortly afterward while you were out there saving our asses. Of course, you got hit by the cannon's recoil and slammed into that concrete slab. But as soon as I got back, I tore this office apart until I found it." He concluded, gesturing at the document in front of me as if I should be proud of him.

"Why did you kill them?" I asked, ignoring the paper. Bane sighed dramatically, rolling his eyes in clear disappointment at my question.

"Because Father would have," my stepbrother replied tersely. I started to shake my head, rejecting that answer.

"He killed the other guards. What makes you think Alexei and Dimiter would have been any different?" he pressed, his green eyes piercing me with a strange new darkness.

"Because I had a choice," I stated. My stepbrother scoffed and rolled his eyes again.

"Dear adopted sister, first off, Alexei was a joke. That man was too scared to tell you how he felt about you. What makes you think he could have handled a woman like you?" Bane asked patronizingly. I thought about that for a moment before reluctantly agreed with him, though I didn't admit it out loud. Instead, I kept my face carefully composed, not wanting to give Bane a hint of what I was feeling.

"And Dimiter?" I whispered, the pain of saying his name out loud evident in my voice. My stepbrother bristled slightly before responding.

"Yes, well, that giant fool and... and... *his legend* might have entertained you for a while. However, we both know he would never have committed to you. He could never commit to anything."

"What if I was really falling for one of them?" I argued.

Bane snorted. "Angel, think about it. Would you have seriously considered either of those men if they were not already in an inappropriate position to be with you? As soon as that thrill was gone, or if Father would have just accepted it, you would have dropped them faster than a man after hearing the pregnancy results."

I stared at my hands, not answering Bane. Somewhere deep down, I knew he was right, but he was never going to hear me admit it.

"I hate being called Angel," I whispered.

"But you are an Angel. To this family and to me," Bane said, balking before softening. He reached a hand out to me, which I ignored.

"Wherever I go, this path of destruction follows. Just about everyone I've ever slept with is dead. The only Angel I am is the Angel of Death," I said, meeting Bane's gaze. His green eyes looked colder than usual today.

Bane shook his head and dismissed my comment.

"Father had a point, you know. They didn't have the money. How could they possibly expect to take care of you? It would all be great and romantic at first, but feelings fade, and then you'd be left with some mid-class working man struggling to meet your greatness."

I sighed, a wave of depression washing over me, numbing all other emotions.

"What's the plan now? Are you going to confess your love to me?" I challenged Bane. I had become well-versed in the looks he'd been giving me since I first woke up today. He no longer saw me as a sister, but as a *woman*.

"Well, about that. I did find another document in my search," Bane sighed. "A signed marriage contract to, well, Mikhail Volkov. It was dated a year after *Arousal* was burned down. The contract stated that the two of you would be married if you hadn't found a suitable husband," Bane paused to let the news sink in.

"Father... Emilio?... Father said he didn't. That he wouldn't..." I stumbled through my thoughts.

"I know," Bane said seriously. "But we both know he was prone to anger, and I suspect he had it created after the *Arousal* incident, preparing to punish you anyway."

I looked down at my hands again. *Controlling me beyond the grave. Thanks, Father.*

"I threw it in the fire when I found it, but I cannot guarantee it was the only copy, and burning a contract does not break it," Bane let that sink in before continuing. "So I wanted to offer you an out."

"I have an out," I took a deep breath.

"Oh." Bane rested his chin on his knuckles, looking more like a boy dreaming of playing mob boss than a man now in charge of a gun-running empire.

"The Bear," I stated.

"Who?"

I sighed again. "The Panther."

"You cannot be serious," Bane said, his voice sharp with disbelief.

"He said he was going to marry me; I just needed to say when," I pushed, my voice steady with defiance.

"The Panther is dead," Bane announced, a twisted joy lighting up his face.

The words hit me like a physical blow. I closed my eyes and hid my face behind my hands, trying to hold back the torrent of emotions threatening to drown me. My mind raced, struggling to process the finality of it all.

Bane sighed, clearly irritated by my reaction. "The conflict escalated between the two groups, leading to a complete massacre. Only a few survivors remain from both sides. Although his body has yet to be accounted for, it's assumed he died in the clash with his 'Azteca Kings,'" Bane sneered.

I thought back to the last time I saw The Bear.

I will find you, I promise, echoed in my mind again, this time fainter, slowly fading into nothing. The Bear became just a memory as I shed a few silent tears. Feeling uncomfortable and vulnerable, I brushed them away quickly and met my stepbrother's eyes once more, defeated.

Bane reached into the desk again, this time pulling out a book and placing it on top of the adoption certificate. *Rotten Ryan: Weapons and Wives* was written in large letters on the cover. The book looked brand new, unlike the worn copies of *Rotten Ryan* he used to read to me, now aged from years of use.

"Now, back to my proposal," he said.

He gestured toward the book, encouraging me to open it. I just blinked at him, refusing to move. Eventually, Bane couldn't wait any longer, his excitement to reveal his grand plan clearly growing unbearable. He opened the cover to show that the book had been hollowed out. Inside, a ten-carat pear-shaped halo diamond ring rested in the center, surrounded by the words "Will you marry me?" written in elegant, scripted calligraphy.

I looked up at my adopted brother again, hoping he was joking. Instead, he was smiling at me, clearly pleased with himself.

"Angel, I *am* in love with you. It's been a brotherly type of love up to now, but I've been thinking since Father's death," Bane chuckled softly to himself. He seemed pleased, as if he were on the verge of sharing a profound thought.

"After Father told me the truth, I had to confirm it immediately. When I found the adoption papers, I just stared at them and thought about our lives and the last year. Do you know what I realized?" he asked me.

"That you watch too much incest porn?" I snorted. Bane flashed me an angry look for my insolence.

"No. That this makes sense. That me being in love with you makes sense," Bane smiled at me again, trying to come across warmly, but instead looked as if he was on the edge of insanity.

"Bane," I tried to say, but he cut me off.

"I mean, who else in this world is going to know you better than the man who grew up next to you, thinking they were your twin brother? Who else is going to relate to this life we live? Who else is going to be able to provide you the life you deserve?" He smiled at me, again pleased with himself.

I stared down at the ugly ring.

"I would love the chance to spend the rest of my life making you happy. But if you are not comfortable with it yet, consider it a temporary union. To keep you out of that marriage contract. I won't touch you without your consent; you have my word." He leveled his eyes with mine.

I stared back at my stepbrother, waiting for him to tell me he was just joking, that all of this was just a farce. Instead, he continued to look at me with disgusting adoration in his eyes.

"I will spend every day trying my best to prove I am worthy of your trust and that I deserve to be your husband," he enunciated every word gently.

I snatched the ring out of the book and put it on my finger just to make him shut up. A growing headache throbbed behind my eyes.

"So you accept?" my brother cheered.

"It's not like I have a choice," I snapped, then stood up and walked toward the door to leave.

"Angel," Bane's voice made me stop.

I grabbed an expensive vodka from the top of the liquor table by the door, a now familiar move to me, and turned toward my new fiancée.

"I think you made an excellent decision; you will see," he whispered, his voice laced with unearned confidence.

I twisted open the vodka bottle.

"No one in this world knows you like I do," he continued, his words hanging heavy between us.

I took a large gulp from the bottle, letting the alcohol burn its way down my throat. Without another word, I turned and walked out of the room, feeling the heat of his gaze lingering on me.

CHAPTER THIRTY-FIVE

The wedding came together in a rushed, muted blur, as if the world had lost all color. It was small, almost as though everyone knew it was more of a formality than a celebration.

I spent most of my days with a drink in hand, numbing myself to the grief and depression that had settled like a weight in my chest. The wedding planner, a woman with a forced smile and a clipboard seemingly glued to her arm, hovered incessantly, trying to get me to make decisions. My answers were nonexistent, and with each uncommitted shrug I gave, her patience frayed a little more. Eventually, she abandoned her efforts and went straight to Bane, the only one who seemed to care about the wedding at all.

When I refused to pick out a dress, Bane took over, ensuring I was gowned to his liking on the day itself. Staring at my reflection in the mirror before being rushed down the aisle, I was horrified. He had chosen a tight, corseted mermaid gown with off-the-shoulder sleeves and a trailing skirt that flowed behind me. Rhinestones covered the white fabric, shimmering under the lights. Two cloth wings adorned the back, designed to be raised in an angelic display or lowered to trail behind. Instead of a veil, he had chosen a gold double halo crown with spikes radiating outward.

His Angel.

Green and blue light filtered through the stained glass windows as I painfully marched down the center of the small church. My fiancé stood at the altar, dressed in a sharp gray suit, his eyes trailing up my body with possessive zeal as I moved closer to him.

Tears rolled down my face, unchecked, as I reached the shrine. The priest stared at me, his confusion evident.

"Please, just start," Bane insisted gently, his voice firm yet calm.

The priest hesitated, his eyes on me, concern etched in his expression. Leaning in slightly, he whispered, "Do you want me to continue, miss?"

I nodded slowly and took Bane's arm, feeling the weight of the moment settle deep into my bones.

At the conclusion of the ceremony, Bane leaned in to kiss me for the first time as his spouse. He moved carefully, his lips brushing uncomfortably against the side of mine. I could feel him try to deepen the kiss, but I pulled back quickly.

"I'd like to introduce to everyone for the first time—wait, miss!" the priest called after me. The marriage was done, my duty fulfilled. Ignoring his objections, I turned and walked back up the aisle, tossing my bridal bouquet somewhere into the audience.

My husband had planned a reception, but I refused to attend. Instead, I wandered around the house alone, naked, finishing off another bottle of vodka. It almost felt like old times, though the mansion was painfully quiet. Bane had given everyone the day off, and the eerie stillness made the mansion feel as though it was haunted by ghosts.

Bane eventually came to find me, holding a big, soft, fluffy robe in his hands. He had left the reception early since I had not attended.

"I got you a wedding present," he said, clearly irritated by my initial slight of not attending his reception. I took the robe to cover myself, not bothering to respond. The weight of unspoken expectations began to radiate from my husband, pressing heavily on me.

Bane gently took my hand and led me to our parents' bedroom. He had quickly moved into the master bedroom, but I was reluctant to join him. Instead, I had mostly fallen asleep in a drunken haze on various couches and chairs around the house.

"Close your eyes!" he instructed excitedly.

I stared at him with a dead-to-the-world look, already deep into my drunken slur. Bane knew I was testing his patience on purpose. With a heavy sigh, he moved behind me and placed a hand over each of my eyes. Then he guided me carefully into the bedroom.

When his hands pulled away in an excited flash, I looked up and gawked.

There it was, right over the bed, the painting of the woman with the gun pressed to the roof of her mouth. A man behind her holding her perfect tits in the air.

It was the painting I had fallen in love with at Andonis's art house during our first sale. I felt myself growing a little breathless at the irony. My husband's attempt at a romantic gesture was disturbingly symbolic of how I felt. I turned to Bane and saw him studying me intently.

"Do you like it?" he asked, hopeful and hesitant.

"I love it," I replied, my eyes glassy as I attempted a half smile. Bane sighed in relief, visibly pleased with my response.

After a stiff hug, I wandered back into the house and fell asleep late into the night in the library.

By the time I woke up the next day, it was well into the evening. Someone had moved me from where I had fallen asleep to the master bedroom.

As I dragged myself to the dining area, hungover, I noticed something strange: the hallway had suddenly changed. Stopping to look around, I saw that a solid wall now blocked the entrance that Dimiter had once used to swing Alexei into the room.

The library had disappeared, replaced by a normal, nondescript wall that felt oddly oppressive, as if it were holding its breath. On it hung a large, painted family portrait of the great Zorics, adding an unsettling touch to the transformation.

"It's a great family photo of us, don't you think?" Bane asked, seemingly materializing from nowhere. He approached me down the hall with the measured pace of a predator closing in on its prey. His eyes locked on me with dangerous power, studying me for any outbursts or negative reactions.

I stared at him for several long seconds, understanding the unspoken message loud and clear. This argument was over; I was expected to accept the situation, let my men go, and move on.

"Of course," I whispered, my voice barely audible. Bane nodded once, satisfied with my response.

"We have a business that's been disrupted with our father's departure," he said, his tone serious.

"I will allow you to eat, but I think it would be beneficial for you to help me get things back in order," he instructed. I nodded in agreement, my response lazy.

"Good. I'm in our new office, cleaning it out. It has proven to be a great way to find new connections and opportunities," Bane continued. "So please, go shower and come help me," he concluded, his tone more instructive than anything else. His eyes glossed over my sloppy demeanor with visible disgust. A flare of anger ignited deep in my stomach at my husband.

"Of course," I sneered softly.

I stormed into the office an hour later, wearing the tightest crop top I owned and a pleated skirt that swayed with every step. A simmering wrath had started to course through my veins since I had seen the vanished library. I wanted Bane to feel the sting of something he would never have, and I was determined to make an impression. For once, I had gone through the effort of doing my hair and make-up, the bold colors and styled curls a stark contrast to my previously drunken and disheveled appearance.

My husband sat in our father's chair, his focus intently fixed on some documents spread across the desk. I plopped down into my usual seat, my legs dangling casually over the arm of the chair, my posture relaxed but deliberately defiant.

Bane glanced up when he heard the sound, then did a double take as he noticed my outfit. I saw the smallest flicker of lust in his gaze before he quickly masked it and met my eyes.

"It's good to see some things don't change, I guess," Bane remarked, his tone tinged with bemusement.

"What, would you prefer if I suddenly started dressing like Mom now that I'm married?" I asked, twisting a strand of hair around my finger nonchalantly. Bane ignored my comment, his gaze lingering on my outfit with interest before he returned to the papers in front of him, trying to hide his reaction.

"What are you looking at?" I asked, barely interested.

"Divorce papers," Bane mumbled.

"What?"

Bane got up and moved to the seat next to me, bringing the stack of papers with him.

"These were signed this past year," he mused, confusion apparent as he settled into the chair next to mine. Leaning over, Bane showed me the documents.

I skimmed the page and confirmed what Bane said was correct. The documents were indeed divorce papers between Emilio and Morana Zoric. The decree outlined a settlement in which fifty million dollars was awarded to Morana Zoric as part of the terms for their separation. The wet signatures at the bottom of the page, dated within the last year, confirmed that both parties had agreed to the terms.

"She's alive," Bane said, a hopeful edge to his voice.

"So?" I snorted, thinking back to our dreadful mother.

"So, my mother is alive! Angel, this changes everything!" Bane leaped from his seat, clutching the papers. He rifled through the documents, scanning them eagerly for more information.

"We're going to find her," he whispered with determination.

"Whatever," I mumbled, moving to the other side of my father's desk. Bane had several drawers open, their contents scattered in the chaos of my father's haphazard and illogical filing system.

I sank into the massive, foreboding chair and leaned back into it.

"So this is what it was like, huh?" I mused aloud, nodding approvingly at my father's choices.

"Sophia, will you please take this seriously?" my brother pleaded, pacing in the middle of the office, his attention focused on the divorce decree. I eyed him carefully, noting that he had slipped and called me by my real name—a detail that hadn't escaped my notice.

Turning my attention back to the desk, it was clear that Bane had already organized several important formal documents. Each was stacked into categories only he would understand. I glanced at the top of one of the documents and drew it closer for examination.

"Hey twi... I mean Bane," I fumbled. Luckily, my husband paid me no mind.

"Did you know that Father hired that intruder when I was eighteen? The one he used to justify hiring me dedicated guards? For five hundred dollars, apparently. Didn't he end up shooting that man?" I asked, searching my memories to recall what had happened.

My husband didn't even bother to listen to me. I watched him pace back and forth a few times, mumbling to himself about his mother, before giving up on trying to get his attention.

I turned back to the desk, drawn to one of the drawers that seemed oddly shaped, as if it wasn't as deep as it should have been.

Leaning over, I began removing the few thick, dusty volumes that had been stored inside, which looked as if they hadn't been touched in ages.

Why does Father still have 1987 Northern Mineva tax codes? I wondered, quietly placing the outdated volumes on the floor.

With the drawer now empty, I reached my hand deep into it, feeling around the back for anything else. My fingers found an unusual groove along the side. It felt like a cutout, with a small indent in the center. I pressed the indent, and the bottom of the drawer lifted silently, revealing a hidden compartment.

A quick glance at Bane confirmed he was still absorbed in his discovery, paying me no mind. My husband was no longer pacing but was now standing in the center of the office with his back to me, staring intently at the last page of the divorce papers. I turned my attention back to the drawer.

When I removed the false bottom, there sat a large yellow envelope with my name on it in Mom's careful handwriting. Scowling in confusion, I pulled the envelope out of its resting place and set it in my lap. Then I carefully opened it and took out a stack of papers and newspaper clippings.

"FAMOUS BOIKO FAMILY KILLED!" a headline jumped out at me. I continued to read the article: "Casimeer and Ganna Boiko, of the Boiko Family Enterprises, were found dead this morning by the docks. Speculation has arisen as reports of potentially stolen military technology have recently come to light. Zaria Boiko, the three-year-old daughter of Casimeer and Ganna, was not found at the scene and has been reported missing. It is unclear if Zaria was with her parents at the time of the attack."

I flipped to the next article. At the top, written clearly in my adopted mother's handwriting and circled three times with large red ink, was the note:

"Zaria Boiko = Sophia Boiko = Sophia Zoric"

Did my adoptive father kill my parents over military guns?

I looked up toward Bane, only to find he was nowhere to be seen.

"Father mentioned that Mother tried to figure out where you came from. No one seemed to question how I suddenly had a twin at the age of three." I heard my husband's voice behind me, icy and menacing, causing the hairs on my neck to prickle.

I turned toward him slowly, my heart pounding as I looked up into his piercing eyes, finding them cold and unyielding. Bane glared down at me with such spite that warning bells blared in my mind.

"He actually, very specifically, told me not to let *you* find these documents," Bane said, his voice cutting through the air with a chilling edge. "He warned me that with your fits of unhinged rage, you might not be able to handle the truth. That they were desperate for money and willing sell him the goods. But they too cowardly to go through with the deal, so he had no choice but to kill them. It wasn't until after that he caught a glimpse of the the beautiful raven-haired Angel daughter, peering through the Boikos' car door," he sneered, each word dripping with mockery.

With a sudden, violent movement, Bane's eyes hardened as he swung his fist down, aiming to knock me out swiftly. I saw the attack coming and reacted on pure instinct. Leaping up, I seized his wrist mid-air, halting the punch with a jarring force. My grip unrelenting, as I held his arm in a crushing hold between us.

We locked eyes, both of us breathing heavily as my husband and I stared each other down.

For the first time since I witnessed my lovers' deaths, a fierce, unrelenting anger surged within me. It was as if a dormant rage had awoken, consuming me completely. My hand tightened around Bane's wrist, my grip becoming increasingly vice-like. A pained expression began to flicker across Bane's face, a subtle yet telling sign of his discomfort.

"I warned you," I whispered, my voice cold and resolute. My husband winced as I tightened my grip on his wrist, uncompromising.

"Angel," he begged, his free hand clawing at my arm in a desperate attempt to free himself. His fingernails dug into my skin, but the searing rage inside me rendered me numb to the pain.

Ignoring his pleas, I spoke each word with deliberate precision.

"I warned you. I am destruction, and I would break you if you stand in my way."

EPILOGUE

BANE, A FEW MONTHS LATER

I t was a beautiful day outside at our private beach. The wind was blowing softly, only serving to cool us from the hot sun.

I turned to look at my companion, sunbathing herself. Ava had expensive blonde hair and was shielding her green eyes behind black, sexy sunglasses. My eyes lingered down to her luscious C-cups, barely being contained in the bikini I arranged for her to wear.

"Bane, what are you looking at?" Ava giggled when she caught me looking at her breasts.

"Sorry Kitten, I was just thinking about that chocolate I licked off of you last night," I responded, running my tongue across my lips seductively and winking at her. This spurred another giggle from the ditzy, young woman.

Nope, nothing at all like my cunt of a wife, I confirmed.

"I'm going to get another drink, Kitten. Do you want anything?" I asked, standing up with my empty glass.

"Oh, I don't know. I probably shouldn't drink. It will age me," my beautiful woman sighed as she spoke. I leaned over and kissed her on the nose, then fully on her soft lips. She returned the kiss shyly, until I crawled on top of her. My lips remained locked on hers as she tittered beneath me.

"Bane," she chuckled at me, her tone mockingly scolding. My lips trailed down her neck and halted briefly at the top of her breasts, before stopping over one of her perfect nipple. The only barrier between my tongue and my prize being the rich, luxurious fabric of her swimwear.

Ava's laughter turned into moaning at once as I started to suck on her tit slightly. I pulled away before either of us wanted me to.

"How about a Cape Cod?" I asked, stepping toward the bar.

"A what?" she inquired airily.

"Vodka cranberry," I explained, a small, satisfied smirk resting on my lips as I looked down at how adorable my Kitten was.

To this, Ava eagerly nodded 'yes.' I winked at her and approached our private beach bar, humming along to the ♫ *classic power ballad* ♫ blasting loudly through the hut's speakers. When I reached the bar, I held up my empty glass to the bartender and then requested my lover's drink as well. The barkeep busied himself with the order while I picked at a bowl of nuts sitting on the aged wood.

I probably got a good two to three months left before Ava will start begging me for some commitment, I thought, staring out at nothing in particular as I waited.

The drinks were placed in front of me, pulling me from my thoughts, and I threw some small bills at the man. The bartender didn't respond to the money, so I looked at him to draw his attention to it. That was when I noticed he was staring at something behind me, a worried look on his face.

I turned sharply and froze, shocked by the sight before me.

Ava was being held in the air by her pretty blonde hair, a gun pointed right at her temple. The perpetrator stared at me with her clear blue eyes, dressed head to toe in black despite the warmth of the day. An evil smirk began to spread across her face, darkening her features with a knowing intent.

"So, this is the one, huh?" she said hotly, inspecting Ava with a careful, chilling eye. My mistress sobbed against the gun barrel.

I took a step toward my wife, and she cocked the firearm. When I stopped in my tracks, my Kitten began wailing louder.

"Who is this, Bane?" Ava asked, trembling with fear.

"Angel!" I shouted, my voice laden with frustration as I chastised my wife.

"I already told you," Angel's voice was laced with a haunted edge as she spoke. She locked her eyes on me, her stare cutting through my core. Then she muttered through gritted teeth, "I am no *Angel*, only the ♫ *Angel of Death*." ♫

Then my bitch of my wife pulled the trigger.

WIDE AWAKE
ANGEL OF DEATH

ABOUT THE AUTHOR

E.M. Cummings began writing in 2022, emerging from a lifetime of avid reading with bold inspiration sparked by the trailblazing erotic authors who came before her. Specializing in erotic thrillers, weird science fiction, and low fantasy, she crafts stories that push boundaries and captivate the imagination.

As for what inspires her to write, first and foremost, she is a reader. When telling stories, E.M. strives to create the kind of narratives she, as a reader, would enjoy—breaking tropes, developing well-rounded characters, and weaving compelling plot points that carry the reader through each novel. Writing about topics and emotions she has personally experienced also serves as a therapeutic outlet, adding authenticity and depth to her work.

When not writing, E.M. runs an eclectic book club that explores literature ranging from the timeless *Hamlet* to the modern *Paris: The Memoir*. This passion for diverse reading informs and enriches her writing style. Influenced by the provocative works of Blanka Lipińska's *365 Days* series, Anne Rice's *The Claiming of Sleeping Beauty* (written under the pseudonym A.N. Roquelaure), and the seminal *Twilight* series by Stephenie Meyer, E.M. strives to create stories that enthrall and inspire readers.

Currently, E.M. is working on a unique creative project: developing soundtracks for each short story and book she publishes. These soundtracks, available under the name "Sinful Spins," can be streamed on Spotify.

Stay tuned for more captivating novels from E.M. Cummings.

ALSO BY E.M. CUMMINGS

That ending was pretty depressing, wasn't it? Ready for something a little different? Step out of the shadows of *Angel of Death* and into the melody of *Angel of Music,* where Erik, the infamous Opera Ghost, finally gets his happily ever after.

Check out E.M. Cummings' one and only attempt at gothic romanticism in

Unmasked

A reimagining of *The Phantom of the Opera* by Gaston Leroux.

Not your great-grandmother's *Phantom of the Opera*. This is *Unmasked*.

Christine Daaé is no longer the damsel in distress. She is an ambitious chorus girl, spending long nights perfecting her craft with dreams of becoming a star.

Raoul de Chagny is not the naive boy in love. He is an arrogant viscount of his time, chasing Christine with the ruthless determination of a man who cannot stand to be denied.

Erik, the legendary Opera Ghost, is no longer unloved. When he finally starts to get what he wants, will the very obsession that once fueled his genius completely unravel him?

Unmasked takes the soul of *Phantom* and transforms it into a seductive, haunting reimagining that asks: **What happens when ambition, obsession, and desire strip you bare, forcing you to face what truly lies beneath the mask?**

Unmasked is a dark, gothic reimagining of The Phantom of the Opera, featuring passion, obsession, and sensual romance.

Turn the page for a sneak peek into the world of *Unmasked*.

Novels

Gunrunner's Daughter

24601

Delectable

Short Stories

The Lycan's Claim

PROLOGUE

The flickering chandeliers of the Palais Garnier cast golden ripples across the towering mirrors of the Grand Foyer. Shadows stretched along the gilded walls, warping with every drunken sway of Joseph Buquet's steps. The half-empty bottle dangled from his fingers, swaying precariously as he staggered forward. A wet slosh spilled onto the marble floor, darkening the pristine surface.

His voice erupted, brash and unsteady, sending a garbled rendition of ♫ "Vive le vin, vive l'amour" ♫ echoing off the grand gilded walls. He threw his arms out wide, the half-empty bottle swinging dangerously from his fingers as he staggered forward. His boots clapped unevenly against the marble, each step a drunken waltz that he conducted with exaggerated flourishes.

He stopped in front of a marble statue of Apollo, thrusting a hand toward it as if to offer a toast.

"To you, my celestial friend!" he declared, tilting his bottle in reverence before taking a long swig. Wine dribbled from the corner of his mouth, staining his collar as he twirled, nearly knocking over a nearby candelabrum.

"A toast to music! A toast to love!"

He lurched toward another statue, a muse frozen in elegant repose.

"Oh, my lady, do you spurn my advances?" He clutched his chest dramatically, staggering back with the flair of a dying performer. "No matter! You are as cold as all the rest!"

He spun in place, arms splaying out as he hummed another off-key line of his song, his body moving in a ridiculous parody of a ballroom dance.

His steps turned wild, one boot slipping against the polished surface. His weight pitched forward, knees buckling as the world tilted around him. A sharp curse sputtered from his lips as he caught himself against a gilded column, the impact jarring through his drunken haze.

Laughter bubbled up from his chest, reckless and loud.

"Too much love, not enough wine," he slurred, dragging the bottle to his lips once more.

He twirled, the force of his movement sending him staggering into a clumsy half-spin. A triumphant flourish followed as he attempted to regain his balance, his free hand sweeping through the air like a maestro guiding an invisible orchestra. The room tilted, the chandeliers above shimmering in his blurred vision. His foot lifted for a final grand step, meant to carry him toward the next waiting partner of stone and silence, but something unexpected met his boot.

The impact jolted his entire frame, a shockwave shooting up his leg as if the opera house itself had turned against him. His arms flailed, grasping at empty air. The bottle slipped from his fingers, the dark liquid spilling in a wild arc before shattering against the marble. The world reeled, golden embellishments blurring into streaks as his vision tilted with the force of his stumble.

His knees slammed against the floor, a dull, bone-rattling thud reverberating through his body. A hiss of pain escaped his lips, lost in the vast emptiness of the Grand Foyer.

His hands shot out, palms pressing against the cool stone to brace himself. A wave of nausea twisted in his stomach, the drunken warmth that had carried him moments ago now a sickly fog clouding his senses. He inhaled sharply, his chest rising and falling in uneven gulps of air.

Liquid pooled around his wrist, the rich scent of spilled wine mixing with the lingering perfume of candle wax and old velvet. His feet skidded slightly as he attempted to shift, the slickness of the spilled drink threatening to betray him further.

Twisting his torso, he threw a wild glance over his shoulder, eyes burning with irritation. His heart pounded against his ribs, the pulse in his ears nearly deafening. He expected to see a fallen rope, a loose tile, some mundane explanation for the misstep. Instead, only the pristine marble stretched out before him, gleaming under the dim glow of candlelight, undisturbed and perfect save for the mess he had made.

Confusion crept into his bleary gaze. He pushed himself upright, swaying as he squinted down at the floor, searching for the unseen adversary that had dared to interrupt his revelry. His fingers dragged over the ground, their tips brushing against something unfamiliar, a thin, deceptive break in the otherwise flawless expanse of stone. The haze of alcohol dulled the pain radiating through his limbs, but curiosity flared hot and insistent.

His fingers ghosted over the floor, seeking the culprit. There, just beside the intricate inlay of gold leaf, a break in the seamless pattern. A sliver of something darker.

The cool edge of something unnatural met his touch, sending a spark of intrigue through his inebriated mind. His lips parted, fascination overtaking any lingering irritation.

A hidden mechanism? A secret meant to be forgotten?

His breath hitched as his fingers worked over the surface, feeling the slight give beneath his press. Someone had buried this here, concealed it within the grandeur of the opera house, but he had found it. He, Joseph Buquet, had stumbled upon a secret meant for no man's hands. A hidden switch, nestled within the elaborate design. Someone had gone through great lengths to disguise it.

His fingers hovered for only a moment before curiosity bested hesitation. He pressed down, anticipation bubbling in his chest.

Nothing happened.

A wicked delight slithered across his expression. He pressed again, his fingers tapping an uneven rhythm, coaxing the switch to reveal its mystery. Each push sent a small thrill through his spine, as if each movement pulled back the curtain of a great unseen performance just for him.

A game now, his fingers drumming the surface in an bumpy tempo. The wine, the night, the secrecy, his body swayed with the sheer delight of the discovery.

"Come on, little trick. Show me something good."

He hammered the switch again, then again, his grin stretching as the marble refused to respond. His fingers drummed with impatience, his laughter bouncing off the high-arched ceiling.

"Come on now, show me something!"

Another press, then another, the rhythm of his drunken amusement building into something feverish. Then the floor shuddered beneath him.

The groan of hidden gears rasped through the silence, rattling up from deep below, ancient and restless. The very air seemed to tighten. The final click snapped into place, sharp as a guillotine's release.

The marble beneath his feet was gone.

A gasp barely formed in his throat before the world dropped away. His chest jerked as gravity tore him downward, his arms flailing wildly for purchase that did not exist. A strangled sound, too raw to be a proper scream, escaped him. The abyss welcomed him with open arms.

The fall ended with a brutal jolt. His body struck a cold, hard surface, the impact forcing the breath from his lungs in a ragged wheeze. Pain radiated through his ribs as he lay sprawled on his back, the world a dizzying blur of shadows and dull metallic gleams. His pulse pounded in his ears, drowning out the silence that pressed in around him.

A groan slipped from his lips as he forced himself onto his side, fingers splaying against the surface beneath him. Smooth, icy glass met his touch, unsettling in its perfect seamlessness. He blinked rapidly, trying to clear his muddled vision, but the world around him twisted and shifted, an endless maze of reflections.

The walls, the floor, even the ceiling, all mirrors, their surfaces without borders, without edges, trapping him in an infinite, distorted version of reality.

His image stretched unnaturally, refracted a thousand times over, turning his drunken, disheveled form into a grotesque, shifting phantasm. Every motion sent ripples of movement through the mirrored abyss, warping the space around him. There was no point of reference, no grounding, only the eerie illusion of a bottomless void swallowing him whole.

A shudder crawled up his spine as he struggled to steady himself, but the weight of a long night spent drinking and roughhousing clung to his bones, making it harder to stay upright.

In the center of the room stood a massive steel tree, its thick trunk bolted to the floor, branches reaching upward in rigid, unnatural angles. The metallic bark gleamed faintly in the scarce light, its surface cold beneath his tentative touch. He clung to it, muscles straining as he pulled himself to his feet. His head spun from the abrupt movement, but the fall had shaken the worst of the wine's haze from his mind.

He swallowed hard, chest rising and falling in unsteady rhythm as he steadied himself against the cold metal.

Then a sharp click echoed through the chamber. Light flooded the room, searing through the dark and sending daggers of pain into his skull. His hands flew up to shield his face, breath hitching as he stumbled back against the steel tree. His pulse hammered in his throat, the sudden brightness disorienting and oppressive.

Blinking furiously, he lowered his hands, squinting as his eyes adjusted. The mirrors shimmered in the artificial glow, their warped images now painfully clear.

One in particular drew his attention, standing apart from the others. Unlike the rest, this one did not reflect his own form. Instead, beyond the glass, a figure loomed in the harsh light.

The man stood motionless, his posture rigid with barely concealed irritation. The sharp lines of his coat, the shadows draped around his frame, the way his head tilted ever so slightly in restrained impatience all carried an air of silent authority.

A stark crimson mask covered most of his face, leaving only his mouth and part of one cheek exposed. His mouth remained unreadable, but the weight of his gaze burned through the barrier between them.

Joseph inhaled sharply, his breath shuddering as he took an unsteady step forward. His knees trembled, though whether from the lingering effects of drink or the sudden grip of fear, he could not say. His tongue felt heavy in his mouth, words slow and clumsy as they fought their way past his lips.

"It's... you..." The slurred whisper barely carried in the oppressive stillness. His throat bobbed as he swallowed, eyes locked onto the masked man through the glass. "The... Opera Ghost..."